Praise for Harlan Coben

'It is always satisfying to discover a new crime writer – and this is the business . . . this book will keep you up until 2 a.m.' *The Times*

'Harlan Coben. He's smart, he's funny, and he has something to say' Michael Connelly

'An increasingly frightening conspiracy with an unguessable ending . . . hard to put down' *Sunday Telegraph*

'At last a British publisher has given British readers the chance to discover something every US mystery fan already knows – that Harlan Coben is one of the most entertaining and intriguing crime writers around'
Val McDermid, *Manchester Evening Guardian*

'What sets Harlan Coben above the crowd are wit and . . . an entertaining plot' *Los Angeles Times Book Review*

'Fast action, snappy dialogue and plenty of insider hoops material make this a fast, enjoyable read' *Toronto Star*

'Coben . . . scores a hole in one! The characters are deftly etched and the details keenly observed'
Publishers Weekly

'Coben is still one of America's masters of the hook, the twist and the surprise ending' *Literary Review*

'Intelligent and gripping, this is a real white-knuckle read of a thriller' *Daily Mail*

By Harlan Coben

Play Dead
Miracle Cure
Deal Breaker
Drop Shot
Fade Away
Back Spin
One False Move
The Final Detail
Darkest Fear
Tell No One
Gone for Good
No Second Chance
Just One Look
The Innocent
Promise Me
The Woods
Hold Tight
Long Lost
Caught
Live Wire
Shelter
Stay Close
Seconds Away
Six Years
Missing You

Harlan Coben is one of the most exciting talents in crime writing. He is an international number one bestseller, gracing the charts of the *Sunday Times* and the *New York Times*. His books are published in more than forty languages and there are more than fifty million of his novels in print worldwide. Harlan lives in New Jersey with his wife and four children. Visit his website at www.harlancoben.com

Deal Breaker

HARLAN COBEN

An Orion paperback

First published in Great Britain in 2001
by Orion Books
This new paperback edition published in 2014
by Orion Books,
an imprint of The Orion Publishing Group Ltd,
Orion House, 5 Upper St Martin's Lane,
London WC2H 9EA

An Hachette UK company

Published by arrangement with Dell Publishing,
an imprint of The Bantam Dell Publishing Group,
a division of Random House, Inc.

A CIP catalogue record for this book
is available from the British Library.

Printed and bound by the CPI Group (UK) Ltd, Croydon, CR0 4YY

The Orion Publishing Group's policy is to use papers
that are natural, renewable and recyclable products and
made from wood grown in sustainable forests. The logging
and manufacturing processes are expected to conform to
the environmental regulations of the country of origin.

www.orionbooks.co.uk

This, like everything else, is for Anne.

Acknowledgements

The author wishes to thank the Sunandan B. Singh, MD, Chief Medical Examiner of Bergen County, New Jersey; Bob Richter; Rich Henshaw; Richard Curtis; Jacob Hoye; Shawn Coyne; and, of course, Dave Bolt.

Chapter 1

Otto Burke, the Wizard of Schmooze, raised his game another level.

'Come on, Myron,' he urged with neoreligious fervor. 'I'm sure we can come to an understanding here. You give a little. We give a little. The Titans are a team. In some larger sense I would like all of us to be a team. You included. Let's be a real team, Myron. What do you say?'

Myron Bolitar steepled his fingers. He had read somewhere that steepled fingers made you look like a thoughtful person. He felt foolish.

'I'd like nothing more, Otto,' he said, returning the pointless volley for the umpteenth time. 'Really I would. But we've given as much as we can. It's your turn now.'

Otto nodded vigorously, as if he had just heard some philosophical whimsy that put Socrates to shame. He tilted his head, angling the painted-on smile toward his team's general manager. 'Larry, what do you think?'

Taking his cue, Larry Hanson pounded the conference

table with a fist hairy enough to be a gerbil. 'Bolitar can go to hell!' he shouted, playing enraged to the hilt. 'You hear me, Bolitar? You understand what I'm telling you? Go to hell.'

'Go to hell,' Myron repeated with a nod. 'Got it.'

'You being a wiseass with me? Huh? Answer me, dammit! You being a wiseass?'

Myron looked at him. 'You have a poppy seed stuck in your teeth.'

'Goddamn wiseass.'

'And you're beautiful when you're angry. Your whole face lights up.'

Larry Hanson's eyes widened. He swung his line of vision toward his boss, then back to Myron. 'You're out of your league here, Bolitar. And you fucking know it.'

Myron said nothing. The truth of the matter was, Larry Hanson was partially right. Myron was out of his league. He had been in sports representation for only two years now. Most of his clients were borderline cases – guys who were lucky to make the cut and grabbed the league's minimum. And football was far from his specialty. He had only three NFL players, only one of whom was a starter. Now Myron sat across from thirty-one-year-old wunder-kind Otto Burke, the youngest owner in the NFL, and Larry Hanson, former-football-legend-turned-exec, nego-tiating a contract that even in his inexperienced hands would be the biggest rookie contract in NFL history.

Yes, he – Myron Bolitar – had landed Christian 'Hot Prop' Steele. Two time Heisman trophy-winning quarter-back. Three straight AP and UPI number-one rankings. All-American four years in a row. If that wasn't enough, the kid was an endorsement wet dream. An A student, good-looking, articulate, polite, and white (hey, it mattered).

Best of all, he was Myron's.

'The offer is on the table, gentlemen,' Myron continued. 'We think it's more than fair.'

Otto Burke shook his head.

'It's a load of crap!' Larry Hanson shouted. 'You're a goddamn idiot, Bolitar. You're going to flush this kid's career down the toilet.'

Myron spread his arms. 'How about a group hug?'

Larry was about to offer up another expletive, but Otto stopped him with a raised hand. In Larry's playing days Dick Butkus and Ray Nitzchke couldn't stop him with body blows. Now this one-hundred-fifty-pound Harvard grad could silence him with but a wave.

Otto Burke leaned forward. He hadn't stopped smiling, hadn't stopped the hand gestures, hadn't stopped the eye contact – like an Anthony Robbins Personal Power infomercial come to life. Disconcerting as all hell. Otto was a small, fragile-looking man with the tiniest fingers Myron had ever seen. His hair was dark and heavy-metal long, flowing to his shoulders. He was baby-faced with a silly goatee that looked as if it'd been sketched on in pencil. He smoked a very long cigarette, or maybe it just appeared long against his tiny fingers.

'Now, Myron,' Otto said, 'let's speak rationally here, okay?'

'Rationally. Let's.'

'Great, Myron, that'll be helpful. The truth is, Christian Steele is an unknown, untested quantity. He hasn't even put on a pro uniform yet. He may be the bust of the century.'

Larry snorted. 'You should know something about that, Bolitar – about players who amount to nothing. Who crap out.'

Myron ignored him. He had heard the insult before. It no longer bothered him. Sticks and stones and all that. 'We are talking about perhaps the greatest quarterback prospect in history,' he replied steadily. 'You made three trades and gave up six players to get his rights. You didn't do all that if you didn't believe he has what it takes.'

'But this proposal' – Otto stopped, looked up as though searching the ceiling tiles for the right word – 'it's not sound.'

'Crap is more like it,' Larry added.

'It's final,' Myron said.

Otto shook his head, the smile unfazed. 'Let's talk this through, okay? Let's look at it from every conceivable angle. You're new at this, Myron – an ex-jock reaching for the executive brass ring. I respect that. You're a young guy trying to give it a go. Heck, I admire that. Really.'

Myron bit down. He could have pointed out that he and Otto were the same age, but he so loved being patronized. Didn't everybody?

'If you make a mistake on this,' Otto continued, 'it could be the sort of thing that destroys your career. Do you know what I mean? Plenty of people already feel that you're not up to this – to handling such a high-profile client. Not me, of course. I think you're a very bright guy. Shrewd. But the way you're acting . . .' He shook his head like a teacher disenchanted with a favorite pupil.

Larry stood, glowering down at Myron. 'Why don't you give the kid some good advice?' he said. 'Tell him to get a real agent.'

Myron had expected this whole good-cop, bad-cop routine. He had, in fact, expected worse; Larry Hanson had not yet attacked the sexual appetites of anyone's mother. Still, Myron preferred the bad cop to the good

4

cop. Larry Hanson was a frontal assault, easily spotted and handled. Otto Burke was the snake-infested high grass with buried land mines.

'Then I guess we have nothing more to discuss,' Myron said.

'I believe a holdout would be unwise, Myron,' Otto said. 'It might soil Christian's squeaky-clean image. Hurt his endorsements. Cost you both a great deal of money. You don't want to lose money, Myron.'

Myron looked at him. 'I don't?'

'No, you don't.'

'Can I jot that down?' He picked up a pencil and began scribbling. 'Don't . . . want . . . . to . . . lose . . . money.' He grinned at both men. 'Am I picking up pointers today or what?'

Larry mumbled, 'Goddamn wiseass.'

Otto's smile remained locked on autopilot. 'If I may be so bold,' he continued, 'I would think Christian would want to collect quickly.'

'Oh?'

'There are those who have serious reservations about Christian Steele's future. There are those' – Otto drew deeply on his cigarette – 'who believe he may have had something to do with that girl's disappearance.'

'Ah,' Myron said, 'that's more like it.'

'More like what?'

'You're starting to fling mud. For a second there I thought I wasn't asking for enough.'

Larry Hanson stuck a thumb in Myron's direction. 'Do you believe this fucking sliver of pond film we're sitting with? You raise a legitimate issue about Christian's ex-bimbo, one that goes to the heart of his value as a public relations commodity—'

'Pitiful rumors,' Myron interrupted. 'No one believed them. If anything, they made the public more sympathetic to Christian's tragedy. And don't call Kathy Culver a bimbo.'

Larry raised an eyebrow. 'Well, well, aren't we touchy,' he said, 'for a low-life pissant.'

Myron's expression did not change. He had met Kathy Culver five years ago when she was a sophomore in high school, already a budding beauty. Like her sister Jessica. Eighteen months ago Kathy had mysteriously vanished from the campus of Reston University. To this day no one knew where she was or what had happened to her. The story had all the media's favorite tasty morsels – a gorgeous co-ed, the fiancée of football star Christian Steele, the sister of novelist Jessica Culver, a strong hint of sexual assault for extra seasoning. The press could not help themselves. They attacked like ravenous relatives around a buffet table.

But just recently a second tragedy had befallen the Culver family. Adam Culver, Kathy's father, had been murdered three nights earlier in what police were calling a 'botched robbery.' Myron wanted very much to contact the family, to do more than merely offer simple condolences, but he had decided to stay away, not knowing if he was welcome, fairly certain he wasn't.

'Now if—'

There was a knock on the door. It opened a crack, and Esperanza stuck her head in. 'Call for you, Myron,' she said.

'Take a message.'

'I think you'll want to take it.'

Esperanza stayed in the doorway. Her dark eyes gave away nothing, but he understood.

'I'll be right there,' he said.

She slipped back through the door.

Larry Hanson gave an appreciative whistle. 'She's a babe, Bolitar.'

'Gee, thanks, Larry. That means a lot coming from you.' He rose. 'I'll be right back.'

'We don't have all goddamn day to jerk off here.'

'I'm sure you don't.'

He left the conference room and met up with Esperanza at her desk.

'The Meal Ticket,' she told him. 'He said it was urgent.'

Christian Steele.

From her petite frame most would not guess that Esperanza used to be a professional wrestler. For three years she had been known on the circuit as Little Pocahontas. The fact that Esperanza Diaz was Latina, without a trace of American Indian blood, did not seem to bother the FLOW (Fabulous Ladies of Wrestling) organization. A minor detail, they said. Latino, Indian, what's the difference?

At the height of her pro wrestling career, the same script was played out every week in arenas all over the US of A. Esperanza ('Pocahontas') would enter the ring wearing moccasins, a suede-fringed dress, and a headband that lassoed her long black hair away from her dark face. The suede dress came off before the fight, leaving a somewhat flimsier and less traditional Native American garb in its stead.

Professional wrestling has a pretty simple plot with painfully few variations. Some wrestlers are bad. Some are good. Pocahontas was good, a crowd favorite. She was cute and small and quick and had a tight little body.

Everyone loved her. She would always be winning the fight on skill when her opponent would do something illegal – throw sand in her eyes, use a dreaded foreign object that everyone in the free world except the referee could see – to turn the tide. Then the bad wrestler would bring in a couple of extra cronies, ganging up three against one on poor Pocahontas, pounding mercilessly on the brave beauty to the unequivocal shock and chagrin of the announcers, who had seen the same thing happen last week and the week before.

Just when it seemed there was no hope, Big Chief Mama, a mammoth creature, charged out of the locker room and threw the beasts off the defenseless Pocahontas. Then together Big Chief Mama and Little Pocahontas would defeat the forces of evil.

Massively entertaining.

'I'll take it in my office,' Myron said.

As he entered he saw the nameplate on his desk, a gift from his parents.

MYRON BOLITAR
SPORTS AGENT

He shook his head. Myron Bolitar. He still couldn't believe someone would name a kid Myron. When his family first moved to New Jersey, he had told everyone in his new high school that his name was Mike. Nope, no dice. Then he tried to nickname himself Mickey. Unhunh. Everyone reverted to Myron; the name was like a horror-movie monster that would not die.

To answer the obvious question: No, he never forgave his parents.

He picked up the phone. 'Christian?'

'Mr Bolitar? Is that you?'

'Yes. And please call me . . . Myron.' Acceptance of the inevitable, a sign of a wise man.

'I'm sorry to interrupt you. I know how busy you are.'

'I'm busy negotiating your contract. I have Otto Burke and Larry Hanson in the next room.'

'I appreciate that, Mr Bolitar, but this is very important.' His voice was trembling. 'I have to see you right away.'

He switched hands. 'Something wrong, Christian?' Mr Perceptive.

'I – I'd rather not discuss it over the phone. Would you be able to meet me at my room on campus?'

'Sure, no problem. What time?'

'Now, please. I – I don't know what to make of this. I want you to see it.'

Myron took a deep breath. 'No problem. I'll throw Otto and Larry out. It'll be good for the negotiations. I'll be there in an hour.'

It took a lot longer.

Myron entered the Kinney garage on Forty-sixth Street, not too far from his Park Avenue office. He nodded to Mario, the garage attendant, walked past the pricing sheet, which had a small disclaimer on the bottom that read 'not including 97% tax,' and headed to his car on the lower level. A Ford Taurus. Your basic Babe Magnet.

He was about to unlock the door when he heard a hissing sound. Like a snake. Or more likely, air escaping from a tire. The sound emanated from his back right tire. A quick examination told Myron that it had been slashed.

'Hi, Myron.'

He spun around. Two men grinned at him. One was

the size of a small Third World nation. Myron was big – nearly six-four and two hundred twenty pounds – but he guessed that this guy must have been six-six and closing in on three hundred. A heavy-duty weight lifter, his whole body was puffed up as if he were wearing inflatable life vests under his clothes. The second man was of average build. He wore a fedora.

The big man lumbered toward Myron's car. His arms swung stiffly at his sides. He kept tilting his head, cracking the part of the anatomy that on a normal human being might be called a neck.

'Having some car trouble?' he asked with a chuckle.

'Flat tire,' Myron said. 'There's a spare in the trunk. Change it.'

'I don't think so, Bolitar. This was just a little warning.'

'Oh?'

The human edifice grabbed the lapels of Myron's jacket. 'Stay away from Chaz Landreaux. He's already signed.'

'First change my tire.'

The grin increased. It was a stupid, cruel grin. 'Next time I won't be so nice.' He grabbed a little tighter, bunching up the suit and tie. 'Understand?'

'You are aware, of course, that steroids make your balls shrink.'

The man's face reddened. 'Oh, yeah? Maybe I oughta smash your face in, huh? Maybe I oughta pulverize you into oatmeal.'

'Oatmeal?'

'Yeah.'

'Nice image, really.'

'Fuck you.'

Myron sighed. Then his whole body seemed to snap into motion at the same time. He started with a head-butt that landed square on the big man's nose. There was a squelching noise like beetles being stepped on. Blood gushed from the nose.

'Son of a—'

Myron cradled the back of the big man's head for leverage and smashed his elbow into the sweet of the Adam's apple, nearly caving the windpipe all the way in. There was a painful, gurgling choke. Then silence. Myron followed up with a knife-hand strike to the back of the neck below the skull.

The big man slid to the ground like wet sand.

'Okay, that's enough!'

The man with the fedora stepped closer, a gun drawn and pointed at Myron's chest.

'Back away from him. Now!'

Myron squinted at him. 'Is that really a fedora?'

'I said, back off!'

'Okay, okay, I'm backing.'

'You didn't have to do that,' the smaller man said with almost childlike hurt. 'He was just doing his job.'

'A misunderstood youth,' Myron added. 'Now I feel terrible.'

'Just stay away from Chaz Landreaux, okay?'

'Not okay. Tell Roy O'Connor I said it's not okay.'

'Hey, I ain't hired to get no answer. I'm just delivering.'

Without another word the man with the fedora helped his fallen colleague to his feet. The big man stumbled to their car, one hand on his nose, the other massaging his windpipe. His nose was busted, but his throat would hurt even worse, especially when he swallowed.

They got in and quickly drove away. They did not stop to change Myron's tire.

Chapter 2

Myron dialed Chaz Landreaux's number on his car phone.

Not being what one would call mechanically inclined, it had taken Myron half an hour to change the tire. He rode slowly for the first few miles, fearing his handiwork would encourage the tire to slip off and flee. When he felt more confident, he accelerated and started back on the road to Christian's.

When Chaz answered, Myron quickly explained what happened.

'They was already here,' Chaz told him. Lots of noise in the background. An infant cried. Something fell and broke. Children laughed. Chaz shouted for quiet.

'When?' Myron asked.

'Hour ago. Three men.'

'Did they hurt you?'

'Nah. Just held me down and made threats. Said they was going to break my legs if I didn't honor my contract.'

Breaking legs, Myron thought. How original.

Chaz Landreaux was a senior basketball player at Georgia State and a probable first-round NBA pick. He was a poor kid from the streets of Philadelphia. He had six brothers, two sisters, no father. The ten of them lived in an area that – if daringly improved – might one day be charitably dubbed 'poor ghetto.'

During his freshman year, an underling of a big-time agent named Roy O'Connor had approached Chaz – four years before Chaz was eligible to talk to an agent. The man offered Chaz a five-thousand-dollar 'retainer' up front, with monthly payments of $250, if he signed a contract making O'Connor his agent when he turned pro.

Chaz was confused. He knew that NCAA rules forbade him from signing a contract while he still had eligibility. The contract would be declared null and void. But Roy's man assured him this would be no problem. They would simply postdate the contract to make it appear Chaz had signed on after his final year of eligibility. They'd keep the contract in a safety deposit box until the proper time arrived. No one would be the wiser.

Chaz was not sure. He knew it was illegal, but he also knew what that kind of money would mean to his mom and eight siblings living in a two-room hellhole. Roy O'Connor then entered the picture and pitched the final inducement: If Chaz changed his mind at some future date, he could repay the money and tear up the contract.

Four years later Chaz changed his mind. He promised to pay back every cent. No way, said Roy O'Connor. You have a contract with us. You'll stick with it.

This was not an uncommon setup. Dozens of agents did it. Norby Walters and Lloyd Bloom, two of the country's biggest agents, had been arrested for it. Threats too were not uncommon. But that was where it usually ended: with threats. No agent wanted to risk being exposed. If a kid stood firm, the agent backed off.

But not Roy O'Connor. Roy O'Connor was using muscle. Myron was surprised.

'I want you out of town for a little while,' Myron continued. 'You got someplace to lay low?'

'Yeah, 'I'll crash with a friend in Washington. But what we going to do?'

'I'll take care of it. Just stay out of sight.'

'Okay, yeah, I hear ya.' Then: 'Oh, Myron, one other thing.'

'What?'

'One of the dudes who held me down said he knew you. A monster, man. I mean, huge. Slick-looking mother-fucker.'

'Did he say his name?'

'Aaron. He said to tell you Aaron said hi.'

Myron's shoulders slumped. Aaron. A name from his past. Not a good name either. Roy O'Connor not only had muscle behind him – he had serious muscle.

Three hours after leaving his office, Myron shook off all thoughts about the garage incident and knocked on Christian's door. Despite the fact that he'd graduated two months earlier, Christian still lived in the same campus dorm he had occupied throughout his senior year, work-ing as a counselor at Reston U's football summer camp. The Titans minicamp, however, started in two days, and Christian would be there. Myron had no intention of having Christian hold out.

Christian opened the door immediately. Before Myron

14

had a chance to explain his tardiness, Christian said, 'Thanks for getting here so fast.'

'Uh, sure. No problem.'

Christian's face was completely devoid of its usual healthy color. Gone were the rosy cheeks that dimpled when Christian smiled. Gone was the wide-open, aw-shucks smile that made the co-eds swoon. Even the famed steady hands were noticeably quaking.

'Come on in,' he said.

'Thanks.'

Christian's room looked more like a 1950s sitcom set than a modern-day campus dorm room. For one thing, the place was neat. The bed was made, the shoes in a row beneath it. There were no socks on the floor, no under-wear, no jock straps. On the walls were pennants. Actual pennants. Myron couldn't believe it. No posters, no calendars with Claudia Schiffer or Cindy Crawford or the Barbi twins. Just old-fashioned pennants. Myron felt as if he'd just stepped into Wally Cleaver's dormitory.

Christian didn't say anything at first. They both stood there uncomfortably, like two strangers stuck together at some cocktail party with no drinks in their hands. Christian kept his eyes lowered to the floor like a scolded child. He hadn't commented on the blood on Myron's suit. He probably hadn't noticed it.

Myron decided to try one of his patented silver-tongued ice-breakers. 'What's up?'

Christian began to pace – no easy accomplishment in a room slightly larger than the average armoire. Myron could see that Christian's eyes were red. He'd been crying, his cheeks still showing small traces of the tear tracks.

'Did Mr Burke get mad about canceling the meeting?' Christian asked.

Myron shrugged. 'He had a major conniption, but he'll survive. Means nothing, don't worry about it.'

'Minicamp starts Thursday?'

Myron nodded. 'Are you nervous?'

'A little, maybe.'

'Is that why you wanted to see me?'

Christian shook his head. He hesitated and then said, 'I – I don't understand it, Mr Bolitar.'

Every time he called him mister, Myron looked for his father.

'Don't understand what, Christian? What's this all about?'

He hesitated again. 'It's . . .' He stopped, took a deep breath, started again. 'It's about Kathy.'

Myron thought he'd heard wrong. 'Kathy Culver?'

'You knew her,' Christian said. Myron couldn't tell if it was a statement or a question.

'A long time ago,' Myron replied.

'When you were with Jessica.'

'Yes.'

'Then maybe you'll understand. I miss Kathy. More than anyone can ever know. She was very special.'

Myron nodded, encouraging. Very Phil Donahue.

Christian took a step back, nearly banging his head into a bookshelf. 'Everybody sensationalized what happened to her,' he began. 'They put it in tabloids, had stories about the disappearance on *A Current Affair*. It was like a game to everyone. A TV show. They kept calling us "idyllic," the "idyllic couple."' He made quote marks in the air with his fingers. 'As if *idyllic* meant unreal. Unfeeling. Everyone kept saying I was young, I'd get over it quickly. Kathy was just a pretty blonde, millions more like her for a guy like me. I was expected to get on with my life. She was gone. It was over and done with.'

Christian's boyish quality – something that Myron thought would help make him the future endorsement king – had suddenly taken on a new dimension. Instead of the shy, gee-whiz, modest little Kansas boy, Myron saw reality: a scared child huddled in a corner, a child whose parents were dead, who had no real family, probably no real friends, just hero-worshipers and those who wanted a piece of him (like Myron himself?).

Myron shook his head. No way. Other agents, yes, but not him. Myron wasn't like that. But still something akin to guilt stayed there, poking a sharp finger into his ribs.

'I never really believed Kathy was dead,' Christian continued. 'That was part of the problem, I guess. The not-knowing gets to you after a while. Part of me – part of me almost hoped they'd find her body already, anything to end it. Is that an awful thing to say, Mr Bolitar?'

'I don't think so, no.'

Christian looked at him solemnly. 'I kept thinking about the panties. You know about that?'

Myron nodded. The lone clue in the mystery was Kathy's ripped panties, found on top of a campus Dumpster. Rumor had it that they were covered with semen and blood. To the world at large, the panties had confirmed what had long been suspected: Kathy Culver was dead. It was a sad though not uncommon story. She had been raped and murdered by a random psychopath. Her body would probably never be found – or maybe some hunters would stumble across the skeletal remains in the woods one day, giving the press a great eleven o'clock commercial teaser, bringing the cameras back into the story with undying hopes of catching a grief-stricken relative on film.

'They made it seem like it was a dirty thing,' Christian continued. ' "Pink," they said. "Silk," they said. They never called them underwear or undergarments or even just plain panties. It was always pink silk panties. Like that was important. One TV station even interviewed a Victoria's Secret model for her comment on them. Pink silk panties. Like that meant she was asking for it. Trashing Kathy like that . . .'

His voice sort of faded away then. Myron said nothing. Christian was working up to something. Myron only hoped it wasn't a breakdown.

'I guess I should get to the point,' Christian finally said.

'Take your time. I'm not going anywhere.'

'I saw something today. I—' Christian stopped and swung his eyes toward Myron's. They looked at him, pleading. 'Kathy may still be alive.'

His words hit Myron like a wet slap. Whatever Myron had been preparing himself for, whatever he imagined Christian was leading up to, hearing Kathy Culver might still be alive was not a part of the equation.

'What?'

Christian reached behind him and opened his desk drawer. The desk too was something out of *Leave It to Beaver*. Completely uncluttered. Two cans, one with Bic pens, the other with sharpened number-two pencils. Gooseneck lamp. Desk blotter with calendar. Dictionary, thesaurus, and *The Elements of Style* all in a row between two globe bookends.

'This came in the mail today.'

He handed Myron a magazine. On the cover was a naked woman. Calling her well endowed would be tantamount to calling World War II a skirmish. Most men are somewhat mammary obsessed, and Myron was not above having similar sentiments, but this was positively freakish. The woman's face was far from pretty, kind of harsh looking. She was giving the camera a look that was supposed to be come-hither but looked more like constipation. Her tongue was licking her lips, her legs spread, her finger beckoning the reader to come closer.

Very subtle effect, Myron thought.

The magazine was called *Nips*. The lead story, according to the words emblazoned across her right breast: 'How to Get Her to Shave Dat Thang.'

Myron looked up sharply. 'What's this all about?'

'The paper clip.'

'What?'

But Christian seemed too weak to repeat it. He just pointed. On the top of the magazine Myron spotted a glint of silver. A paper clip was being used as a bookmark.

'It came with that on there,' Christian said by way of explanation.

Myron fingered through the pages, catching quick glimpses of flesh, until he arrived at the page marked off by the paper clip. His eyes squinted in confusion. It was an ad page, though it had as many erotic photos as any other. The top of the page read:

Live Fantasy Phone – Pick Your Girl!

There were three rows, four girls in each row, all the way down the page. Myron's eyes scanned down. He could not believe what he was seeing. 'Oriental Girls Are Waiting!' 'Wet and Juicy Lesbos!' 'Spank Me, Please!' 'Bitches in

Heat!' 'Tiny Titties!' (for those who didn't like the cover shot, no doubt) 'I Want You to Ride Me!' 'Pick My Cherry!' 'Make Me Beg for More!' 'Wanted: Robocock.' 'Mistress Savannah Demands You Call Now!' 'Horny Housewife!' 'Overweight Men Wanted.' Each with matching photo – provocative poses involving telephones.

There were some that were far more raunchy. Crossdressers. Women with men's equipment. There were some Myron could not even understand. Like unfathomable science experiments. The telephone numbers were what you'd expect. 1–800–888-SLUT. 1–900–46-TRAMP. 1–800-REAM-MEE. 1–900-BAD-GIRL.

Myron made a face. He wanted to wash his hands.

Then he saw it.

It was in the bottom row, second from the right. It read, 'I'll Do Anything!' The phone number was 1–900–344-LUST. $3.99 per minute. Discreetly billed to your telephone or charge card. Visa/MC accepted.

The woman in the picture was Kathy Culver.

Myron felt a coldness seep into him. He turned back to the cover and checked the date. It was the current issue.

'When did you get this?'

'It came in today's mail,' Christian said, picking up an envelope. 'In this.'

Myron's head began to swim. He tried to fight the dizziness and get some kind of footing, but the picture of Kathy kept tipping him back over. The envelope was plain manila. There was no return address – that would have been too easy. It was not postmarked and had no stamps, merely reading:

CHRISTIAN STEELE
BOX 488

No city, no state. That meant it'd been mailed on campus. The address had been handwritten.

'You get lots of fan mail, right?' Myron asked.

Christian nodded. 'But they go somewhere else. This was in my private box. The number is unlisted.'

Myron handled the envelope carefully, trying not to smudge any potential fingerprints. 'It could be trick photography,' Myron added. 'Someone might have super-imposed her head on—'

Christian stopped him with a shake of his head. His eyes were back on the floor. 'It's not just her face, Mr Bolitar,' he said, embarrassed.

'Oh,' Myron said, ever swift on the uptake. 'I see.'

'Do you think we should give this to the police?' Christian asked.

'Perhaps.'

'I want to do the right thing,' Christian said, his hands balling into fists. 'But I won't let them drag Kathy through the mud again. You saw what they did when she was the victim. What will they do when they see this?'

'They'll go animal,' he agreed.

Christian nodded.

'But it's probably just a prank,' Myron continued. 'I'll check it out before we do anything else.'

'How?'

'Let me worry about that.'

'There's one other thing,' Christian said. 'The hand-writing on the envelope.'

Myron glanced at it again. 'What about it?'

'I can't say for sure, but it looks a lot like Kathy's.'

Chapter 3

Myron stopped short when he saw her.

He had just stumbled into the bar in something of a daydream, his mind like a movie camera that couldn't stay in focus. He tried to sift through what he had just seen and learned from Christian, tried to compute the facts and form a solid, well-conceived conclusion.

He came up with nothing.

The magazine was jammed into the right pocket of his trench coat. Porn mag and trench coat, Myron thought. Jesus. The same questions echoed ad nauseam in his head: Could Kathy Culver still be alive? And if she was, what had happened to her? What could have led Kathy from the innocence of her dorm room to the back pages of *Nips* magazine?

That was when he spotted the most beautiful woman he had ever seen.

She was sitting on a stool, her long legs crossed, sipping gently at her drink. She wore a white blouse opened at the throat, a short gray skirt, and black stockings. Everything clung just right. For a fleeting moment Myron thought she was just a by-product of his daydream, a dazzling vision to tantalize the senses. But the knot in his stomach made him quickly dismiss that notion. His throat went dry. Deep, dormant emotions crashed down upon him like a surprise wave at the beach.

He managed to swallow and commanded his legs to move forward. She was, quite simply, breathtaking. Everything else in the bar faded into the background, as though they were only stage props set for her.

Myron approached. 'Come here often?' he asked.

She looked at him like he was an old man jogging in a Speedo. 'Original line,' she said. 'Very creative.'

'Maybe not,' he said. 'But what a delivery.' He smiled. Winningly, he thought.

'Glad you think so.' She turned back to her drink. 'Please leave.'

'Playing hard to get?'

'Get lost.'

Myron grinned. 'Stop it already. You're embarrassing yourself.'

'Pardon me.'

'It's obvious to everyone in this bar.'

'Oh?' she remarked. 'Do enlighten.'

'You want me. Bad.'

She almost smiled. 'That obvious, huh?'

'Don't blame yourself. I'm irresistible.'

'Uh-huh. Catch me if I swoon.'

'I'm right here, sweetcakes.'

She sighed deeply. She was as beautiful as ever, as beautiful as the day she had walked out on him. He hadn't seen her in four years, but it still hurt to think about her. It hurt even more to look at her. Their weekend at Win's house on Martha's Vineyard came to him. He could still remember the way the ocean breeze blew her hair, the way she tilted her head when he spoke, the way she looked and felt in his old sweatshirt. Simple fragile bliss. The knot in his stomach tightened.

'Hello, Myron,' she said.

'Hello, Jessica. You're looking well.'

'What are you doing here?' she asked.

'My office is upstairs. I practically live here.'

She smiled. 'Oh, that's right. You represent athletes now, don't you?'

'Yes.'

'Better than working all that undercover stuff?'

Myron did not bother answering. She glanced at him but did not hold the gaze.

'I'm waiting for someone,' Jessica said suddenly.

'A male someone?'

'Myron . . .'

'Sorry. Old reflex.' He looked at her left hand. His heart back-flipped when he saw no rings. 'You never married what's-his-name?' he asked.

'Doug.'

'That's right. Doug. Or was it Dougie?'

'You're making fun of someone's name?'

Myron shrugged. She had a point. 'So what happened to him?'

Her eyes studied a beer ring on the bar. 'It wasn't about him,' she said. 'You know that.'

He opened his mouth and then closed it. Rehashing the bitter past was not going to do any good. 'So what brings you back to the city?'

'I'm going to be teaching a semester at NYU.'

24

His heart sped up again. 'You moved back to Manhattan?'

'Last month.'

'I'm really sorry about your father's—'

'We got your flowers,' she interrupted.

'I wanted to do more.'

'Better you didn't.' She finished her drink. 'I have to go. It was nice seeing you.'

'I thought you were meeting someone.'

'My mistake, then.'

'I still love you, you know.'

She stood, nodded.

'Let's try again,' he said.

'No.'

She walked away.

'Jess?'

'What?'

He considered telling her about her sister's picture in the magazine. 'Can we have lunch sometime?' he asked. 'Just talk, okay?'

'No.'

Jessica turned and left him. Again.

Windsor Horne Lockwood III listened to Myron's story with his fingers steepled. Steepling looked good on Win, a lot better than on Myron. When Myron finished, Win said nothing for a few moments, doing more of that steepled-hands-concentration thing. Finally he rested his hands on the desk.

'My, my, haven't we had a special day?'

Myron rented his space from his old college roommate, Windsor Horne Lockwood III. People often said that Myron looked nothing like his name – an observation

Myron took as high praise; Windsor Horne Lockwood III, however, looked exactly like his name. Blond hair, perfect length, parted on the right side. His features were classical patrician, almost too handsome, like something crafted in porcelain.

His attire was always thoroughbred prep – pink shirts, polo shirts, monogrammed shirts, khaki pants, golf (read, ugly) pants, white bucks (Memorial Day to Labor Day) or wing tips (Labor Day to Memorial Day) on his feet. Win even had that creepy accent, the one that did not originate from any particular geographical location as much as from certain prep schools like Andover and Exeter. (Win had gone to Exeter.) He played a mean game of golf. He had a three handicap and was the fifth-generation member of stuffy Merion Golf Club in Philadelphia and third-generation at equally stuffy Pine Valley in southern New Jersey. He had a perennial golf tan, one of those where the color could be found only on the arms (short-sleeve shirts) and a V-shape in the neck (open alligator shirt), though Win's lily-white skin never tanned. It burned.

Win was full-fledged whitebread. He made star quarterback Christian Steele look like a Mediterranean houseboy.

Myron had hated Windsor on sight. Most people did. Win was used to it. People liked to form and keep an immediate impression. In Win's case that impression was old money, elitist, arrogant – in a phrase, a flaming asshole. There was nothing Win could do about it. People who relied solely on first impressions meant little to him.

Win gestured to the magazine on his desk. 'You chose not to tell Jessica about this?'

Myron stood, paced, and then sat back down. 'What was I going to say? "Hi, I love you, come back to me,

26

here's a photo of your supposedly dead sister advertising a sex phone in a porno mag?"'

Win thought a moment. 'I'd refine the wording a bit,' he said.

He flipped through the porno rag, his eyebrow arched as if to say Hmmm. Myron watched. He had decided not to tell Win about Chaz Landreaux or the incident in the garage. Not yet anyway. Win had a funny way of reacting when someone tried to hurt Myron. It wasn't always pretty. Better to save it for later, when Myron would know exactly how he wanted to handle Roy O'Connor. And Aaron.

Win dropped the magazine on his desk. 'Shall we begin?'

'Begin what?'

'Investigating. That is what you planned for us, correct?'

'You want to help?'

Win smiled. 'But of course.' He turned his phone around so that it faced Myron. 'Dial.'

'The number in the magazine?'

'Well, golly, Myron, I thought we'd call the White House,' Win said dryly. 'See if we can get Hillary to talk dirty.'

Myron took hold of the phone. 'You ever call one of these lines?'

'I?' Win feigned shock. 'The Debutantes' Darling? The Society Stud? Surely you jest.'

'Neither have I.'

'Perhaps you'd like to be alone, then,' Win said. 'Loosen your belt, pull down your trousers, that kind of thing.'

'Very funny.'

Myron dialed the 900 number under Kathy's photograph. He had made thousands of investigative calls, both during his years in the FBI and in his private work for team owners and commissioners. But this was the first time he'd felt self-conscious.

An awful beeping noise blasted his ear, followed by an operator: 'We're sorry. Your call is being blocked.'

Myron looked up. 'The call won't go through.'

Win nodded. 'I forgot. We have a block on all 900 calls. Employees were calling them all the time and ringing up quite a bill – not just the sex phones but astrologers, sports lines, psychics, recipes, even dial-a-prayers.' He reached behind him and pulled out another phone. 'Use this one. It's my private line. No blocks.'

Myron redialed. The phone rang twice before being picked up. A woman's voice on tape husked, 'Hello, there. You've reached the fantasy phone line. If you're under eighteen or do not wish to pay for this call, please hang up now.' Less than a second passed before she continued. 'Welcome to the fantasy phone line, where you can talk to the sexiest, most willing, most beautiful, most desirous women in the world.'

Myron noticed that the taped voice was speaking far more slowly now, as if she were reading to a kindergarten class. Each word was its own sentence.

'*Welcome. To. The. Fantasy . . .*'

'In a moment you will talk directly to one of our wondrous, gorgeous, voluptuous, hot girls who are here to heighten your pleasure to new boundaries of ecstasy. One-on-one private conversation. Discreetly billed to your phone. You will talk live with your personal fantasy girl.' The voice droned on with its own form of iambic pentameter. Finally the tape gave instructions: 'If you have a touch-tone phone, press one if you'd like to talk about the secret confessions of a naughty schoolteacher. Press two if . . .'

Myron looked up at Win. 'How long have I been on?'

'Six minutes.'

'Twenty-four dollars already,' Myron said. 'Does the term "total scam" mean anything to you?'

Win nodded. 'Talk about jerking off.'

Myron pressed a button, anything to get off this revolving tape. The phone rang ten times – Christ, they knew how to stretch the time – before he heard another female voice say, 'Hi, there. How are you today?'

Her voice was exactly what Myron had expected. Low and husky.

'Uh, hi,' Myron fumbled. 'Look, I'd like—'

'What's your name, honey?' she asked.

'Myron.' He slapped his forehead and held back a profanity. Had he really been stupid enough to use his real name?

'Mmmmm, Myron,' she said as if testing it out. 'I like that name. It's so sexy.'

'Yeah, well, thanks—'

'My name is Tawny.'

Tawny. Sure.

'How did you get my number, Myron?'

'I saw it in a magazine.'

'What magazine, Myron?'

The constant use of his name was beginning to unnerve him. '*Nips*.'

'Oooo. I like that magazine. It makes me so, you know.'

A way with words. 'Listen, uh, Tawny, I'd like to ask you about your ad.'

'Myron?'

29

'Yes.'

'I love your voice. You sound really hot. Do you want to know what I look like?'

'No, not real—'

'I have brown eyes. I have long brown hair, kinda wavy. I'm five-six. And I'm a 36–24–36. C cup. Sometimes a D.'

'You must be very proud but—'

'What do you like to do, Myron?'

'Do?'

'For fun.'

'Look, Tawny, you seem very nice, really, but can I talk to the girl in the ad?'

'I am the girl in the ad,' she said.

'No, I mean, the girl whose picture is in the magazine on top of this phone number.'

'That's me, Myron. I'm that girl.'

'The girl in the photo is a blonde with blue eyes,' Myron said. 'You said you had brown eyes and brown hair.'

Win gave him a thumbs-up, scoring one for the detailed eye of Myron Bolitar, ace investigator.

'Did I say that?' Tawny asked. 'I meant blonde with blue eyes.'

'I need to talk to the girl in the ad. It's very important.'

Her voice went down another octave. 'I'm better, Myron. I'm the best.'

'I don't doubt that, Tawny. You sound very professional. But right now I need to talk to the girl in the ad.'

'She's not here, Myron.'

'When will she be back?'

'I'm not sure, Myron. But just sit back and relax. We're going to have fun—'

'I don't want to be rude, but I'm really not interested. Can I talk to your boss?'

'My boss?'

'Yes.'

Her tone was different now. More matter-of-fact. 'You're kidding, right?'

'No. I'm serious. Please put your boss on.'

'Okay, then,' she said. 'Hold on a second.'

A minute passed. Then two. Win said, 'She's not coming back. She's just going to see how long the chump will stay on the line and pour dollars down her pants.'

'I don't think so,' Myron said. 'She liked my voice, said I sounded hot.'

'Oh, I didn't realize. Probably the first time she's ever said that.'

'My thinking exactly.' A few minutes later Myron put the receiver back in its cradle. 'How long was I on for?'

Win looked at his watch. 'Twenty-three minutes.' He grabbed a calculator. 'Twenty-three minutes times three ninety-nine per minute.' He punched in the numbers. 'That call cost you ninety-one dollars and seventy-seven cents.'

'A rare bargain,' Myron said. 'You want to hear something weird? She never said anything dirty.'

'What?'

'The girl on the phone. She never said anything dirty.'

'And you're disappointed.'

'Don't you find that a bit strange?'

Win shrugged, skimming through the magazine. 'Have you looked through this at all?'

'No.'

31

'Half the pages are advertisements for sex phones. This is clearly big business.'

'Safe sex,' Myron said. 'The safest.'

There was a knock on the door.

'Enter,' Win called out.

Esperanza opened the door. 'Call for you. Otto Burke.'

'Tell him I'll be right there.'

She nodded and left.

'I have some time on my hands,' Win said. 'I'll try to find out who placed the ad. We'll also need a sample of Kathy Culver's handwriting for comparison.'

'I'll see what I can come up with.'

Win resteepled his hands, bouncing the fingertips gently against one another. 'You do realize,' he began, 'that this photograph probably means nothing. Chances are there is a very simple explanation for all this.'

'Maybe,' Myron agreed, rising from his chair. He had been telling himself the same thing for the past two hours. He no longer believed it.

'Myron?'

'What?'

'You don't think it was a coincidence – Jessica being in the bar downstairs, I mean.'

'No,' Myron said. 'I guess I don't.'

Win nodded. 'Be careful,' he said. 'A word to the wise.'

Chapter 4

Damn him.

Jessica Culver sat in her family's kitchen, in the very seat she had sat in innumerable times as a child.

She should have known better. She should have thought it through, should have come prepared for any occurrence. But what had she done instead? She had gotten nervous. She had hesitated. She had stopped for a drink in the bar below his office.

Stupid, stupid.

But that wasn't all. He had surprised her, and she had panicked.

Why?

She should have told Myron the truth. She should have told him in a plain unemotional voice the real reason she was there. But she hadn't. She had been drinking unaware, and suddenly he had appeared, looking so handsome and yet so hurt and—

Oh shit, Jessie, you are one fucked-up chick . . .

She nodded to herself. Yup. Fucked up. Self-destructive. And a few other hyphenated words she couldn't come up with right now. Her publisher and agent did not see it that way, of course. They loved her 'foibles' (their term – Jessie preferred 'fuck-ups'), even encouraged them. They were what made Jessica Culver such an exceptional writer. They were what gave Jessica Culver's writing that certain 'edge' (again, their term).

Perhaps that was so. Jessie really couldn't say. But one thing was certain: These foibling fuck-ups had turned her life to shit.

Oh, pity the suffering artist! Thy heart bleeds for such torment!

She dismissed the mocking tone with a shake of her head. She was unusually introspective today, but that was understandable. She had seen Myron, and that had led to a lot of 'what if-ing' – a verifiable avalanche of useless 'what if-ing' from every conceivable height and angle.

What if. She pondered it yet again.

In her typically self-centered way, she had seen the 'what if-ing' only in terms of herself, not Myron. Now she wondered about him, about what his life had really been like since the world crumbled down upon him – not all at once – but in small, decaying bits. Four years. She had not seen him in four years. She had shoved Myron into some back closet in her mind and locked the door. She'd thought (hoped?) that would be the end of it, that the door could stand up to a little pressure without opening. But seeing him today, seeing the kind, handsome face high above those broad shoulders, seeing the still why-me stare in his eyes – the door had blown off its hinges like something in a gas explosion.

Jessica had been overwhelmed by her feelings. She

wanted to be with him so badly that she knew she had to get out right away.

Makes sense, she thought, *if you're a total fuck-up*.

Jessica glanced out the window. She was waiting for Paul's arrival. Bergen County police Lieutenant Paul Duncan – Uncle Paul to her, since infancy – was two years away from retirement. He had been her father's closest friend, the executor of Adam Culver's will. They had both worked in law enforcement – Paul as a cop, Adam as the county medical examiner – for more than twenty-five years.

Paul was coming to finalize the details for her father's memorial service. No funeral for Adam Culver. He wouldn't hear of it. But Jessica wanted to talk to Paul about another matter. Alone. She did not like what was going on.

'Hi, honey.'

She turned to the voice. 'Hi, Mom.'

Her mother came up through the basement. She was wearing an apron, her fingers fiddling with the large wooden cross around her neck. 'I put his chair in storage,' she explained in a forced matter-of-fact tone. 'Just cluttering space up here.'

For the first time Jessica realized that her father's chair – the one her mother must have been referring to – was gone from the kitchen table. The simple unpadded four-legged chair her father had sat in for as long as Jessica could remember, the one closest to the refrigerator, so close that her father could turn around, open the door, and stretch for the milk on the top shelf without getting up, had been taken away, stored in some cobwebbed corner of the basement.

But not so Kathy's.

35

Jessie's gaze touched down on the chair to her immediate right. Kathy's chair. It was still here. Her mother had not touched it. Her father, well, he was dead. But Kathy – who knew? Kathy could, in theory, walk through the back door right this very minute, banging it against the wall as she always did, smile brightly, and join them for dinner. The dead were dead. When you lived with a medical examiner, you understood just how useless the dead were. Dead and buried. The soul, well, that was another matter. Jessie's mom was a devout Catholic, attending mass every morning, and during crises like these her religious tenacity paid off – like someone who spent time in a gym finally finding a use for their new muscles. She could believe without question in a divine and joyous afterlife. Such a comfort. Jessica wished she could do the same, but over the years her religious fervor had become a strict couch potato.

Except, of course, Kathy might not be dead. Ergo the chair – Mom's lantern kept lit to guide her youngest back home.

Jessica awoke most mornings bolting upright in her bed, thinking about – no, inventing new possibilities for – her younger sister. Was Kathy lying dead in a pit somewhere? Buried under brush in the woods? A skeleton gnawed on by animals and inhabited by maggots? Was Kathy's corpse stuck in some cement foundation? Was it weighed down in the bottom of some river like the little undersea man in the living-room aquarium? Had she died painlessly? Had she been tortured? Had her body been chopped into small bits, burned, broken down with acid . . .

Or was she still alive?

That eternal spring.

Had Kathy possibly been kidnapped? Was she living in white slavery under the thumb of some Middle East sheikh? Or was she living chained to a radiator on a farm in Wisconsin like something on *Geraldo*? Could she have banged her head, forgotten who she was, and was now living as a street person with amnesia? Or had she simply run away to a different world?

The possibilities were endless. Even those lacking creativity can come up with a million different horrors when their loved one suddenly vanishes – or more painfully, a million different hopes.

Jessica's thoughts were chased away by the tired chugging of a car engine. A familiar Chevy Caprice blanketed with tiny dents pulled up. It looked like a retrieval car at a driving range. She stood and hurried out the front door.

Paul Duncan was a stocky man, compact, with salt-and-pepper hair now turning defiantly toward salt. He walked purposely, the way cops do. He greeted her on the front stoop with a big smile and kiss on the cheek. 'Hey, beautiful! How are you?'

She hugged him. 'I'm okay, Uncle Paul,' she said.

'You look great.'

'Thanks.'

Paul shaded his eyes from the sun. 'Come on, let's go inside. It's hot as hell out here.'

'In a minute,' she said, putting a hand on his forearm. 'I want to talk to you first.'

'What about?'

'My father's case.'

'I'm not handling that, honey. I don't do homicides anymore, you know that. Besides, it would be a conflict of interest – me being Adam's friend and all.'

'But you have to know what's going on.'

Paul Duncan nodded slowly. 'I do.'

'Mom said the police think he was killed in a robbery attempt.'

'That's right.'

'You don't believe that, do you?'

'Your father was robbed,' he said. 'His wallet was gone. His watch. Even his rings. The guy stripped him clean.'

'To make it look like a robbery.'

Paul smiled then, gently – the way, she remembered, he had at her confirmation and Sweet Sixteen party and high school graduation. 'What are you getting at, Jess?'

'You don't find this whole thing odd?' she asked. 'You don't see a connection between this and Kathy?'

He stumbled a step back, as if her words had given him a gentle push. 'What connection? Your sister vanished from her college campus. Your father was murdered by a robber a year and a half later. Where do you see a connection?'

'Do you really believe that they have nothing to do with each other?' she asked. 'Do you honestly believe that lightning struck twice in the same place?'

He put his hands in his pockets. 'If you mean do I think your family has been the victim of two separate awful tragedies, the answer is yes. It happens all the time, Jess. Life is rarely fair. God doesn't go around divvying out the bad in equal doses. Some families go through life with nary a scratch. Some get too much. Like yours.'

'So it's fate,' she said. 'That's your answer. Fate.'

He threw his hands up. 'Fate, lightning striking twice – these are your phrases. You're the writer here, not me. I just call it a tragedy. I just call it a tragic, somewhat bizarre coincidence. I've seen a lot stranger. So had your dad.'

The front door opened. Mom stood in the doorway. 'What's going on?'

'It's nothing, Carol. We were just talking.'

Carol looked at her daughter. 'Jessica?'

Her eyes stayed on Paul's, probing. 'Just talking, Mom.'

Jessica turned away and stepped back inside. Paul Duncan watched her, letting loose a silent breath. He had suspected she would be a problem – Jessica never accepted easy solutions to anything in life, even when the answer was simple. Yep, he had hoped it wouldn't happen, but he had definitely foreseen this possibility.

He just wasn't sure what he should do about it.

Midnight.

At ten P.M. Christian Steele had crawled under the blanket, read for ten minutes, and then switched off the light. Since then he had lain on his back in the dark, staring at the ceiling, not moving, not fooling himself into even hoping that sleep was imminent.

'Kathy,' he said out loud.

His mind floated about aimlessly, settling like a butterfly for only brief moments before moving on. Darkness surrounded him, but not silence. There was no such thing as silence at football camp. Christian heard kegs being thrown, loud music, laughter, singing, swearing. He could distinctly hear Charles and Eddie, his offensive tackles, in the next room. They were permanently set on loud, like a radio turned up before the knob was ripped out. Christian was not above partying too, having fun by consuming alcohol until he hugged the porcelain god and puked up his offering. But not tonight.

God, not tonight.

'Kathy,' he said again.

Was it possible? After all this time . . .

So many things were happening at once. School was over. The Titans' minicamp began the day after tomorrow. The scrutiny of the press had grown more intense than ever. He liked the attention, liked being on the cover of *Sports Illustrated*, liked the awe in people's faces when they spoke to him. Nice kid, they always said. Real nice. As though they expected him to be rude just because he could throw a pigskin with precision. As though he should somehow feel as though he belonged to a higher species, far above them, because he happened to be a good athlete.

Christian was excited. He was scared. He knew he had to think about the future. Myron had told him of the dangers and of how short-lived fame could be. Myron was, after all, a classic example. He had told Christian about the importance of cashing in now, that his career would at best last ten years. So much was at stake. So much. He was famous now, but there was a big difference between college famous and pro famous. Soon he'd have it all. Competition. Fame. Real money – not just the alumni secret handouts . . .

But so what?

'Kathy . . .'

His phone rang.

Christian shot up, his heart beating like a rabbit's. Fast reflexes. Sometimes they played against you. It was only the phone. Probably Charles or Eddie telling him, hey, it's party time! They'd both gotten drafted too. Charles had gone in the second round to Dallas. Eddie in the fifth to the Rams.

He picked up the phone. 'Hello?'

No response.

'Hello?' he said again.

Nothing. But the phone had not been hung up. Someone was there, silently holding the receiver to their ear.

'Who is this?'

Nothing.

Christian hung up. He began to lie back down when the phone rang again. He picked up the receiver.

'Hello?'

Silence again. Christian tried to listen more closely. Nothing. Or – or was that breathing? Panic seized him. He couldn't say why. It was just a prankster calling on his unlisted phone. It might even be Charles or Eddie playing some kind of joke. Nothing to get upset about.

Except he was upset.

He cleared his throat. 'What do you want?'

Still nothing.

'If you call back again, I'll call the cops.'

He slammed the phone down. His hand shook. He was just about to try to settle back down when he remembered something.

Star. Six. Nine.

The phone company had sent something in the mail today. There had been advertisements on the TV – a pregnant woman trying to get to the ringing phone, trudging across the room toward the phone, but when she arrived the caller had already hung up. Then what? She picked up the phone and the voice-over – Cliff Robertson's or someone like that – said something like 'You just missed the call. Was it important? Was it someone you wanted to talk to? There is only one way to find out. Press the star and then six and nine.' They demonstrated it on the screen now, in case anyone wasn't sure how to use a phone. Then the voice-over continued.

'You'll be connected to your previous caller, even if the number is busy. We'll keep dialing for you, leaving your phone line free to make or receive other calls.'

The pregnant woman listened to a phone ring and then spoke to her relieved husband, who was working on some drafting board at work.

Christian picked up the phone. Then he hit the star, the six, and the nine.

The phone rang.

He rubbed his chin. A moment later a robotic operator came on. 'The number is currently busy. We will ring you back when the line is free. Thank you.'

Christian replaced the receiver. He sat up and waited. The partying was still going on. He could hear three or four distinct partying areas. Someone shouted, 'Yahooo!' A window crashed. People cheered. His larger teammates were playing keg toss, a sort of discus throw involving beer kegs.

The phone rang.

He snatched the receiver as if it were a loose ball on the turf. The phone was ringing back the number – just like the pregnant lady's on the television. After the fourth ring the phone was picked up.

An answering machine.

A voice said, 'Hi. We're not in right now. Please leave a message at the beep, and we'll be sure to call you back. Thanks.'

The phone slipped from Christian's grip. A chilly hand caressed the back of his neck. A sound – some kind of choking noise – escaped his lips. Christian tried to form words but he couldn't.

The answering machine. The voice.

It was Kathy.

Chapter 5

Myron staggered into his office, punch-drunk from lack of sleep. He had not even bothered climbing into bed the night before. He tried to read, but the words swam in front of his eyes in meaningless waves. He put on the television. Nick at Nite, the cultural equivalent of aerosol cheese. Back-to-back episodes of *F Troop* for three hours. Larry Storch's portrayal of Agarn was, in a phrase, pure thespian genius. Who knew that hitting someone repeatedly with a big hat could be so funny?

But not even such highbrow entertainment could stop his mind from going back to one thought: Jess was back. And like Win had said, it was no coincidence.

At midnight his mother had come down in her robe.

'Hon, you all right?'

'I'm fine, Mom.'

'You seemed distracted all night.'

'It's nothing. Just have a lot of work.'

She looked at him with her a-mother-is-psychic-and-knows look of disbelief. 'Whatever you say.'

At the age of thirty-one Myron still lived at home. True, he had his own space, his own bedroom and bathroom in the basement. But there was no denying it. Myron still lived with Mommy and Daddy.

Five minutes after his mother had gone back to bed, Christian Steele called Myron on his private line, the one that rang softly in the basement so as not to wake up his parents, both of whom slept so lightly, Myron was sure they'd been some kind of ghetto lookouts in a previous life. He filled Myron in on the weird phone calls.

Myron was familiar with the star-six-nine, known as Return Call. The phone company charged on a 'pay-per-use' basis – around seventy-five cents per use. The problem was, Return Call did not trace the number. It automatically redialed the number of the last incoming call received, not letting you know the number. Star-five-seven – Call Trace – would have done the job, though the number is merely reported to the local phone company, which gives it only to the proper authorities.

Still, Myron would call some of his old sources at the phone company, see what he could find out. He knew that star-six-nine worked only for certain local areas. That meant the call was not long distance. A start. Better than nothing. He would also put Caller ID or a trace on Christian's phone. Taps were no longer like you saw on television, the hero anxiously trying to get the caller to stay on the line until it was completed. They were automatic. Caller ID actually showed you the incoming number before you picked up the phone.

But of course, none of that answered the larger questions:

44

Was it really Kathy's voice Christian had heard? And if so, what did that mean?

Lots of *preguntas*. Not too many answers.

He approached Esperanza's desk. 'How's it going?'

She pierced him with a glare, shook her head in disgust, and looked back down at her desk.

'Back on decaf?' he asked.

Another glare. Myron shrugged. 'Any messages?'

A head shake. Esperanza muttered something. Myron thought he picked up the Spanish equivalent of 'ass-wipe.'

'You want to tell me why you're so upset?'

'Right,' she said bitingly. 'Like you don't know.'

'I don't.'

The glare was back. Women had a talent for glares. Esperanza had a divine gift.

'Forget it,' he said. 'Just get me Otto Burke on the phone.'

'Now?' Esperanza said, her voice dripping with sarcasm. 'Won't you be busy?'

'Just do it, please, okay? You're starting to piss me off.'

'Oooo. I'm quaking.'

Myron shook his head. He had no time for her moods right now. He crossed the room and opened his office door. He stopped short.

'Hi.'

He cleared his throat and closed the door behind him. 'Hello, Jessica.'

For most athletes, Jessica thought, the spotlight fades slowly. But for a tragic few, it vanishes as though from a sudden power failure, bathing the athlete in dazzling darkness.

Such was the case with Myron.

45

For most athletes the expectation game helps dim the light gradually. A high school star becomes a college bench warmer. The light dims. A college starter realizes he will not be the team's high scorer. The light dims. The college superstar realizes he will never make it to the pros. The light dims. And then there are those very few, those who are one in a million, those with almost Wolfean 'right stuff,' who become professional athletes.

For those, the light is blinding, forever damaging the vision of the ones who stare directly into it. That was what made the dimming so important. An athlete could get used to losing the light slowly. His career would peak before tapering off just slightly. He would brighten from the inexperienced rookie to the player in his prime, and then the light would begin to fade as he moved past seasoned vet.

For Myron that had not happened.

He had been one of those select few who basked in the most potent wattage imaginable, as if the spotlight shone on him and from inside of him. His basketball talent had first became apparent in the sixth grade. He had gone on to break every scoring and rebounding record in Essex County, New Jersey, a perennial basketball stronghold. Myron was short for a forward, a program six-six (really only six-four), but he was a physical brute, a bull, and a hell of a leaper for a white man. He was highly recruited, chose Duke, and won two NCAA titles in four years.

The Boston Celtics had drafted him in the first round, the eighth pick overall. Myron's spotlight grew impossibly bright.

And then the fuse blew.

A freak injury, they called it. It was a preseason game against the Washington Bullets. Two players weighing a combined six hundred pounds sandwiched the rookie Myron Bolitar. The doctors threw all kind of terms at the man-child who had never been injured before, not even a twisted ankle. Multiple fractures, they said. Shattered kneecap. Casts. Wheelchair. Crutches. Cane.

Years.

Sixteen months later Myron could walk, though the limp lasted another two years. He never came back. His career was over. The only life he had ever known had been stripped from him. The press had done a story or two, but Myron was quickly forgotten.

Complete blackout.

Jessica frowned. Spotlight. Bad metaphor. Too cliché and inaccurate. She shook her head and looked up at him.

'That explains it,' Myron said.

'Explains what?'

'Esperanza's mood.'

'Oh.' She smiled at him. 'I told her we had an appointment. She didn't seem pleased to see me.'

'No kidding.'

'She'd still kill me for a nickel, huh?'

'Or half that much,' he replied. 'Want some coffee?'

'Sure.'

He picked up his phone. 'Can you get me a black coffee? Thanks.' He put the receiver back in its cradle and looked up at her.

'How's Win?' she asked.

'Good.'

'His family owns the building?'

'Yes.'

'I understand Win's become quite a financial whiz – despite himself.'

Myron nodded, waited.

'So you're still hanging around with Win,' she continued. 'You still have Esperanza. Not a lot changes.'

'Plenty changes,' he said.

Esperanza appeared at the door, the scowl still on her face. 'Otto Burke was in a meeting.'

'Try Larry Hanson.'

She handed the coffee to Jessica, smiled eerily, and left. Jessica studied the cup. 'Think she spat in it?'

'Probably,' Myron replied.

She put it down. 'I need to cut back anyway.'

Myron moved around his desk and sat down. The wall behind him was covered with theater posters. All musicals. His fingers drummed the desk.

'I'm sorry about yesterday,' she said. 'I wanted to surprise you, catch you off guard. Not the other way around.'

'Still seeking the upper hand?'

'I guess so, yeah. Old habit.'

He shrugged but said nothing.

'I need your help,' she said.

He waited.

She took a breath and plunged. 'The police say my father was killed in a robbery attempt. I don't believe it.'

'What do you believe?' he asked.

'I think his murder has something to do with Kathy.'

Myron was not surprised. He leaned forward, his eyes never staying on hers for very long. 'What makes you say that?'

'The police dismiss it as a coincidence,' she said simply. 'I'm not big on coincidences.'

'What about your dad's friend on the force, what's-his-name?'

'Paul Duncan.'

48

'Right, him. Have you spoken to him?'

'Yes.'

'And?'

She began tapping her foot, an old, subconscious, annoying habit. She made herself stop. 'Paul says it was a robbery too. He spews out all the facts about the crime scene, the missing wallet, the missing jewelry, that kind of thing. He is perfectly logical and objective, which is not his way.'

'What do you mean?'

'Paul Duncan is a passionate man. A hothead. Here his best friend has been murdered, and he seems almost blasé about it. It's not like him.' She stopped, shifted in her chair. 'Something isn't right here, I don't know how else to explain it.'

Myron rubbed his chin but kept quiet.

'Look, you know I was never very close to my father,' she continued. 'He wasn't an easy man to love. He was far better with his corpses than with breathing entities. He liked the ideal of family, the concept – it was the actual execution he found wearisome. But I still have to find out the truth. For Kathy.'

'How did your father and Kathy get along?' Myron asked.

She thought about it a moment. 'Better lately. When we were kids, they weren't very close. Kathy was a mama's girl, always hanging around my mom, wanting to be like her, the whole bit. But when she vanished, I'd venture to guess she was closer to my dad than my mom. He was crushed when she disappeared. He became obsessed. No, "obsessed" isn't strong enough. All of us were obsessed, of course. But not like my father. It consumed him entirely. Everything about him changed. He had always been the quiet county medical examiner, the man who made no waves. Now he was using his position to keep the pressure on twenty-four hours a day. He became paranoid, convinced the police weren't doing all they could do to find her. He even started his own investigation.'

'Did he find anything?'

'No. Not that I know of.'

Myron looked away. At the far wall. A movie still of the Marx Brothers. *A Night at the Opera*. Groucho looked back but offered no answers.

'What is it?' she asked.

'Nothing. Go on.'

'There isn't much else. I can only tell you that my father was acting very strangely the past few weeks. He started calling me all the time when previously we'd only talked maybe three times a year, sounding a little teary. It was like he was play-acting the part of perfect daddy with renewed vigor. I couldn't tell if it was a serious change or just a phase.'

Myron nodded, looking off again. He said nothing. Jessica almost thought he'd completely drifted off when he finally spoke, his voice almost inaudibly soft. 'What do you think happened to Kathy?' he asked.

'I don't know.'

'Do you think she's dead?'

'I—' She stopped. 'I miss her. It's . . . I don't want to think she's dead.'

He nodded again. 'So what do you want me to do?'

'Look into it. Find out what's going on.'

'Assuming something is going on.'

'Right.'

'Why me?'

50

She thought about it a moment. 'I'm not sure,' she said. 'I thought you'd believe me. I thought you'd help.'

'I'll help,' he said. 'But understand one thing: I have an important business interest in settling this whole thing.'

'Christian?'

'I'm his agent,' he continued. 'I'm responsible for his well-being.'

'He still misses my sister,' she said.

'Yes.'

'Is he okay?'

Myron's face remained set. 'He's fine.'

'He's a good kid. I like him.'

Myron nodded.

Jessica rose and stepped toward the window. Myron averted his eyes. He did not like to look at her for too long at one time. She understood. It hurt her too. She looked down at Park Avenue, twelve stories below. A taxi driver with a turban was shaking his fist at an old woman with a cane. The old woman whacked him and ran. The driver fell. The turban did not even shift.

'Hiding your feelings from me has never been your forte,' she said, still staring out the window. 'What don't you want to tell me?'

He did not reply.

'Myron . . .'

Esperanza saved him, bursting through the door without knocking. 'Larry Hanson is out of the office,' she said.

Win came in behind her. 'I got something for us on that magazine . . .' His voice died out when he saw Jessica.

'Hi, Win,' she said.

'Hello, Jessica Culver.' They embraced. 'My goodness, you look utterly fantastic. I read an article on you the other day, calling you the Literary Sex Symbol.'

'You shouldn't read such trash.'

'It was in my dentist's waiting room. Honest.'

An uncomfortable pause followed. Esperanza broke it by pointing at Jessica, making a gagging motion by sticking her finger in her mouth, and then storming out.

'Ever the enchantress,' Jessica muttered.

Myron stood. 'Where are you staying?'

'At my mom's.'

'Same number?'

'Yes.'

'I'll call you later. Right now I've got to go with Win.'

Jessica looked toward Win. He grinned at her. His face, as always, gave away nothing. 'I have a meeting with my editor this afternoon,' she said. 'But I'll be home all night.'

'Fine. I'll call you then.'

An awkward impasse. No one knew exactly how to say good-bye. A wave? A handshake? A kiss?

'We've got to go,' Myron said. He sprinted past her, never getting too close. Win shrugged at her in a what-can-you-do fashion and followed. She watched them disappear around the corner. Batman and Robin heading to the Bat-poles.

She left then. She had seen Myron twice now, and they had not yet touched – not even brushed up against one another.

It was an odd thing to wonder about.

Chapter 6

'What did you find out?' Myron asked.

Win whipped the wheel to the right. The Jag XJR responded with nary a squeal. They had been driving without speaking for the past ten minutes, Win's CD player the only sound. Win favored show tunes. *Man of La Mancha* was on now. Don Quixote serenaded his beloved Dulcinea.

'*Nips* magazine is published by HDP,' Win answered.

'HDP?'

'Hot Desire Press.' Another Bat-turn. The Jag accelerated past eighty.

'Speed limits,' Myron said. 'Heard of them?'

Win ignored him. 'Their editorial office is located in Fort Lee, New Jersey.'

'Editorial office?'

'Whatever. We have an appointment with Mr Fred Nickler, managing editor.'

'His mother must be proud.'

'Moralizing,' Win mused. 'Nice.'

'What did you tell Mr Nickler?' Myron asked.

'Nothing. I called and asked if we could see him. He said yes. Seemed like a very pleasant fellow.'

'I'm sure he's a prince.' Myron looked out the window. Buildings blurred. They fell back into silence. 'You're probably wondering what Jessica was doing in my office.'

Win gave a halfhearted shrug. It was not his way to pry.

'It's her father's murder. The police say it was a robbery. She thinks otherwise.'

'How does she see it?'

'She thinks there's a connection between his murder and Kathy.'

'So the plot thickens. Are we going to help her?'

'Yes.'

'Goodie. So do we think there is a connection?'

'Yes.'

'Yes,' Win agreed.

They pulled into the driveway of a building that could have been either a nice warehouse or low-rent office space. No elevator, but then again, only three levels. HDP, Inc., was on the second floor. When they entered the outer office, Myron was a bit surprised. He was not sure what he'd expected, but he had thought the dwellings of a sleaze merchant would not be so . . . nondescript. The walls were white with inexpensive but tastefully framed art posters – McKnight, Fanch, Behrens. Mostly scenery shots of beaches and sunset. Nothing with naked breasts. Surprise number one. Surprise number two was the unremarkable receptionist. She was strictly standard issue, not an over-aged, bleach-blond, flabby ex-bunny/sexpot/porno starlet with a breathy giggle and seductive wink.

54

Myron was almost disappointed.

'May I help you?' the receptionist asked.

Win said, 'We're here to see Mr Nickler.'

'Your names, please?'

'Windsor Lockwood and Myron Bolitar.'

She picked up the phone, buzzed in, and a moment later said, 'Right through that door.'

Nickler greeted them with a firm handshake. He was dressed in a blue suit, red tie, white shirt – conservative as a Republican senatorial candidate. Surprise number three. Myron had expected gold chains or a Joey Buttafuoco earring or at the very least a pinkie ring. But Fred Nickler wore no jewelry, except for a plain wedding band. His hair was gray, his complexion a bit washed out.

Win whispered, 'He looks like your uncle Sid.'

It was true. The publisher of *Nips* magazine looked like Sidney Griffin, popular suburban orthodontist.

'Please have a seat,' Nickler said, moving back behind his desk. He smiled at Myron. 'I was at the Final Fours when you guys beat Kansas. Twenty-seven points including the game winner. Hell of a performance. Incredible.'

'Thank you,' Myron said.

'Never seen anything like it. The way that final shot kissed the backboard.'

'Thank you.'

'Just incredible.' Nickler renewed his smile, shaking his head in awe at the memory. Then he sat back. 'So, what can I do for you gentlemen?'

Myron said, 'We have a couple of questions about an ad in one of your, uh, publications.'

'Which one?'

'*Nips*.' Saying the word felt grungy. Myron tried not to make a face.

'Interesting,' Nickler replied.

'What makes you say that?'

'*Nips* is a relatively new publication, and it's doing poorly – far and away the worst of HDP's monthlies. I'm going to give it another month or two, and then it'll probably fold.'

'How many magazines do you publish?'

'Six.'

'Are they all like *Nips*?'

Nickler chuckled lightly. 'They are all pornographic magazines, yes. And they are all completely legal.'

Myron handed him the magazine Christian had given him. 'When was this printed?'

Fred Nickler barely glanced at it. 'Four days ago.'

'That's all?'

'It's our most recent issue – they've barely hit the stands. I'm surprised you found one.'

Myron opened to the proper page. 'We'd like to know who paid for this advertisement.'

Nickler put on a pair of half-moon glasses. 'Which one?'

'Bottom row. The Lust Line.'

'Oh,' he said. 'A sex phone.'

'Is there a problem?'

'No. But this ad wasn't paid for.'

'What do you mean?'

'It's the nature of the business,' Nickler explained. 'Someone calls me up to place an ad for a dial-a-porn line. I tell him it costs X amount. He says, wow, I'm just starting out, I can't afford it. So if it looks like a good idea, I go in fifty-fifty with him. In other words, I take care of the marketing, if you will, while my partner takes care of the technical side – phones, cables, girls to work the phones, whatever else. Then we split it down the middle. It limits both of our risks.'

'Do you do this a lot?'

He nodded. 'Ninety percent of my advertising comes for fantasy lines. I'd say I have a piece of the action in three-quarters of them.'

'Can you give us the name of your partner on this particular venture?'

Nickler studied the picture in the magazine. 'You're not with the police, are you?'

'No.'

'Private investigators?'

'No.'

He took off his glasses. 'I'm fairly small-time,' he said. 'I have my own little niche. It's the way I like it. No one bothers me, and I don't bother anybody else. I have no interest in a lot of publicity.'

Myron shot a glance at Win. Nickler had a family, probably a nice house in Tenafly, told the neighbors he was in publishing. Pressure could be applied. 'I'll be frank with you,' Myron said. 'If you don't help us out, it may blow up into something major. Newspapers, TV, the works.'

'Is that a threat?'

'Absolutely not.' Myron reached into his wallet and took out a fifty-dollar bill. He placed it on the desk. 'We just want to know who put this ad in.'

Nickler pushed the bill back toward Myron, his expression suddenly irritated. 'What is this, a movie? I don't need a payoff. If the guy has done something wrong, I want no part of him. This business has enough problems as it is. I run a straight operation. No underage girls, nothing illegal in any way, shape, or form.'

Myron looked at Win. 'Told you he was a prince.'

'Think what you want,' Nickler said in a voice that said he'd been down this road many times before. 'This is a business like any other. I'm just an honest guy trying to make an honest buck.'

'Real American of you.'

He shrugged. 'Look, I don't defend everything about this business. But there are plenty of worse. IBM, Exxon, Union Carbide – these are the real monsters, the real exploiters. I don't steal. I don't lie. I satisfy a societal need.'

Myron had a quick comeback, but Win stopped him with a shake of his head. He was right. What was the point in antagonizing the guy?

'Could we have the name and address, please?' Myron asked.

Nickler opened a drawer behind him and pulled out a file. 'Is he in some sort of trouble?'

'We just need to talk to him.'

'Can you tell me why?'

Win spoke to Nickler for the first time. 'You don't want to know.'

Fred Nickler hesitated, saw Win's steady gaze, then nodded. 'The company is called ABC. They have a PO box in Hoboken, number 785. The guy's name is Jerry. I don't know anything else about him.'

'Thanks,' Myron said, standing. 'One more question if you don't mind: Have you ever seen the girl in the ad?'

'No.'

'You're sure?'

'Positive.'

'If you do or if you think of anything else, will you give me a call?' Myron handed him a card.

58

Nickler looked as if he wanted to ask a question, his gaze continually drifting back to Kathy's photograph, but he settled for saying 'Sure.'

Once outside, Win asked, 'What do you think?'

'He's lying,' Myron said.

Back in the car Myron asked, 'Can I use the phone?'

Win nodded, his foot not slackening on the pedal. The speedometer was hovering at seventy-five. Myron watched it as if it were a taxi meter on a long ride, keeping his gaze averted from the blur of a street.

Myron dialed the office. Esperanza answered the phone after one ring.

'MB SportReps.'

MB SportReps. The M stood for Myron, the B for Bolitar. Myron had thought of the name himself, though he rarely bragged about it. 'Did Otto Burke or Larry Hanson call?'

'No. But you have lots of messages.'

'Nothing from Burke or Hanson?'

'You deaf?'

'I'll be back in a little while.'

Myron hung up. Otto and Larry should have called by now. They were avoiding him. The question was, why?

'Trouble?' Win asked.

'Maybe.'

'I believe we need a rejuvenation.'

Myron looked up. He recognized the street immediately. 'Not now, Win.'

'Now.'

'I have to get back to the office.'

'It'll keep. You need inner energy. You need focus. You need balance.'

'I hate it when you talk like that.'

Win smiled, pulling into the parking lot. 'Come along now. I'd hate to kick your ass right here in the car.'

The sign read MASTER KWAN'S TAE KWON DO SCHOOL. Kwan was nearing seventy now and rarely conducted classes any longer, choosing instead to hire well-tutored underlings to handle that work. Master Kwan stayed in his high-tech office, surrounded by four television screens so he could monitor the classes. Occasionally he leaned forward and barked something into a microphone, scaring some poor student into attention. Like something out of *The Wizard of Oz*.

If Master Kwan's English improved a bit, it might reach the level of pidgin. Win had brought him over from Korea fourteen years ago, when Win was only seventeen. It seemed to Myron that Master Kwan had spoken better English back then.

Win and Myron changed into their white uniforms called *dobok*. Both men wrapped black belts around their stomachs. Win was a sixth-degree black belt, about as high a ranking as anybody in the United States. He had been studying tae kwon do since the age of seven. Myron had picked it up in college, giving him a dozen years of studying and a third-degree black belt.

They approached Master Kwan's door, paused in the doorway until he acknowledged their presence, then bowed at the waist. 'Good afternoon, Master Kwan,' they said in unison.

Kwan smiled toothlessly. 'You here early.'

'Yes, sir,' Win replied.

'Need help?'

'No, sir.'

Kwan dismissed them by spinning back to his television

screens. Myron and Win bowed once more and moved into the private *dojang* for the upper-ranked black belts. They began with meditation, something Myron had never quite gotten the full grasp of. Win loved it. He did it for at least an hour a day. Win folded himself into a lotus position. Myron settled for sitting Indian style. Both men closed their eyes, placed their thumbs on the palm directly below the pinkie, and tilted their palms toward the ceiling. They rested their hands on their knees. Instructions echoed through Myron's mind like a mantra. Back straight. Bottom of tongue curled up against the back of the upper teeth. He breathed in through his nose for six seconds, concentrating on pushing the air down into the pit of his gut, making sure that his chest did not move, that only his abdomen expanded. Then he held the air down deep, counting to himself to prevent his mind from wandering. After seven seconds he slowly released the air through the mouth for a ten count, making sure to empty completely his contracting gut. Then he waited four seconds before breathing in again.

Win did this painlessly. He did not count. His mind went blank. Myron always counted, needing it to keep his mind from wandering back to the problems of the day – especially on a day like today. But in spite of himself he began to relax, to feel the tension leave his body with every long exhalation. It almost tingled.

They meditated for ten minutes before Win opened his eyes and said, '*Barro*.' Korean for stop.

They performed deep stretching exercises for the next twenty minutes. Win had the flexibility of a ballet dancer, performing full splits effortlessly. Myron had gained a lot of flexibility since taking up tae kwon do. He believed it had helped him gain six inches on his vertical leap in college. He could almost do a full split, but he couldn't hold it long.

In short Myron was flexible; Win was Gumby.

They went through their forms or *poomse* next, a complicated set of moves not unlike a violent dance step. What many exercised-crazed junkies never realized is that the martial arts are the ultimate aerobic workout. You are in constant motion – jumping, turning, spinning – propelling both arms and both legs nonstop for a half hour at a time. Low block and front kick, high block and punch, middle block and roundhouse kick. Inside blocks, outside blocks, knife-hand, fists, palm strikes, knees and elbows. It was an exhausting and exhilarating workout.

Win moved through his routine flawlessly – ever the contradiction and deception. See Win on the street, and people said arrogant Waspy wimp who couldn't bruise a peach with his best punch. See him in a *dojang*, and he struck fear and awe. Tae kwon do is considered a martial art. Art. The word was not used by accident. Win was an artist, the best Myron had ever seen.

Myron remembered the first time he'd seen Win demonstrate his talent. They were freshmen in college. A group of large football players decided to shave Win's blond locks because they didn't like the way he looked. Five of them sneaked into Win's room late at night – four to hold down his arms and legs and one to carry the razor and shaving cream.

Simply put, the football team had a poor season that year. Too many guys on the injured list.

Myron and Win finished up with light free sparring. Then they dropped to the mat and performed one hundred push-ups on their fists – Win counting out loud in

Korean. That done, they sat again for meditation, this time lasting fifteen minutes.

'*Barro*,' Win said.

Both men opened their eyes.

'Feeling more focused?' Win asked. 'Feeling the flow of energy? The balance?'

'Yes, Grasshopper. You want me to snatch the pebble from your hand now?'

Win moved from his lotus position into a full stance in one graceful, effortless move. 'So,' he said, 'have you reached any decisions?'

'Yes.' Myron struggled to stand in one motion, tipping from side to side as he ascended. 'I'm going to tell Jessica everything.'

Chapter 7

Yellow stick-on phone messages swarmed Myron's phone like locusts on a carcass. Myron peeled them away and shuffled through them. Nothing from Otto Burke or Larry Hanson or anyone in the Titans organization.

Not good.

He strapped on his headset telephone. He had resisted using one for a long time, figuring they were more suited for air traffic controllers than agents, but he quickly learned that an agent is but a fetus, his office a womb, his telephone an umbilical cord. It was easier with the headset. He could walk around; he could keep his hands free; he could forgo neck cramps from cradling a phone against his shoulder.

His first call was to the advertising director for Burger-City, a new fast-food chain. They wanted to sign up Christian and were offering pretty good money, but Myron wasn't sure about it. BurgerCity was only region-al. A national chain might come up with a better offer.

Sometimes the hardest part of the job was saying no. He'd discuss the pros and cons with Christian, let him make the final decision. In the end it was his name. His money.

Myron had already signed Christian to several very lucrative endorsement deals. Wheaties would have Christian's likeness on cereal boxes starting in October. Diet Pepsi was coming up with some promotion involving Christian throwing a two-liter bottle on a perfect spiral to nubile women. Nike was developing a sweatsuit line and cleats known as the Steele Trap.

Christian stood to earn millions from endorsements, far more than he would make playing for the Titans, no matter how reasonable Otto Burke wanted to be. It was strange in a way. Fans grew agitated at the idea of a player trying to get the most out of his playing contract. They called him boorish, selfish, and egomaniacal when he demanded a great deal of money from a wealthy team owner – but they had no problem when he grabbed vault-loads from Pepsi or Nike or Wheaties for promoting products he'd probably never used or even liked. It made no sense. Christian would make more money for spending three days shooting a thirty-second hypocritical spot than he would for spending the season getting blindsided by drooling men with overactive pituitary glands – and that was how the fans wanted it.

No agent minded that setup. Most agents got between three and five percent of their players' total negotiated salary (Myron took four percent), compared with twenty or twenty-five percent for all endorsement money. (Myron took fifteen percent – hey, he was new.) In other words, sign a million-dollar deal with a team, and the agent gets around forty grand. Sign him for a million-dollar commercial, and the agent can nab as much as a quarter mil.

Myron's second call was to Ricky Lane, a running back for the New York Jets and a former college teammate of Christian's. Ricky was one of his most important clients, and Myron was fairly certain it had been Ricky who'd convinced Christian to hire him in the first place.

'I have a kids' camp appearance for you,' Myron began. 'They're paying five grand.'

'Sounds good,' Ricky said. 'How long do I have to be there?'

'Couple hours. Do a little talk, sign a few autographs, that kind of thing.'

'When?'

'A week from Saturday.'

'What about that mall appearance?'

'That's Sunday,' Myron said. 'Livingston Mall. Morley's Sporting Goods.' Ricky would get paid another five thousand dollars for sitting at a table for two hours and signing autographs.

'Cool.'

'You want me to send a limo to pick you up?'

'No, I'll drive. You hear anything about next year's contract yet?'

'We're getting there, Ricky. Another week at the most. Listen, I want you to come in and see Win soon, okay?'

'Yeah, sure.'

'You in shape?'

'The best of my life,' Ricky said. 'I want that starting job.'

'Keep working. And don't forget to make that appointment with Win.'

'Will do. Later, Myron.'

'Yeah, later.'

The calls continued, one blurring into another. He

returned calls from the press. They all wanted to know about a pending deal between the Titans and Christian. Myron politely no-commented. Occasionally it was good to use the media as leverage in negotiating, but not with Otto Burke. Matters were proceeding, he told them. An agreement could be expected at any time.

He then called Joe Norris, an old-time Yankee who appeared almost every weekend at a baseball card show. Joe made more in a month now than he had in an entire season in his heyday.

Next up was Linda Regal, a tennis pro who had just cracked the top ten. Linda was worried about aging, offended because a broadcaster had referred to her as a 'familiar veteran.' Linda was almost twenty.

Eric Kramer, a UCLA senior and probable second round NFL draft pick, was in town. Myron managed to arrange a dinner with him. That meant Myron was a finalist – he and a zillion other agents. The competition was incredible. Example: There are twelve hundred NFL-authorized agents who court the two hundred college players who will be drafted in April. Something has to give. It's usually ethics.

Myron called the New York Jets general manager, Sam Logan, to discuss Ricky Lane's contract.

'The kid is in the best shape of his career,' Myron raved. He stood and paced. Myron had a large, fairly gorgeous office on Park Avenue between Forty-sixth and Forty-seventh streets. It impressed people, and appearance was important in a business dominated by sleaze-balls. 'I've never seen anything like it. I'm telling you, Sam, the kid is Gayle Sayers all over again. It's amazing, really.'

'He's too small,' Logan said.

'What are you talking about? Is Barry Sanders too small? Is Emmitt Smith too small? Ricky's bigger than both of them. And he's been lifting. I'm telling you, he's going to be a great one.'

'Uh-huh. Look, Myron, he's a nice kid. He works hard. But I can't go any higher than . . .'

The number was still too low. But it was better.

The calls continued without a break. Sometime during the day Esperanza brought him a sandwich, which he inhaled.

At eight o'clock Myron placed his final office call of the day.

Jessica answered. 'Hello?'

'I'll be at your house in an hour,' Myron said. 'We need to talk.'

Myron watched Jessica's face for a reaction. She kept looking at the magazine as if it were just another issue of *Newsweek*, her expression frighteningly passive. Every once in a while she nodded, looked over the rest of the page, and glanced at the front and back covers of the magazine, always returning to the picture of Kathy. She was so nonchalant, Myron almost expected her to whistle.

Only her knuckles gave her away. They were bloodless white, the pages crinkling in her death grip.

'Are you okay?' he asked.

'I'm fine,' she said, her voice calm, almost soothing. 'You said Christian got this in the mail?'

'Yes.'

'And you and Win spoke to the man who publishes this' – she hesitated, her face finally showing some signs of disgust – 'this thing?'

'Yes.'

She nodded. 'Did he give you the address of whoever put this ad in?'

'Just a PO box. I'm going to scout it out tomorrow, see who picks up the mail.'

She looked up for the first time. 'I'll go with you.'

He almost protested but stopped himself. He didn't stand a chance. 'Okay.'

'When did Christian give this to you?'

'Yesterday.'

That got her attention. 'You knew about this yesterday?'

He nodded.

'And you didn't tell me?' she snapped. 'I was pouring my heart out to you, feeling like some paranoid schizophrenic, and you knew about this the whole time?'

'I wasn't sure how to tell you.'

'Anything else you haven't told me?'

'Christian got a phone call last night. He thinks it was from Kathy.'

'What?'

He quickly told her about it. When he reached the part about Christian hearing Kathy's voice, her face drained of all color.

'Has your friend at the phone company learned anything?' she asked.

'No. But we know Return Call only works for specific towns within the 201 area codes.'

'How many towns?'

'About three-quarters of them.'

'So you're talking about three-quarters of the northern part of New Jersey, the most densely populated state in the US? That limits it down to what, two, three million people?'

'It's not a big help,' he admitted, 'but it's something.'

Her eyes settled back on the magazine. 'I didn't mean to jump all over you. It's just—'

'Forget it.'

'You're the best person I've ever known,' she said. 'I mean that.'

'And you're the biggest pain in the ass.'

'Tough to argue that one,' she said, but there was a hint of a smile.

'Do you want to tell the police about this?' he asked. 'Or Paul Duncan?'

She thought a moment. 'I'm not sure.'

'The press will eat it up,' he said. 'They'll drag Kathy through the mud.'

'I don't give a rat's ass what the press does.'

'I'm just telling you,' Myron said.

'They can call her a slut a million different ways. I don't care.'

'What about your mom?'

'I don't give a rat's ass what she wants either. I just want Kathy found.'

'So you want to tell them,' Myron said.

'No.'

He looked at her, confused. 'Care to elaborate?'

Her words came slow, measured, the ideas coming to her even as she spoke. 'Kathy has been gone for more than a year now,' she began. 'In all that time the cops and the press have come up with zip. Not one thing. She's just vanished without a trace.'

'So?'

'But now we get this magazine. Someone sent it to Christian, which means someone – maybe Kathy, maybe not – is trying to make contact. Think about it. For the first time in over a year there is some form of communication. I don't want that taken away. I don't want a lot of attention scaring away whoever is out there. Kathy might disappear again. This' – she held up the magazine – 'this thing is disgusting, but it's also encouraging. It's something. Don't get me wrong. I'm shocked by this. But it's a solid thread – a thread as confusing as all hell, but nonetheless a thread of hope. If the cops and the press are called in, whoever did this might get scared and vanish again. Permanently this time. I can't risk that. We have to keep this to ourselves.'

Myron nodded. 'Makes sense.'

'So what's next?' she asked.

'We go to the post office in Hoboken. I'll pick you up early. Say six.'

Chapter 8

Jessica smelled great.

They were at Uptown Station in Hoboken. She stood very close to him. Her hair had that freshly washed smell he had tried for four years to forget. Inhaling made him feel light-headed.

'So this is playing detective,' she said.

'Exciting, isn't it?'

They had been trying to look inconspicuous – no easy task when a man is six-four and a woman is a total knee-knocker – for the better part of an hour, having arrived at the post office at six-thirty in the morning. No one had touched Box 785 yet.

Boredom set in quickly. Jessica looked over the prices of different mailing containers. Not very interesting. She read the wanted ads, all of them, found them a bit more interesting. Wanted posters in a post office. Like they wanted you to write the guy a letter.

'You sure know how to show a girl a good time,' she said.

'That's why they call me Captain Fun.'

She laughed. The melodic sound twisted his stomach.

'Do you like being an agent, Captain Fun?'

'Very much.'

'I always thought of agents as a bunch of sleazeballs.'

'Thank you.'

'You know what I mean. Leeches. Vipers. Greedy, money-hungry, bloodsucking parasites, swindling naïve jocks, doing lunch at Le Cirque, destroying everything that's good about sports—'

'The problems in the Middle East,' he interrupted. 'That's our fault too. And the budget deficit.'

'Right. But you're not any of those things.'

'Not a leech, viper, or parasite. That's quite a rave.'

'You know what I mean.'

He shrugged. 'There are plenty of sleazy agents. There are also plenty of sleazy doctors, lawyers—' He stopped, the words sounding familiar. Hadn't Fred Nickler used the same argument in justifying his magazines? 'Agents are a necessary evil,' he continued. 'Without them, athletes get taken advantage of.'

'By whom?'

'Owners, management. Agents have done some good for the athletes. They've helped raise their salaries, assure free agency, get them endorsement money.'

'So what's the problem?'

Myron thought a moment. 'Two things,' he said. 'First of all, some agents are crooks. Plain and simple. They see a young, rich kid, and they take advantage. But as the athletes get more sophisticated, as more stories like what

73

happened to Kareem Abdul-Jabar become known, most of the crooks will be weeded out.'

'And second?'

'Agents have to wear too many hats,' he said. 'We're negotiators, accountants, financial planners, hand-holders, travel agents, family counselors, marriage counselors, errand boys, lackeys – whatever it takes to get the business.'

'So how do you do it all?'

'I give two of the biggest hats to Win – accountant and financial planner. I'm the lawyer. He's the MBA. Plus we have Esperanza, who can do almost anything. It works well. We all check and balance one another.'

'Just like the branches of the federal government.'

He nodded. 'Jefferson and Madison would be proud.'

A hand reached out and opened Box 785.

'Show time,' Myron said.

Jessica snapped her head around to look. The man was slim. Everything about him was too long, eerily elongated, as if he had spent time on a medieval rack. Even his face seemed stretched like a cartoon imprint on Silly Putty.

'Recognize him?' Myron asked.

She hesitated. 'Something about him . . . but I don't think so.'

'Come on, let's get out of here.'

They hurried down the steps and got in the car. Myron had parked illegally in front of the building, putting a police emergency sign in his front windshield. A gift from a friend on the force. The emergency sign came in handy – especially during sale days at the mall.

The slim man came out two minutes later. He got into a yellow Oldsmobile. New Jersey plates. Myron shifted into drive and followed. Slim took Route 3 to the Garden State Parkway north.

'We've been driving almost twenty minutes,' Jessica said. 'Why would he go to a mailbox so far from his home?'

'Could be that he's not going to his house. Maybe he's going to work.'

'The dial-a-porn office?'

'Maybe,' Myron said. 'Or it could be that he travels a long way so no one will see him.'

He got off at Exit 160, jumped on Route 208 heading north, and pulled off at Lincoln Avenue, Ridgewood.

Jessica sat up. 'This is my exit,' she said.

'I know.'

'What the hell is going on here?'

The yellow Oldsmobile turned left at the end of the ramp. They were now within three miles of Jessica's house. If he took Lincoln Avenue all the way to Godwin Road, they'd be . . .

Nope.

Mr Slim turned on Kenmore Road, a half-mile before the Ridgewood border. They were still in the heart of suburbia – the suburb in question being Glen Rock, New Jersey. Glen Rock was so named because of a giant rock that sat on Rock Road. The key word here is *rock*.

The yellow Olds pulled into a driveway. 78 Kenmore Drive.

'Look casual,' he said. 'Don't stare.'

'What?'

He didn't answer. He drove past the house without pausing, turned at the next street, and stopped the car behind some shrubs. He picked up the car phone and dialed the office. It was picked up midway through the first ring.

'MB SportReps,' Esperanza said.

'Get me all you can on 78 Kenmore Street, Glen Rock, New Jersey. Owner's name, credit check, the works.'

'Got it.' Click.

He dialed another number. 'My friend at the phone company,' he explained to Jessica. Then: 'Lisa? It's Myron. Look, I need a favor. Seventy-eight Kenmore Road, Glen Rock, New Jersey. I don't know how many lines the guy has, but I need you to check them all. I want to know every number he calls for the next two hours. Right. Hey, what did you find out about that 900 number? What? Oh, okay, I understand. Thanks.'

He hung up.

'What did she say?'

'The 900 number isn't operated by the phone company. Some small outfit out of South Carolina takes care of it. She can't get anything on it.'

'So what do we do now?' she asked. 'Just watch his house?'

'No. I go inside. You wait here.'

She arched an eyebrow. 'Excuse me?'

'You were the one who didn't want to scare anyone away,' he continued. 'If this guy has something to do with your sister, how do you think he'll react to seeing you?'

She folded her arms across her chest and fumed. She knew he was right, but that didn't mean she had to be happy about it. 'Go,' she said.

He got out of the car. It was one of those no-variety neighborhoods, each house cookie-cut from the same mold – split-levels on three-quarters of an acre. Sometimes the house was backward, the kitchen on the right instead of the left. Most had aluminum siding. The street reeked of middle class.

Myron knocked. The thin man opened the door.

'Jerry?'

Slim's face registered confusion. Up close he was better looking, his face more brooding than freakish. Give him a cigarette and a black turtleneck, and he could be reading poetry in a village café. 'May I help you?'

'Jerry, I'm—'

'You must have the wrong house. My name isn't Jerry.'

'You look like Jerry.'

Something dark crossed his face. 'I'm sorry,' he said, closing the door. 'I really don't have time right now.'

'Sure about that, Jer?'

'I already told you—'

'Do you know Kathy Culver?'

It was a sneak attack. And it drew blood. 'Wha – what's this all about?' he snapped.

'I think you know.'

'Who are you?'

'My name is Myron Bolitar.'

'Am I supposed to know you?'

'Well, if you're a big basketball fan . . . actually, no. But I'd like to ask you a few questions.'

'I have nothing to say.'

Ace of spades time. Myron pulled out the magazine. 'Sure about that, Jerry?'

The whites of Slim's eyes grew tenfold, looking like Wedgwood china on the elongated face. 'You have me mixed up with someone else. Good-bye.'

He slammed the door.

Myron shrugged, headed back to the car.

'Well?' Jessica asked.

'We shook him,' Myron said. 'Let's see what falls out.'

The neighborhood newsstand.

Win remembered a time when the phrase conjured up nostalgia and Rockwellian images of real America. No more. Any street, any corner, any hickville town was the same. Candy, newspapers, greeting cards – and porno mags. Kids could pick up a Snickers bar and get an eyeful, all in one. Porno had become a staple of American life. Hardcore porn. The kind of porn that made *Penthouse* look like *Highlights* magazine.

Win approached the man behind the lottery ticket dispenser. 'Pardon me,' Win said.

'Yeah?'

'Would you be able to tell me if you have the most recent issues of *Climaxx*, *Jiz*, *Orgasm Today*, *Licks*, *Quim*, and *Nips*?'

An elderly woman gasped and gave him an icy stare. Win smiled at her. 'Let me guess,' he said. 'Playmate of the Month, June 1926?'

She made a harumph noise and turned away.

'Check over there,' the man said. 'Between the comic books and Disney videos.'

'Thank you.'

Win found three of them – *Climaxx*, *Orgasm Today*, and *Quim*. He tried three other newsstands and was able to pick up *Lick*, but there was no sign of *Jiz* or *Nips*. He finally found copies of them at a hardcore shop on Forty-second Street called King David's Smut Palace. They had a big sign out front that said OPEN 24 HOURS. How very convenient. Win considered himself fairly worldly, but the items and photographs in the 'palace' proved that both his life experiences and his imagination had at best been limited.

It was almost noon when he exited the palace. A productive and quasi-educational morning.

With a total of eight magazines lodged under his arm, Win caught a taxi to midtown. He skimmed through a few in the backseat.

'So far so good,' he said out loud.

The driver glanced at him in the rearview mirror, shrugged, looked back to the road.

When Win arrived at his office, he spread the magazines across the vast breadth of his desk. He studied them closely, comparing them. Incredible. His suspicion had been sound. It was just as he thought.

Five minutes later, Win put the magazines in his desk drawer. Then he buzzed Esperanza.

'Kindly send Myron to my office as soon as he comes in.'

Chapter 9

'I have a confession,' Jessica said.

They were coming out of the Kinney garage on Fifty-second Street, the smell of fumes and urine dissipating as they hit the relatively fresh air on the sidewalk. They turned down Fifth Avenue. The line for passports stretched past the statue of Atlas. A black man with long dreadlocks sneezed repeatedly, his hair flapping about like dozens of snakes. A woman behind him tsk-tsked a complaint. Many of the people waiting faced St Patrick's across the street as though pleading for divine intervention, their faces lined with anguish. Japanese tourists took pictures of both the statue and the line.

'I'm listening,' Myron replied.

They kept walking. Jessica did not face him, her gaze fixed on nothing straight ahead. 'We weren't close anymore. In fact, Kathy and I barely spoke.'

Myron was surprised. 'Since when?'

'The last three years or so.'

'What happened?'

She shook her head, but she still did not look at him. 'I don't know exactly. She changed. Or maybe she just grew up and I couldn't handle it. We just drifted apart. When we saw each other, it was as if she couldn't stand to be in the same room with me.'

'I'm sorry to hear that.'

'Yeah, well, it's no big thing. Except Kathy called me the night she disappeared. First time in I don't know how long.'

'What did she want?'

'I don't know. I was on my way out the door. I rushed her off.'

They fell into silence the rest of the way to Myron's office.

When they got off the elevator, Esperanza handed him a sheet of paper and said, 'Win wants to see you right away.' She glared at Jessica the way a linebacker might glare at a limping quarterback on a blindside blitz.

'Otto Burke or Larry Hanson call?' Myron asked.

She swerved her glare toward Myron. 'No. Win wants to see you right away.'

'I heard you the first time. Tell him I'll be up in five minutes.'

They moved into Myron's office. He closed the door and skimmed over the sheet. Jessica sat in front of him. She crossed her legs the way few women could, turning an ordinary event into a moment of sexual intrigue. Myron tried not to stare. He also tried not to remember the luscious feel of those legs in bed. He was unsuccessful in both endeavors.

'What's it say?' she asked.

He snapped to. 'Our slim friend on Kenmore Street in Glen Rock is named Gary Grady.'

Jessica squinted. 'The name sounds familiar.' She shook her head. 'But I can't place it.'

'He's been married seven years, wife Allison. No kids. Has a $110,000 mortgage on that house, pays it on time. Nothing else yet. We should know more in a little while.' He put the paper on his desk. 'I think we have to start attacking this on a few different fronts.'

'How?'

'We have to go back to the night your sister disappeared. Start with that, and move forward. The whole case needs to be reinvestigated. The same with your father's murder. I'm not saying the cops weren't thorough. They probably were. But we now know some things they don't.'

'The magazine,' she said.

'Exactly.'

'How can I help?' she asked.

'Start finding out all you can about what she was up to when she disappeared. Talk to her friends, roommates, sorority sisters, fellow cheerleaders – anyone.'

'Okay.'

'Also get her school records. Let's see if there's anything there. I want to see what courses she was taking, what activities she was involved with, anything.'

Esperanza threw open the door. 'Meal Ticket. Line two.'

Myron checked his watch. Christian should be in the middle of practice by now. He picked up the phone. 'Christian?'

'Mr Bolitar, I don't understand what's going on.'

Myron could barely hear him. It sounded as if he were standing in a wind tunnel. 'Where are you?'

'A pay phone outside Titans Stadium.'

'What's the matter?'

'They won't let me in.'

Jessica stayed in the office to make a few calls. Myron rushed out. Fifty-seventh Street to the West Side Highway was unusually clear. He called Otto Burke and Larry Hanson from the car. Neither one was in. Myron was not astounded.

Then he dialed an unlisted phone in Washington. Few people had this particular number.

'Hello?' the voice answered politely.

'Hi, P.T.'

'Ah shit, Myron, what the fuck do you want?'

'I need a favor.'

'Perfect. I was just telling someone, gee, I wish Bolitar would call so I could do him a favor. Few things bring me such joy.'

P.T. worked for the FBI. FBI chiefs come and go. P.T. was a constant. The press didn't know about him, but every president since Nixon had had his number on their speed dial.

'The Kathy Culver case,' Myron said. 'Who's the best guy to talk to about it?'

'The local cop,' P.T. answered without hesitation. 'He's an elected sheriff or something. Great guy, good friend of mine. I forget his name.'

'Can you get me an appointment?' Myron asked.

'Why not? Serving your needs gives my life a sense of purpose.'

'I owe you.'

'You already owe me. More than you can pay. I'll call you when I have something.'

Myron hung up. The traffic was still clear. Amazing. He crossed the Washington Bridge and arrived at the Meadowlands in record time.

The Meadowlands Sports Authority was built on useless swampland off the New Jersey Turnpike in a place called East Rutherford. From west to east stood the Meadowlands Race Track, Titans Stadium, and the Brendan Byrne Arena, named for the former governor who was about as well liked as a whitehead on prom night. Angry protests equal to the French Revolution had erupted over the name, but to no avail. Mere revolutions are hardly worthy adversaries for a politician's ego.

'Oh, Christ.'

Christian's car – or he assumed it was Christian's – was barely visible under the blanket of reporters. Myron had expected this. He had told Christian to lock himself in his car and not say a word. Driving away would have been useless. The press would have just followed, and Myron was not up for a car chase.

He parked nearby. The reporters turned toward him like lions smelling a wounded lamb.

'What's going on, Myron?'

'Why isn't Christian at practice?'

'You pulling a holdout or what?'

'What's happening with his contract?'

Myron no-commented them, swimming through the sea of microphones, cameras, and flesh, squeezing his way into the car without allowing any of the slime to ooze in with him.

'Drive off,' Myron said.

Christian started the car and pulled out. The reporters parted grudgingly. 'I'm sorry, Mr Bolitar.'

'What happened?'

'The guard wouldn't let me in. He said he had orders to keep me out.'

'Son of a bitch,' Myron muttered. Otto Burke and his damn tactics. Little weasel. Myron should have been looking for something like this. But a lockout? That seemed a tad extreme, even by Otto Burke's standards. Despite the posturing, they had been fairly close to signing. Burke had expressed strong interest in getting Christian to minicamp as soon as possible, to get him ready for the season.

So why would he lock Christian out?

Myron didn't like it.

'Do you have a car phone?' he asked.

'No, sir.'

It didn't matter. 'Turn back around,' Myron said. 'Park by Gate C.'

'What are you going to do?'

'Just come with me.'

The guard tried to stop them, but Myron pushed Christian past him. 'Hey, you're not allowed in there!' he called after them. 'Hey, stop!'

'Shoot us,' Myron said without stopping.

They strode onto the field. Players were hitting the tackle dummies hard. Very hard. No one was holding back. These were tryouts. Most of these guys were fighting for a spot on the team. Most had been high school and college superstars, accustomed to unadulterated greatness on the field. Most would get cut. Most would not allow the dream to end there, scrounging other teams' rosters for a possible opening, holding on, slipping endlessly, dying slowly all the while.

A glamour profession.

The coaches blew whistles. The running backs practiced

wind sprints. Kickers were knocking down field goals at the far goal post. Punters boomed slow lazy arcs high into the air. Several players turned and spotted Christian. A buzz developed. Myron ignored it. He had spotted his target, sitting in the first row on the fifty-yard line.

Otto Burke sat like Caesar at the Colosseum, that damn smile still plastered to his face, his arms spread over the seats on either side of him. Behind him sat Larry Hanson and a few other executives. Caesar's senate. Occasionally Otto would lean back and award his entourage a comment that brought on aneurysm-like fits of laughter.

'Myron!' Otto called out pleasantly, waving one of those tiny hands. 'Come on over. Have a seat.'

'Wait here,' Myron told Christian. He climbed the steps. The entourage, led by Larry Hanson, stood in unison and marched away.

Myron snapped a salute at them. 'Hut two, three, four. Right face.' No one laughed. Big surprise.

'Sit down, Myron,' Otto said, beaming. 'Let's have a chat.'

'You haven't been returning my calls,' Myron said.

'Did you call?' He shook his head. 'I'll have to get on my secretary about that.'

Myron let out a deep breath and sat. 'Why was Christian locked out?'

'Well, Myron, it's pretty simple, actually. Christian hasn't signed his contract yet. The Titans don't have time to invest in someone who may not be part of our future.' He nodded toward the field. 'Do you see who's here for a tryout? Neil Decker from Cincinnati. Fine quarterback.'

'Yeah, he's great. He can almost throw a spiral.'

Otto chuckled. 'That's funny, Myron. You're a very amusing man.'

'I'm so glad you think so. Mind telling me what's going on?'

Otto Burke nodded. 'That's fair, Myron. So let's talk frankly, shall we?'

'Rationally, frankly, whatever you want.'

'Great. We'd like to renegotiate your client's contract,' he said. 'Downward.'

'I see.'

'We feel your client's value has depreciated.'

'Uh-huh.'

Burke studied him. 'You don't seem surprised, Myron.'

'So what is it this time?' Myron asked.

'What is what this time?'

'Well, let's start with Benny Keleher. You invited him to your house, plied him with booze, then had a cop arrest him on his ride home for drunk driving.'

Otto looked properly shocked. 'I had nothing to do with that.'

'Amazing how he signed the next day. And then there's Eddie Smith. You had compromising photographs of him taken by a private eye and threatened to send them to his wife.'

'Another lie.'

'Fine, a lie. So let's cut to the chase, then. What has caused this sudden devaluation?'

Otto sat back. He withdrew a cigarette from a gold case with a Titans emblem on the cover. 'It's something I saw in a rather lewd magazine,' he said. 'Something that truly disheartened me.' He didn't look disheartened. He looked rather pleased.

'A new low,' Myron said. 'You should be proud.'

'Pardon me?'

'You set it up. The magazine.'

Otto smiled. 'Ah, so you knew about it.'

'How did you get that picture?'

'What picture?'

'The one in the ad.'

'I had nothing to do with it.'

'Sure,' Myron said. 'I guess you're just a charter subscriber to *Nips*.'

'I had nothing to do with that ad, Myron. Honestly.'

'Then how did you get a hold of the magazine?'

'Someone pointed it out to me.'

'Who?'

'I am not at liberty to discuss it.'

'Very convenient.'

'I'm not sure I like your tone, Myron. And let me tell you something else: You're the one who has done wrong in the case. If you knew about the magazine, you had an ethical responsibility to tell me.'

Myron looked up at the sky. 'You used the word *ethical*. Lightning did not strike. There is no God.'

The smile flickered but stayed on. 'Much as we'd like to, Myron, we can't just wish this away. The magazine exists, and it must be dealt with. So let me tell you what I've come up with.'

'I'm all ears.'

'You're going to take our current offer and knock it down by a third. If not, the picture of Ms Culver goes public. Think about it. You have three days to decide.' Otto watched Neil Decker throw a pass. It looked like a duck with a broken wing, crashing well short of the receiver. He frowned, stroked his goatee. 'Make that two days.'

Chapter 10

Dean of Students Harrison Gordon made sure the door to his office was locked. Double-locked, in fact. He was taking no chances. Not with this.

He sat back down and stared out his office window. Esteemed Reston University in all its glory. The view was a mesh of green grass and brick buildings. No ivy adorned these towers of learning, but it should have. The students were gone for summer break, but the commons still had a sprinkling of people on it – campers from the football and tennis camps, local people who used the campus as a park, the old throwback hippies who pilgrimage to liberal arts institutions like Moslems to Mecca. Lots of red bandannas and ponchos and granola-types. A bearded man tossed a Frisbee. A small boy caught it.

Harrison Gordon saw none of it. He had not spun his chair around to enjoy the view. He had done so to avert his gaze from the . . . thing on his desk. He wanted simply to destroy the damn thing and forget about it. But he couldn't. Something held him back. And something kept drawing him toward it, toward that page near the back . . .

Destroy it, you fool. If somebody finds it . . .

What?

He did not know. He spun his chair back around, keeping his eyes away from the magazine. The student file marked CULVER, KATHERINE lay to the right. He swallowed. With a shaking hand he sifted through the stacks of transcripts and recommendation letters. It was an impressive file, but Harrison had no time for that now.

The buzz of his intercom – a horrid noise – startled him upright.

'Dean Gordon?'

'Yes,' he said, nearly shouting. His heart was beating like a rabbit's.

'I have someone here to see you. She doesn't have an appointment, but I thought you might want to see her.'

Edith's voice was hushed, a church-whisper.

'Who is it?' he asked.

'It's Jessica Culver. She's Kathy's sister.'

Panic punctured his heart like an icicle.

'Dean Gordon?'

He clamped his hand over his mouth, afraid he might scream.

'Dean Gordon? Are you there?'

There were no true options. He would have to see her and find out what she wanted. To act in any other manner would raise suspicion.

He opened his bottom drawer and scooped the contents of his desk into it. He shut it, took out his key ring, and locked his desk. Better safe than sorry. Last, he unbolted his door.

'Send Ms Culver in,' he said.

Jessica was at least as beautiful as her sister, which was saying something quite extraordinary. He debated on how to greet her and settled for funeral director mode – detached sympathy, warm professionalism.

He shook her hand with gentle firmness. 'Miss Culver, I'm so sorry we have to meet under such circumstances. Our prayers are with your family during this difficult time.'

'Thank you for seeing me without an appointment.'

He waved his hand as if to scoff, It's nothing. 'Please have a seat. Can I get you something to drink? Coffee, soda?'

'No, thank you.'

He moved back to his chair. He sat and folded his hands on the desk. 'Is there something I can do for you?'

'I need my sister's file,' Jessica replied.

Harrison felt his fingers bunch, but he kept his face steady. 'Your sister's school file?'

'Yes.'

'May I inquire as to why?'

'It involves her disappearance.'

'I see,' he said slowly. His voice, he was surprised to hear, remained calm. 'I believe the police were very thorough with the file. They made copies of everything in it—'

'I understand that. I'd like to see the file for myself.'

'I see,' he said again.

Several seconds passed. Jessica shifted in her chair. 'Is there a problem?' she asked.

'No, no. Well, perhaps. I'm afraid it may not be possible to give you the file.'

'What?'

'What I mean to say is, I'm not sure you have any legal right to it. Parents certainly do. But I'm not sure about siblings. I'll need to check this with a university attorney.'

'I'll wait,' Jessica said.

'Uh, fine. Would you mind waiting in the other room, please?'

She stood, turned, stopped. She looked back over her shoulder at him. 'You knew my sister, didn't you, Dean Gordon?'

He managed a smile. 'Yes, I did. Wonderful young lady.'

'Kathy worked for you.'

'Filing, answering the phone, that sort of thing,' he said quickly. 'She was a terrific worker. We all miss her very much.'

'Did she seem okay to you?'

'Okay?'

'Before she disappeared,' Jessica continued, her eyes boring into his. 'Was she acting strangely?'

Beads of sweat popped onto his forehead, but he dared not wipe them away. 'No, not that I could see. She seemed perfectly fine. Why do you ask?'

'Just checking: I'll wait out front.'

'Thank you.'

She closed the door.

Harrison let loose a long breath. What now? He would have to give her the file; to do otherwise would do far more than merely raise suspicion. But he could not, of course, just pull the file out of his bottom drawer and hand it to Jessica. No, he would wait a few minutes, walk down to the filing room to handle her case 'personally,' then return with the file.

Why, he wondered, did Jessica Culver need the file? Was there something he had missed?

No. He was sure of that.

Harrison had spent the last year hoping, praying, that it was over. But he should have known better. Matters like this never truly die. They hide, take root, grow stronger, prepare for a fresh onslaught.

Kathy Culver was not dead and buried. Like some gothic ghost, she had arisen, haunting him, crying out from some great beyond.

For vengeance.

Myron returned to the office.

'Win buzzed down twice,' Esperanza said. 'He wants to see you. Now.'

'On my way.'

'Myron?'

'What?'

Esperanza's lovely dark eyes were solemn. 'Is she back? Jessica, I mean.'

'No. She's just visiting.'

Her face registered doubt. Myron did not press it. He no longer knew what to think himself.

He ran up the stairs two at a time. Win was two floors above him, but he might as well have been in another dimension. As soon as he opened the big steel door, the tireless clamor swarmed in, attacking. The large open space was in perpetual motion. Two, maybe three hundred desks covered the huge floor like throw rugs. Every desk had at least two computer terminals on it. There were no partitions. Hundreds of men sat and stood at every angle, each wearing a white button-down shirt with tie and suspenders, suit jackets draped from the back of their chairs. There were painfully few women. The men were all on the phone, most covering the mouthpiece to scream at someone else. They all looked alike. They all sounded alike. They were all pretty much the same person.

Welcome to Lock-Horne Investments & Securities.

All six floors were exactly the same. In fact, Myron often suspected that Lock-Horne had only one floor and that the elevator was set to stop on the same floor no matter which number you hit from floor fourteen to floor nineteen, giving the illusion of a bigger company.

Office after office made up the compound's perimeter. These were saved for the head honchos, the top dogs, the numero unos, or in securities talk, the Big Producers. The BPs all had windows and sunshine, unlike the peons on the inside, who sickened and paled from the unnatural light.

Win had a corner office with a view of both Forty-seventh Street and Park Avenue – a view that screamed major dinero. His office was decorated in Early American Wasp. Dark-paneled walls. Forest green carpet. Wing-back chairs. Paintings of a fox hunt on the wall. Like Win had ever seen a fox.

Win looked up from his massive oak desk when Myron entered. The desk weighed slightly less than a cement mixer. He'd been studying a computer print-out, one of those never-ending reams with green and white stripes. The desk was blanketed with them. They sort of matched the carpet.

'How did your morning rendezvous go with our friend Jerry the Phone-icator?' Win asked.

'Phone-icator?'

Win smiled. 'I spent the whole morning working that one.'

'It was worth it,' Myron said.

He filled Win in on his encounter with Gary 'Jerry' Grady. Win sat back and steepled. Myron then filled him in on his encounter with Otto Burke. Win leaned forward and unsteepled.

'Otto Burke,' Win said, his voice measured, 'is a scoundrel. Perhaps I should pay him a private visit.' He looked up at Myron hopefully.

'No. Not yet. Please.'

'Are you quite positive?'

'Yes. Promise me, Win. No visits.'

He was clearly disappointed. 'Fine,' Win said, grudgingly.

'So what did you want to see me about?'

'Ah.' Win's face lit up again. 'Take a look at this.'

He lifted the reams of computer print-outs and unceremoniously dumped them on the floor. Underneath were a pile of magazines. The top one was called *Climaxx*. The subheadline read, 'Double Xs for Double the Pleasure.' Nifty sales technique. Win fanned them out as if he were doing a card trick.

'Six magazines,' he said.

Myron read the titles. *Climaxx, Licks, Jiz, Quim, Orgasm Today*, and of course, *Nips*. 'Nickler's publications?'

'God, you are good,' Win said.

'Years of training. So what about them?'

'Take a look at the pages I have marked off.'

Myron started with *Climaxx*. The cover featured another freakishly endowed woman, this time licking her own nipple. Handy. Win had used leather bookmarks to mark the page. Leather bookmarks in porno magazines. Like cigarettes in an aerobics class.

The page marked off was already too familiar. Myron felt his stomach churn all over again.

Live Fantasy Phone – Pick Your Girl

There were still three rows, still four in each row. His eyes immediately moved down to the bottom row, second from the right. It still read, 'I'll Do Anything!' The phone number was still 1–900–344-LUST. Still $3.99 per minute. Still discreetly billed to your telephone or charge card, Visa and MasterCard accepted.

But the woman in the picture was not Kathy Culver.

He quickly scanned the rest of the page. Nothing else was different. The same Oriental girl was still waiting. The same buttock still craved a spanking. 'Tiny Titties' had not pubesced.

'This same advertising page is in all six magazines,' Win explained. 'But only *Nips* has Kathy Culver's picture.'

'Interesting.' Myron thought a moment. 'Nickler probably sells package deals to advertisers – buy space in six for the price of three, that kind of thing.'

'Precisely. I would venture to say that all six magazines have the exact same ads.'

'But someone stuck Kathy's picture in *Nips*.' Myron was getting used to saying the name of the magazine. It no longer felt grimy on his lips, which in itself made him feel grimier.

Win said, 'Do you remember Nickler telling us that *Nips* was doing poorly?'

Myron nodded.

'Well, I had a devil of a time locating it. Most of the other rags were fairly easy to find on corner newsstands.

But I had to go to a hardcore porno palace on Forty-second Street to come up with *Nips*.'

'Yet,' Myron added, 'Otto Burke was able to get a copy.'

'Precisely. I am sure you've considered the possibility that Mr Burke is behind it.'

'The idea has crossed my mind.'

There was a knock on the door. Esperanza entered.

'Your handwriting expert is on the phone,' she said. 'I put it on Win's line.'

Win picked up the receiver and handed it to Myron.

'Hello.'

'Hey, Myron, it's Swindler. I just went over the two samples you gave me.'

Myron had given Swindler the envelope *Nips* had come in as well as a letter in Kathy's handwriting.

'Well?'

'They match. It's her or a very professional forgery.'

Myron felt his stomach dive. 'You're sure?'

'Positive.'

'Thanks for calling.'

'Yeah, no problem.'

Myron handed the receiver back to Win.

'A match?' Win asked.

'Yep.'

Win tilted back in his chair and smiled. 'Yowzer.'

Chapter 11

Myron ran into Ricky Lane in the corridor. He hadn't seen him in three months. Ricky looked a lot bigger. The Jets would be pleased.

'What are you doing here?' Myron asked.

'I made an appointment with Win,' Ricky said with a big grin. 'Just like my agent advised.'

'Good to see you listen to your agent.'

'Always. The man is brilliant.'

'And he never argues with a client.'

Ricky laughed. 'Say, I heard Christian got locked out of camp.'

News traveled fast. 'Where did you hear that?'

'The FAN.'

WFAN was New York's all-sports radio station. 'Have you spoken to him lately?'

Ricky made a face. 'Christian?'

'Yeah.'

'Not since my last college football game, what, year and a half ago.'

'I thought you were friends.' Myron had, in fact, assumed that Ricky had recommended his services to Christian.

'We were teammates,' Ricky replied steadily. 'We were never friends.'

'You don't like him?'

Ricky shrugged. 'Not really. None of us did.'

'Who is "us"?'

'Guys on the team.'

'What's wrong with him?'

'Long story, man. Not worth telling.'

'I'd be interested.'

'Put it like this,' Ricky said. 'Christian was a little too perfect for most of us, okay?'

'An egomaniac?'

Ricky paused, considering. 'Not really. I mean, to be straight, I guess a lot of it was jealousy. Christian wasn't just good. Shit, he wasn't even just great. He was incredible. Best I ever seen.'

'So?'

'So he expected the same from everyone else.'

'He got on people's case when they made mistakes?'

Ricky paused again, shook his head. 'No, that ain't it either.'

'You're being a tad obtuse, Ricky.'

Ricky Lane looked up, looked down, looked left, looked right, looked very uneasy. 'I can't explain it,' he said. 'It's going to sound like a lot of griping, but guys weren't crazy about all the attention he was getting. I mean, we won two national championships, and the only guy they ever talked to was Christian.'

'I heard those interviews. He always gave his team-mates all the credit.'

'Yeah, a real gentleman,' Ricky replied with more than a hint of sarcasm. 'All that "it's a team effort" bullshit just made the press love him even more. Guys on the team thought he was a promo-hog, you know? His own best PR firm. They blamed him for being too popular.'

'Did you?'

'I don't know. Maybe. Truth was, I just didn't really like him. We had nothing in common except football. He's a pure Midwest white boy. I'm a city-slicking black man. It ain't a winning combination.'

'That's all it was?'

He gave a half-shrug. 'I guess so. But man, this is all ancient history. I don't know why I brought it up. It don't matter no more. Christian just didn't fit in, okay. He was a nice guy, I guess. He was always polite. But that don't play so well in a locker room, you know?'

Myron knew. Juvenile, sexist, homophobic bantering – that was the stuff of locker-room popularity.

'I gotta go, man. Win will be wondering where I am.'

'Okay. I'll see you around.'

Ricky had almost turned away when Myron thought of something else. 'What can you tell me about Kathy Culver?'

Ricky's face blanched. 'What about her?'

'Did you know her?'

'A little, I guess. I mean, she was a cheerleader and dated the quarterback. But we never hung out or anything.' He looked very unhappy now. 'Why you asking?'

'Was she popular? Or was she hated too?'

Ricky's eyes darted about like birds trying to find a safe

place to land. 'Look, Myron, you always been straight with me, I always been straight with you, right?'

'Right.'

'I don't want to say nothing else. She's dead. Might as well let her be.'

'What does that mean?'

'Nothing. I just don't like talking about her, okay. It's kinda creepy. I'll see you later.'

Ricky hurried down the corridor as if Reggie White were chasing him. Myron watched him. He debated following him but decided against it. Ricky would say no more today.

Chapter 12

Esperanza stuck her head in the door. 'Someone – or something – is here to see you.'

Myron held up a silencing hand. The headset had been on since his return to his office. 'Look, I have to go,' he said. 'See if you can get him upgraded to first class. He's a big guy. Thanks.' He took off the headset. 'Who is it?'

She made a face. 'Aaron. He didn't give a last name.'

He didn't have to. 'Send him in.'

Seeing Aaron was like falling into a time warp. He was as big as Myron remembered, as big as the lummox in the garage. He was dressed in a freshly pressed white suit, but he wore no shirt with it, displaying plenty of tan pectoral cleavage. He wasn't wearing socks either. Nifty haircut, the swept-back look à la Pat Riley. A saunter for a walk. Designer sunglasses. Designer cologne that smelled suspiciously like insect repellent. Aaron was the pure definition of 'supersmooth' – just ask him, he'd tell you.

He smiled widely. 'Nice to see you, Myron.'

They shook hands. Myron did not squeeze. He was far too mature. That, and Aaron could probably squeeze harder. 'Have a seat.'

'Wonderful.' Aaron made a production of it, spreading out his arms as if he were wearing a cloak. He removed his sunglasses with an audible snap. 'I like your office. It's really great.'

'Thank you.'

'Great address. Great view.'

The password is *great*. 'You looking to rent space?'

Aaron laughed as if that were the gem of gems. 'No,' he said. 'I don't like being cooped in an office. It's not my style. I like my freedom. I like being out on my own, on the road. I wouldn't do well chained to a desk.'

'Wow, that's fascinating, Aaron. Really.'

He laughed again. 'Ah, Myron, you haven't changed a bit. I'm glad to see it.'

They hadn't seen each other since high school. Myron had gone to Livingston High School in New Jersey. Aaron had gone to his archenemy, West Orange High. The teams played each other twice a year, and it was rarely a pleasant encounter.

In those days Myron's best friend was a huge ox named Todd Midron. Todd was a big, softhearted, simple kid with a lisp. He played Lenny to Myron's George. He was also the toughest kid Myron had ever met.

Todd never lost a fight. Never. No one ever came close to him. He was just too powerful. During a game in their senior year, Aaron undercut and nearly injured Myron. Todd took exception. He went after Aaron. Aaron destroyed him. Myron tried to help his friend, but Aaron shrugged Myron off like a dandruff flake. He continued to pulverize Todd, steadily, methodically, glaring at Myron the whole time, not even glancing at his limp victim. The beating was ferocious. By the time it ended, Todd's face was an unrecognizable pulpy mess. Todd spent four months in a hospital. His jaw was wired shut for nearly a year.

'Hey,' Aaron said. He pointed to a movie still on the wall. 'That's Woody Allen and what's-her-name.'

'Diane Keaton.'

'Right, Diane Keaton.'

'Is there something I can do for you?' Myron asked.

Aaron turned his whole body toward Myron. The glare from his shaved chest was nearly blinding. 'I think there is, Myron. In fact, I think there's something we can do for each other.'

'Oh?'

'I represent a competitor of yours. A certain dispute has arisen between the two of you. My client wishes to settle it peacefully.'

'Are you an attorney now, Aaron?'

He smiled. 'Not likely.'

'Oh.'

'I am referring to a young man named Chaz Landreaux. He recently signed a contract with your company, MB SportReps.'

'I thought of the name myself.'

'Pardon me.'

'MB SportReps. I came up with the name by myself.'

Aaron renewed his smile. It was a good smile. Lots of teeth. 'There is a problem with the contract.'

'Do tell.'

'You see, Mr Landreaux has also signed a contract with Roy O'Connor at TruPro Enterprises, Incorporated. The contract predates yours. So you see the problem: Your contract is invalid.'

'Why don't we let a court of law decide that?'

He sighed deeply. 'My client feels it is in everyone's best interest to avoid litigation.'

'Gee, what a surprise. So what does your client suggest?'

'Mr O'Connor would be willing to pay you for your time.'

'Very generous of him.'

'Yes.'

'And if I say no?'

'We hope it won't come to that.'

'But if it does?'

Aaron sighed, stood, leaned on Myron's desk. 'I'll be forced to make you disappear.'

'Like in a magic trick?'

'Like in dead.'

Myron put his hand to his chest. 'Gasp. Oh. Gasp.'

Aaron laughed again, this time without humor. 'I know all about your tae kwon do display in the garage. But that guy was a stupid musclehead. I am not. I boxed professionally. I'm a black belt in jujitsu and a grand master in aikido. I've killed people.'

'I bet that looks good on a résumé,' Myron said.

'Let me put this in very simple terms for you, Myron: You fuck with us, I'll kill you.'

'Shiver. Tremble.' Myron was not quite as confident as his sarcasm, but he knew better than to show fear. Guys like Aaron are like dogs. They smell fear, they pounce.

Aaron laughed again. He was laughing a lot today. He was either very amused or had been sniffing gas. He turned his back and walked to the door. 'This is your final warning,' he said. 'Landreaux honors his contract with Mr O'Connor, or both of you end up worm food.'

Worm food. First oatmeal. Now worm food.

'I like you, Myron. I'd really hate to see something bad happen. But you understand.'

'Business is business.'

'Exactly.'

Esperanza appeared at the door.

Aaron gave her a sharklike smile. 'Well, well,' he said. Then he followed up with his best big-guy wink. Esperanza managed to keep her clothes on. Amazing restraint.

'Pick up line two,' she said.

'Listen to this call closely, Myron,' Aaron added with a final grin. 'Appreciate the gravity of the situation. And remember. Worm food.'

'Worm food. I'll keep it in mind.'

Aaron winked at Esperanza again, blew her a kiss, and left.

'Charming,' she said.

'Who's on the phone?'

'Chaz Landreaux.'

Myron picked up the headset. 'Hello.'

'Motherfuckers were at my mom's!' Chaz shouted. 'They told her they were going to cut off my nuts and send them to her in a box! My mother, man! They said this to my mother!'

Myron felt his fingers tighten into fists. 'I'll take care of it,' he said slowly. 'They won't bother her again.'

Enough game playing. It was time to act.

It was time to tell Win about Roy O'Connor.

Win smiled like a kid on a snow day listening to the radio for a school closing. 'Roy O'Connor,' he said.

'I don't want him hurt. Promise me.'

Win's eyes drifted dreamily. He might have nodded a yes, but Myron couldn't say for sure.

Chapter 13

Baumgart's on Palisades Avenue. Their old stomping grounds.

Peter Chin greeted them at the door, his eyes widening in delight and surprise when he spotted Jessica, 'Miss Culver! How wonderful to see you again.'

'Nice to see you, Peter.'

'You look as lovely as ever. You beautify my restaurant.'

Myron said, 'Hi, Peter.'

'Yeah, whatever.' He dismissed Myron with a hand wave. His full attention was on Jessica; a crocodile gnawing on his foot wouldn't have changed that. 'You look a little too thin, Miss Culver.'

'The food's not as good in Washington.'

'Funny,' Myron said. 'I was thinking she looked a little chunky.'

Jessica eyed him. 'Dead man.'

Baumgart's was an institution in Englewood, New Jersey. For fifty years it was an old Jewish deli and soda fountain, noted for its superb ice cream and desserts. When Peter Chin bought it eight years ago, he kept all of the tradition but added the best nouvelle Chinese cuisine in the state. The combination was a smash. The normal order might consist of Peking duck, sesame noodles, chocolate milk shake, French fries and a death-by-chocolate sundae for dessert. When Myron and Jessica had lived together, they ate at Baumgart's at least once a week.

Myron still came once a week. Usually with Win or Esperanza. Sometimes alone. He never brought a date here.

Peter walked them past the soda fountain and put them in a booth under a huge painting. Modern art. It was a portrait of either Cher or Barbara Bush. Maybe both. Very esoteric.

Myron and Jessica sat across the table from each other, silently. The moment seemed weighed down, overwhelming. Being here together again – they had expected it to generate some light nostalgia. But the effect was more like a body blow.

'I've missed this place,' she said.

'Yes.'

She reached her hand across the table and took his. 'I've missed you.'

Her face was aglow, the way it used to be when she looked at him as though he were the only person in the entire world. Myron felt something squeeze his heart, making it nearly impossible to breathe. The rest of the world broke apart, diffused. There were only the two of them.

'I'm not sure what to say.'

She smiled. 'What? Myron Bolitar at a loss for words?'

'Ripley's, huh?'

Peter came by. Without preamble, he said, 'You'll start with the crispy duck appetizer and squab package with pine nuts. For your main course you'll have soft-shell crab in special sauce and the Baumgart lobster and shrimp.'

'Can we choose dessert?' Myron asked.

'No. Myron, you'll have the pecan pie à la mode. And for Miss Culver.' He stopped, building suspense like a game-show host.

She smiled expectantly. 'You don't mean . . .'

Peter nodded. 'Banana pudding cake with vanilla wafers. There's only one piece left, but I put it away for you.'

'Bless you, Peter.'

'Each man does what he can. You didn't bring wine?' Baumgart's was BYO.

'We forgot,' Jessica said. She was dazzling Peter with her smile. Not fair. Jessica's looks were like a *Star Trek* laser set on stun. Her smile, kill.

'I'll send someone across the street to get a bottle. Kendall-Jackson Chardonnay?'

'You have a good memory,' she said.

'No. I just remember what is important.' Myron rolled his eyes. Peter bowed slightly and left.

She turned the smile back to Myron. He felt frightened and helpless and deliriously happy.

'I'm sorry,' she said.

He shook his head. He was afraid to open his mouth.

'I never meant—' She was unsure how to continue. 'I made a lot of mistakes in my life,' she said. 'I am dumb. I am self-destructive.'

'No,' Myron said. 'You're perfect.'

Her voice grew dramatic, her hand against her chest.

' "Take the blinders from your eyes and see me as I really am." '

He thought a moment. 'Dulcinea to Don Quixote in *Man of La Mancha*. And it's "take the clouds," not blinders.'

'Very impressive.'

'Win was playing it in the car.' This was an old game of theirs. Guess the Quote.

She fiddled with her water glass, making little water circles and then inspecting them for clarity and definition. Eventually she created an aquatic Olympics logo. 'I'm not sure what I'm trying to say to you,' she said at last. 'I'm not sure what I want to happen here.' She looked up. 'One last confession, okay?'

He nodded.

'I came to you because I thought you would help. That was true. But that wasn't the only reason.'

'I know,' he said. 'I try not to think about it too much. It terrifies me.'

'So what do we do now?'

His chance. He hoped there would be others. 'Did you get your sister's file?'

'Yes.'

'Have you gone through it yet?'

'No. I just picked it up.'

'Then why don't we open it now?'

She nodded. The crispy duck and squab package with pine nuts appeared. Jessica took out a manila envelope and slit the seal. 'Why don't you look at it first?'

'Okay,' he said. 'But save me some food.'

'Chance.'

He started sifting through the papers. The top page was Kathy's high school transcript. After her junior year her ranking had been twelfth in a class of three hundred. Not bad. But by the end of senior year her ranking had slipped considerably – to fifty-eighth.

'Her grades dropped senior year of high school,' Myron said.

'Whose didn't drop senior year?' Jess countered. 'She was probably just goofing off.'

'Probably.' But usually that meant A students got B's or C's. Kathy had gotten one A, three D's and an F in her final semester. Her clean record was also muddied with several detentions – all in her senior year. Strange. But probably meaningless.

'Do you want to fill me in on what happened today?' Jessica asked between bites.

She was even beautiful when pigging out. Amazing. He started by telling her about Win's discovery in the six magazines.

'So what does it mean,' she asked, 'her picture being only in that one rag?'

'I'm not sure.'

'But you have an idea?'

He did. But it was too early to say anything. 'Not yet.'

'Did you hear from your friend at the phone company?'

He nodded. 'Gary Grady placed two calls after we left. One was to Fred Nickler's office at Hot Desire Press. The other was someplace in the city. There was no answer when we called it. We got the information kind of late in the day.'

'And the handwriting analyst?'

Best to dive right in. 'The handwriting matches. It's either Kathy's or a very good forger.'

That slowed her chopsticks. 'My God.'

'Yes.'

'Then she's alive?'

'It's still just a possibility. Nothing more. That envelope could have been written before she died. Or like I said, it could be a clever forgery.'

'You're reaching.'

'I'm not so sure,' he said. 'If she's alive, where is she? Why is she doing all this?'

'Maybe she's been kidnapped. Maybe she's being forced to.'

'Forced to address envelopes? Now who's reaching?'

'Do you have a better explanation?' she asked.

'Not yet. But I'm working on it.' He started looking through the file again. 'You ever hear of a guy named Otto Burke?'

'The big record company magnate who owns the Titans?'

'Right. He also knew about the magazine.' Myron quickly summarized his visit to Titans Stadium.

'So you think Otto Burke might be behind it?' she asked.

'Otto has a motive: knocking down Christian's asking price. He certainly has the resources: lots of money. And it would also explain why Christian got a copy in the mail.'

'He was sending Christian a message,' she added.

'Right.'

'But how would Burke forge my sister's handwriting?'

'He could have hired an expert.'

'Where did he get a writing sample?'

'Who knows? It can't be that difficult.'

Her eyes glazed over. 'So this was all a hoax? This was all some plot to gain leverage in a negotiation?'

'It's possible. But I don't think so.'

'Why not?'

'Something just doesn't mesh. Why would Burke go through all that trouble? He could have blackmailed us with just the photo. He didn't have to put it in a magazine. The photo was enough.'

She grasped on to his hope as if it were a life preserver. 'Good point,' she said.

'The question then becomes,' he continued, 'how did Otto get a copy of the magazine?'

'Maybe someone in his organization picked up a copy at a newsstand.'

'Very unlikely. *Nips*' – the word felt grungy again, good – 'has a very low circulation rate. The chances that someone in the Titans organization bought that particular magazine, had time to read it carefully, somehow spotted Kathy's picture in the bottom row on a page of ads in the back – it's fairly remote at best.'

Jessica snapped her fingers. 'Someone mailed it to him too.'

He nodded. 'Why should Christian have been the only one? For all we know, dozens of people were sent that magazine.'

'How do we find out?'

'I'm working on it.'

He managed to salvage a sliver of crispy duck before it was sucked into the black hole. It was delicious. He turned his attention back to Kathy's files. Her bad grades continued during her first semester at Reston. By second semester, her grades had picked up considerably. He asked Jessica about this.

'She settled into college life, I guess,' she said. 'She joined the drama group, became a cheerleader, started dating Christian. She went through culture shock in her first semester. It's not uncommon.'

'No. I guess not.'

'You don't sound convinced.'

He shrugged. Myron Bolitar, Señor Skepticalo.

Kathy's recommendation letters were next. Three of them. Her high school guidance counselor called her 'unusually gifted.' Her tenth-grade history teacher said, 'Her enthusiasm for life is contagious.' Her twelfth-grade English teacher said, 'Kathy Culver is bright, witty, and fun-spirited. She will be a welcome addition to any institution of learning.' Nice comments. He scanned down to the bottom of the page.

'Uh-oh,' he said.

'What is it?'

He handed her the glowing recommendation letter from Kathy's twelfth-grade English teacher at Ridgewood High School. A Mr Grady.

A Mr Gary, aka 'Jerry' Grady.

Chapter 14

Myron was startled awake by the telephone. He'd been dreaming about Jessica. He tried to remember specifics, but the details disintegrated into small pieces and blew away, leaving behind only a few frustrating snippets. The clock on his nightstand read seven o'clock. Someone was calling him at home at seven o'clock in the morning. Myron had a pretty good idea who it was.

'Hello?'

'Good morning, Myron. I hope I didn't wake you.'

Myron recognized the voice. He smiled and asked, 'Who is this?'

'It's Roy O'Connor.'

'*The* Roy O'Connor?'

'Uh, yes, I guess so. Roy O'Connor, the agent.'

'The superagent,' Myron corrected. 'To what do I owe this honor, Roy?'

'Would it be possible for us to meet this morning?' The voice had a discernible quake to it.

'Sure thing, Roy. My office, okay?'

'Uh, no.'

'Your office, Roy?'

'Uh, no.'

Myron sat up. 'Should I keep guessing places and you can say hotter or colder?'

'You know Reilly's Pub on Fourteenth Street?'

'Yes.'

'I'll be in the booth in the back right-hand corner. One o'clock. We'll have lunch. If that's okay with you.'

'Peachy, Roy. Want me to wear anything special?'

'Uh, no.'

Myron hung up, smiled. A night visit from Win, usually while sleeping soundly in your bedroom, your innermost sanctuary. Worked every time.

He got out of bed. He heard his mother in the kitchen above him, his father in the den watching television. Early morning at the Bolitar house. The basement door opened.

'Are you awake, Myron?' his mother shouted.

Myron. What a goddamn awful name. He hated it with a passion. The way he looked at it, he'd been born with all his fingers and toes, he didn't have a harelip or a cauliflower ear or a limp of any kind – so to compensate for his lack of ill fortune, his parents had christened him Myron.

'I'm awake,' he answered.

'Daddy bought some fresh bagels. They're on the table.'

'Thanks.'

He got out of bed and climbed the steps. With one hand he felt the rough beard he'd have to shave; with the other he picked the yellow sleep-buggers out of the corner of his eyes. His father was sprawled on the den couch like a wet

116

sock, wearing an Adidas sweatsuit and eating a bagel
oozing with whitefish spread. As he did every morning,
Myron's father was watching a videocassette of people
exercising. Getting in shape through osmosis.

'Good morning, Myron. There're some bagels on the
table.'

'Uh, thanks.' It was like one parent never heard the
other.

He entered the kitchen. His mom was nearly sixty, but
she looked much younger. Say, forty-five. She acted much
younger too. Say, sixteen.

'You came in late last night,' she said.

Myron made a grunting noise.

'What time did you finally get home?'

'Really late. It was almost ten.' Myron Bolitar, the late-
night scream machine.

'So,' Mom began, struggling to look and sound casual,
'who were you out with?' Mistress of the Subtle.

'Nobody,' he said.

'Nobody? You were out all night with nobody?'

Myron looked left and right. 'When are you going to
bring in the hot lights and jumper cables?'

'Fine, Myron. If you don't want to tell me—'

'I don't want to tell you.'

'Fine. Was it a girl?'

'Mom . . .'

'Okay, forget I asked.'

Myron reached for the phone and dialed Win's number.
After the eighth ring he began to hang up when a weak,
distant voice coughed. 'Hello?'

'Win?'

'Yeah.'

'You okay?'

'Hello?'

'Win?'

'Yeah.'

'What took you so long to answer the phone?'

'Hello?'

'Win?'

'Who is this?'

'Myron.'

'Myron Bolitar?'

'How many Myrons do you know?'

'Myron Bolitar?'

'No, Myron Rockefeller.'

'Something's wrong,' Win said.

'What?'

'Terribly wrong.'

'What are you talking about?'

'Some asshole is calling me at seven in the morning pretending to be my best friend.'

'Sorry, I forgot the time.' Win was not what one would call a morning person. During their years at Duke, Win was never out of bed before noon – even on the days he had a morning class. He was, in fact, the heaviest sleeper Myron had ever known or imagined. Myron's parents, on the other hand, woke up when somebody in the Western hemisphere farted. Before Myron moved into the basement, the same scenario was played out nightly:

Around three in the morning, Myron would get out of bed to go to the bathroom. As he tiptoed past his parents' bedroom, his father would stir ever so slowly, as though someone had dropped a Popsicle on his crotch.

'Who's that?' his father would shout.

'Just me, Dad.'

'Is that you, Myron?'

'Yes, Dad.'

'Are you okay, son?'

'Fine, Dad.'

'What are you doing up? You sick or something?'

'I'm just going to the bathroom, Dad. I've been going to the bathroom by myself since I was fourteen.'

During their sophomore year at Duke, Myron and Win lived in the smallest double on campus with a bunk bed that Win said 'creaks slightly' and Myron said 'sounds like a duck being run over by a back hoe.' One morning, when the bed was quiet and he and Win were asleep, a baseball crashed through their window. The noise was so deafening that their entire dorm jumped out of bed and rushed to see if Myron and Win had survived the wrath of whatever gigantic meteorite had fallen through the roof. Myron rushed to the window to yell obscenities. Dorm members stamped across the underwear-carpeted floor to join in the tirade. The ensuing reverberations were loud enough to disturb a diner waitress on her coffee break.

Win just lay asleep, a blanket of broken glass strewn over his blanket.

The next night, Myron called through the darkness of his bottom bunk. 'Win?'

'Yes.'

'How do you sleep so soundly?' But Win didn't answer because he'd fallen asleep.

On the phone Win asked, 'What do you want?'

'Did all go well last night?'

'Mr O'Connor hasn't called you yet?'

'He has.' End of subject. Myron didn't want details.

'I know,' Win continued, 'that you did not awaken me to question my effectiveness.'

'Kathy Culver got only one A in her senior year at Ridgewood High. Guess who her teacher was.'

'Who?'

'Gary Grady.'

'Hmm. Dial-a-porn and high school English. Interesting vocational mix.'

'I was thinking we could go see Mr Grady this morning.'

'At the school?'

'Sure. The two of us can pretend we're concerned parents.'

'For the same kid?'

'Putting the rainbow curriculum to the test.'

Win laughed. 'This is going to be fun.'

Chapter 15

'How do we find him?' Win asked.

They arrived at Ridgewood High School at nine-thirty. It was a warm June day, the kind of day where you stared at the window and daydreamed about the end of school. Not much movement around the building – as though the entire school, even the edifice, were coasting toward summer vacation.

Myron remembered how miserable such days were. It gave him an idea.

'Let's pull the fire alarm,' he said.

'I beg your pardon.'

'We'll get everyone outside. It'll be easier to spot him.'

'Idiotically ingenious,' Win said.

'Besides, I always wanted to pull a fire alarm.'

'Walk on the wild side.'

No one noticed them when they entered the school. There were no guards, no locks on the door, no hall monitors of any kind. This was not an urban high school. Myron found a fire alarm not too far from the entrance.

'Kids, don't try this at home,' Myron said. He pulled. Bells went off. Then cheers from the kids. Myron felt good about his deed. He thought about pulling alarms more often but decided some might construe the act as immature.

Win held the door open and pretended to be a fire marshal. 'Single file,' he told the students. 'And remember: Only you can prevent fires.'

Myron spotted Grady. 'Bingo.'

'Where?'

'Turning the corner. On the left. Mr Fashion.'

Gary Grady was wearing a yellow Century 21-like blazer with Keith Partridge orange-striped pants. Win looked visibly pained at the sight. They made their approach.

'Hi, Jerry.'

Grady's head shot around. 'That's not my name.'

'Yeah, you told me. It's your alias, right? When you do business with Fred Nickler. Your real name is Gary Grady.'

Nearby students stopped walking.

'Keep moving!' Gary snapped.

The students restarted their grudging trudge.

'Impatient teachers,' Myron said.

'Sad,' Win agreed.

Gary's thin face seemed to stretch even further. He stepped closer so that no one could overhear.

'Perhaps we can continue this conversation later,' he whispered.

'I don't think so, Gary.'

'I'm in the middle of a class.'

'Tough tittie,' Myron said.

Win arched an eyebrow. 'Tough tittie?'

'Something about being back in high school,' Myron said. 'Besides, I thought it appropriate considering the situation.'

Win considered for a moment. 'Okay, I can accept that.'

Myron turned back to Gary. 'The fire drill will last a little while. Then it will take a little while for the kids to file back in. Then they'll want to goof around in the halls for a while. By then we'll be all done.'

Gary crossed his arms over his chest. 'No.'

'Option two, then.' Myron took out a copy of *Nips*. 'We can play Show and Tell with the principal.'

Grady coughed into his fist. A loud fire whistle sounded. Sirens came closer. 'I don't know what you're talking about,' he said, taking a few more steps away from the kids.

'I followed you.'

'What?'

Myron sighed, gave him exasperation. 'You were in Hoboken yesterday morning. You picked up the mail at an address used for advertising sex lines in porno rags. Then you went home to Glen Rock, saw me, panicked, and called Fred Nickler, the managing editor of said rags.'

'Amateur,' Win added with disgust.

'Now, we can discuss this with you or with the school board. Up to you.'

Gary glanced at his watch. 'You have two minutes.'

'Fine.' Myron gestured to the right. 'Why don't we step into the teachers' lavatory? I assume you have a key.'

'Yes.'

He opened the door. Myron had always wanted to see

a teachers' bathroom, see how the other half lives. It was unremarkable in every way.

'Okay, you have me here,' Gary said. 'What do you want?'

'Tell me about this ad.'

Gary swallowed. His enlarged Adam's apple bobbed up and down like a boxer's head avoiding jabs. 'I don't know anything about it.'

Myron and Win exchanged a glance.

'Can I stick his head in a toilet?' Win asked.

Gary straightened his back. 'If you are trying to frighten me, it won't work.'

Win's voice was semipleading. 'One quick dunk?'

'Not yet.' Myron turned his attention back to Gary. 'I have no interest in busting you, Gary. You're a perv, that's your business. I want to know about your connection with Kathy Culver.'

Sweat appeared above Gary's upper lip. 'She was a student of mine.'

'I know. Why is her picture in *Nips*? In your ad?'

'I have no idea. I saw it for the first time yesterday.'

'But that's your ad, right?'

He hesitated, giving silent half-shrugs to no one in particular. 'Okay,' he said, 'I admit it. I advertise in Mr Nickler's publications. No law against that. But I did not put that picture of Kathy in the ad.'

'Who did?'

'I don't know.'

'But you admit operating sex lines?'

'Yes. It's harmless. I do it to make extra money. Nobody gets hurt.'

'Another prince,' Myron said. 'How much extra money?'

'In the business's heyday I was making twenty thousand dollars a month.'

Myron wasn't sure he heard right. 'Twenty thousand dollars a month from phone sex?'

'In the mid-eighties, yes. Before the government got involved and began to crack down on 900 lines. Now I'm lucky to clear eight grand a month.'

'Damn bureaucrats,' Myron said. 'So how does Kathy Culver fit into all this?'

'What do you mean?'

'Gee, Gary, a naked picture of her is in your ad this month. Maybe that's what I mean.'

'I already told you. I had nothing to do with that.'

'Then I guess it's a coincidence, her being a student of yours and all.'

'Yes.'

'I won't hold him under long,' Win promised. 'Please.'

Myron shook his head. 'You wrote her a glowing recommendation letter for college, correct?'

'Kathy was a wonderful student,' Gary replied.

'And what else?'

'If you are suggesting that my relationship with Kathy was something other than student-teacher—'

'That's exactly what I'm suggesting.'

Once again he crossed his arms over his chest. 'I will not dignify that with a response. And I am now terminating this conversation.'

Gary was addressing them in that way teachers do. Sometimes teachers forget that life is not a classroom.

'Dunk him,' Myron said.

'With pleasure.'

Gary probably had two inches on Win. He leaned up on his toes and gave Win his most withering glare.

'I'm not afraid of you,' Gary said.

'Mistake number one.'

Win moved with a speed that videocameras would not catch. He took hold of Gary's hand, twisted it, and pulled down. Hapkido move. Gary dropped to the tile floor. Win pressed his knee against the point of Gary's elbow. Gently. Not too much pain. Just enough to let him know who was in control.

'Damn,' Win said.

'What?'

'All the toilets are clean. I hate when that happens.'

'Anything to add before the dunk?' Myron asked.

Gary's face was white. 'Promise me you won't tell anyone,' he managed.

'You'll tell us the truth?'

'Yes. But you have to swear you won't tell anyone. Not the principal, no one.'

'Okay.' Myron nodded to Win. Win let go. Gary took back his hand and caressed it as though it were an abused puppy.

'Kathy and I had an affair,' he said.

'When?'

'Her senior year. It lasted a few months, that's all. I haven't seen her since, I swear.'

'And that's everything?'

He nodded. 'I don't know anything else. Somebody else put that picture in the ad.'

'If you're tying, Gary—'

'I'm not. Hand to God.'

'Okay,' Myron said. 'You can go.'

Gary rushed out. He had not even paused to check his hair in the mirror.

'Scum,' Myron said. 'The man is pure unadulterated scum. Seduces his students, operates a dial-a-porn line.'

'But a snappy dresser,' Win said. 'So what next?'

'We finish the investigation. Then we go to the school board. We tell them all about Mr Grady's extracurricular activities.'

'Didn't you just promise him you weren't going to tell?'

Myron shrugged. 'I lied.'

Chapter 16

In something of a trance, Jessica thanked Myron and hung up the phone. She half-stumbled into the kitchen and sat down. Her mother and her younger brother Edward looked up.

'Honey,' Carol Culver began, 'are you okay?'

'Fine,' she managed.

'Who was on the phone?'

'Myron.'

Silence.

'We were talking about Kathy,' she continued.

'What about her?' Edward asked.

Her brother had always been Edward, not Ed or Eddie or Ted. He was only a year out of college and already he owned a successful computer business, IMCS (Interactive Management Computer Systems), which developed software systems for several prestigious corporations. Edward wore only jeans, even in the office, and obnoxious T-shirts, the kind with chintzy iron-on decals that say stuff like

'Keep on Truckin'.' He didn't own a tie. He had a wide, almost-feminine face with delicate porcelain features. Women would kill for his eyelashes. Only the buzz-cut hair – and the pithy phrase on his T-shirt – hinted at what Edward was proud to be: COMPUTER WEENIES HAVE THE BEST HARDWARE.

Jessica took a deep breath. She could not be concerned with delicacies or feelings anymore. She opened her purse and pulled out a copy of *Nips*. 'This magazine hit the stands a few days ago,' she said.

She tossed it on the table, cover up. A cross between puzzlement and disgust blanketed her mother's face.

Edward remained stoic. 'What the hell is this?' he asked.

Jessica flipped to the page in the back. 'There,' she said simply, pointing to the picture of Kathy in the bottom row.

It took a few moments for them to comprehend what they were seeing, as though the information had been waylaid somewhere between the eye and brain. Then Carol Culver let out a groan. Her hand flew to her mouth, smothering a scream. Edward's eyes narrowed into thin slits.

Jessica did not give her time to recover. 'There's more,' she said.

Her mother looked up at her with hollow, haunted eyes. There was no life behind them anymore, as though a final cold gust had put out a flickering flame.

'A handwriting expert checked the envelope it came in. The writing matches Kathy's.'

Edward inhaled sharply. Carol's legs finally gave out, folding at the knees. She landed hard in her chair and crossed herself. Tears came to her eyes.

'She's alive?' Carol managed.

'I don't know.'

'But there's a chance?' Edward followed up.

Jessica nodded. 'There's always been a chance.'

Stunned silence.

'But I need some information,' Jessica continued. 'I need to know what happened to Kathy. What made her change.'

Edward's eyes narrowed again. 'What do you mean?'

'Kathy had an affair with her high school English teacher. Senior year.'

More silence. Jessica was not so sure it was stunned.

'The teacher, a maggot named Gary Grady, has admitted it.'

'No,' her mother said weakly. She lowered her head, her crucifix dangling like a pendulum. She began to weep. 'Sweet Jesus, not my baby . . .'

Edward stood. 'That's enough, Jess.'

'It's not enough.'

Edward grabbed his jacket. 'I'm out of here.'

'Wait. Where are you going?'

'Good-bye.'

'We need to talk this out.'

'The hell we do.'

'Edward—'

He ran out the back door, slamming it behind him.

Jessica turned back to her mother. Her sobs were gut-wrenching. Jessica watched for a minute or two. Then she turned and left the kitchen.

Roy O'Connor was already in the back booth when Myron arrived. His glass was empty, and he was sucking on an ice cube. He sounded like an aardvark near an anthill.

'Hey, Roy.'

O'Connor nodded to the seat across the table, not bothering to stand. He wore gold rings that disappeared under the folds of flesh in his chubby unstained hands. His fingernails were manicured. He was somewhere between forty-five and fifty-five years old, but it was impossible to tell where. He was balding, wearing the ever-desirable swept-over look, parting his hair just below the armpit.

'Nice place, Roy,' Myron said. 'A table in the back, low lights, soft romantic music. If I didn't know better—'

O'Connor shook his head. 'Look, Bolitar, I know you think you're a regular Buddy Hackett, but give it a rest, okay?'

'I guess flowers are out, then.' Pause. Then: 'Buddy Hackett?'

'We need to talk.'

'I'm all ears.'

A waitress came over. 'Can I get you gentlemen something to drink?'

'Another,' Roy said, pointing to his glass.

'And for you?'

'Do you have Yoo-Hoo?' Myron asked.

'I think so.'

'Great. I'll have one.'

She left. Roy shook his head. 'A fucking Yoo-Hoo,' he mumbled.

'Did you say something?'

'Your goon visited me last night.'

'Your goons visited me first,' Myron said.

'I had nothing to do with that.'

Myron gave him his best 'come off it' look of pure

skepticism. The waitress put down the drinks. Roy scooped up his whiskey as if it held a life-saving antidote. Myron, by contrast, sipped his Yoo-Hoo daintily. Ever the gentleman.

'Look, Myron,' O'Connor continued, 'it's like this. I signed Landreaux. I gave him money up front. I gave him money every month. I kept my part of the bargain.'

'You signed him illegally.'

'I'm not the first guy to do it,' he said.

'Nor the last. What's your point, Roy?'

'Look, you know me. You know how I operate.'

Myron nodded. 'You're a chicken-shitted crook.'

'I might have threatened the kid. Fine. I've done that before. But that's it. I'd never really hurt anybody.'

'Uh-huh.'

'Word would get out to the athletes. I'd be ruined.'

'Damn shame that would be.'

'Bolitar, you're not making this any easier.'

'I'm not trying to.'

O'Connor grabbed the drink again. He finished it and signaled to the waitress for another. 'I've gotten involved with the wrong people,' he said.

'What do you mean?'

'I worked up some big-time gambling debts. Debts I couldn't pay off.'

'So they took a piece of your business.'

Roy nodded. 'They control me now. Your – your friend from last night.' A Geiger counter could have registered the quake in his voice when he mentioned Win. 'I want to do just what he said, but I don't have the power any-more.'

Myron took another sip of his Yoo-Hoo, hoping he

wasn't getting one of those chocolate mustaches. 'My friend won't be pleased to hear that.'

'You have to tell him it's not me.'

'Then who is it?'

Roy sat back, shaking his head. 'I can't say. But I can tell you they play for keeps. And they don't understand a thing about this business. They think they can just scare everyone into compliance. They want to make an example out of someone.'

'And Landreaux is the example?'

'Landreaux. And you. They want to hurt Landreaux. They want to kill you. They're putting out a contract on your head.'

Another cool sip. Myron said nothing.

'You don't seem very worried,' Roy said.

'I laugh in the face of death,' Myron replied. 'Well, maybe not laugh. More like a snicker. A quiet snicker.'

'Jesus, you're a lunatic.'

'And I wouldn't do it directly in death's face. So it's more like a quiet snicker behind his back.'

'Bolitar, this isn't funny.'

'No,' Myron agreed. 'It's not. I strongly suggest you call them off.'

'Haven't you heard a word I've said? I got no control here.'

'If something happens to me, my friend will be very upset. He'll take it out on you.'

Roy swallowed. 'But I'm powerless. You have to believe that.'

'Then tell me who's calling the shots.'

'I can't.'

Myron shrugged. 'Maybe we can be buried next to one another. One of those romantic tragedy things.'

'They'll kill me if I say anything.'

'What do you think my friend will do to you?'

Roy shuddered. He sucked on the ice again, trying to salvage the last remnants of the whiskey. 'Where is that damn bimbo with my drink?'

'Who's calling the shots, Roy?'

'You didn't hear it from me, right?'

'Right.'

'You won't tell them?'

'Mum's the word.'

One more ice suck. Then Roy said, 'Ache.'

'Herman Ache?' Myron asked, surprised. 'Herman Ache is behind this?'

Roy shook his head. 'His younger brother. Frank. He's out of control. I don't know what the psycho will do next.'

Frank Ache. It made sense. Herman Ache was one of New York's leading mobsters, responsible for countless misery. But next to his younger brother Frank, Herman was an Alan Alda clone. Aaron would enjoy working for someone like Frank.

This was not good news. Myron toyed with the idea of dropping the snicker altogether. 'Anything else you can tell me?'

'No. I just don't want anyone hurt.'

'You're some guy, Roy. So selfless.'

O'Connor stood. 'I got nothing more to say.'

'I thought we were going to have lunch.'

'Have it by yourself,' O'Connor said. 'It's on my tab.'

'Won't be the same without your company.'

'Yet somehow you'll muddle through.'

Myron picked up the menu. 'I'll try.'

Chapter 17

Who else to call?

The answer, Jessica realized, was obvious.

Nancy Serat. Kathy's roommate and closest friend.

Jessica sat at her father's desk. The lights were turned off, the shades were pulled down, but the sunlight was still strong enough to sneak through and cast shadows.

Adam Culver had done everything he could to make his home office radically different from the cement, institutional, macabre feel of the county morgue. The results were mixed. The converted bedroom had bright yellow walls, plenty of windows, silk flowers, white Formica desk. Teddy bears encircled the room. William Shakesbear. Rhett Beartler with Scarlett O'Beara. Bear Ruth. Bearlock Holmes. Humphrey Beargart with Lauren Bearcall. The whole atmosphere was cheerful, albeit a forced cheerful, like a clown you laugh at but find a little scary.

She took her phone book from her purse. Nancy had sent the family a card a few weeks ago. She had won some fellowship and was staying on campus to work in admissions. Jessica looked up her number and dialed.

On the third ring the answering machine picked up. Jessica left a message and hung up. She was about to start going through the drawers when a voice stopped her.

'Jessica.'

She looked up. Her mother stood in the doorway. Her eyes were sunken, her face a skeletal death mask. Her body swayed as though she were about to topple over.

'What are you doing in here?' Carol asked.

'Just looking around,' she said.

Carol nodded, her head bobbing on the string that was her neck. 'Find anything?'

'Not yet.'

Carol sat down. She stared straight ahead, her eyes unfocused. 'She was always such a happy child,' she said slowly. Her fingers fiddled with prayer beads, her gaze still far off. 'Kathy never stopped smiling. She had such a wonderful, happy smile. It lit up any room she entered. You and Edward, well, you were both more brooding. But Kathy – she had a smile for everyone and everything. Do you remember?'

'Yes,' Jessica said. 'I remember.'

'Your father used to joke that she had the personality of a born-again cheerleader,' Carol added, chuckling at the memory. 'Nothing ever brought her down.' She stopped, the chuckle fading away. 'Except, I guess, me.'

'Kathy loved you, Mom.'

She sighed deeply, her chest heaving as though even a sigh took great effort. 'I was a strict mother with you girls. Too strict, I guess. I was old-fashioned.'

Jessica did not reply.

'I just didn't want you or your sister to . . .' She lowered her head.

'To what?'

She shook her head. Her fingers moved across the beads at a more fervid pace. For a long time neither of them spoke. Then Carol said, 'You were right before, Jessica. Kathy changed.'

'When?'

'Her senior year.'

'What happened?'

Tears sprang to Carol's eyes. Her mouth tried to form words, her hands moving in gestures of helplessness. 'The smile,' she replied with something like a shrug. 'One day it was gone.'

'Why?'

Her mother wiped her eyes. Her lower lip quivered. Jessica's heart reached out to her, but for some reason the rest of her couldn't. She sat and watched her suffering, strangely uninvolved, as if she were watching a late-night tearjerker on cable.

'I'm not trying to hurt you,' Jessica said. 'I just want to find Kathy.'

'I know, sweetheart.'

'I think,' Jessica continued, 'that whatever changed Kathy is connected to her disappearance.'

Her mother's shoulders sagged. 'Merciful God.'

'I know it hurts,' Jessica said. 'But if we can find Kathy, if we can find who killed Dad—'

Carol's head shot up. 'Your father was killed in a robbery.'

'I don't think so. I think it's all connected. Kathy's disappearance, Dad's murder, everything.'

'But – how?'

'I don't know yet. Myron is helping me find out.'

The doorbell rang.

'That'll be Uncle Paul,' her mother said, heading for the door.

'Mom?'

Carol stopped but did not turn around.

'What's going on? What are you afraid to tell me?'

The doorbell rang again.

'I better get that,' Carol said. She hurried down the stairs.

'So,' Win began, 'Frank Ache wants to kill you.'

Myron nodded. 'Seems so.'

'A shame.'

'If he'd only get to know me. The real me.'

They sat in the front row at Titans Stadium. Out of the goodness of his heart, Otto had agreed to let Christian practice. That, and the fact that veteran quarterback Neil Decker was beyond horrendous.

The morning session had been a lot of wind sprints and walking through plays. The afternoon session, however, was a bit of a surprise. The players were in full gear, almost unheard of this early on in the year.

'Frank Ache is not a kind fellow,' Win said.

'He likes torturing animals.'

'Excuse me?'

'A friend of mine knew him growing up,' Myron explained. 'Frank Ache's favorite hobby was to chase down cats and dogs and bash in their heads with a base-ball bat.'

'I bet that impressed the girls,' Win said.

Myron nodded.

'I assume, then, that you will be in need of my unique services.'

'For a few days, anyway,' Myron replied.

'Goodie. May I also assume that you have a plan?'

'I'm working on it. Feverishly.'

Christian jogged out on the field. He moved in that effortless way great athletes do. He got into the huddle, broke it, and approached the line of scrimmage.

'Full contact!' a coach yelled out.

Myron looked at Win. 'I don't like this.'

'What?'

'Full contact on the first day.'

Christian started calling out numbers. Then he gave a few hut-huts before the ball was snapped to him. He faded back to pass.

'Oh, shit,' Myron said.

Tommy Lawrence, the Titans' All-Pro linebacker, charged forward unblocked. Christian saw him too late. Tommy placed his helmet into Christian's sternum and slammed him to the ground – the kind of tackle that hurts like hell but doesn't do any permanent damage. Two other defenders piled on.

Christian got up, wincing and holding his chest. Nobody helped him.

Myron stood.

Win stopped him with a shake of his head. 'Sit down, Myron.'

Otto Burke came down the stairs, entourage in tow.

Myron glared at him. Otto smiled brightly. He made a tsk-tsk noise. 'I traded a lot of popular veterans to get him,' he said. 'It looks like some of the guys aren't too thrilled.'

'Sit down, Myron,' Win repeated.

Myron hesitated, then complied.

Christian limped back to the huddle. He called the next play and again approached the line of scrimmage. He surveyed the defense, yelled out numbers and hut-huts, then took the snap from the center. He stepped back. Tommy Lawrence blitzed again over left guard, completely untouched. Christian froze. Tommy bore down on him. He leaped like a panther, his arms stretched out for a bone-crushing tackle. Christian moved at the very last moment. Not a big move. Just a slight shift, actually. Tommy flew by him and landed on the ground. Christian pumped and threw a bomb.

Complete pass.

Myron turned around, grinning. 'Hey, Otto?'

'What?'

'Kiss my grits.'

Otto's smile did not falter. Myron wondered how he did that, if his mouth was frozen that way, like the threat a little kid hears from his mom when he's making faces. Otto nodded and walked away. His entourage followed in a row, like a family of mallard ducks.

Win looked at Myron. 'Kiss my grits?'

Shrug. 'Paying homage to Flo on *Alice*.'

'You watch too much television.'

'Listen, I've been thinking.'

'Oh?'

'About Gary Grady,' Myron said.

'What about him?'

'He has an affair with a student. She vanishes a year or so later. Time passes and her picture ends up in a porno ad he runs.'

'Your point being?'

'It's crazy.'

140

'So is everything about this case.'

Myron shook his head. 'Think about it. Grady admits having an affair with Kathy, right? So what would be the last thing he'd want to do?'

'Publicize it.'

'Yet her picture ends up in his ad.'

'Ah.' Win nodded. 'You believe someone is setting him up.'

'Exactly.'

'Who?'

'Fred Nickler would be my bet,' Myron said.

'Hmm. He did hand over Grady's PO box without much debate.'

'And he has the power to switch photos in his own magazine.'

'So what do you suggest?' Win asked.

'I'd like you to check out Mr Fred Nickler very thoroughly. Maybe talk to him again. *Talk*,' Myron repeated. 'Not visit.'

On the field Christian was fading back again. For the third straight time Tommy Lawrence blitzed over left guard untouched. In fact, the left guard stood with his hands on his hips and watched.

'Christian's own lineman is setting him up,' Myron said.

Christian side-stepped Tommy Lawrence, cocked his arms, and whipped the ball with unearthly velocity directly into his left guard's groin. There was a short *oomph* sound. The left guard collapsed like a folding chair.

'Ouch,' Win said.

Myron almost clapped. '*The Longest Yard* revisited.'

The left guard was, of course, wearing a cup. But a cup was far from full protection against a speeding missile. He rolled on the ground, back curved fetal-like, eyes wide. Every man in the general vicinity gave a collective, sympathetic 'Ooo.'

Christian walked over to his left guard – a man weighing in excess of 275 pounds – and offered him a hand. The left guard took it. He limped back to the huddle.

'Christian has balls,' Myron said.

Win nodded. 'But can the same be said of the left guard?'

Chapter 18

As soon as Myron entered the Reston University campus, his car phone rang.

'Listen, putz, I got what you want,' P.T. said. 'My friend's name is Jake Courter. He's the town sheriff.'

'Sheriff Jake,' Myron said. 'You're kidding, right?'

'Hey, don't let the title fool you. Jake used to work homicide in Philly, Boston, and New York. Good man. He said he'd meet with you today at three.'

Myron checked his watch. It was one o'clock now. The station was five minutes away. 'Thanks, P.T.'

'Can I ask you something, Myron?'

'Shoot.'

'Why you looking into this?'

'It's a long story, P.T.'

'This have to do with her sister? That great piece of tail you used to nail?' He cackled.

'You're all class, P.T.'

'Hey, Myron, I want to hear about it sometime. The whole story.'

'It's a promise.'

Myron parked the car and headed into the old athletic center. The corridor was a bit more beaten up than Myron had expected. Three rows of framed photographs of past athletic teams – some from as far back as a hundred years ago – lined the walls. Myron approached a beaded-glass door that looked like something out of an old Sam Spade film. The word FOOTBALL was stenciled in black. He knocked.

The voice was like an old tire on an unpaved road. 'What?'

Myron stuck his head. 'Busy, Coach?'

Reston University football coach Danny Clarke looked up from his computer. 'Who the hell are you?' he rasped.

'Fine, thanks. But let's dispense with the pleasantries.'

'That supposed to be funny?'

Myron tilted his head. 'You didn't think so?'

'I'll ask one more time: Who the hell are you?'

'Myron Bolitar.'

The coach's scowl did not change. 'Am I supposed to know you?'

It was a hot summer day, the campus was practically empty, and here sat the school's legendary football coach wearing a suit and tie, watching videotapes of high school prospects. A suit and tie and no air conditioning. If the heat bothered Danny Clarke, it didn't show. Everything about him was well groomed and tidy. He was shelling and eating peanuts, but no mess was visible. His jaw muscles bunched as he chewed, making little knobs appear and disappear near his ears. He had a prominent vein in his forehead.

'I'm a sports agent.'

He flicked his eyes away like a ruler dismissing an underling. 'Get out of here. I'm busy.'

'We need to talk.'

'Out of here, asshole. Now.'

'I just—'

'Listen up, shithead.' He pointed a coach finger at Myron. 'I don't talk to bottom-feeders. Ever. I run a clean program with clean players. I don't take payoffs from so-called agents or any of that bullshit. So if you got an envelope stuffed with green, you can go shove it up your ass.'

Myron clapped. 'Beautiful. I laughed, I cried, it became a part of me.'

Danny Clarke looked up sharply. He wasn't used to having his orders questioned, but part of him seemed almost amused by it. 'Get the hell out of here,' he growled, but more gently now. He turned back to the television. On the screen a young quarterback threw a long, tight spiral. Caught. Touchdown.

Myron decided to disarm him with tact. 'The kid looks pretty good,' he said.

'Yeah, well, it's a good thing you're a scum-sucking leech and not a scout. The kid can't play a lick. Now take a hike.'

'I want to talk to you about Christian Steele.'

That got his attention. 'What about him?'

'I'm his agent.'

'Oh,' Danny Clarke said. 'Now I remember. You're the old basketball player. The one who hurt his knee.'

'At your service,' Myron said.

'Is Christian okay?'

Myron tried to look noncommittal. 'I understand he didn't get along with his teammates.'

'So? You his social coordinator?'

'What was the problem?'

'I can't see how it matters now,' he said.

'Then humor me.'

It took the coach some time to relax his glare. 'It was a lot of things,' he said. 'But I guess Horty was the main problem.'

'Horty?' Clever interrogation techniques. Pay attention.

'Junior Horton,' he explained. 'A defensive lineman. Good speed, good size, good talent. The brains of a citrus beverage.'

'So what does this Horty have to do with Christian?'

'They didn't see eye to eye.'

'How come?'

Danny Clarke thought a moment. 'I don't know. Something to do with that girl who disappeared.'

'Kathy Culver?'

'Right. Her.'

'What about her?'

He turned back to the VCR and changed tapes. Then he typed something on his computer. 'I think maybe she dated Horty before Christian. Something like that.'

'So what happened?'

'Horty was a bad apple from the get-go. In his senior year I found out he was pushing drugs to my players: cocaine, dope, Lord knows what else. So I bounced him. Later, I heard he'd been supplying the guys with steroids for three years.'

Later my ass, Myron thought. But for once he kept the

146

thought to himself. 'So what does this have to do with Christian?'

'Rumors started circulating that Christian had gotten Horty thrown off the team. Horty fueled them, you know, telling the guys that Christian was turning them all in for using steroids, stuff like that.'

'Was that true?'

'Nope. Two of my best players showed up game day so stoned, they could barely see. That's when I took action. Christian had nothing to do with it. But you know how it is. They all figured Christian was the star. If he wanted his ass wiped, the coaches asked Charmin or Downy.'

'Did you tell your guys Christian had nothing to do with it?'

He made a face. 'You think that would have helped? They would have thought I was covering for him, protecting him. They would have hated him even more. As long as it didn't affect their play – and it didn't – it was not my concern. I just let it be.'

'You're a real character developer, Coach.'

He gave Myron his best intimidate-the-freshman glare. The forehead vein started pulsing. 'You're out of line, Bolitar.'

'Wouldn't be the first time.'

'I care about my boys.'

'Yeah, I can tell. You let Horty stay as long as he pumped your boys with dangerous albeit play-enhancing drugs. When he graduated to the big leagues – to the stuff that had a negative on-the-field impact – all of a sudden you became a righteous drug czar.'

'I don't have to listen to this bullshit,' Danny Clarke ranted. 'Especially from a no-good, bloodsucking vampire. Get the hell out of my office. Now.'

Myron said, 'You want to catch a movie together sometime? Maybe a Broadway show?'

'Out!'

Myron left. Another day, another friend. Charm was the key.

He had plenty of time to kill before he visited Sheriff Jake, so he decided to take a stroll. The campus was like a ghost town, except no tumbleweeds were skittering along the ground. The students were gone for summer break. The buildings stood lifeless and sad. In the distance a stereo was playing Elvis Costello. Two girls appeared. Co-ed types wearing crotch-riding shorts and halter tops. They were walking a hairy, little dog – a shih-tzu. It looked like Cousin It after one too many spins in the dryer. Myron smiled and nodded as the girls passed him. Neither one fainted or disrobed. Astonishing. The little dog, however, snarled at him. Cujo.

He was nearly at his car when he spotted the sign:

Campus Post Office

He stopped, looked around the grounds, saw nobody. Hmm. It was worth a try.

The inside of the post office was painted institutional green, the same color as the school bathroom. A long V-shaped corridor was wallpapered with PO boxes. He heard the distant sound of a radio. He couldn't make out the song, just a strong, monotonous bass beat.

Myron approached the mail window. A kid sat with his feet up. The music was coming from the kid's ears. He was listening to one of those Walkman clones with the minispeakers that bypass the ears and plug directly into the cerebrum. His black high-tops rested on a desk, his baseball hat tipped down like a sombrero at siesta time. There was a book on his lap. Philip Roth's *Operation Shylock*.

'Good book,' Myron said.

The kid did not look up.

'Good book,' Myron said again, this time yelling.

The kid pulled the speakers out of his ears with a sucking pop. He was pale and red-haired. When he took off his hat, his hair was Afro-wild. Bernie from *Room 222*.

'What?'

'I said, good book.'

'You read it?'

Myron nodded. 'Without moving my lips.'

The kid stood. He was tall and lanky.

'You play basketball?' Myron asked.

'Yeah,' the kid said. 'Just finished my freshman year. Didn't play much.'

'I'm Myron Bolitar.'

The kid looked at him blankly.

'I played ball for Duke.'

Blink, blink.

'No autographs, please.'

'How long ago did you play?' the kid asked.

'Graduated ten years ago.'

'Oh,' the kid replied, as though that explained everything. Myron did some quick math in his head. The kid had been seven or eight when Myron won the national title. He suddenly felt very old.

'We used peach baskets back then.'

'What?'

'Never mind. Can I ask you a few questions?'

The kid shrugged. 'Go ahead.'

'How often are you on duty in the post office?'

'Five days a week in the summer, nine to five.'

'Is it always this quiet?'

'This time of year, yeah. No students, so there's almost no mail.'

'Do you do the mail sorting?'

'Sure.'

'Do you do pick-ups?'

'Pick-ups?'

'Campus mail.'

'Yeah, but there's only that slot by the front door.'

'That's the only campus mailbox?'

'Um-hmm.'

'Been getting a lot of campus mail lately?'

'Next to none. Three, four letters a day.'

'Do you know Christian Steele?'

'Heard of him,' the kid said. 'Who hasn't?'

'He got a big manila envelope in his box a few days ago. There was no postmark, so it had to be mailed from campus.'

'Yeah, I remember. What about it?'

'Did you see who mailed it?' Myron asked.

'No,' the kid said. 'But they were the only pieces of mail I got that whole day.'

Myron cocked his head. 'They?'

'What?'

'You said "they. They were the only pieces." '

'Right. Two big envelopes. Exact same except for the address.'

'Do you remember who the other one was addressed to?'

'Sure,' the kid said. 'Harrison Gordon. He's the dean of students.'

Chapter 19

Nancy Serat dropped her suitcase on the floor and rewound the answering machine. The tape raced back, shrieking all the way. She had spent the weekend in Cancún, a final vacation before starting her fellowship at Reston University, her alma mater.

The first message was from her mother.

'I don't want to disturb you on vacation, dear. But I thought you'd want to know that Kathy Culver's father died yesterday. He was stabbed by a mugger. Awful. Anyway, I thought you'd want to know. Give us a call when you get back in. Your father and I want to take you out to dinner for your birthday.'

Nancy's legs felt weak. She collapsed into the chair, barely hearing the next two messages – one from her dentist's office reminding her of a teeth cleaning on Friday, the other from a friend planning a party.

Adam Culver was dead. She couldn't believe it. Her mother had said it was a mugger. Nancy wondered. Was it really random? Or did it have something to do with his visit on . . . ?

She calculated the days.

Kathy's father had visited on the day he died.

A voice on the machine jarred her back to the present.

'Hello, Nancy. This is Jessica Culver, Kathy's sister. When you get in, please give me a call. I need to talk to you as soon as possible. I'm staying with my mom. The number here is 555–1477. It's kind of important. Thank you.'

Nancy suddenly felt very cold. She listened to the rest of the messages. Then she sat without moving for several minutes, debating her options. Kathy was dead – or so everyone believed. And now her father, hours after talking to Nancy, was dead too.

What did it mean?

She remained very still, the only sound her own breaths coming in short, hitching gasps. Then she picked up the phone and dialed Jessica's number.

The dean's office was closed, so Myron proceeded straight to his house. It was an old Victorian with cedar shingles on the west end of the campus. He rang the doorbell. A very attractive woman opened the door. She smiled solicitously.

'May I help you?'

She wore a tailored cream suit. She was not young, but she had a grace and beauty and sex appeal that made Myron's mouth a little dry. In front of such a lady Myron wanted to remove his hat, except he wasn't wearing one.

'Good afternoon,' he said. 'I'm looking for Dean Gordon. My name is Myron Bolitar, and—'

'The basketball player?' she interrupted. 'Of course. I should have recognized you right away.'

To grace, beauty, and sex appeal, add knowledge of basketball.

'I remember watching you in the NCAAs,' she continued. 'I cheered you all the way.'

'Thank you—'

'When you got hurt—' She stopped, shook the head attached to the Audrey Hepburn neck. 'I cried. I felt like a part of me was hurt too.'

Grace, beauty, sex appeal, basketball knowledge, and alas, sensitivity. She was also long-legged and curvy. All in all, a nice package.

'That's very kind of you, thank you.'

'It's a pleasure to meet you, Myron.'

Even his first name sounded good coming from those lips. 'And you must be Dean Gordon's wife. The lovely dean-nessa.'

She laughed at the Woody Allen rip-off. 'Yes, I'm Madelaine Gordon. And no, my husband is not home at the moment.'

'Are you expecting him soon?'

She smiled as though the question were a double entendre. Then she gave him a look that flushed his cheeks. 'No,' she said slowly. 'He won't be home for hours.'

Heavy accent on the word *hours*.

'Well then, I won't bother you anymore.'

'It's no bother.'

'I'll come by another time,' he said.

Madelaine (he liked that name) nodded demurely. 'I'll look forward to it.'

'Nice meeting you.' With Myron, every line was a lady-slayer.

'Nice meeting you too,' she singsonged. 'Goodbye, Myron.'

The door closed slowly, teasingly. He stood there for another moment, took a few deep breaths, and hurried back to his car. Whew.

He checked his watch. Time to meet Sheriff Jake.

Jake Courter was alone in the station, which looked like something out of Mayberry RFD. Except Jake was black. There were never any blacks in Mayberry. Or Green Acres. Or any of those places. No Jews, Latinos, Asians, ethnics of any kind. Would have been a nice touch. Maybe have a Greek diner or a guy named Abdul working for Sam Drucker at the grocery store.

Myron estimated Jake to be in his mid-fifties. He was in plainclothes, his jacket off, his tie loosened. A big gut spilled forward like something that belonged to someone else. Manila files were scattered across Jake's desk, along with the remnants of what might be a sandwich and an apple core. Jake gave a tired shrug and wiped his nose with what looked like a dishrag.

'Got a call,' he said by way of introduction. 'I'm supposed to help you out.'

'I'd appreciate it,' Myron said.

Jake leaned back and put his feet on the desk. 'You played ball against my son. Gerard. Michigan State.'

'Sure,' Myron said, 'I remember him. Tough kid. Monster on the boards. Defensive specialist.'

Jake nodded proudly. 'That's him. Couldn't shoot worth a lick, but you always knew he was there.'

'An enforcer,' Myron added.

'Yep. He's a cop now. In New York. Made detective second grade already. Good cop.'

'Like his old man.'

Jake smiled. 'Yeah.'

'Give him my regards,' Myron said. 'Better yet, give him an elbow to the ribcage. I still owe him a few.'

Jake threw back his head and laughed. 'That's Gerard. Finesse was never his forte.' He blew his nose into the dishrag. 'But I'm sure you didn't come all this way to talk basketball.'

'No, I guess not.'

'So why don't you tell me what this is all about, Myron?'

'The Kathy Culver case,' he said. 'I'm looking into it. Very surreptitiously.'

'Surreptitiously,' Jake repeated with a raised eyebrow. 'Awfully big word, Myron.'

'I've been listening to self-improvement tapes in the car.'

'That right?' Jake blew his nose again. Sounded like a ewe's mating call. 'So what's your interest in this – aside from the fact that you represent Christian Steele and you used to have a thing for Kathy's sister.'

Myron said, 'You're thorough.'

He took a bite out of the half-eaten sandwich on his desk, smiled. 'Man does love to be flattered.'

'It's like you said. Christian Steele. He's a client. I'm trying to help him out.'

Jake studied him, waiting again. It was an old trick. Stay silent long enough, and the witness would start talking again, elaborating. Myron did not bite.

After a full minute had passed Jake said, 'So let me get this straight. Christian Steele signs on with you. One day you start chatting. He says, "You know, Myron, the way you been licking my lily-white ass and all, I'd like you to go play Dick Fuckin' Tracy and find my old squeeze who's been missing for the last year and a half and the cops and feds can't find." That how it went, Myron?'

'Christian doesn't curse,' Myron said.

'Okay, fine, you want to skip the dance? Let's skip it. You want me to give, you have to give back.'

'That's fair enough,' Myron said. 'But I can't. Not yet, anyhow.'

'Why not?'

'It could hurt a lot of people,' Myron said. 'And it's probably nothing.'

He made a face. 'What do you mean, hurt?'

'I can't elaborate.'

'Fuck you can't.'

'I'm telling you, Jake. I can't say anything.'

Jake studied him again. 'Let me tell you something, Bolitar. I'm no glory hound. I'm like my son was on the court. Not flashy but a workhorse. I don't look for clippings so I can climb up the ladder. I'm fifty-three years old. My ladder don't go no higher. Now this may seem a bit old-fashioned to you, but I believe in justice. I like to see truth prevail. I've lived with Kathy Culver's disappearance for eighteen months. I know her inside and out. And I have no idea what happened that night.'

'What do you think happened?' Myron asked.

Jake picked up a pencil and tapped it on the desk. 'Best guess based on the evidence?'

Myron nodded.

'She's a runaway.'

Myron was surprised. 'What makes you say that?'

A slow smile spread across Jake's face. 'That's for me to know and you to find out.'

'P.T. said you would help.'

Jake shrugged and took another bite from yet another sandwich scrap. 'What about Kathy's sister? I understand you two were pretty heavy.'

'We're friends now.'

Jake gave a low whistle. 'I've seen her on TV,' he said. 'Hard to be friends with a woman who looks like that.'

'You're a real nineties guy, Jake.'

'Yeah, well, I forgot to renew my subscription to *Cosmo*.'

They stared at each other for a while. Jake settled back in his chair and examined his fingernails. 'What do you want to know?'

'Everything,' Myron said. 'From the beginning.'

Jake folded his arms across his chest. He took a deep breath and let it loose slowly. 'Campus security got a call from Kathy Culver's roommate, Nancy Serat. Kathy and Nancy lived in the Psi Omega sorority house. Nice house. All pretty white girls with blond hair and white teeth. Kind that all look alike and sound alike. You get the picture.'

Myron nodded. He noticed that Jake was not reading or even consulting a file. This was coming from memory.

'Nancy Serat told the rent-a-cop that Kathy Culver hadn't returned to her room for three days.'

'Why did Nancy wait so long to call?' Myron asked.

'Seems Kathy wasn't spending too many nights in the sorority house anyhow. She slept in your client's room most of the time. You know, the one who doesn't like to curse.' Brief smile. 'Anyhow, your boy and Nancy got to talking one day, both figuring Kathy had been spending all her time with the other. That's when they realized she was missing and called campus security.

'Campus security told us about it, but no one got very excited at first. A co-ed missing for a few days is hardly an earth-shattering event. But then one of the rent-a-cops found the panties on top of a waste bin, and well, you know what happened then. The story spread like a grease stain on Elvis's pillow.'

'I read there was blood on the panties,' Myron said.

'A media exaggeration. There was a bloodstain, dry, probably from a menstrual cycle. We typed it. B negative. Same type as Kathy Culver's. But there was also semen. Enough antibodies for a DNA and blood test.'

'Did you have any suspects?'

'Only one,' Jake said. 'Your boy, Christian Steele.'

'Why him?'

'Usual reasons. He was the boyfriend. She was on her way to see him when she vanished. Nothing very specific or damaging. But the DNA test on the semen cleared him.' He opened a small refrigerator behind him. 'Want a Coke?'

'No, thanks.'

Jake grabbed a can and snapped it open. 'Here's what you probably read in the papers,' he continued. 'Kathy is at a sorority cocktail party. She has a drink or two, nothing serious, leaves at ten P.M. to meet Christian, and disappears. End of story. But now let me fill it in a little.'

Myron leaned forward. Jake took a swig of Coke and wiped his mouth with a forearm the size of an oak trunk.

'According to several of her sorority sisters,' he said, 'Kathy was distracted. Not herself. We also know she got a phone call a few minutes before she left the house. She told Nancy Serat the call was from Christian and she was going to meet him. Christian denies making the call. These were all intracampus calls, so there is no way for us to tell. But the roommate says Kathy sounded strained on the phone, not like she was talking to her true love, Mr Clean-Mouth.

'Kathy hung up the phone and went back downstairs with Nancy. Then she posed for the now-famous last photograph before leaving for good.'

He opened his desk drawer and handed Myron the photograph. Myron had, of course, seen it countless times before. Every media outlet in the country had run the photograph with morbid fascination. A picture of twelve sorority sisters. Kathy stood second from the left. She wore a blue sweater and skirt. Pearls adorned her neck. Very preppy. According to Kathy's sorority sisters, Kathy left the house alone immediately after the picture was taken. She never returned.

''Okay,' Jake said, 'so she leaves the cocktail party. Only one person saw her for sure after that.'

'Who?' Myron asked.

'Team trainer. Guy named Tony Gardola. He saw her, strangely enough, entering the team's locker room around quarter after ten. The locker room was supposed to be empty at that hour. Only reason Tony was there was that he forgot something. He asked her what she was doing there, and she said she was meeting Christian. Tony figured what the hell, kids today. Might be having a kinky locker-room encounter. Tony decided it was in his best interest not to ask too many questions.

'That's our last *firm* report on her whereabouts. We have a possible sighting of her on the western edge of campus at around eleven P.M. Someone saw a blond woman wearing a blue sweater and skirt. It was too dark to make a positive ID. The witness said he wouldn't have even noticed, except she seemed in a rush. Not running but doing one of those quick walks.'

'Where on the western edge of campus?' Myron asked.

Jake opened a file and took out a map, still studying Myron's face as though it held a clue. He spread the map out and pointed. 'Here,' he said. 'In front of Miliken Hall.'

'What's Miliken Hall?' Myron asked.

'Math building. Locked tight by nine o'clock. But the witness said she was moving west.'

Myron's eyes traced a path to the west. There were four other buildings labeled FACULTY HOUSING. Myron remembered the spot.

It was where Dean Gordon lived.

'What is it?' Jake asked.

'Nothing.'

'Bullshit, Bolitar. You see something.'

'It's nothing.'

Jake's eyebrows furrowed. 'Fine. You want to play it that way? Then get the fuck out. I still got my ace in the hole, and I ain't showing it.'

Myron had planned for this. Jake Courter would have to be given something. That was fine, as long as Myron could turn it to his advantage.

'It seems to me,' Myron said slowly, 'that Kathy was walking in the general direction of the dean's house.'

'So?'

Myron said nothing.

'She worked for him,' Jake said.

Myron nodded.

'What's the connection?'

'Oh, I'm sure it's completely innocent,' Myron said. 'But you might want to ask him about it. You being so thorough and all.'

'Are you saying—'

'I'm not saying anything. I am merely making an observation.'

Again Jake studied him. Myron looked back coolly. A visit from Jake Courter would probably not crack Dean Gordon, but it should soften him a bit. 'Now about that ace in the hole . . . ?'

Jake hesitated. 'Kathy Culver inherited money from her grandmother,' he said.

'Twenty-five grand,' Myron added. 'All three kids got the same. It's sitting in a trust account.'

'Not exactly,' Jake said. He stood, hitched his pants up. 'You want to know why I said the evidence pointed to Kathy being a runaway?'

Myron nodded.

'The day Kathy Culver vanished, she visited the bank,' Jake continued. 'She cleared out her inheritance. Every penny.'

Chapter 20

Myron started back toward New York. He flipped on the radio. Wham's classic hit 'Careless Whisper' was playing. George Michael was bemoaning the fact that he would never dance again because 'guilty feet have got no rhythm.' Deep, Myron thought. Very deep.

He picked up the car phone and dialed Esperanza.

'What's up?' he asked.

'You coming back to the office?'

'I'm on my way there now.'

'I wouldn't make any stops,' she said.

'Why?'

'You have a surprise client waiting for you.'

'Who?'

'Chaz Landreaux.'

'He's supposed to be hiding in Washington.'

'Well, he's here. And he looks like shit.'

'Tell him to sit tight. I'm on my way.'

*

'It's like this,' Chaz began. 'I want to cancel our contract.'

He paced the office like an expectant father, and he did indeed look like shit. The cocky grin was nowhere to be seen. The swagger was more like a hunch. He kept licking his lips, darting his eyes, bunching and unbunching his fingers.

'Why don't you start at the beginning?' Myron tried.

'Ain't no beginning,' Chaz snapped. 'I want out. You gonna fight me on it?'

'What happened?'

'Nothing happened. I changed my mind, is all. I want to go with Roy O'Connor at TruPro now. They're big-time. You're a nice guy, Myron, but you don't have their connections.'

'Uh-huh.'

Silence. More pacing.

'Can I have the contract or what?'

'How did they get to you, Chaz?'

'I don't know what the fuck you're talking about. How many times do I have to say it? I don't want you, okay?' Chaz was on the edge and teetering. 'I want TruPro.'

'It's not that easy,' Myron said.

'You gonna fight me on this?' he asked again.

'They won't stop with this, Chaz. You're in over your head. You have to let me help you.'

He stopped. 'Help me? You wanna help me? Then give me back my contract. And don't pretend you give a shit about me. You just want your piece.'

'Do you really believe that?' Myron asked.

He shook his head. 'You don't get it, man. I don't want you. I want to go with TruPro.'

'I get it. And like I said before, it's not that easy. These guys got you by the balls. You think you can make them let

163

go by doing what they say. But you can't. Not for good anyway. Whenever they want something, they'll just reach back into your pants and give another squeeze. They won't stop, Chaz. Not until they've squeezed you for everything they can.'

'Man, you don't know shit. I don't have to explain nothing to you.' He approached the desk, but his eyes looked away. 'I want that goddamn contract. I want it now.'

Myron picked up his phone. 'Esperanza, bring me Chaz's contract. The original.' He hung up. 'It'll just be a moment.'

Chaz said nothing.

'You don't know what you're mixed up in,' Myron continued.

'Fuck off, man. I know exactly what I'm mixed up in.'

'Let me help, Chaz.'

He snorted. 'What can you do?'

'I can stop them.'

'Oh yeah, I can tell. You done a great job so far.'

'What happened?'

But he just shook his head.

Esperanza came in and handed Myron the contract. Myron in turn handed it to Chaz. He grabbed it and hurried to the door.

'Sorry, Myron. But this is business.'

'You can't beat them, Chaz. Not on your own. They'll suck you dry.'

'Don't worry about me. I can take care of myself.'

'I don't think you can.'

'Just stay the fuck out. It ain't your business no more.'

He took off without a backward glance. When he was gone, Win opened the door between the conference room and Myron's office. 'Interesting conversation,' Win said.

Myron nodded, thinking.

'We've lost a client,' Win said. 'Too bad.'

'It's not that simple, Win.'

'That's where you're mistaken,' Win replied steadily. 'It's just that simple. He dumped you for another agency. As he so eloquently put it, "It ain't your business no more."'

'Chaz is being pressured.'

'And you offered to help him. He refused.'

'He's a scared kid.'

'He's an adult who makes his own decisions. One of which was to tell you to fuck off.'

Myron looked up. 'You know what they'll do to him.'

'It's a world of free will, Myron. Landreaux chose to take the money in college. And he chose to go back to them now.'

'Will you follow him?'

'Pardon?'

'Follow Chaz. See where he takes those contracts.'

'You complicate the simple, Myron. Just let it be.'

'I can't. You know I can't.'

Win nodded. 'I guess I do.' He thought a moment. 'I'll do it for the sake of our business,' he said. 'For the added revenue. If we get Landreaux back in our stable, it will be very profitable. You may enjoy playing superhero, but as far as I'm concerned, this is no moral crusade. I am doing this for the money. That is the only reason. The money.'

Myron nodded. 'I wouldn't want it any other way.'

'Fine. As long as we are clear on that point. And I want you to take this.'

Win handed him a Smith & Wesson .38 and a shoulder holster. Myron put it on. Carrying a gun was incredibly uncomfortable, yet the weight felt good, like a reminder

165

of some kind of protective bubble. Sometimes the sensation made you feel heady, invincible even.

That was usually when you got popped.

'Be extra careful,' Win said. 'The word has hit the streets.'

'What word?'

'A price has officially been put on your head,' Win said, as if it were amusing cocktail conversation. 'Thirty thousand dollars to the man who takes you out.'

Myron made a face. 'Thirty thousand? Hell, I used to be a fed. I should be worth sixty, seventy grand minimum.'

'Bad economy. Times are tough.'

'I'm being discounted?'

'Appears so, yes.'

Myron opened the revolver and checked the bullets. Just as he suspected. Win had loaded the gun with dumdums – bullets with cross-hatched tips to expose the lead. Wasn't enough to be using hollow-point Winchester Silvertip bullets. Win had to doctor them for that extra little crunch. 'These are illegal.'

Win put his hand against his chest. 'My. Oh. My. How. Awful.'

'And unnecessary.'

'If you say so.'

'I say so.'

'They are effective.'

'I don't want them,' Myron said.

'Fine.' He handed Myron uncut bullets. 'Be a wimp.'

Chapter 21

Jessica listened to the message on the answering machine.

'Hi, Jessica. It's Nancy Serat. I'm so sorry to hear about your father. He was such a nice man. I can't believe it. He was here the morning he died. So weird. He was so nostalgic that day. He told me all about that favorite yellow sweater he gave Kathy. Such a sweet story. I wish I could have been more helpful. I just can't believe – well, I'm rambling, sorry. I do that when I'm nervous. Anyway I'll be out until ten o'clock tonight. You can come by then or give me a call. Bye.'

Jessica rewound the message and played it back. Then a third time. Nancy Serat had seen her father on the morning of his murder.

Another coincidence?

She thought not.

Myron called his mother. 'I won't be home for a few days.'

'What?'

'I'm going to stay with Win.'

'In the city?'

'Yes.'

'New York City?'

'No, Mom. Kuwait City.'

'Don't be such a wise guy with your mother, save it for your friends,' she said. 'So why are you staying in the city?'

Hmm. Should he tell her the truth? *Because, Mom, a mobster has a contract out on my head and I don't want to put you and Dad in danger.* Nah. Might make her worry. 'I'm going to be working late the next few nights.'

'You sure about this?'

'Yes.'

'Be careful, Myron. Don't walk around alone at night.'

Esperanza opened the door. 'Urgent call on line three,' she said, loud enough for Myron's mother to hear.

'Mom, I gotta go. Urgent call.'

'Call us.'

'I will.' He hung up and looked up at Esperanza. 'Thanks.'

'Don't mention it.'

'Is there anyone on the phone?'

She nodded. 'Timmy Simpson again. I tried to handle it, but he says his problem needs your particular expertise.'

Timmy Simpson was a rookie shortstop for the Red Sox. A major-league pain in the ass.

'Hi, Timmy.'

'Hey, Myron, I've been waiting here two goddamn hours for your call.'

'I was out. What's the problem?'

'I'm here in Toronto, okay, at the Hilton. And this hotel's got no hot water.'

Myron waited. Then he said, 'Did I hear you correctly, Timmy? Did you say—'

'Unfuckinbelievable, ain't it?' Timmy shouted. 'I go in the shower, right, wait five minutes, then ten minutes. The water's fucking freezing, Myron. Ice cold. So finally I call down to the front desk, right? Some pissant manager tells me they're having some kind of plumbing problem. Plumbing problem, Myron, like I'm staying in a fuckin' trailer park or something. So I say, when's it going to be fixed? He gives me this whole long spiel how he don't know. Can you believe this shit?'

No, Myron thought. 'Timmy, why exactly are you calling me?'

'Jesus Christ, Myron, I'm a pro, right? And I'm stuck in this hellhole with no hot water. I mean, isn't there something in my contract about that?'

'A hot water clause, perhaps?' Myron tried.

'Or something. I mean, come on. Where do they get off? I need a shower before a game. A *hot* shower. Is that too much to expect? I mean, what am I going to do?'

Stick your head in the toilet and flush, Myron thought, massaging his temples with his fingertips. 'I'll see what I can do, Timmy.'

'Talk to the hotel manager, Myron. Make him understand the importance.'

'As far as I'm concerned,' Myron said, 'those orphans in Eastern Europe are a minor annoyance in comparison to this. But if the hot water doesn't come back on soon, check into another hotel. We'll send the bill to the Red Sox.'

'Good idea. Thanks, Myron.'

Click.

Myron stared at the phone. Unbelievable. He leaned back and wondered how to handle his three big problems: Chaz Landreaux's sudden departure, Kathy Culver's possible re-emergence, and the Toronto Hilton's plumbing. He decided to forgo the last. Only so much one man can do.

Problem 1: Chaz Landreaux was climbing into bed with Frank Ache. There was only one way out of that. Big brother Herman.

Myron picked up the phone and dialed. He still knew the number by heart. It was picked up on the first ring. 'Clancy's Tavern.'

'It's Myron Bolitar. I'd like to see Herman.'

'Hold on.' Five minutes passed before the voice came back on. 'Tomorrow. Two o'clock.'

Click. No need to wait for an answer. Whatever time Herman Ache agreed to see you, you were free.

Problem 2: Kathy Culver. *Nips* magazine had been mailed from a campus box. It had been mailed not only to Christian Steele but also to Dean Harrison Gordon. Why? Myron knew that Kathy had worked for the dean. Was there more to her job than just filing? An affair, perhaps? And what about the dean's lovely wife? Did she wear underwear?

But Myron was digressing.

The catalyst of this whole thing was the ad in *Nips*. Gary Grady claimed he had nothing to do with it. Maybe. Maybe not. But either way the picture had to go through Fred Nickler. Good ol' Freddy was at the center of this.

Myron looked up the number and dialed.

'HDP. May I help you?'

'I'd like to speak to Fred Nickler.'

'Whom shall I say is calling?'

'Myron Bolitar.'

'Please hold.'

A minute passed. Then Fred Nickler came on. 'Hello?'

'Mr Nickler, this is Myron Bolitar.'

'Yes, Myron. What can I do for you?'

'I'd like to come by and ask you a few more questions about the ad.'

'I'm afraid I'm quite busy right now, Myron. Why don't you give me a call tomorrow? Maybe we can set something up.'

Silence.

'Myron? You there?'

'Do you know who took that picture, Mr Nickler?'

'Of course not.'

'Your friend Jerry denies any knowledge of it.'

'Myron, please. You're a man of the world. What did you expect him to say?'

'He says he had nothing to do with putting that picture in the ad.'

'Well, that's quite impossible. He was the advertiser. He submitted the photograph.'

'Then you have a copy of the photo?'

Pause. 'It has to be in the file somewhere.'

'Maybe you can pull it out, and I'll come pick it up.'

'Listen, Myron, I hate to be rude, but I'm really busy right now. It will just be the same photograph you already saw.'

'Kathy's picture was only in *Nips*,' Myron said.

'Pardon me?'

'Her picture. It wasn't in any of your other magazines. Only *Nips*.'

Pause. 'So?' But his voice was suddenly tottery.

'So the same ad was in all six magazines. The same exact page with the same exact pictures. Except for one small change in *Nips*. Someone had changed just one photograph in the bottom row. Someone had switched pictures for just that one magazine and not the others. Why?'

Fred Nickler coughed. 'I really don't know, Myron. Tell you what: I'll check on it and let you know. Gotta zillion calls waiting. Gotta run. Bye.'

Another click.

Myron sat back. Fred Nickler was starting to panic.

With a shaking hand Fred Nickler dialed the number. After three rings the phone was picked up.

'County police.'

Fred cleared his throat. 'Paul Duncan, please.'

Chapter 22

Nine P.M.

Myron called Jessica. He filled her in on his dean discovery.

'Do you really think Kathy was having an affair with the dean?' Jessica asked.

'I don't know. But after seeing his wife, I'd tend to doubt it.'

'Good-looking?'

'Very,' Myron said. 'And she knows her basketball. She even cried when I got hurt.'

Jessica made a noise. 'The perfect woman.'

'Do I detect a note of jealousy?'

'Dream on,' Jessica said. 'The fact that a man is married to a beautiful woman does not preclude him from having affairs with pretty co-eds.'

'True enough. So the question is: How did Dean Gordon get his name on this infamous mailing list?'

'I haven't got a clue,' she said. 'But I too found out

something interesting today. My father visited Nancy Serat, Kathy's roommate, the morning he died.'

'Why?'

'I don't know yet. Nancy just left a message on my machine. I'm meeting her in an hour.'

'Good. Call me if you hear anything else.'

'Where are you going to be?' she asked.

'I work nights at Chippendale's,' Myron said. 'Stage name Zorro.'

'Should be Tiny.'

'Ouch.'

An uncomfortable silence engulfed them. Jessica finally broke it. 'Why don't you come by the house tonight?' she asked, struggling to keep her tone level.

Myron's heart pounded. 'It'll be late.'

'That's okay. I'm not sleeping much. Just knock on my bedroom window. Zorro.'

She hung up. For the next five minutes Myron sat perfectly still and thought about Jessica. They had first started dating a month before his career ended. She stayed with him. She nursed him. She loved him. He pushed her away under some macho disguise of protecting her. But she wouldn't leave. Not then, anyway.

Esperanza opened the door without knocking. She looked at him and snapped, 'Stop it.'

'What?'

'You're making that face again.'

'What face?'

She imitated him. 'That repulsive lovesick-puppy face.'

'I wasn't making any face.'

'Right. You disgust me, Myron.'

'Thank you.'

'You know what I think? I think you're more interested

in getting back in Jessica's pants than you are in finding her sister.'

'Jesus, what the hell is with you?'

'I was there, remember? When she left.'

'Hey, I'm a big boy. I can take care of myself.'

Esperanza shook her head. 'Déjà vu all over again.'

'What?'

'Take care of yourself. Bullshit. You sound just like Chaz Landreaux. Both of you have your head up your ass.'

Esperanza's dark face reminded him of Spanish nights, golden sand, full moons against starless skies. There had been moments of temptation between them, but one or the other had always realized what it would mean and stopped it. Such temptations no longer came their way anymore. Aside from Win, Esperanza was his closest friend. Her concern, Myron knew, was genuine.

He changed subjects. 'Was there a reason for your unannounced entrance?'

'I found something.'

'What?'

She read from a steno pad. Why she had a steno pad he could not say. She could not take dictation or type a lick. 'I finally tracked down the other number Gary Grady called after your visit. It belongs to a photography studio called – get this – Global Globes Photos. Located off Tenth Avenue, near the tunnel.'

'Sleazy area.'

'The sleaziest,' she said. 'I think the studio specializes in pornography.'

'Nice to have a specialty.' Myron checked his watch. 'Any word from Win?'

'Not yet.'

'Leave the photographer's address on his voice mail. Maybe he'll finish in time to meet me.'

'You going tonight?' she asked.

'Yes.'

Esperanza closed the pad with a snap. 'Mind if I tag along?'

'To the photography studio?'

'Yes.'

'Don't you have class tonight?' Esperanza was getting her law degree from NYU at night.

'No. And I've done all my homework, Daddy. Really I have.'

'Shut up and come on.'

Chapter 23

Hookerville.

There were all kinds. White, Black, Asian, Latino – a verifiable United Nations of prostitutes. Most were young, very young, stumbling on too-high heels, like children playing dress-up, which in a real sense they were. Most were thin, dried-up, needle tracks covering their arms like dozens of tiny insects, their skin pulled tightly around cheekbones, giving their faces a haunted skull look. Their eyes were hollow and set deep, their hair lifeless and strawlike.

Myron muttered, 'Don't they know they're making love to what's already dead?'

Esperanza paused, thinking. 'Don't know that one.'

'Fontine in *Les Misérables*. The musical.'

'I can't afford Broadway musicals. My boss is cheap.'

'But cute.'

He watched a blond girl in sixties hot-pants negotiate with a sleazeball in a Ford station wagon. He knew her story. He had seen girls (boys sometimes) just like her get off the bus at the Port Authority, a Greyhound bus that had originated in West Virginia or western Pennsylvania or that great, barren mono-expanse New Yorkers simply referred to as the Midwest. She had run away from home – maybe to avoid abuse, but more likely because she was bored and 'belonged' in a big city. She had high-stepped off the bus with a wide smile, mesmerized, without a penny. Pimps would eye her and wait with the patience of a vulture. When the time was right, they would sweep down and claim their carcass. They'd introduce her to the Big Apple, get her a place to stay, some food, a hot shower, maybe a room with a Jacuzzi and dazzling lights and a cool CD player and cable TV with a remote. They'd promise to set her up with a photographer, get her a few modeling gigs. Then they'd teach her how to party, *really* party, not that candy-ass shit she'd done in Hicks Falls with some beer and a zit-infested senior pawing at her in the backseat of a pickup. They'd show her how to have a good time with the prime stuff, the numero-uno white powder.

But things would change. Someone would have to pay for all these good times. The modeling job would fall through, and she couldn't just be a freeloader. Besides, the partying was more a need now than a luxury. Like food or breathing. She could no longer exist without a snort or a pinch from her favorite needle.

It didn't take long to plummet and hit bottom. And once there she didn't have the strength – not even the desire, really – to get up.

She ended up here.

Myron parked. He and Esperanza got out of the car

silently. Myron felt his stomach churn. It was night, of course. Places like this existed only at night. They fled with the onslaught of sunlight.

Myron had never been with a whore, but he knew Win had engaged their services on plenty of occasions. Win liked the convenience. His favorite spot was an Asian whorehouse on Eighth Street called Noble House. Back in the mid-eighties, Win and a few friends would have what they called 'Chinese night' in Win's apartment – Hunan Garden would deliver food. Noble House women. The truth was, Win had no feelings for women. He didn't trust them. Whores were what he wanted. It wasn't just the lack of attachment. Win never let women attach. But prostitutes were throwaways. Disposable.

Myron didn't think Win still partook in such events – not in this disease-ridden era – but he didn't know for sure. They never talked about it.

'Pretty spot,' Myron said. 'Scenic.'

Esperanza nodded.

They passed a nightclub of some sort. The music was loud enough to crack the sidewalk. A teen – Myron couldn't say if it was male or female – with green spiked hair bumped into him. Looked like the Statue of Liberty. There were lots of motorcycles, ear and nipple rings, tattoos, chain jewelry. A constant whore chorus of 'Hey, baby' pelted him from every conceivable angle, their faces blurring into one mass of human debris. The place was like a carnival freak show.

The sign above the door read CLUB F.U. The logo was a raised middle finger. Subtle. A chalkboard read the following:

HEAVY 'MEDICAL' NIGHT!
LIVE BANDS!
Featuring the only local appearances by:
PAP SMEAR
and RECTAL THERMOMETER

Myron could see through the open door. People weren't dancing. They were jumping up and down, heads lolling lifelessly as if their necks were rubber bands, their arms tucked against their sides. Myron focused in on one kid, maybe fifteen years old, lost in the violet bliss, sweat matting his long hair to his face. He wondered if the group onstage was Pap Smear or Rectal Thermometer. Didn't matter. Sounded like someone had jammed a rutting pig into a Cuisinart.

The whole scene was like Dickens meets *Blade Runner*.

'The studio is next door,' Esperanza said.

The building was either a disastrous brownstone or a small warehouse. Whores hung out the windows like shreds of leftover Christmas decorations.

'This is it?' Myron asked.

'Third floor,' Esperanza answered. She did not seem intimidated by the surroundings in the least, but she had come from streets not much better than this. Her face remained a placid pool. Esperanza never showed weakness. Her temper flared often, but for all their times together, Myron had never seen her cry. She could not say the same of him.

Myron approached the stoop. An overweight whore stuffed into a bodysuit that doubled as sausage casing licked her lips and stepped in front of him.

'Hey, yo, want a blow job? Fifty bucks.'

Myron tried not to close his eyes. 'No,' he said softly,

lowering his head. He wanted to offer words of wisdom, words that could transform her, change her circumstances. But he just said, 'I'm sorry,' and hurried past. The fat girl shrugged and moved on.

It was a walk-up. No surprise there. The stairwells were littered with people, most unconscious or maybe dead. Myron and Esperanza carefully climbed over them. A cacophony of music – everything from Neil Diamond to what might have been Pap Smear bellowed through the corridor. There were other sounds too. Broken bottles, shouts, curses, crashing, a baby crying. An orchestra from hell.

When they reached the third floor, they saw a glassed-in office. No one was inside, but the pictures on the wall – not to mention the bullwhip and handcuffs – left little doubt that they had arrived at the right place. Myron tried the knob. It turned.

'You stay out here,' he said.

'Okay.'

He moved in. 'Hello?'

No one answered him, but music was coming from the other room. Sounded like calypso music. He called out again and stepped into the studio.

Myron was struck by how professional the setup was. It was clean, brightly lit, with one of those big white umbrella things you always see in photo studios. There were half a dozen cameras set up on tripods, and overhead was a variety of different-colored lights.

Of course, the setting was not the first thing that struck him. Other things caught his eye first. The naked woman sitting on a motorbike, for example. To be accurate, she wasn't fully naked – she had on a pair of black boots. Nothing else. Not a look every woman could pull off, but it seemed to work for her. She had not seen him yet, intensely studying the magazine in her hand. *The National Sun*. Headline: Boy 16 Becomes Grandmother. Hmm. He stepped closer. She was big-breasted, very Russ Meyer, but Myron could see scars under the large swellings. Implants, the fashion accessory of the eighties.

She looked up, startled.

Myron smiled warmly. 'Hi.'

She screamed. Piercingly. 'Get the fuck out of here!' she shrieked, covering her chest. Modesty. So rare nowadays. It was nice to see.

Myron said, 'My name—'

Another piercing scream. Myron heard a noise behind him and spun. A skinny kid wearing no shirt stood smiling. He popped open a switchblade, a maniacal grin plastered across his face. His Bruce Lee-like build shimmered in the light. He crouched low and beckoned Myron forward. Very *West Side Story*. If only the kid would snap his fingers.

Another door opened, and red light leaked out. A woman stepped into view. She had what looked like curly red hair, but Myron couldn't be sure if that was her color or if it just appeared red because of the light from the darkroom.

'You're trespassing,' she said to Myron. 'Hector has the right to kill you where you stand.'

'I don't know where you got your law degree,' Myron said, 'but if Hector isn't careful, I'm going to take away his toy and shove it where the sun don't shine.'

Hector giggled. He began to toss the knife back and forth between his hands.

'Wow,' Myron said.

The topless model fled to the dressing room, which was

cleverly marked UNDRESSING ROOM. The woman from the darkroom stepped fully into the studio and closed the darkroom door. Her hair was indeed red, more like burnt auburn actually. Her skin was what some might call peaches and cream. She was maybe thirty and looked, strange as it might sound, perky. The Katie Couric of the porno world.

'Are you the owner?' Myron asked.

'Hector is very good with a blade,' she replied coolly. 'He could slice out a man's heart and show it to him before he died.'

'That must liven a party.'

Hector stepped closer. Myron did not move.

'I could demonstrate my skills in the martial arts,' Myron began. He quickly withdrew his gun and aimed it at Hector's chest. 'But I just showered.'

Hector's eyes widened in surprise.

'Let this be a lesson to you, Blade Boy,' Myron continued. 'Half the people in this building probably carry guns. You go around waving that toy, and someone without my tender heart will ace you.'

The redhead did not seem taken aback by the gun. 'Get out of here,' she said to Myron. 'Now.'

'Are you the owner?' Myron tried again.

'You got a warrant?'

'I'm not a cop.'

'Then get your ass out of here.' She undulated a lot when she talked. Her hips and legs in constant motion. She signaled to Hector, who closed up the switchblade. 'You can go, Hector.'

'Not so fast, Hector,' Myron said. 'Get in the darkroom. I don't want you getting any ideas about coming back with a gun.'

Hector looked toward the redhead. She nodded, and he went.

'Close the door,' Myron said.

He closed it. Myron walked over and pulled the dead bolt.

The redhead put her hands on her hips. 'Happy now?'

'Nearly ecstatic.'

'Now get out.'

'Listen,' Myron said with his melt-'em, warm smile, 'I don't want any trouble. I'm just here to buy some photographs. My name is Bernie Worley. I work for a new porno magazine.'

She made a face. 'Do I really look that stupid? Bernie Worley, here to buy some photographs. Give me a fuckin' break.'

There was a sudden noise. People. Lots of them. A commotion, even by this place's standard. In the corridor. Right where he had left Esperanza. Alone.

Myron turned and ran, feeling his heart leap to his throat. If something had happened to her—

He threw open the door. Dozens of people surrounded Esperanza, most kneeling. She stood in the middle, smiling and – he couldn't believe it – signing autographs.

'It's Pocahontas!' someone shouted.

'Make mine out "With love to Manuel."'

'You're still my favorite!'

'I remember when you beat Queen Carimba. What a fight!'

'That Highway Hannah. Such a dirty fighter. When she threw salt in your eyes, I could have killed her.'

Esperanza caught Myron's eye, shrugged, went back to signing old matchbooks and scraps of paper. The redhead followed him out the door. When she saw Esperanza, her entire being lit up. 'Poca?'

Esperanza looked back up. 'Lucy?'

They hugged. They stepped back into the studio, Myron following.

'Where you been, girl?' Lucy asked.

'Here, there.'

The two women kissed. On the lips. A little too long. Esperanza turned around. 'Myron?'

'Huh?'

'Your eyes are bulging.'

'They are?'

'I don't tell you everything.'

'Apparently not,' he said. 'But at least I know why my startling good looks didn't faze your friend.'

Both women found that laughable. 'Lucy, this is Myron Bolitar.'

Lucy looked him up and down. 'He your boyfriend?'

'No. Just a good friend. And my boss.'

'He looks like a guy I know, worked a kinky show at a club down the street. He had this act where he peed on different women.'

'It wasn't me,' Myron assured her. 'I have enough trouble peeing in a public urinal.'

Lucy turned her attention to Esperanza. 'You look good, Poca.'

'Thanks.'

'Out of the wrestling game, huh?'

'Completely.'

'But you're still working out?'

'As often as I can.'

'Nautilus?'

'Um-hmm.'

'It shows,' Lucy said with a wicked smile. 'You really look hot.'

Myron cleared his throat. 'Hey, how about those Knicks?'

The women ignored him. 'You still taking pictures of the wrestlers?' Esperanza asked.

'Not much anymore. I'm mostly into this shit.'

Esperanza looked back at Myron. 'Lucy – that isn't her real name, we just call her that because of her hair – she used to do the promo photos of all the wrestlers.'

'So I gathered,' Myron said. 'Do you think she can help us out?'

'What do you want to know?' Lucy asked.

Myron handed her the copy of *Nips*. He pointed to Kathy's picture. 'I want to know about this,' he said.

Lucy studied the photograph for a second. 'He a cop?' she asked Esperanza.

'A sports agent.'

'Oh.' She did not ask for further elaboration. 'Because this could get us in trouble.'

'How so?' Myron asked.

'The photograph. The girl is topless.'

'So?'

'So it's illegal. Topless girls aren't allowed in 900 ads. We're going to get screwed if the government sees this.'

'We?' Myron repeated. Again the clever interrogation techniques.

'I'm one of the owners of these dial-a-porn companies. A lot of the lines work out of this building.'

'I'm not sure I understand,' Myron said. 'What do you mean, topless girls are illegal? Almost every girl in that magazine is naked.'

'Not in the ads for 900 lines,' Lucy corrected. 'Couple years back a law was passed. 900 lines had to go clean. Look here.' She turned a page and pointed at another ad.

'The girl might look suggestive, but she can't be naked. And look at the name of the lines. Stuff like "Secret Confessions" or "Talk to Girls." Now look at the ones for the 800 lines. Hard core. "Cum Between My Tits," stuff like that.'

Myron remembered his conversation with Tawny on the 900 line. He had been struck by the fact that she said nothing dirty. 'So you can only have phone sex on the other lines?'

'Right. You see, you need real permission for those. That's how the government sees it. Any asshole can call a 900 line. The charges are automatic. They start almost immediately after your call is answered. But not with an 800 line or one of the other numbers. You have to use either your credit card or a callback. That's the way you get billed.'

'So all that talk about 900 lines being dirty—'

'Is bullshit,' Lucy finished. 'They're cons. We can't say one dirty thing on those lines. We use them as lures mostly, because they're so easy to use. A guy just has to dial. No credit card. No callbacks. Most of the time we talk about skinny-dipping or massages – suggestive but not sexual. Get him excited, you know what I mean?'

'I think so, yes.'

'These guys call horny anyway. I mean, most are so hard up, they'll stick it in a knothole to get relief. What we try to do is get him to say the first dirty word, which usually isn't too difficult. Once he does, we say, "Oh, baby, I can't talk dirty on this line, but you should call me back at X number with a credit card." The guys calls it and gets charged all over again.'

'Aren't they afraid of how it'll look on their credit card bill?' Myron asked.

Lucy shook her head. She was still undulating. It was a combination of irritating and erotic. 'The company names are usually pretty discreet,' she explained. 'We bill under names like Norwood Incorporate or Telemark – not Hot Lesbos or Sucking Starlet. You want to see it?'

'See what?'

'The operation upstairs. Where we answer some of the calls. Lots of people work out of their homes, but I got a crew of six or seven working the lines now.'

Myron shrugged. 'Yeah, sure.'

Lucy took them up one level. Some sort of sickening stench engulfed the stairwell. When they reached the landing, Lucy opened a door. They stepped through and quickly closed it behind them.

'This is Fantasies Forever Lines,' Lucy said. 'Not to mention Dick-a-Lick, Hootersline, Telefun, and a dozen others.'

Myron could not believe what he was seeing. His mouth dropped open. He had expected ugly women or fat women or old women. But he had not expected this.

They were men. All but one of the workers were male.

'Gay lines?' Myron asked.

Lucy shook her head, smiling. 'Very few gay calls come in. Maybe one in a hundred.'

'But . . . these are men.'

Myron Bolitar, the essence of keen observation.

He heard a man in a gruff, truck-driver voice say, 'Yeah, big man, slide it all the way in. That's it. Oh, yeah, that feels good.'

Lucy smiled at the man. The man rolled his eyes and continued, 'Don't stop, Stallion. Ride me.'

Esperanza, Myron was glad to see, looked equally confused. 'What's going on, Lucy?' she asked.

'It's the times,' Lucy said. 'In this economy men are a cheaper source of labor. Most of the girls are on the streets. These are brothers, cousins, street kids.'

'But their voices—'

'They use a voice changer. Sharper Image sells them, but I get them cheaper in the Village. You can make little girls sound like Barry White, or vice versa. These guys can become a husky woman, a teenage virgin, a little girl – whatever the line calls for.'

Myron was stunned. 'Do the customers know this?'

'Of course not.' She turned to Esperanza. 'Dumb. But he is kinda cute.'

Myron Bolitar, Lesbian Fantasy Man.

The room looked like any telemarketing office. The phones were high-tech. Dozens of lines lit up, each marked for what role was to be played. Horny House-wife. Dominatrix. Cross-dressers. Busty Babes. Even Foot Fetish. Each employee also had another phone for Visa and MasterCard verification.

'The lines with a C next to them got to be kept clean,' Lucy explained. 'We also have another hundred or so people working phones from their homes. Most of those are women.'

'Horny housewives?'

'Some of them. Most are just plain housewives. Anyway, that's why I found the ad strange. A 900 line shouldn't have a topless girl.'

They left the room and walked back down to the studio. Myron almost tripped over a wino who chose the moment Myron was stepping over him to stand up.

'Is ABC one of the companies upstairs?' Myron asked.

'Yeah.'

'And we know Gary Grady called you yesterday. Can you tell us why?'

'Who?'

'Gary Grady.'

Lucy shook her head. 'Don't know him.'

'How about Jerry?'

'Oh yeah, him,' She gave a small laugh. 'I figured that wasn't his real name. He was always real secretive.'

'So what did he want?'

She nodded as though something had just occurred to her. 'I get it now.'

'Get what?'

'He was asking me about a photograph I'd taken a couple years back.'

'This one?' Myron asked, pointing to Kathy's picture again.

'Yeah. One of his girls.'

Myron and Esperanza exchanged a glance. 'You mean there were others?'

'Few. Half dozen, maybe more.'

Myron felt the rage consume again. 'Underage girls?'

'How the fuck am I supposed to know?'

'You didn't ask?' Myron asked.

'Do I look like a cop? Look, man, if you're here to hassle me—'

'He's not,' Esperanza said. 'You can trust him.'

'The fuck I can, Poca. He comes busting in here with a fucking gun, scares the piss out of my model.'

'We need your help,' Esperanza said. '*I* need your help.'

'I don't want to hurt you, Lucy,' Myron said. 'I'm just interested in the girl in the picture.'

Lucy hesitated. 'All right,' she said at last. 'But back off.'

Myron gave a quick nod of agreement. 'Jerry brought this girl to you?'

'Yeah, when I had my other studio a couple blocks away. Like I said, he brought in a few girls over the years. He wanted their photos for all kinds of stuff. Porno mags, smut film stills, that kind of thing. Most were a cut or two above the average hosebag who comes through the door. But he usually keeps the photos under wraps until they're a little older. Legal age, I guess.'

The rage again. Myron's hands tightened into fists. 'So Jerry asked you about this picture yesterday?'

'Yeah.'

'What did he want to know?'

'If I sold any copies recently.'

'Have you?'

Pause. 'Yeah. Couple months ago.'

'Who bought them?'

'You think I keep records?'

'A he or a she?'

'A he.'

'Do you remember what he looks like?'

She took out a cigarette, lit it, took a deep puff. 'I'm not real good with faces.'

'Anything, Lucy,' Esperanza added. 'Young, old, anything you can remember.'

Another puff. Then: 'Old. Not ancient, but not a young guy. Might have been my father's age. And he knew what he was doing.' She looked at Myron. 'Not like you. Bernie Worley. Jesus.'

Myron pressed on. 'What do you mean, he knew what he was doing?'

'The man paid me top dollar under one condition: I hand over every photo and negative in front of him right now. Smart. He wanted to make sure I didn't have time to make any extra copies or an extra set of negatives.'

'How much did he pay you?'

'Sixty-five hundred altogether. In cash. Five grand for the photos and negatives. Plus another grand for Jerry's phone number. Said he wanted to get in touch with the girl personally. Then he gave me another five hundred if I didn't say anything to Jerry.'

In the background there was yet another bloodcurdling scream. It went ignored. 'Would you know the man if you saw him again?' Myron asked.

'I don't know,' she said. 'I can't picture him now, but if we met up face to face . . . who knows?' There was a pounding noise from the darkroom. 'Mind if I let Hector out now?'

'We were just leaving,' Myron said. He handed her a card. 'If you remember anything else—'

'Yeah, I'll call.' She looked over to Esperanza. 'Don't be a stranger, Poca.'

Esperanza nodded but said nothing. They were quiet the entire way down. When they stepped into the hot air, surrounded by the night street, she said, 'Didn't mean to shock you in there.'

'Not my business,' he said. 'I was a little surprised, that's all.'

'Lucy is a lesbian. I experimented with it a little. Long time ago.'

'You don't have to explain,' he said. But he was glad she told him. Myron had no secrets from Esperanza. He didn't like thinking she had some from him.

They were about to head back to the car when Myron felt the muzzle of a gun against his ribs.

A voice said, 'Stay cool, Myron.'

It was the man with the fedora hat from the garage. He reached into Myron's jacket and took out the .38. A second man, this one with a Gene Shalit-like mustache, grabbed Esperanza and pressed his gun against her temple.

'If Myron moves,' Fedora said to the other man, 'blow the bitch's brains all over the sidewalk.'

The man nodded, half smiling.

'Come on,' Fedora said, nudging Myron forward with the gun. 'Let's take a little walk.'

Chapter 24

Jessica parked in front of the house Nancy Serat was renting for the semester. It was more a cottage really, located at the end of a dark street about a mile from the campus of Reston University. Even at night Jessica could see the house's salmon-pink hue, which seemed to clash with the planet earth. The landscape looked like the trees had vomited – the front yard of *The Munsters*. A faded 118 ACRE STREET was stenciled on the weather-beaten sign. A blue Honda Accord with a Reston University bumper sticker sat in the driveway.

Jessica headed down the broken remnants of what must have once been a cement path. She rang the bell and immediately heard a scurrying sound. Several seconds passed. No one approached the door. She tried again. No scurrying sound this time. No sound at all.

'Nancy?' she called out. 'It's Jessica Culver.'

She hit the bell a few more times, though in a house this small there was not much chance she hadn't been heard.

Unless Nancy was in the shower. A possibility. The lights, she could see through the window shades, were on. The car was in the driveway. Jessica had heard movement.

Nancy had to be home.

Jessica reached out for the knob. Under normal conditions some filter in her mind would probably have stopped her from simply trying to open the door of a virtual stranger (she had only met Nancy once). But these conditions were hardly normal. She took hold of the knob and turned.

Locked.

Now what?

She stood at the door five more minutes ringing the bell. Still nothing. Jessica circled the house, using a distant streetlight and the house's glow-in-the-dark properties to guide her. She stumbled over a tricycle that looked like something recovered from an archaeological dig. Her feet got tangled in the high grass, the prickly ends tickling her calves. As she circled, Jessica peeked through the small openings in the window shades. She could make out rooms and spotted an occasional piece of furniture or wall hanging, but no people.

In the backyard she saw the shades were not pulled down in the kitchen. The lights were off too. It was pitch black here, the pink not getting the illumination of the streetlight to cast its glow. She peered through the kitchen window, cupping her hands around her face to cut off the reflection. A sliver of light from the front room slashed across the room. On the table sat a purse. And a set of keys.

Someone was home.

A sound behind her made her jump. Jessica spun, but it was too dark to make out what it was. Her heart beat wildly in her chest. Crickets singsonged unceasingly. She pounded on the door with both fists.

'Nancy! Nancy!'

She heard the panic in her voice and scolded herself for it. *Get a grip. You're spooking yourself.*

She stopped, took a few deep breaths, felt herself relax. She took another look through the window, pressing her face right up against the glass. She was watching the sliver of light when it happened.

Someone walked by.

Jessica jumped back. She hadn't seen the person, hadn't seen anything, except the sliver of light disappear for the briefest of seconds. She looked again. Nothing. But someone had gone past and blocked off the light. She put her hand on the kitchen doorknob.

This time the door was not locked. The knob turned easily.

Don't just go in, dodo! Call the cops!

And say what? I knocked on a door and no one answered? That I then started peeking through windows and saw someone moving around?

That doesn't sound so bad.

Sounds bad enough to me. Besides, I'd have to find a phone. By the time I do that, whatever is going on may be over. I may have lost my one opportunity . . .

Opportunity for what?

She pushed the voice away. Then she opened the door. She waited for the door to squeak madly, but it slid open with remarkable silence. She stepped into the kitchen and left the door open. Better for the quick getaway.

'Nancy?

'*Kathy?*'

She clasped her hand over her mouth. She hadn't meant

that. Kathy wasn't here. Jessica wished like hell she were, but that would be too easy. Kathy wasn't here. And if she were, she certainly would not be afraid to open the door for her sister. Her baby sister. The sister with the bright smile. The sister whom she loved . . .

The sister you let slip away. The sister you impatiently rushed off the line the night she vanished.

For several minutes Jessica just stayed in the kitchen. There were no sounds, except those maddening crickets. No running water. No shower. No scurrying. No footsteps. She opened the purse and extracted the wallet. Driver's license and assorted credit cards – all in the name of Nancy Serat. She flipped to the back and stopped suddenly at a wallet-size photograph.

The picture. The sorority sisters picture. The last picture of Kathy.

She dropped the wallet as though it were something scary and alive. Enough, Jessica said to herself. She moved toward the light. One foot slid out, the other followed. In a matter of seconds Jessica was at the door. It was open a crack, allowing the light to cast its sliver now unimpeded. She pushed through, crouching like a cop with a gun, preparing for the worst.

And the worst was what she got.

Jessica stumbled back. 'Jesus Christ—'

Nancy lay flat on her back, her hands at her sides. Her eyes stuck out like two golf balls, staring at Jessica. Her face was a deep purplish-blue, like a giant bruise. Her mouth was wide and twisted in pure agony. The tongue lolled out like a dead fish. Nancy Serat's entire expression was still frozen in a look that begged and screamed with its every cell for oxygen. A thin line of still-wet saliva clung to her chin.

A cord of some kind – no, a wire – was wrapped around Nancy's neck, barely visible. Most of it had sliced clean through the skin and was embedded deep in the flesh. A circling lash of blood marked the spot where the wire had entered.

Jessica stared, lost. The world vanished for several moments, leaving behind only the horror. She forgot about the scurrying when she first rang the bell. She forgot the shadow that had cut off the sliver of light.

Jessica did not hear the approaching footsteps. Still staring at Nancy's face, unable to tear her eyes away, she felt a sudden, sharp pain in her head. She saw white flashes. Her body folded at the waist and pitched forward. A tingling numbness followed.

Then nothing.

Chapter 25

Fedora Hat knew what he was doing.

'Stay a few steps behind me,' he barked at his new partner.

In the garage Fedora and Musclehead (who, Myron was happy to see, seemed to be out of commission) had underestimated Myron. Fedora would not make the same mistake twice. Not only had he always kept eyes and gun on Myron but he was making sure that his new partner (the Mustache) kept both himself and Esperanza a safe distance away.

Smart.

Myron had been tempted to make a move, but even his best move was useless in this circumstance. If he managed to get the gun away from Fedora, there was no way he'd be able to turn it on the Mustache before he'd shoot either him or Esperanza.

He would have to wait and watch. He knew what Fedora and Mustache intended to do. They hadn't been hired to buy him ice cream or teach line dancing or even beat him up. Not this time.

'Let her go,' Myron said. 'She has nothing to do with this.'

'Keep moving,' Fedora replied.

'You don't need her.'

'Move.'

Mustache spoke for the first time. 'I might want a little company later,' he sneered. Then he stopped and pressed the gun against Esperanza's right cheek while he licked – actually licked – her left cheek with a wet cow-like tongue. Esperanza stiffened. Mustache looked at Myron. 'You got a problem with that, pal?'

Myron knew words would be either superfluous or harmful at this stage. He kept his mouth shut.

They turned a corner. The stench of garbage was over-whelming. It was piled at least six feet high on both sides of the narrow alley. Fedora quickly scanned the area. It appeared to be abandoned.

'Go,' he said, giving Myron another poke with the gun. 'End of the alley.'

Myron felt as if he were walking a plank. He tried to take it as slowly as possible.

'What are we going to do with the piece of ass?' Mustache asked.

Fedora's eyes never left Myron. 'She's seen us,' he said. 'She's a witness.'

'But we weren't hired to ace her,' Mustache whined.

'So?'

'So let's not just waste a piece like this' – he smiled – 'especially when we can fuck it first.'

Mustache laughed at his suggestion. Fedora did not. He stepped back, aiming the gun at Myron's back. Myron turned to face him. They were separated by about six feet. Myron was against the back wall. There was no avenue of escape. The nearest window was at least twelve feet off the ground. No room to move at all.

Fedora raised the gun so that it stared Myron right in the face. Myron did not blink. He looked into Fedora's eyes.

And then they were gone. Fedora's eyes were gone. Along with half his head.

The bullet had ripped off the skull at the midway point, splitting Fedora's head open like a coconut. He slid to the ground, the fedora floating down after him.

A dum-dum bullet.

Mustache cried out and dropped the gun. He held his hands up. 'I surrender!'

Myron ran forward. 'Don't! He's surren—'

But the gun exploded again. Mustache's face disappeared in a spray of red mist. Myron stopped, closed his eyes. Mustache joined Fedora on the filthy cement. Esperanza came over and wrapped her arms around Myron. They both turned toward the alley's entrance.

Win stepped into view, studying his handiwork as though it were a statue he wasn't sure he liked. He was dressed in a gray suit, his red tie still in a perfect Windsor knot. His blond hair was neat, conservative, parted as always on the left. The .44 was in his right hand. His cheeks were rosy, and there was just a hint of a smile on his face.

'Good evening,' Win said.

'How long have you been here?' Myron asked. He hadn't spotted Win when they exited the photography studio. But he had known he was there. With Win you just knew. One of life's constants.

'I arrived as you entered the dwelling of ill repute,' Win answered. He smiled. 'But I wanted my appearance to have that flair of drama.'

Myron let go of Esperanza.

'We better get moving,' Win said. 'Before the authorities arrive.'

They walked away from the corpses in silence. Esperanza was shaking. Myron did not feel so hot either. Only Win seemed completely unaffected by what had transpired. As they approached the car, the same fat young prostitute clad in sausage casing approached Win.

'Hey, yo, want a blow job? Fifty bucks.'

Win looked at her. 'I would rather have my semen sucked out with a catheter.'

'Okay,' the girl said. 'Forty bucks.'

Win laughed and walked away.

Chapter 26

'All units. One-eighteen Acre Street. All units. One-eighteen Acre Street.'

Paul Duncan heard the call on his police scanner. He was only a few blocks from the scene, but this was not his district. Far from it. He could certainly not answer the call. That would only draw attention and questions. Questions like what was he doing here.

Pieces were starting to come together. Fred Nickler, the publisher of those sleazy rags, had called him earlier in the day. What he had told Paul explained a lot. Not everything. Not by a long shot. But he now understood Jessica's behavior the other night. She had learned about Kathy's picture. Myron Bolitar must have told her.

But how had Myron gotten a copy of it?

Not important. Not really. What was important was that Myron Bolitar was involved. He could not be under-estimated. Jessica was a big enough pain in the ass on her own. But now she had Myron on her side and probably that Win Lockwood, Myron's psychotic Tonto. Paul knew something about their past work for the feds. Not a lot. Myron and Win had answered only to top government officials. Their work was almost always classified. But Paul knew their reputations. That was enough.

A police car sped past Paul, sirens screaming. They were probably on their way to 118 Acre Street. Paul turned up his scanner. He wanted to hear every word that was said.

He debated calling Carol, but what could he tell her? She hadn't been specific on the phone, just telling him about the phone message from Nancy to Jessica. So what did Jessica know? How had she found out?

And what would Carol ultimately be pressured into saying?

Two ambulances flew by him. They too had their sirens on full blast. Paul swallowed. He wanted to pull over, but he wanted more to drive as far away as possible.

Once again Paul Duncan thought of his friend Adam Culver. Dead. Murdered. With everything that had happened, there had been no time for Paul to mourn.

Yes, mourn.

That might sound strange – Paul Duncan mourning Adam Culver. Especially if anyone knew how Adam had spent the last precious hours of his life.

Win and Myron dropped Esperanza off at the apartment she shared with her sister and cousin in the east part of Greenwich Village. Myron escorted her to the door.

'You okay?'

She nodded. Her face was deathly pale. She had not spoken a word since the shooting. 'Win—' She stopped, shook her head. It took her a full minute to pull herself together. 'He saved us. I guess that's what counts.'

'Yes.'

'I'll see you in the morning.'

Myron returned to the car. He called Jessica. She wasn't home yet, but Myron did manage to wake her mother. They drove to a twenty-four-hour diner on Sixth Avenue – one of those Greek diners with a menu the approximate length of a Tolstoy novel. Win was a vegetarian. He ordered a salad and French fries. Myron ordered a Diet Coke. He couldn't eat.

After they were settled in, Myron asked, 'What happened with Chaz?'

Win was picking at a basket of stale bread. His face registered displeasure, but he settled on a small packet of Saltines. 'Mr Landreaux hurried straight from our esteemed offices to a building at 466 Fifth Avenue,' he began. 'He took the elevator to the eighth floor, which is rented by Roy O'Connor and TruPro Enterprises. When Landreaux entered the elevator, he had your contract tightly clutched in his paw. When he exited, the contract was no longer visible. He had no pockets that could hold such a document. Conclusion: Mr Landreaux gave the contract to someone at TruPro Enterprises.'

'Your powers of deduction,' Myron said. 'In a word: uncanny.'

Win smiled. 'I assume you are feeling better.'

Myron shrugged.

'We are not the same, you and I,' Win added. 'You call it execution, what I did to that vermin. I call it extermination.'

'You didn't have to kill him.'

'I *wanted* to kill him,' Win said with flat inflection.

'And I doubt any of us will mourn his death for very long.'

True enough, but the argument did not ease Myron's mind. He wanted to drop the subject. 'Where did Chaz go after he left TruPro?'

Win took a dainty bite out of the corner of the Saltine. 'Before I get into that, I should point out that Mr Landreaux was escorted from the building by a large man who fit the description of your friend Aaron. Large. Confident. Athletic. Suit with no shirt. Sunglasses, though the sun had already set.'

'Sounds like Aaron.'

'They split up on the street. Aaron got into a stretch limousine. Chaz Landreaux walked to the Omni Hotel.'

'Which Omni?' Myron asked. Manhattan had several.

'The one near Carnegie Hall. Landreaux met up with his mother in the lobby. Their reunion was rather moving. Mother and son embraced. Both were crying.'

'Hmm,' Myron said.

The waitress arrived with the food and drinks. She put them down, scratched her butt with a pencil, and returned to the kitchen.

'So where did they go after that?'

'Upstairs. They ordered room service.'

Myron thought a moment. 'What is Chaz's mother doing up from Philadelphia?'

'I would assume,' Win said, pulling a napkin out of the dispenser and spreading it on his lap, 'based on their mutual anguish, that Frank Ache reached Chaz Landreaux through a family member.'

'A kidnapping?'

Win shrugged. 'A possibility. Frank just sent two men

to try to kill you. I highly doubt he is going to become squeamish over a ghetto abduction.'

Silence.

'We're wading in some deep doo-doo,' Myron said.

'Indeed. Too deep.'

Chaz had a big family. If Frank really wanted to hit him where he lived, he'd take one of his siblings. 'We'll settle it tomorrow,' Myron said. 'I scheduled a meeting with Herman Ache. Two o'clock. Usual place.'

'Should I attend?'

'Most definitely.'

Win ate his salad. 'You do know that this won't be easy.'

Myron nodded.

'Herman Ache does not like to intervene in his brother's business.'

'I know.'

Win put down his fork. 'If I may be so bold as to offer a suggestion.'

'I'm listening.'

'Frank Ache sent two professionals after you. Their untimely deaths will not dissuade him from trying again.'

'Uh-huh. So what's your suggestion?'

'Cut your losses now. Make an exchange. You let them keep Landreaux. They call off the contract on your head.'

'I can't do that.'

'You can. You choose not to.'

'Semantics.'

'You don't have to help him.'

'I *want* to help him,' Myron answered.

Win sighed. 'A man must try to illuminate even those who prefer to sit in the darkness. Do you have a plan yet?'

'I'm still working on it.'

'Feverishly?'

Myron nodded.

'In the meantime,' Win said, 'what did you learn from the photographer?'

Myron filled him in on the meeting with Lucy.

'So who bought the nude pictures?' Win asked.

'A name springs to mind,' Myron said.

'Who?'

'Adam Culver.'

'Kathy's father?'

Myron nodded. 'Think about it. The buyer was in his fifties. He wanted all copies and all negatives on the spot. He left nothing to chance.'

'The father protecting the daughter?'

'It makes sense,' Myron said.

'But Kathy was missing for over a year. How did Adam Culver suddenly learn about the photographs?'

'Maybe he knew about them all along.'

'Then why did he wait so long to buy them?'

Myron shrugged. 'We'll know more tomorrow. I'm going to send Esperanza over to the studio with a picture of Adam, see if Lucy recognizes him.'

Win took another bite of his salad. 'It's a rather strange development.'

'Yes.'

'But' – Win stopped to finish chewing – 'here is something else you may not have considered: If Adam Culver purchased all the pictures and negatives in order to protect his daughter, how did her photograph end up in the magazine?'

Myron had considered that. He just didn't have an answer.

The waitress put down the check. Myron picked up

the tab for both of them. The total was $8.50. Mr Magnanimous. They drove uptown. Win lived in the San Remo building overlooking Central Park West. Very fancy address. They were on Seventy-second Street when the car phone rang.

Myron looked at his multicolored Swatch. A gift from Esperanza.

Past midnight.

'Rather late for a call to your car,' Win noted.

Myron picked up the phone. 'Hello?'

The voice came fast. 'Bolitar, it's Jake Courter. Get your ass down to St Barnabas Hospital in Livingston right away.'

'What happened?'

'Just get down here. Now.'

Chapter 27

'We got the call around eleven-thirty,' Jake said, ushering Myron through the lobby of St Barnabas. Jake's face was set, his eyes red and puffy. They hurried past the circular visitors' desk and waited for an elevator.

'Is Jessica okay?' Myron asked.

'She is going to be fine,' he said. Then he added, 'Wish I could say the same about Nancy Serat.'

'What happened?'

'She was garroted with a wire.' The elevator arrived. Jake pressed the button for the fifth floor. 'When no one answered the door, Jessica let herself in through the back. The killer must have still been there. He knocked her over the head and ran. When she came to, she called us. I'd say she's pretty lucky the perp didn't waste her.'

The elevator opened with a *ding*. 'What room is she in?' Myron asked.

'Five fifteen.'

Myron sprinted down the corridor. He turned the

corner. Jessica was in the bed, her face ashen. A doctor stood next to her, preparing a needle. Jake came up behind Myron but stayed in the doorway.

Her voice was wobbly. 'Myron?'

'I'm here,' he said, taking her hand. She looked small and frail and alone. 'I won't leave.'

The doctor pricked her with the needle. 'You need your rest,' he said.

'I'm fine,' Jessica insisted weakly. 'I want to get out of here.'

'We think it's best if you stay overnight for observation.'

'But—'

'Listen to him, Jess,' Myron interrupted. 'There's nothing we can do tonight.'

The drug began to take effect. Her eyes fluttered back. 'Nancy . . .'

'It's okay,' Myron soothed.

'Her face was blue . . .'

'Shhh.'

Jessica slipped into unconsciousness. Myron looked up at the doctor. 'Is she going to be okay?'

'She'll be fine. I think the shock of what she saw was worse than the blow to her head.'

Jake put his hand on Myron's shoulder. 'Come on, I'll buy you a cup of coffee.'

'I want to stay.'

'You can come back later. Right now we need to talk.'

Myron gazed down at Jessica. She was deep in sleep.

'She'll be out for a while,' the doctor assured him.

They walked down the corridor silently and took the elevator back to the lobby. The place had that hospital smell – that unique combo of something antiseptic and the hospital food. Win had parked the car and was now sitting in the waiting area. He stood when he saw them.

'That your friend Win?' Jake asked, motioning with his chin. 'The one P.T. told me about?'

'Yes.'

'Tell him to stay here. I want to talk to you alone.'

Myron signaled to Win. Win nodded, sat back down, picked up a newspaper, crossed his legs. Jake looked him over for a minute. 'He as crazy as P.T. says?'

'Pretty much.'

'Come on.'

They grabbed coffee and found a table in the corner. 'The crime scene unit is going over Nancy's house now. They'll beep me if they find anything.'

'So what do you know so far?' Myron asked.

'Not much. Nancy spent the last few days in Cancún – a graduation present from her parents.'

'Have they been told?'

He shook his head. 'I'm going over there right after we talk.'

Silence. Jake broke it. 'So how did Jessica get involved in this?'

'She wanted me to look into her father's murder. She didn't buy the fact that he was killed in a botched robbery.'

Jake nodded. 'She thought her old man's murder had something to do with her sister.'

'Yes.'

'I figured as much. I got the file in the car.'

Myron sat up. 'Adam Culver's homicide file?'

'Hey, I ain't an idiot, Bolitar. You start investigating after eighteen months. Why? Had to be the father's murder. You saw a connection. But I gotta be honest. I don't see it. No connections in that file at all. A few inconsistencies maybe. But no connection.'

'What sort of inconsistencies?' Myron asked.

'Adam Culver was supposed to be in Denver when he was killed. At a medical examiners' conference at the Hyatt Regency. But he never showed, missed his morning flight.'

'Does the file say why?'

'Adam didn't feel well. A reasonable explanation.'

'Who told them that?'

'His wife.'

Pause. 'What else?'

'Nothing else. The crime scene – a quiet street – was unremarkable. He was stabbed through the heart.'

'What was he doing out?'

'The wife said he went out to buy some groceries.'

Myron chewed that one over for a moment. 'Odd thing to do,' he said, 'when you're not feeling well.'

'Yeah, that's easy for us to say, sitting here like this. But the cops were concentrating on finding a mugger. No one really gave a shit about a missed flight or what it might mean.'

'Any witnesses to the murder?'

'None. The file is pretty bare-bone.' Jake leaned forward and tried to stare Myron down. Myron did not look away. 'Now,' Jake said slowly, 'you start talking to me. And don't give me no "I don't want no one hurt" crap. Too late for that now. Why are you really involved in all this?'

'I told you. Jessica.'

Jake leaned farther forward until their faces were only inches apart. 'Stop jerking me around,' he spat out. 'I ain't blind. I can see Jessica Culver is great tail. But don't start giving me this bullshit that you just decided to drop everything and help on a whim. You ain't that hard up.'

'There was also Christian to consider,' Myron said.

'What about him?'

'He's my top client. He was still upset about his fiancée's disappearance.'

Jake made a snorting nose. 'Yeah, I bet.'

'What's that supposed to mean?'

'It means,' Jake said, 'that I'm not convinced Christian is completely innocent in all this.'

'But you said the DNA test on the semen—'

'I'm not saying he raped her.'

'Then what are you saying?'

'That he might be involved,' Jake replied. 'Your client had no solid alibi for the time of the disappearance. He claims he was in bed at eleven o'clock, but no one can confirm it.'

'He has a single room,' Myron said. 'Who's going to confirm he was in bed when he lived alone?'

'It's suspicious,' Jake replied.

'How? Kathy Culver was seen entering the team locker room after ten, right?'

Jake nodded.

'And you know Christian was meeting with the offensive coordinator until ten-thirty,' Myron continued. 'That's confirmed.'

'But that's where his alibi ends.'

'He went to bed after that. Kathy was seen wandering around on the other side of the campus at eleven o'clock. I don't see the connection.'

'Maybe there is none,' Jake said simply. 'But he's the boyfriend. The boyfriend is always a prime suspect. And there was something else.'

'What?'

'His teammates.'

'What about them?'

Jake finished his coffee. He tapped the cup to get the last few drops. 'They were cooperative, I guess, but some of them seemed awfully vague. Nothing I could pin down, but some of them looked more nervous than they should. Like they were covering something up. Like maybe, just maybe, they were protecting their star quarterback before the big game.'

Except, Myron thought, nobody on the team liked Christian. His teammates would not have gone out of their way to protect him. Just the opposite, in fact.

So why were they nervous?

Jake settled back and smiled, marking a change in tactics. 'Now, Myron, I've been awfully sweet, haven't I? I've told you all I know, and you're still holding back on me. That ain't nice. Something else – something you haven't shared with me yet – put a real hairy bug in your ass. Now I visited our friend Dean Gordon a few hours ago, just like you suggested. The man was cordial, friendly, not at all a pompous ass. Which ain't like him. In fact, I think he was scared shitless. Now why's that?'

'Did he tell you anything?'

'Oh, he was real helpful. Kathy was a wonderful girl, an honor student, a hard worker, blah, blah, blah. Oh, yeah. He also told me your ex upstairs paid him a visit. Seems Jessica wanted her sister's file. Imagine that.'

'We were trying to gather as much info as possible.'

'Information on what?'

Myron eyed his coffee. It looked like sewer sludge. 'On the morning Adam Culver was murdered, he visited Nancy Serat.'

Jake's eyes widened a bit. 'How do you know that?'

'Nancy left a message on Jessica's phone to meet her at ten o'clock tonight. She also said that she'd seen Adam Culver on the morning of the murder.'

'Jesus Christ.' Jake crossed his arms, resting them on his belly. 'So Adam Culver visits Nancy Serat in the morning. He finds something out. Something big. Something so big he cancels his trip.'

'Something so big,' Myron added, 'it gets him killed.'

Jake nodded, thinking. 'Then the killer has to get rid of the source.'

'Nancy Serat.'

'Right.' Jake stopped. 'But I questioned that girl for hours. I asked her everything . . .' His voice faded off, and a shadow crossed his face. Myron knew what he was wondering. Any cop worth a damn would be asking the same questions. Did I fuck up? Did I miss something? Is a young girl dead because of me?

'If Nancy knew something that important,' Myron said, 'the killer wouldn't have waited eighteen months to silence her. I think it's a little more complicated than our scenario. I think Adam Culver had already put most of it together. Nancy had the final piece, a piece that by itself meant nothing to anyone – except Adam Culver.'

'You trying to make me feel better?'

'No. It's how I see it. If I thought you fucked up, I'd say so.'

'You didn't see her body,' Jake said quietly. 'Strangulation ain't pretty. The damn wire nearly sliced her head off. Not a nice way to go, Myron.' He stopped, shook his head. 'After seeing that, I know what Jessica is asking herself, because I keep asking myself the same thing.'

'What's that?'

'Did Kathy meet a similar fate?'

Silence. They drank some coffee. Myron's was already cold, but he didn't complain. Cold, sludgelike coffee seemed to fit the occasion.

'P.T. told me all about you,' Jake said after a massive slurp. 'Said you were smart, that I could trust you. He don't say that about too many folks. Said you and that Win fella were as good as they come. A little too maverick, but right now I could use that. I'm a cop. I have to follow rules. You don't. More power to you. But this is my territory, and I ain't gonna sit around like some fucking movie extra.' He put his hands on the table. They were big and callused and had no rings. 'So now I want you to tell me everything, Myron. Right now. Just you and me. It won't get out, you have my word. Don't hold anything back. You understand?'

Myron nodded.

'So start talking, boy. I'm all ears.'

Myron took out the magazine and handed it to Jake. 'It all started with this.'

Chapter 28

The morning papers had no mention of Nancy Serat's murder, but the radio was beginning to pick up early reports of a murdered woman. Just a question of time. Myron took Route 280 east to the New Jersey Turnpike north. Scenic road. Like driving through west Beirut on a good day. Problem was, people unfairly judged New Jersey by this road. It was like judging a woman's beauty by the size of her feet.

Billy Joel was on the radio, singing, 'I love you just the way you are.' Big talk, Myron mused, when you've been married to Christie Brinkley.

Exit 16W led him directly into the Meadowlands parking lot. Murder and intrigue were all well and good, but agenting paid the bills. He had a meeting with Otto Burke. Otto was expecting a response to his demand vis-à-vis Christian's contract. Myron had prepared one for him.

He had spent the night in Jessica's hospital room, trying

to get comfortable in a chair that doubled as a medieval torture device. But he had not minded. He liked watching her sleep. It brought back memories. He'd always hoped they'd one day sleep together again, though last night was not precisely what he had had in mind.

Jess had woken up two hours ago. Belligerent. Testy. Demanding. In a word: herself. Before her brother Edward took her home, Myron had told her all he knew – especially about his visit to Lucy's photo studio. She had given him a photograph of her father to show Lucy. Myron was surprised to see Jessica carried one in her wallet. But he was far more surprised to catch a fleeting glimpse of a picture from four summers ago – a picture she tried to skip past without his seeing. But he had seen it, and he remembered the precise moment it had been taken. Their last weekend in Martha's Vineyard. Just the two of them. Tan, happy, relaxed. A barbecue at Win's summer house. The pinnacle before the inevitable slide.

Myron had not had a chance to change clothes. He looked as if he'd spent the evening in the bottom of a laundry hamper.

Otto was waiting for him in the owner's box on Titans Stadium mezzanine level. Larry Hanson was with him. Otto greeted Myron with a bony handshake and a wide smile. Mr Sunshine. Larry offered a quick wave. He did not meet Myron's eye. It was no wonder. Larry Hanson was a tough guy, a loud brute even, but he tried to play fair. He didn't like to cheat, and he did not like what Otto was doing now. He looked, in fact, as if he wanted to blend into the wall.

'Please, Myron,' Otto said, spreading his arms like Carol Merrill on *Let's Make a Deal*, 'sit wherever you like.'

'Always the perfect host, Otto.'

'I do try, Myron. Thank you for noticing.'

'Sarcasm, Otto. It's called sarcasm.'

Otto kept the smile aglow. His goatee was exactly the same as always, never heavier or lighter. Must trim it every day, Myron thought. They sat in two seats facing the field. Fifty yard line. Fans would kill for these seats. Down below, players were scattered across the field. Myron spotted Christian walking toward the sideline. His helmet was off, his head held high. Christian didn't know about Nancy Serat's murder – her name had not yet been released – but the press would be all over him soon enough. Myron could protect him only so much, though he did entertain hopes that the news of Christian's signing would deflect some attention away from the murder.

'So,' Otto said with a clap of his hands, 'are you ready to sign?'

Down on the field Christian was being introduced to a bunch of long-haired men. Myron recognized the men from a video on MTV. They were Otto Records' latest find. A group called StillLife. Good sound, but did they have the raw talent, of, say, Pap Smear?

'Sure,' Myron said. 'We would like nothing more.'

'Great. I have a pen.'

'How handy. I have a contract.' He handed it to Otto. Otto read it quickly. His mouth was smiling, but his eyes frowned. He passed it to Larry Hanson.

'I'm confused, Myron. This looks like your last offer.'

'Very perceptive, Otto.'

'I thought we had an agreement,' he said.

'We do. There it is.'

'I think you're forgetting' – he paused, searching for the right word – 'Christian's sudden devaluation.'

'You make him sound like a foreign currency.'

Otto laughed. He looked over to Larry as if to say, laugh too. Larry could only muster a smile. 'Okay, Myron, I'll accept that. We are all, to some extent, commodities. Your client, however, is now trading at a lower rate against the US dollar.'

'Thanks for keeping within the metaphor, Otto, but I don't see it that way.' Myron looked at Larry Hanson. 'How's his play been, Larry?'

'Well, it's very early,' Larry said, clearing his throat. 'You really can't tell too much after such a short time period.'

'But if you had to grade him so far?'

Another throat clear. 'Let's just say,' he replied, 'that Christian's play has not been a disappointment.'

'There you go,' Myron said, matching Otto's smile. 'His value has, if anything, increased with his recent on-the-field display. You have now had a tasty morsel of his potential. I don't see how you could expect us to drop our asking price.'

Otto rose, nodding his head. He clasped his hands behind his back and walked to the bar. 'Care for a drink, Myron?'

'Do you have any Yoo-Hoo?'

'No, I don't.'

'Nothing, then.'

Otto poured himself a 7-Up. He did not ask Larry Hanson if he wanted anything. 'I will admit,' Otto said, 'that Christian's play so far has been impressive, though I must caution you, Myron – and you too, Larry – that there is a big difference between practice and games. Between how an athlete performs in a scrimmage and how he performs in a pressure situation.'

Myron and Larry exchanged a glance. The glance said, Pretentious asshole.

'But let me also add,' Otto continued, 'that our product is dependent on more than just performance. If, for example, our team were to win the Super Bowl but were also involved in a major drug or sex scandal, the overall value of the product may decline.'

'Can you demonstrate that with a graph?' Myron asked. 'I'm not sure I understand.'

'It means,' Otto said, 'that the photograph in that sleazy publication makes Christian worth less money to us.'

'But it's not a picture of him.'

'It's a picture of his fiancée.'

'Ex-fiancée.'

'His fiancée who vanished under mysterious circumstances.'

'Christian and I are willing to take the chance,' Myron said. 'It was in a small publication. It hasn't gotten out so far. We don't think it will.'

Otto sipped his 7-Up. He seemed to enjoy it, even adding an 'aaah' like he was taping a commercial. 'But the press might find out.'

'I don't think so,' Myron said. 'I've discussed it with Christian. We both feel the same.'

'Then you are both fools.'

The facade had dropped open a crack.

'Now, Otto, that wasn't very nice.'

The facade slid back up, smooth as an electric car window. 'Let me remind you of our previous discussion on this very subject, Myron. See if you can follow this. You were to take our agreement and knock if down by a third. If not, the picture of the au naturel Ms Culver goes public, thereby ruining your player's endorsement career.'

'But he didn't do anything, Otto. It's only a picture of Kathy Culver.'

'It doesn't matter. Advertisers do not like the smallest whiff of controversy. Remember this, Myron: In business, appearance is far more important than reality.'

'Appearance versus reality,' Myron said. 'That I have to write down.'

Otto took out a contract of his own. 'Sign it,' he said. 'Now.'

Myron just smiled at him.

'Sign it, Myron. Or I'll ruin you.'

'I don't think so, Otto.'

Myron began to unbutton his shirt.

'What do you think you're doing?'

'Don't get excited, Otto. I'm stopping after the third button. Just enough to show you this.' He pointed to the small microphone on his chest.

'What the hell—?'

'It's a wire, Otto. It leads to a tape recorder stuck in my belt. You can make the picture public, that's up to you. It may damage Christian, it may not. I, in turn, will make this tape public. I will also sue your sorry ass for any damages Christian may have suffered because of your actions, and I will also see to it that you are arrested for extortion and blackmail.' Myron smiled. 'I always wanted to own a record company. Chicks dig that, don't they, Otto?'

Otto looked at him coolly. 'Larry?'

'Yes, Mr Burke.'

'Take the tape away from him. Forcibly, if necessary.'

Myron looked at Hanson. 'You're a big guy, Larry,'

223

Myron said. 'And I know you were one of the toughest fullbacks ever to play this game. But if you get out of that chair, I'll put you in a body cast.'

Larry Hanson merely nodded. Not afraid, but not moving either.

'There are two of us,' Otto urged. 'I can call in security guards to help.'

'I don't think so, Mr Burke.' Larry was almost smiling. 'And I don't think a few security guards are going to scare him very much. Are they, Myron?'

'Not likely.'

'I think we should sign his contract, Mr Burke. I think it's best for all.'

'I've even drawn up a press release,' Myron said. 'Says how happy Christian is to be playing for such an outstanding and reputable organization as the Titans.'

Otto thought a moment. 'If I sign,' he said, 'you'll hand over the tape?'

'Not likely.'

'Why not?'

'You keep the magazine and I keep the tape. Think of it as our own little balance of terror. A throwback to the cold war.'

'But you have my word—'

'Please, Otto, it hurts when I laugh.'

Otto thought a moment. He was shaken but calm. A guy his age doesn't reach this level without learning to take a few knocks.

'Myron?'

'Yes.'

'I can't tell you how thrilled the Titans are to have Christian Steele, the quarterback of the future, with us.'

'Just sign right here, Otto.'

224

'My pleasure, Myron.'

'No, Otto. Mine.'

Otto signed. Myron and Otto shook hands. The deal was done.

'Shall we meet the press jointly, Myron?'

'Sounds wondrous, Otto.'

'There's a shower downstairs. I'll make sure you're provided with shaving equipment, if you like.'

'Very kind of you.'

Otto's smile was back. The man was never down long. He picked up the phone. 'Christian Steele has been signed,' Otto said. Then, looking back and winking at Myron, he added, 'At the highest salary ever given to a rookie.'

Myron winked back and gave him the thumbs up. Lifelong chums. He checked his watch. There would be just enough time to shower and do the press conference before he would have to head back into the city for his meeting with Herman Ache.

He had no idea how he was going to handle the evil Ache brothers. But he was still working on it. Feverishly.

Chapter 29

Jessica arrived at the house in Ridgewood at ten o'clock. The doctor had wanted to run some more tests in the morning. Jessica refused. They finally reached a compromise whereby Jessica promised to visit him in his office sometime during the week. Edward had driven her home in silence.

When they arrived, Jessica noted that her mother's car was not in the driveway. Good. Not in much of a mood to handle a hysterical mother on top of everything else, Jessica had insisted that no one tell her mother about last night's incident. Mom had enough on her mind. No reason to get her unnecessarily upset.

Jessica headed straight for the study. Her father had been up to something, that much was clear. There were too many weird happenings for it to have been any other way. He had visited Nancy Serat on the morning of his death. He had skipped out on a medical examiners' convention in Denver because he hadn't felt well – something he would never do. He had possibly even purchased nude photographs of Kathy.

You didn't have to be Sherlock Holmes to realize something was amiss.

She flicked on the track lights, illuminating the room a bit too harshly for her taste. She used the dimmer. Downstairs, Edward was in the kitchen opening the refrigerator.

She began to rifle through her father's drawers. She had no idea what she was looking for. Perhaps a small box with the words BIG CLUE scrawled across the top. That would be nice. She tried not to think about Nancy Serat, about her blue face frozen in terror, but the thought stayed anchored front and center. She thought of more pleasant things, like waking to see Myron folded up in that hospital chair like a contortionist from Le Cirque du Soleil. The image made her smile.

In the file drawer she found a folder marked CMA. Her father's Merrill Lynch Cash Management Account. She pulled it out. The CMA statement is a financial instrument of great beauty. Everything in one statement – your stocks, bonds, other holdings, checks, Visa card transactions. Jessica had one of her own.

She checked the charges and checks cleared on the most recent statement. Nothing unusual. Problem was, the statement ended three weeks ago. She needed something more recent.

She flipped to the last page. On the bottom in small print it read 'You have an alphabetic character in your Merrill Lynch account number. Please use nine-eight-two-three-three-four as your account access number for CMA-DATA.'

CMA-DATA. The 800 line. She had used it before with

her own account, whenever she found a discrepancy. She dialed the number and immediately heard a taped voice say, 'Welcome to the Merrill Lynch Financial Service Center. Enter your Merrill Lynch account number or your account access number.'

Jessica entered the number.

'Enter your selection. You may interrupt the dialogue at any time. For your current balance and purchasing power, enter one. For check clearing information, enter two. For most recent funds received, enter three. For most recent Visa transactions, enter six.'

She decided to start with the charges and then look at the checks. She pressed six.

The voice said, 'Visa draft for $28.50 is on delay debit as of May twenty-eighth. Visa draft for $14.75 is on delay debit as of May twenty-eighth.'

The machine was not telling her where the charges were coming from. The same would be true for the checks. Knowing just the amounts would do her no good.

'Visa draft for $3,478.44 is on delay debit as of May twenty-seventh.'

She froze. Three thousand dollars? For what? She hung up, hit the redial button, and put in the account access number.

'Enter your selection.'

This time she pressed zero for a customer service representative.

'Good morning,' a pleasant-voiced woman singsonged. 'May I help you?'

'Yes, there's a Visa charge on my account for over three thousand dollars. I'd like to know where the charge came from.'

'Your account number, please?'

'Nine-eight-two-three-three-four.'

There was some keyboard clacking in the background. 'And you are?' the rep asked.

Jessica checked the statement. A joint account, thank God. 'Carol Culver,' she said.

'Hold one moment, Mrs Culver.'

More clacking. 'Yes, I have it here. $3,478.44. Eye-Spy Shop in Manhattan.'

Eye-Spy? What the hell was that all about?

'Thank you,' Jessica said.

'Anything else today, Mrs Culver?'

'Yes. My husband and I have all our records on a personal computer, and I'm afraid the computer has had a disk failure. Can I ask you to give me the most recent checks that have been written against the account?'

'Certainly.'

More clacking. 'Check one-nineteen for $295 to Volvo Finance, written on May twenty-fifth.'

Car payment.

'Check one-eighteen for $649 to Getaway Realty, also written on May twenty-fifth.'

Hold the phone. 'Did you say Getaway Realty?'

'Yes, that's correct.'

'Does it say where they're located?'

'I'm afraid I don't have that information.'

They went through the rest of the month's checks. Nothing unusual. Jessica thanked the woman and hung up.

$649 to Getaway Realty? $3,478.44 to Eye-Spy? More and more amiss.

Edward knocked on the door. 'Hi,' he said.

'Hi.'

He stepped into their father's study, head lowered.

'I'm sorry about the other day,' Edward said. He blinked several times, his to-die-for eyelashes waving up and down. 'About running out like that.'

'It's okay.'

'You hit a raw nerve,' he said. 'Asking all those questions and everything.'

'They need to be asked,' she replied. 'I think everything is connected. What happened to Kathy. What happened to Dad. What made Kathy change.'

Edward flinched at the word *change*. Then he shook his head. His T-shirt of the day featured Beavis and Butthead. 'You're wrong,' he said. 'It doesn't have anything to do with what happened to her.'

'Maybe,' she said. 'Only way to find out is if you tell me.'

'I don't feel comfortable about it. It's painful.'

'I'm your sister. You can trust me.'

'We were never very close,' he said bluntly. 'Not like you and Kathy.'

'Or you and Kathy,' Jessica said. 'But I still love you.'

She waited.

'I don't know where to begin exactly,' he said. 'It started her senior year of high school. You had just moved to Washington. I was at Columbia. I was living off campus with my friend Matt. Remember him?'

'Of course. Kathy dated him for two years.'

'Almost three,' Edward corrected. 'Matt and Kathy were like something out of another century. They were together three years, and he never got, well, below the neck. I mean, never. And it wasn't just from a lack of trying. Matt was as straightlaced as any guy I knew, but that didn't mean he didn't push it now and again. But Kathy held him off.'

Jessica nodded, remembering. Kathy had still been confiding in her at that stage.

'Mom loved Matt,' Edward continued. 'She thought he was the greatest. She used to invite him over for tea like something out of *The Glass Menagerie*. A gentleman caller sitting on the porch with the youngest daughter. Dad liked him too. Everything seemed to be going well. They planned on getting engaged in another year, married after he graduated, the whole Chevy-and-apple-pie love story. Then one day Kathy called him on the phone and just dumped him. No explanation.

'Matt was shocked. He tried to talk to her, but Kathy wouldn't see him. I tried to talk to her too, but she just blew me off. Then I started hearing rumors.'

Jessica shifted in her chair. 'What kind of rumors?' she asked.

'The kind,' Edward said slowly, 'a brother doesn't like to hear about his sister.'

'Oh.'

'Worse than oh. Guys were trashing her nonstop. Someone had finally found the key to Miss Prude's chastity belt, they said, and now they couldn't get it back closed. I even got into a fight. Got the shit beaten out of me protecting Kathy's honor.' He spat out the word *honor* as though it had an offensive taste.

'She changed at home too. She never went to mass anymore. I thought Mom would have a stroke – you know how she gets about stuff like that.'

Jessica nodded. She knew only too well.

'But she never said a word. Kathy started staying out late. She went to college parties. Some nights she wouldn't even come home.'

'Didn't Mom stop her?' Jessica asked.

'She couldn't, Jess. It was unbelievable. Kathy had spent her entire life in fear of the woman. Now it was like Kathy had found Kryptonite. Mom couldn't touch her.'

'What about Dad?'

'He was never as strict as Mom, you know that. He wanted to be everyone's buddy, not the bad guy. But strangely enough, Kathy grew closer to Dad during all this. He was thrilled by the sudden attention. I think he was afraid if he laid down the law, he'd push her away from him.'

Sounded like her father. 'What did you do?' she asked.

'I confronted her.'

'What did she say?'

'Nothing really. She wouldn't deny it or admit it. She would just stand there and smile eerily. She said I didn't understand, that I was "naïve." Naïve. Can you believe Kathy could call someone else naïve?'

Jessica thought a minute. 'But none of that explains what started it, what made her change in the first place.'

Edward opened his mouth, stopped. He spread his hands, then dropped them back to his sides as though they were too heavy to hold up. His voice was barely audible. 'Something with Mom,' he said.

'What with Mom?'

'I don't know. I think maybe Mom does. Kathy became withdrawn from you and me. But she still loved us. It was Mom got the brunt of it.'

Jessica leaned back in her father's chair, considering his last comment. 'I knew Kathy had changed the last couple of years, but I had no idea . . .' Her voice sort of faded away.

'But it ended, Jess. You have to remember that.'

'What ended?' she asked.

'This stage Kathy went through. That's why I don't think it's related to her disappearance. By the time she disappeared, it was all in the past.'

'What do you mean, in the past?'

'She changed back. Oh, I don't mean she started going to mass every Sunday or became buddies with Mom. But whatever had twisted her out of shape had finally let go. She was regaining her old self. I think Christian had a lot to do with that. I think he helped bring her back from the edge. The slutty behavior certainly stopped. So did the drugs, the drinking, the partying. Other things too. The smile even came back a little.'

Jessica remembered Kathy's school transcript. The terrible grades in her senior year and the beginning of college. Then the sudden turnabout back toward excellence that had started her second semester freshman year – when she met Christian. It added up with what Edward was saying.

So was the past irrelevant? Was this period of her life, as Edward had insisted, all behind her? Perhaps. But Jessica doubted it. If it were truly dead and buried, why was her picture now appearing in a pornographic magazine? And that of course led to the central question in all this:

What had made Kathy change in the first place?

Jessica still did not know. But she now had a pretty good idea who might.

Chapter 30

There were several things Myron enjoyed more than visiting Herman Ache. Having his eyeball removed with a grapefruit spoon, for example.

'I heard your press conference on the radio,' Win said. The top was down on Win's racing-green Jaguar XJR. Myron was not big on having the top down. It was just a question of time before a bug got stuck in his teeth. 'I trust that Christian was pleased with the deal.'

'Very.'

'The press still hasn't picked up on Nancy Serat.'

'Jake hasn't released her name yet. Once they do—'

'Party time.'

'Exactly.'

'Does Christian know?' Win asked.

'Not yet. He was so damn happy. I just wanted to let him enjoy it a little longer.'

'You should warn him.'

'I will. Jake promised to let me know the second it got out.'

'You seem to like this Jake fellow,' Win noted.

'He's a good man. We can trust him.'

Win wiggled his fingers, regripped the wheel, accelerated. 'I don't trust officers of the law,' Win said. 'It's safer that way.'

The car was going very fast. The West Side Highway was not built for such speed – a four-lane highway with traffic lights every twenty yards. Plus the 'ongoing' construction didn't help. The construction had been going on for as long as anyone could remember. History books stated that Peter Minuit, the Dutchman who purchased Manhattan from the Indians in 1626, often complained about the delays around Fifty-seventh Street.

But none of that deterred Win's hefty accelerator foot. The Javits Center was a blur. So was the Hudson River, for that matter.

Myron said, 'Could you slow down a tad?'

'No need to worry. The car has a driver-side air bag.'

'Wonderful.'

They were getting closer to Ache's office. Myron's stomach knotted – not helped by the smog blasting into his face because the top was down. His nerves were as taut as a freshly strung tennis racket. Win, on the other hand, looked relaxed. Then again, Frank Ache didn't have a contract out on his head.

Win's car phone rang. He picked it up. 'Hello?' He handed the phone to Myron, 'It's P.T.'

Myron took the receiver. 'What's up?'

'Hey, Myron, how you feeling today?'

'Can't complain.'

'Glad to hear it. Say, you'll never guess what happened last night.'

'What?'

'Two of New York's finest hit men were found dead in an alley. Sad, ain't it?'

'Tragic,' Myron agreed.

'They worked for Frank Ache.'

'That a fact?'

'Forty-four Magnum with dum-dum bullets were used. Blew their heads clean off.'

'Such a loss.'

'Yeah, I'm losing sleep over it too. Anyway, word out on the street is, this ain't over. Corpses don't exactly waylay the wants of a guy like Frank Ache. The contract is still out on whatever ugly slob pissed Frank off.'

Myron said, 'Ugly?'

'Well, it's been nice talking to you, Myron. Take care.'

'You too, P.T.'

Myron hung up.

'The contract is still in place?' Win asked.

'Yep.'

'They won't hit you in Herman's office,' Win said. 'He would never allow it.'

Myron knew that was true. There was a certain code, even among men who have probably ordered the deaths of hundreds of people. Some idiots believed that these codes were based on some sort of ethics. Not even close. The codes were two things to mobsters: (1) a device to make them appear almost human, and (2) a way of protecting themselves and their position. Ethics are to a mobster what honesty is to a politician.

A construction site slowed them near Twelfth Street, but they still made it with time to spare. The air smelled of pizza – probably because they parked in front of a pizzeria called The First Original Ray's Pizza of New York, Really, We're Not Kidding, Honest, We're It. A tall woman in a blue business suit and fancy sunglasses strolled purposefully down the sidewalk. Myron smiled at her, and she returned it. He would have preferred a faint or even a small swoon, but you can't have everything.

At two in the afternoon Clancy's Tavern was already in full swing. Myron stopped right outside the door, fixed his hair, turned left, smiled, turned right, smiled, looked up, smiled.

Win looked a question at him.

'The feds take pictures of everyone who comes in here,' Myron said. 'I just wanted to look my best.'

'Now you tell me, I look like hell.'

Clancy's patrons were all men. Not exactly a swinging pick-up joint. A jukebox played Bob Seger. The decor was Early American Beer. Lots of those neon signs, the ones that spell out company names. Budweiser, Bud Light, Miller, Miller Lite, Schlitz. A clock courtesy of Michelob. A mirror from Coors. Coasters from Pabst. The mugs had Rolling Rock logos emblazoned across them.

Myron knew that there were probably a million FBI bugging devices in here. Herman Ache didn't care. Anybody who said something truly damaging in the tavern itself was beyond stupid and deserved to get nailed. The real talk went on in the back rooms. Ache made sure they were swept for bugs every day.

Win drew a few curious glances when they entered. Prep was not exactly the 'in' style of Clancy's clientele. But no one stared too long. This was a bar where no one stared at anyone too long.

'Is that your friend Aaron?' Win asked.

Aaron was at the back of the bar wearing his customary white suit. This time he wore a shirt, albeit one of those pectoral-displaying sleeveless muscle T's. It was as if Aaron's wardrobe had entered some molecular transformer with issues of *GQ* and *Pumping Iron*. Aaron waved them to come forward with a hand the size of a manhole cover.

'Hello, Myron,' Aaron said. 'A genuine pleasure to see you again.'

Myron Bolitar, Mr Popularity. 'Aaron, I'd like you to meet Win Lockwood.'

Aaron angled the smile at Win. 'Pleasure, Win.' They shook hands with death stares, each sizing the other man up. Neither flinched.

'They're waiting in the back,' Aaron said. 'Come on.'

Aaron led them to a locked door with a one-way mirror. The door opened immediately. They entered. Two hoods stood stonefaced. In front of them was a long corridor. There was – and this was new – a metal detector, like at the airport.

Aaron shrugged, as if to say, A sign of the times. 'Hand over your weapons, if you'd be so kind. Then step through.'

Myron took out his thirty-eight, Win a brand-new forty-four. Last night's forty-four had no doubt been destroyed. They stepped through. The metal detector did not ding, but the two hoods still searched with one of those gizmos that looked suspiciously like vibrators. Then they searched again, this time by hand.

'Very thorough,' Win said.

'Almost enjoyable,' Myron added. 'I thought he was going to ask me to turn my head and cough.'

'Hey, funny man,' one of the hoods groused, 'this way.'

The two hoods took over, escorting them down the corridor. Aaron stayed back and watched. Myron did not like that. The walls were white, the carpet office-orange. Lithographs of the French Riviera lined the walls. The front of Clancy's Tavern looked like a dive; the back like a dentist's office.

Two other men appeared at the other end of the corridor. They were both carrying guns.

Myron leaned toward Win's ear. 'Uh-oh.'

Win nodded.

The two men pointed their guns at Myron and Win. One barked, 'Hey, you, Goldilocks. Get over here.'

Win looked at Myron. 'Goldilocks?'

'I think he means you.'

'Oh. The blond hair. I get it now.'

'Yeah, Goldie, get your butt down here.'

'Later,' Win said. He moved down the corridor. The two hoods from the metal detector took out their guns. Four men, four guns. Lots of firepower. Not taking any chances after last night.

'Hands on your head. Let's go.'

Win and Myron, separated by approximately ten feet, did as they were told. One of the hoods from the metal detector approached Myron. Without warning, he punched the butt of his gun against Myron's kidney.

Myron dropped to his knees. Nausea swam through him. The man followed up with a kick to the ribs. Then another. Myron slid to the ground. The other man joined in. He stomped on Myron's upper legs like they were small brushfires. One stomp landed on the already-sore kidney. Myron thought he was going to vomit.

In something of a haze Myron spotted Win. He had

not moved, his face displaying something akin to non-interest. Win had sized up the situation and made a quick determination: There was nothing he could do to help. Worrying and fretting were worthless. Win was spending his time calmly studying the men. He didn't like to forget a face.

The kicks came in a nonstop flurry. Myron curled into a fetal position and tried to ride it out. The kicks hurt like hell, but they were too rushed to do serious damage. One landed near his eye. He'd have a shiner for sure.

Then a voice shouted, 'What the hell – Stop this moment!'

The kicks halted immediately.

'Get away from him!'

The men backed off. 'Sorry, Mr Ache.'

Myron rolled onto his back. With some effort he managed to sit up. Herman Ache stood by an open door. 'Are you okay, Myron?'

Myron winced. 'Never better, Herman.'

'I can't tell you how sorry I am,' Herman Ache said. Then glaring at his men. 'But some people will be even sorrier.'

The men cowered away from the older man. Myron almost rolled his eyes. This was all an act. Herman Ache's men did not beat up men in Herman's corridor without permission. This had been a setup. Now Myron supposedly owed Herman, even before the negotiating started. Not to mention the fact that pain is a great fear-inducer, the perfect prenegotiation cocktail.

Aaron came down the hall. He helped Myron to his feet and sort of half-shrugged as if to say, Cheap move, but what can you do?

'Come,' Herman beckoned. 'Let's talk in my office.'

Myron moved tentatively into the office. He had not been here in several years, but not much had changed. Golf was still the theme. LeRoy Neiman painting of some golf course on the main wall. Lots of those stupid cartoon/artworks of old-fashioned golfers. Aerial photographs of golf courses. In one corner of the office was a movie screen showing a shot of a fairway. In front of the screen was a golf tee. The player hits the ball against the screen. A computer then calculates where it would have landed and changes the image on the screen to match that. Then the player takes his second shot. Fun city.

'Nice office,' Win said.

Figures.

'Thank you, son.' Herman Ache smiled. Capped teeth. He was in his early sixties, tan, fit, wearing white pants and a yellow golf shirt with a Nicklaus golden bear where an alligator normally went – as if he were on his way to a gin tournament in Miami Beach. Herman Ache had gray hair. Not his own. A toupee or one of those Hair Club systems, a good one, one most people would probably not spot. He had liver spots on his hands. His face was wrinkle free, probably from collagen shots or a face-lift. The neck gave him away. The flesh was baggy and Reaganesque. Looked like a big scrotum.

'Please, gentlemen, have a seat.'

They did so. The door was closed behind them. Aaron, two new hoods, and Herman Ache. Nausea's grip on Myron's stomach began to slacken.

Herman picked up a golf club and sat on the edge of his desk. 'I understand,' he said, 'that you and Frank are having a misunderstanding, Myron.'

'That's what I wanted to talk to you about.'

Herman nodded. 'Frank?'

The door opened. Frank entered. You could tell that they were brothers, both having almost identical facial features, but that was where the similarities ended. Frank had at least twenty pounds on his older brother. He was pear-shaped with small Paul Schaefer shoulders and a rubber tire that would be the envy of the Michelin Man. Frank was completely bald, forgoing the hair weave. His teeth were black with spaces between them. His face was permanently set on angry scowl.

Both brothers had grown up on the streets. Both had started out as small-time hoods and worked their way up. Both had seen their own children gunned down over the years. Both had gunned down plenty of other people's children. Herman liked to pretend that he dwelled on a loftier plane than his coarse younger brother – a plane of fine books, the arts, golf. But the escape was not that easy. Two sides of the same coin. Frank gratingly reminded Herman of his origins and perhaps true nature. But Frank was comfortable and accepted in his world. Herman was not.

Frank was dressed in a powder blue sweat suit with neon yellow trim. The jacket was unzipped and – taking a fashion tip from Yves St Aaron – he wore no shirt. His chest hairs were matted with either some type of oil or sweat. Quite a turn-on. The form-fitting pants were a few sizes too small, outlining a bulge in his crotch. Myron started feeling nauseous again.

Frank did not speak. He sat at his brother's desk and waited.

'Now, Myron,' Herman continued, 'I understand this is all about some black boy who plays basketball.'

'Chaz Landreaux,' Myron said. 'And I'm not sure he'd be crazy about being called "boy."'

'Pardon an old man who is not up on all the politically correct terms. I meant no disrespect.'

Win sat quietly, studying his surroundings.

'Let me tell you how I see it,' Herman continued. 'And I'm trying to be objective here. Your Mr Landreaux made a deal. He took the money. For four years he helped his family with that money. Then when it was time to pay up, he reneged.'

'That's objective? Chaz Landreaux is just a kid—'

'Spare me the lecture,' Herman interrupted gently. 'We're not social workers here. You know that. We are businessmen. We made an investment in this young man. We risked several thousand dollars on him. The investment was finally about to pay dividends when you interfered.'

'I didn't interfere. He came to me. He's a scared kid. O'Connor got his hooks in him when he was eighteen. There are rules against approaching kids that young for a reason. Now the kid's trying to get out before he slides in too deep.'

Herman looked skeptical. 'Oh, come on now, Myron. Kids grow up fast nowadays. He knew exactly what he was doing. So it was against the rules – big deal. The kid knew the rules. He wanted the money anyway.'

'He'll pay it back.'

Frank Ache spoke for the first time. 'Fuck he will.'

Myron waved. 'Hi, Frank. Boss threads.'

'And fuck you too, bug shit. Deal's a deal.'

Myron turned to Win. 'Bug shit?'

Win shrugged.

'The deal,' Myron continued, 'was that Chaz could back out at any time and pay back the money. Roy O'Connor told him that.'

'I don't give a fuck what O'Connor said.'

Herman said, 'Please, Frank, we don't need to get hostile.'

'Ah, fuck him, Herman. This asshole wants to fuck me over. He wants to steal food off my fucking table. Not just this Landreaux nigger. That's just the start. We got dozens of prospects signed like this. We lose one, we lose them all. I say we let the other agents know we ain't to be messed with. I say we waste Bolitar right now.'

Myron said, 'I don't like that idea.'

'Who the fuck asked you?'

'Just giving my opinion.'

'Please, Frank, this isn't helping. You promised to let me handle this.'

'Handle what? Kill the son of a bitch. End of story.'

'Wait in the other room. I'll take care of it, I promise.'

Frank glared at Myron. Myron did not bother glaring back. He knew this was part of the act. He knew that they were trying to intimidate him in much the same way Otto Burke and Larry Hanson had. But for some odd reason, the air of death gave the Mutt and Jeff routine a whole new dynamic.

Win, however, remained pensive.

'Come on, Aaron,' Frank growled. 'Let's get the fuck out of here.' He stood. 'But the contract is still on.'

'Fine,' Herman said. 'If you want to kill him, I won't get in the way.'

'He's as good as dead.'

Frank and Aaron left. Frank slammed the door. Overacting, Myron thought, but an effective cameo appearance.

Myron said, 'He's fun.'

Herman moved to the corner of the room. He took a

slow practice swing with the club. 'I wouldn't mess with him, Myron. Frank is really angry. Me, I've always liked you. From the early days. But I'm not sure I can help you on this one.'

The 'early days' had begun Myron's sophomore year at Duke. It was not something he liked to remember. His father had been gambling. And losing. On the day before a game against Georgia State, Myron returned to his dorm to find his father and two of Herman Ache's hoods. The two hoods told Myron that if Georgia State did not cover the twelve-point spread, his father would lose a finger. His father was crying, the first time Myron had ever seen his father cry. Myron made three turnovers in the last forty seconds to make sure Duke won by only ten.

Father and son never talked about it.

'Why is this kid, this Chaz Landreaux, so important to you, Myron?'

'I think he's worth saving.'

'Saving from what?'

'He's just a kid, Herman. Frank is putting the screws to him. I want it to stop.'

Herman smiled, changed clubs, took a few more swings. Then he picked up his putter. 'Still a crusader, eh, Myron?'

'Hardly. I'm just trying to help the kid.'

'And yourself.'

'Fine. And myself.'

Myron realized that Herman Ache was wearing golf cleats. Jesus. To most people golf is an idiotic excuse for a sport. For others it's a life-consuming obsession. There is no in between.

'I don't think,' Herman said, reading the break in his carpet, 'I can stop Frank. He's very determined.'

'You run the show,' Myron said. 'Everyone knows that.'

'But Frank is my brother. I don't step on his toes unless it's absolutely necessary. I don't think that's the case here.'

'What did Frank do to him?'

'Pardon?'

'How did he scare the kid?'

'Oh,' Herman said. Another club changed. This time he exchanged the putter for a wood. 'He kidnapped his sister. Twin sister, I think.'

Myron felt his stomach dive anew. They'd been right. Not much satisfaction in that. 'Is she okay?'

'Oh, I wouldn't worry,' Herman said, as if that were a truly foolish question. 'They won't hurt her. Long as Landreaux continues to cooperate.'

'When are they going to let her go?'

'Two more days. Something about making sure the contract is official and Landreaux doesn't have second thoughts.'

'What do you want, Herman? What's it going to cost to get Frank off?'

He put on a golf glove and took a very deliberate swing, watching his hands. 'I'm an old man, Myron. A *rich* old man. What could you possibly give me?'

Win sat forward, moving for the first time. 'Your club is too far open on your swing, Mr Ache. Try turning your wrists a little more. Shift your grip to the right a little.'

The sudden change in subject caught everyone by surprise. Herman looked at Win. 'I'm sorry. I never caught the name.'

'Windsor Horne Lockwood III.'

'Ah, so you are the immortal Win. Not exactly what I expected.' He tested the new grip. 'Feels odd.'

'Give it a few weeks,' Win said. 'Do you play often?'

'As often as I can. It's more than just a game to me. It's . . .'

'Sacred,' Win finished for him.

His eyes livened. 'Exactly. You play, Mr Lockwood?'

'Yes.'

'Nothing like it, is there?'

'Nothing,' Win agreed. 'Where do you play?'

'Not easy for my kind to find good courses. I joined a club in Westchester. St Anthony's. You know it?'

'No.'

'It's not much of a course. Eighteen holes, of course. Very rocky. You have to be half mountain goat.'

Golf stories. Myron loved them. Didn't everyone?

'I don't understand something,' Myron said, playing along. 'With all your, uh, influence, why don't you play anywhere you want?'

Herman and Win looked at him as though he were a naked infidel praying in the Vatican. 'Excuse him,' Win said. 'Myron does not understand golf. He thinks a nine iron is a vitamin supplement.'

Herman laughed. The hoods joined suit. Myron didn't get it.

'I understand fine,' Myron said. 'Golf is a bunch of silly-dressed men using massive tracts of real estate to play with a ball and stick.'

Myron laughed. No one joined suit. Golfers are not known for their sense of humor.

Herman put the club back in the bag. 'A man does not force or buy or bully his way onto a golf course,' he explained. 'I have too much respect for the game, for the traditions, to do anything so crass. It would be like putting a gun against a priest's head to get the front pew.'

'Sacrilege,' Win said.

'Exactly. No *real* golfer would do it.'

'He has to be invited,' Win added.

'Right. And you don't merely play a great course. You pay homage to it. I'd love to be invited to one of the world's great courses. It would be my dream. But it is not meant to be.'

'How about being invited to two of them?' Win asked.

'Two—' Herman stopped. His eyes widened for a millisecond, then quickly dimmed as though afraid he was being teased. 'What do you mean?'

Win pointed to a picture on the left wall. 'Merion Golf Club,' he said. Then he pointed to a picture on the far wall. 'And Pine Valley.'

'What about them?'

'I assume you've heard of them?'

'Heard of them?' Herman repeated. 'They're the top two courses on the East Coast, two of the best in the world. Name a hole. Go ahead, any hole, either course.'

'Sixth hole at Merion.'

Herman's face glowed like a little kid's on Christmas morning. 'One of the most underrated holes anywhere. It sets up with a semiblind tee-shot to a fairway that favors a soft fade. Start your tee-shot at middle bunker, then cut back to the center, keeping clear of the boundary, which comes in on the right. Long-to-middle iron to the modestly elevated green, careful of the bunkers on the left and right.'

Win smiled. 'Very impressive.'

Snore.

'Don't tell me, Mr Lockwood, that you've played Merion and Pine Valley.' Something well past awe resonated in Herman's voice.

'I'm a member of both.'

Herman inhaled sharply. Myron half-expected him to cross himself. 'A member,' he began incredulously, 'of both?'

'I'm a three handicap at Merion,' Win continued. 'A five handicap at Pine Valley. And I'd like you to be my guest at both for a weekend. We'll try to get in seventy-two holes a day, thirty-six at each course. We'll start at five A.M. Unless that's too early.'

Herman shook his head. Myron thought his eyes looked teary. 'Not too early,' he managed.

'Next weekend okay for you?' Win asked.

Herman picked up the phone. 'Let the girl go,' he said. 'And the contract is off. Anyone touches Myron Bolitar, they're dead.'

Chapter 31

Win and Myron went back to the office. Myron felt sore from the beating, but nothing was broken. He would persevere. He was that kind of guy. Terribly brave.

Esperanza said, 'You look like shit.'

'You're so hung up on appearances.'

He tossed her the photograph of Adam Culver. 'See if your friend Lucy recognizes him.'

She snapped a salute. '*Jawohl, Kommandant.*' Of all the old shows, Esperanza's favorite was *Hogan's Heroes*. Myron was not a big fan, though he always wished he could have been there when some young TV hotshot said, 'Hey, I got an idea for a sitcom! Set it in a POW camp in Nazi Germany. Laughs galore.'

'How many calls?' he asked.

'About a million. Mostly the press wanting your comments on Christian's signing.' She smiled. 'Nice job on that one.'

'Thank you.'

'That Otto Burke,' she said, a pencil near her mouth. 'Is he single?'

Myron looked at her, horrified. 'Why would you want to know?'

'He's kinda cute.'

The nausea was back. 'You're hitting me up for a raise, aren't you? Please say yes.'

Esperanza smiled coyly but said nothing. He started for his office.

'Hold it,' she said. 'A strange message just came in for you a few minutes ago.'

'From?'

'A woman named Madelaine. Wouldn't give her last name. Sounded sultry.'

The dean-nessa. Hmm.

'She leave a number?'

Esperanza nodded, handed it to him. 'Remember: The condom is your friend.'

'Thanks, Mom.'

'Speaking of which, your mother called twice, your father once. I think they're worried about you.'

He entered his office. His little private sanctuary. He liked it in here. Myron held most of his negotiations and important meetings in the traditionally decorated conference room, freeing him up to make his office whatever he wanted it to be. He had, of course, his view of the Manhattan skyline to his left. On the wall behind his desk he had framed posters from Broadway musicals: *Fiddler on the Roof*, *The Pajama Game*, *How to Succeed in Business Without Really Trying*, *Man of La Mancha*, *Les Misérables*, *La Cage aux Folles*, *A Chorus Line*, *West Side Story*, *Phantom*.

Another wall had movie stills: Humphrey Bogart and

Ingrid Bergman in *Casablanca*, Woody Allen and Diane Keaton in *Annie Hall*. Katharine Hepburn and Spencer Tracy in *Adam's Rib*. Groucho, Chico, and Harpo in *A Night at the Opera*. Adam West and Burt Ward in *Batman*, the TV show, the real Batman, the one where Burgess Meredith played the Penguin and Cesar Romero played the Joker. The Golden Age of Television.

The final wall had photographs of Myron's clients. In a few days Christian Steele cloaked in Titans blue would join the group.

He dialed Madelaine Gordon's number. The answering machine picked up. Her silky voice. Hearing it again made his throat dry. He hung up, not leaving a message. He checked the time on the far wall. The clock was shaped like a giant watch with a Boston Celtics insignia in the center.

Three-thirty.

Still time to get to the campus. Madelaine was not important, but Myron very much wanted to see the dean. And he wanted to show up unexpectedly.

At Esperanza's desk he said, 'I'm going out for a while. You can reach me in the car.'

'Are you limping?' she asked.

'A little. Ache's men roughed me up.'

'Oh. See you later.'

'Hurts like hell, but I can take it.'

'Uh-huh.'

'Don't make a scene.'

'Inside,' she said. 'I'm dying.'

'Please see if you can reach Chaz Landreaux. Tell him we need to talk.'

'Okay.'

He left. He picked up his car in the garage. Win was

252

into cars. He loved his racing-green Jag. Myron drove a blue Ford Taurus. He was not what one might call a car man. A car got him from point A to point B, that was all. It was not a status symbol. It was not a second home. It was not his baby.

The drive didn't take long. Myron took the Lincoln Tunnel. He passed the famed York Motel. Long sign:

$11.99 PER HOUR
$95 PER WEEK
MIRRORED ROOMS
NOW FEATURING SHEETS!

He paid the toll on the Parkway. The woman in the booth was very friendly. She almost looked at him when she tossed him the change.

He called his mother on the car phone and reassured her he was okay. She told him to call his father, he was the worried one. Myron called his father and reassured him he was okay. He told him to call his mother, she was the worried one. Great communication. The secret to a happy marriage.

He thought about Kathy Culver. He thought about Adam Culver. He thought about Nancy Serat. He tried to draw little lines, connecting them. The lines were tenuous at best. He was sure Fred Nickler, Sir Sleaze Rag, was one line. That picture hadn't sneaked into *Nips* by itself. Fred seemed to run a tight operation. He had to know more than he was saying. Win was digging into his background, seeing what he could unearth.

Half an hour later, Myron arrived at the campus. Extra-deserted today. No one on the commons. Very few cars. He parked near the dean's house and knocked on the door. Madelaine (he still liked the name) answered. She smiled when she saw him, clearly pleased, tilting her head a little. 'Well, hello, Myron.'

'Hi.' The Return of Mr Smooth.

Madelaine Gordon was dressed for tennis. Short white skirt. Great legs. White shirt. He noticed that the shirt was see-through. Keen observation, the signs of a master investigator. Madelaine noticed him noticing. She did not seem particularly offended.

'I'm sorry to intrude,' Myron said.

'No intrusion,' she said. 'I was just about to take a shower.'

Hmm. 'Your husband's not in, is he?'

She crossed her hands under her breasts. 'Not for hours yet,' she said. 'You got my message?'

He nodded.

'Would you care to come inside?'

Myron said, ' "Mrs Robinson, you're trying to seduce me, aren't you?" '

'Pardon me?'

The Graduate.

'Oh.' Madelaine wet her lips. She had a very sexy mouth. People overlook the mouth. They talk about the nose, the chin, the eyes, the cheekbones. Myron was a mouth man. 'I guess I should be offended,' she continued. 'I mean, I'm not that much older than you, Myron.'

'Good point. Quote withdrawn.'

'So,' she said. 'I'll ask again. Would you like to come inside?'

Myron said, 'Sure.' Bowling her over with quick wit. What chance did she have against such sparkling repartee?

She disappeared back into the house, creating an air

254

vacuum that sucked Myron – against his will, of course –
in after her. The inside was nice, the kind of house that
obviously saw plenty of company. Big open room on the
left. Tiffany lamps. Persian rugs. Busts of French guys
with long, curly hair. Grandfather clock. Painted portraits of stern-faced men.

'Care to sit down?' she said.

'Thank you.'

Sultry. That had been the word Esperanza used. It fit.
Not just Madeline's voice but her mannerisms, her walk,
her eyes, her persona.

'How about a drink?' she asked.

He noticed she already had one made for herself. 'Sure,
whatever you're having.'

'A vodka tonic.'

'Sounds good.' Myron hated vodka.

She mixed the drink. He sipped it, trying not to make a
face. He wasn't sure if he was successful. She sat down
next to him. 'I've never been this forward before,' she
said.

'That a fact?'

'But I'm very attracted to you. It's one of the reasons I
loved watching you play. You're really very handsome.
I'm sure you're sick of hearing that.'

'Well, I don't know if *sick* is the right word.'

Madelaine crossed her legs. It wasn't Jessica's leg cross,
but it was still worth watching. 'When you came to the
door yesterday, I didn't want to miss out on the opportunity. I decided to throw caution to the wind and just go
for it.'

Myron could not stop grinning. 'I see.'

She stood and reached out her hand to him. 'Now how
about that shower?'

'Uh, can we talk first?'

Puzzlement shadowed her face. 'Is there something wrong?'

Myron feigned embarrassment. 'Aren't you married?'

'And that bothers you?'

Not really. 'Yes. I guess it does.'

'Admirable,' she said.

'Thank you.'

'Stupid too.'

'Thank you.'

She laughed. 'Actually, it's sweet. But Dean Gordon and I have what we call a semi-open marriage.'

Hmm. 'Could you elaborate a little?'

'Elaborate?'

'Just to make me feel more comfortable about all this.'

She sat back down. The white skirt might as well not have been there. Her legs could best be described as scrumptious. 'I've never had to elaborate before,' she said.

'I realize that. But I'm interested.'

Arched eyebrow, 'In?'

'Can we start with your definition of *semi-open*?'

She sighed. 'My husband and I have been close friends since childhood. Our parents summered together in Hyannis Port. We were both from the "right families."' She made little quote marks in the air when she said 'right families.' 'We thought that would be enough. But it wasn't.'

'So why not divorce?'

She looked a question. 'Why am I telling you this?'

'My honest blue eyes,' he said. 'They're hypnotic.'

'Maybe they are.'

Now Myron gave her aw-shucks modesty. Mr Adaptable Face.

'My husband is politically connected. He was an ambassador. He's next in line to be university president. If we get divorced—'

'That ends,' Myron finished.

'Yes. Even these days, the hint of scandal can destroy a career and a lifestyle. But more than that, Harrison and I are still dear friends. Best friends, really. It's just that we need limited outside stimulation.'

'Limited?'

'Once every two months,' she said.

Yikes. 'How did you come up with that number?' he asked. 'Some kind of new algorithm, perhaps?'

She smiled. 'Lots of discussions. Negotiations, really. Once a month seemed like too much. Once a semester too little.'

Myron nodded at her. *Toto, we're not in Kansas anymore.*

'And we always use a condom,' she added. 'That's part of the arrangement.'

'I see.'

'Do you have one?' she asked. 'A condom.'

'On?'

She smiled. 'I have some upstairs.'

'Can I ask one more thing?'

'If you must.'

'How do you and your husband know that the other has kept to their, er, limit?'

'Easy,' she said. 'We tell each other. Everything. Helps spice things up a little.'

Madelaine was seriously strange, which only made her more attractive to Myron.

'Your husband. Does he ever fool around with coeds?'

She leaned forward and put her hand on his thigh.

Upper thigh. Upper, upper thigh. 'That kind of thing turn you on?'

'Yeah.' He tried a rakish smile. But rakish was not him. He could see in her eyes that she wasn't buying it.

Madelaine took back her hand. 'What are you up to, Myron?' she asked.

'Up to?'

'I feel like I'm being used,' she said. 'But not the way I had in mind.'

Man. 'Just getting in the mood.'

'I don't think so, Myron.' She studied him for moment. 'Be honest for a second. Are we going to go to bed?'

'No,' he said. 'We're not.'

'I've never been turned down before.'

'And I've never turned down a proposition like this before,' Myron said. 'Come to think of it, I've never had a proposition like this before.'

'Is it because I'm married?'

'No.'

'Are you involved with someone else?' she asked.

'Worse. I'm on the cusp of something that means a great deal to me. I don't know which way I'm going to fall. I'm confused.'

'That's sweet.'

Again he gave her aw-shucks.

'If it doesn't work out . . . ?' she said.

'I'll be back.'

She kissed him then. Hard. It was a damn good kiss. He felt it in his toes.

'Just the overture,' she said.

He'd be dead before the second scene. 'I really do have to talk to your husband. Do you know when he'll be home?'

'Not for a while. But he's at the office across campus. By himself. You'll have to knock loudly for him to hear you.'

He rose. 'Thanks.'

'Myron?'

'Yes?'

'We never use names when we discuss our affairs. I don't know if Harrison fools around with co-eds. I would doubt it highly.'

'How about Kathy Culver?'

She visibly jumped. Her face stiffened. 'I think you better leave now.'

'The honest blue eyes,' Myron said. 'Watch the honest blue eyes.'

'Not this time. And when I watched you play, it wasn't your eyes I looked at.'

'Oh?'

'Your ass,' she said. 'It looked nice in those little shorts.'

Myron felt cheap. Or ecstatic. Probably ecstatic. 'Were they having an affair?' he asked.

She said nothing.

'I'll shake my ass if I have to.'

'They weren't having an affair,' she said firmly. 'That much I know.'

'So why did you get all bent out of shape?'

'You were asking if my husband had an illicit affair with a co-ed who was probably murdered. I was taken aback.'

'Did you know Kathy Culver?'

'No.'

'Did your husband ever talk about her?'

'Not really. I just know she worked in his office.' She

looked at the grandfather clock, stood, and led him to the door. 'Talk to my husband, Myron. He's a good man. He'll tell you everything you need to know.'

'Like?'

She shook her head. 'Thanks for visiting.'

Madelaine was in shutdown mode. Probably hurt by his interrogation technique. Using his brawny body to get his way. Myron had never done that before. He liked it. Better than pistol-whipping a suspect, anyway.

He turned and left. Madelaine was probably watching his ass. He put a little wiggle in his step and hurried across campus.

Chapter 32

Jessica found Getaway Realty in the Bergen County Yellow Pages. Their office was a converted cottage next to a McDonald's off Route 17 on the New Jersey side of the New York–New Jersey border. The drive was only twenty minutes, but it felt as if she'd arrived in the rural past. She actually saw a feed store.

Only one person was in the office.

'Well, hello there,' the man said with a too-wide smile. He was mid-fifties, bald, with a long, scraggly gray beard, like a college professor's. He wore a flannel shirt, black tie, Levi's jeans, and red Chuck Taylor Converse sneakers.

'I'm Tom Corbett, president of Getaway Realty.' He handed her a card. 'What can I do for you today?'

'I'm Dr Adam Culver's daughter,' she said. 'He wrote a check to your office on May twenty-fifth for $649.'

'Yeah, so?'

'He passed away recently. I'd like to know what it was for.'

Corbett took a step back. 'I'm awfully sorry to hear that,' he said. 'Nice man, your father.'

'Thank you. Can you tell me why he came to you?'

He thought a moment, shrugged. 'Don't see why not. He rented a cabin.'

'Near here?'

'Five, six miles. In the woods.'

'For how long?'

'A month. Starting May twenty-fifth. Still has it for a few more weeks, if you'd like to use it.'

'What kind of cabin?' she asked.

'What kind? Well, it's pretty small. One bedroom, one bathroom with shower stall, living room, kitchenette.'

This made no sense. 'Do you think you could give me the directions and a spare key?'

He thought that one over too, chewing on the inside of his mouth. 'It's a bit remote,' he said. 'Kinda hard to find, darling.'

Aside from *babe* and *honey-bun*, there were few things Jessica enjoyed being called more than *darling*. But now was not the time to explain her sentiments. She bit her lip and held back.

'The cottage's away from it all,' Tom continued. 'Way away, if you know what I mean. A little hunting, a little fishing, but mostly just peace and quiet.' He picked up a key chain as heavy as a barbell. 'I'll drive you.'

'Thank you.'

He drove a Toyota LandCruiser and chatted the whole way, as though she were a client. 'Here's our local grocery store.'

It was an enormous A&P Superstore.

She was surprised when he turned onto an unpaved road. They were heading straight into the woods.

'Nice, ain't it? Real pretty.'

'Uh-huh.'

Green foliage surrounded them. Jessica was not much of the outdoor sort. To her, the great outdoors meant bugs and humidity and dirt and no running water and no bathroom. Man had evolved for millions of years to escape the woods. Why rush back? But more important, her father had felt the same. He hated the woods.

Why would he rent a cabin out here?

Tom pointed to a gully up ahead. 'Two years ago, guy got killed by a hunter over there. Accident. The hunter thought he was a deer, shot him in the head.'

'Uh-huh.'

'Couple of dead bodies been found in the woods. Three in the past two years, I think. Found one girl just a couple months back. Runaway, they guessed. Hard to tell 'cause she was all decayed and stuff.'

'You're a hell of a salesman, Tom.'

He laughed. 'Yeah, well, I can tell when someone ain't a buyer.'

Jessica, of course, knew all about the bodies. The police hadn't caught the killer, but the general consensus was that the psychopath had gotten hold of one more young girl, one that had not yet been found:

Kathy Culver.

Could Kathy's fate have been that simple and that horrible? Had she been another victim of a random psychopath, just as everyone thought?

No, Jessica told herself. Too many holes.

'When I was a kid growing up around here,' Tom said, 'these woods were filled with legends. Guy with a hook hand lived in here, the old-timers said, used to kidnap bad little boys and gut them with his hook.'

'Charming.'

'Sometimes I wonder if he moved on to young ladies.'

Jessica said nothing.

'Used to call him Dr Hook,' he continued.

'What?'

'Dr Hook. That's what we all called him.'

'Isn't that a singer?' she asked.

'A what?'

'Never mind.'

They drove another mile away from civilization. 'That's the house,' Tom said. 'Up there behind the trees.'

It was a small wooden cabin with a big front porch.

'Rustic, ain't it?'

Decrepit would have been a better adjective. Jessica checked the porch, but there were no toothless hillbillies playing dueling banjos.

'Did my father say why he wanted to rent this cabin?'

'Just said he needed someplace to get away from it all in these woods.'

It still made no sense. Dad was going to be gone at a medical examiners' conference for a week out of the month, anyway. And Adam Culver was not the get-away-from-it-all type. He dealt with the dead. On vacations he wanted to be in Vegas or Atlantic City or someplace with lots of people and action. Now he was renting the Waltons' cabin.

Tom used the key to unlock the door. He pushed it open and said, 'After you.'

Jessica stepped into the living room. And stopped short.

Tom came in behind her. His voice was a whisper. 'What the hell is this?' he asked.

Chapter 33

Dean Gordon's office was in Compton Hall. The building was only three stories high but wide. Greek columns
out front screamed House of Learning. Brick exterior.
White double doors. Directly inside was a bulletin board
filled with old notices. Meetings of the usual campus
groups: the African American Change Committee, the
Gay-Lesbian Alliance, the Liberators of Palestine, the
Coalition to Stop the Domination of Womyn (never
spelled *women*, for the sexism the name implies), the
South African Freedom Fighters – all taking the summer
off. College fun days.

There was no one inside the huge lobby. The motif
was marble. Marble floors, banisters, columns. The walls
were covered with huge portraits of men in graduation
robes, most of whom would flip if they could read the
bulletin board. All the lights were on. Myron's footsteps
clacked and reverberated in the still room. He wanted to
shout 'Echo,' but was far too adult.

The dean of students' office suite was at the end of the left corridor. The door was locked. Myron knocked hard. 'Dean Gordon?'

Shuffling behind the dark-paneled doors. Several seconds later, the door opened. Dean Gordon was wearing tortoiseshell glasses. He had wispy hair, conservatively cut, a handsome face with clear brown eyes. His features were gentle, as though the facial bones had been rounded off to soften his appearance. He looked kind, trustworthy. Myron hated that.

'I'm sorry,' the dean said. 'The office is closed until tomorrow morning.'

'We need to talk.'

Confusion crossed his face. 'Do I know you?'

'I don't think so.'

'You're not a student here.'

'Hardly.'

'May I ask who you are?'

Myron looked at him steadily. 'You know who I am. And you know what I want to talk about.'

'I don't have the slightest idea to what you are referring, but I am really quite busy—'

'Read any good magazines lately?'

Dean Gordon's whole body twitched. 'What did you say?'

'I guess I could come back when the office was crowded. Maybe bring some reading material for the school's trustees, though I understand they only read the articles.'

No response.

Myron smiled – knowingly. At least, he hoped that was how it looked. Myron had no idea what part the dean played in this little mystery. He had to step tentatively here.

266

The dean coughed into his fist. Not a real cough or throat-clear. Just something to stall, give him a chance to think. Finally he said, 'Please come in.'

He disappeared back into his office. No sucking vacuum this time, but Myron still followed. They passed a few chairs in the waiting room, a secretary's desk. The typewriter was hidden by a khaki-colored dust cover. Camouflaged in the event of war.

Dean Gordon's office was cookie-cut university executive. Lots of wood. Diplomas. Old sketches of the Reston University chapel. Lucite blocks with clippings or awards on the desk. Bookshelves with all nonfiction titles. The books hadn't been touched. They were props, creating the mood of tradition, professionalism, competence. The prerequisite picture of the family. Madelaine and a girl who looked about twelve or thirteen years old. Myron picked up the photograph.

'Nice family,' he said. Nice wife.

'Thank you. Please have a seat.'

Myron sat. 'Say, where did Kathy work?'

The dean stopped in midseat. 'Pardon me?'

'Where was her desk?'

'Whose?'

'Kathy Culver's.'

Dean Gordon lowered himself the rest of the way, slowly, as into a hot tub of water. 'She shared a desk with another student in the room next door.'

Myron said, 'Convenient.'

Dean Gordon's eyebrows frowned. 'I'm sorry. I missed your name.'

'Deluise. Dom Deluise.'

The dean allowed himself a small brittle smile. He looked tight enough to pop a wine cork with his butt.

No doubt being sent the magazine had put the screws in. No doubt Jake's visit yesterday had tightened them a little. 'What, Mr Deluise, can I do for you?'

'I think you know.' Again the knowing smile. Combined with the honest blue eyes. If Dean Gordon were female, he'd be naked by now.

'I'm afraid I don't have the slightest idea,' the dean said.

Myron continued the knowing smile. He felt like an idiot or a morning network weatherman, if there was a difference. This was an old trick he was trying. Pretend you know more than you do. Get him talking. Play it by ear. Impromptu.

The dean folded his hands and put them on his desk. Trying to look as if he were in control. 'This whole conversation is very strange. Perhaps you could explain why you're here.'

'I thought we should chat.'

'About?'

'Your English department, for starters. Do you still make students read *Beowulf*?'

'Please, whatever your name is, I don't have time for games.'

'Neither do I.' Myron took out his copy of *Nips* and tossed it on the desk. The magazine was starting to look creased and worn from all the handling, as if it belonged to a hormonal adolescent.

The dean barely glanced at it. 'What is this?'

'Now who's playing games?'

Dean Gordon leaned back, his fingers fiddling with his chin. 'Who are you?' he asked. 'Really.'

'It's not important. I am merely a messenger.'

'Messenger for who?'

'For *whom*,' Myron corrected. 'Prepositional phrase. And you a college dean.'

'I don't need any smart talk, young man.'

Myron looked at him. 'Get real.'

The dean sucked in air as if he were about to plunge underwater. 'What do you want?'

'Isn't the pleasure of your company enough?'

'This is not a joking matter.'

'No, it's not.'

'So kindly stop playing games. What do you want with me?'

Myron tried the knowing smile again. Dean Gordon looked puzzled for a brief moment but then returned the smile. It too was knowing.

'Or should I say,' the dean added, 'how much?'

He seemed more in control now. He had dealt with the blow and was carrying on. A problem had arisen. But there was a solution. There always was in his world.

Money.

He took out a checkbook from his top drawer. 'Well?'

'Not that simple,' Myron said.

'What do you mean?'

'Don't you think someone should pay?'

He shrugged. 'Let's talk figures.'

'Don't you think this is worth something more than just money?'

He looked bewildered, as though Myron had just denied the existence of gravity. 'I don't understand what you mean.'

'What about justice?' Myron asked. 'Kathy is owed. Big-time.'

'I agree. And I am willing to pay. But what good is

revenge going to do her now? You are the messenger, are you not?'

'I am.'

'Then go back and tell Kathy to take the money.'

Myron's heart collapsed. This man, a man who was clearly involved in what had happened that night, believed Myron was a messenger for a living, breathing Kathy Culver. Tread gently, fair Myron. Ever gently.

But how to play this . . .

'Kathy is not happy with you,' he tried.

'I meant her no harm.'

Myron put his hand on his chest and lifted his head dramatically. 'Be thy intents wicked or charitable, thou com'st in such a questionable shape.'

'What's that supposed to mean?'

Myron shrugged. 'I like to work Shakespeare into conversations. Makes me sound smart, don't you think?'

The dean made a face. 'Can we return to the matter at hand?'

'Sure.'

'You say Kathy does not want money.'

'Yup.'

'What then does she want?'

Good question. 'She wants the truth to come out.' Noncommittal, vague, open-ended.

'What truth?'

'Stop playing dumb,' Myron snapped, feigning annoyance. 'You weren't about to write a check to her favorite charity, were you?'

'But I didn't do anything,' he half-whined. 'Kathy took off that night. I haven't seen her since. How was I supposed to know what to think or do?'

Myron gave him a skeptical look. He did that because

he had no idea what else to do. He was now playing Jake's game, the keep-silent-and-hope-he-ties-his-own-noose game. This worked especially well with political types. They're born with a defective chromosome that will not allow for prolonged silence.

'She has to understand,' he continued. 'I did my best. She disappeared. What was I supposed to do? Go to the police? Was that what she wanted? I didn't know any-more. I was thinking of her. She might have changed her mind. I didn't know. I was trying to consider her interests.'

The skeptical look came easier after that last sentence. Myron only wished he knew what the hell the dean was talking about. They sat there staring at one another. Then something happened to Dean Gordon's face. Myron wasn't sure exactly what it was, but his whole demeanor seemed to slump. His eyes grew twisted, pained. He shook his head.

'Enough,' he said in a quiet voice.

'What's enough?'

He closed the checkbook. 'I won't pay,' he said. 'Tell Kathy I'll do whatever she wants. I'll stand by her no matter what the cost. This has gone on long enough. I can't live like this. I am not an evil man. She's a sick girl. She needs help. I want to help.'

Myron had not expected this. 'Do you mean that?'

'Yes. Very much.'

'You want to help your former lover?'

His head shot up. 'What did you say?'

Myron had been skating blindly on thin ice. His last comment, it seemed, had been something of a blowtorch.

'Did you say "lover"?'

Uh-oh.

271

'Kathy didn't send you,' he continued. 'She has nothing to do with you, does she?'

Myron said nothing.

'Who are you? What is your real name?'

'Myron Bolitar.'

'Who?'

'Myron Bolitar.'

'Are you a police officer?'

'No.'

'Then what exactly are you?'

'A sports agent.'

'A what?'

'I represent athletes.'

'You – So what do you have to do with this?'

'I'm a friend,' Myron said. 'I'm trying to find Kathy.'

'Is she alive?'

'I don't know. But you seem to think so.'

Dean Gordon opened his bottom drawer, took out a cigarette, lit it.

'Bad for you,' Myron said.

'I quit smoking five years ago. Or so everyone thinks.'

'Another little secret?'

He smiled without humor. 'So you were the one who sent me the magazine.'

Myron shook his head. 'Nope.'

'Then who?'

'I don't know. I'm trying to figure that out. But I know about it. And now I also know you're hiding something about Kathy's disappearance.'

He inhaled deeply and let loose a long stream of smoke. 'I could deny it. I could deny everything we said here today.'

'You could,' Myron countered. 'But of course I have

the magazine. I have no reason to lie. And I also have a friend in Sheriff Jake Courter. But you're right. In the end it would be my word against yours.'

Dean Gordon took off his glasses and rubbed his eyes. 'No,' he said slowly, 'it won't come down to that. I meant what I said before. I want to help her. I *need* to help her.'

Myron was not sure what to think. The man looked in genuine pain, but Myron had seen performances that would put Olivier to shame. Was his guilt real? Was his sudden catharsis the result of having a conscience, or was it self-preservation? Myron didn't know. He didn't much care either, as long as he got to the truth.

'When was the last time you saw Kathy?' Myron asked.

'The night she vanished,' he said.

'She came to your house?'

He nodded. 'It was late. I guess around eleven, eleven-thirty. I was in my study. My wife was upstairs in bed. The doorbell rang. Not once. Repeatedly, urgently. Interspersed with heavy door-pounding. It was Kathy.'

His voice was on autopilot, as if he were reading a fairy tale to a child. 'She was crying. Or rather she was sobbing uncontrollably. So much so that she couldn't speak. I brought her into my study. I poured her some brandy and wrapped an afghan around her shoulders. She looked' – he stopped, considered – 'very small. Helpless. I sat down across from her and took her hand. She jerked it back. That was when the tears stopped. Not slowly, but all at once, as though a switch had been thrown. She became very still. Her face was completely blank, no emotion whatsoever. Then she started talking.'

He reached into the drawer for another cigarette. He put it in his mouth. The match lit on the fourth try.

'She started from the beginning,' he continued. 'Her

voice was remarkably steady. It never cracked or wavered – uncanny, when you consider the fact that she was hysterical just moments earlier. But her words belied her placid tone. She told me stories—' He stopped again, shook his head. 'They were surprising, to say the least. I had known Kathy for almost a year. I considered her a thoughtful, sweet, proper young woman. I am not making moral judgments here. But she had always been what I considered old-fashioned. And here she was telling me stories that would make a sailor blush.

'She started by telling me that she used to be everything I always thought she was. The girl next door. Everyone's favorite. But then she changed. She became, in her own words, "a free-wheeling slut." She started with some boys in her high school class. But she quickly moved onto bigger things. Adults, teachers, friends of her parents. Biracial, homosexual, two-on-ones, even orgies. She took pictures of her encounters. For posterity, she said with a sneer.'

'Did she mention any names?' Myron asked. 'Of the teachers or adults or anyone?'

'No. No names.'

They fell into silence. Dean Gordon looked exhausted.

'What happened next?' Myron prompted.

He lifted his head slowly, as though it took great effort. 'Her story began to change direction,' he said. 'For the better. She said she realized that what she was doing was wrong and stupid. She began, she said, to work through her problems. That was when she met Christian and fell in love. She wanted to put it all behind her, but it wasn't easy. The past wouldn't just go away. She tried and tried, and then . . .' His voice trailed off.

'And then?' Myron prompted.

'Then Kathy just looked at me – I'll never forget this – and she said, "I was raped tonight." Just like that. Out of nowhere. I was stunned, of course. There were six of them, she said. Or seven, she wasn't sure. A gang-rape in the locker room. I asked her when. She told me it had started less than an hour ago. She had gone to the locker room to meet someone. A blackmailer, she said. A former, uh, suitor, who had threatened to reveal her past. She was going to pay for his silence.'

The big cash withdrawal from her trust account, Myron thought.

'But when she got to the locker room, the blackmailer wasn't alone. Several of his teammates were with him, including another past suitor. They didn't hit her, she said. They didn't beat her. And she didn't fight. There were too many of them, and they were too strong.' He closed his eyes, his voice a whisper. 'They took turns with her.'

Silence.

'As I said before, Kathy told me all this in the most dispassionate tone I had ever heard her use. Her eyes were clear, determined. She told me there was only one way to bury her past. Once and for all. She would have to confront it head-on. She'd have to push it out into the bright sunshine where it would wither and die like a medieval vampire. She said she knew what she had to do.'

More silence.

'What?' Myron asked.

'Prosecute the boys who raped her. Face up to her past and then put it behind her. Otherwise it would follow her around for the rest of her life.'

'What did you say?'

Dean Gordon winced at the question. He stamped out

the cigarette. He glanced down at the bottom drawer but didn't reach for another. 'I told her to calm down.' He laughed at the memory. 'Calm down. By now, the girl was so unemotional, so detached, that she could have been reading a telephone directory. And I told her to calm down. Jesus.'

'What else?'

'I told her that I thought she was still in shock. I meant that too. I told her that she should consider everything, weigh all her options, not rush into a decision that would undoubtably affect the rest of her life. I told her to think about what it would mean to have her past dragged out – to her family, to her friends, to her fiancé, to herself.'

'In other words,' Myron said, 'you tried to talk her out of pressing charges.'

'Perhaps. But I never said what I was really thinking: A self-described free-wheeling slut who had gotten involved in pornography and wild sex was going to claim she was raped by a group of college boys, two of whom she admitted having past liaisons with. I wanted her to think about all that before she did something rash.'

'Don't be so easy on yourself,' Myron said. 'You didn't give a damn about her. She came to you for help, and you thought about everything but her. You thought about your precious institution. You thought about the scandal. You thought about the football team on the eve of a national championship. You thought about your own career, how it would come out that she worked for you, how she felt comfortable visiting your house late at night. You'd be tied in. People would investigate you closer, maybe unearth your unusual marital arrangement.'

That prodded him upright. 'What about my marital arrangement?'

'Does the phrase "once every two months" mean anything to you?'

His mouth dropped open. 'How . . . ?' He stopped, almost smiled. 'You are a very well-informed young man.'

'All-knowing,' Myron corrected. 'Godlike.'

'I won't comment on my marriage, but I would be less than honest if I did not admit that those selfish considerations crossed my mind. But I was also concerned for Kathy. A mistake like this—'

'A rape, Dean. Not a mistake. Kathy was raped. She didn't make a "mistake." She wasn't the victim of an indiscretion. A bunch of football players pinned her down in a locker room and took turns with her against her will.'

'You're simplifying the situation.'

'You're the one who simplified the situation. You just put Kathy last.'

'That's not true.'

Myron shook his head. No time for this now. 'So what happened after you bestowed your stellar counsel upon Kathy?'

He tried to shrug but couldn't pull it off. 'She looked at me funny, as though I had betrayed her when all I was trying to do was help. Or maybe she saw in my words the same thing you did. I don't know. She stood up then and said that she would be back tomorrow morning to press charges. Then she left. I never heard from her again until that magazine came in the mail. And the phone call a few nights ago.'

'What phone call?'

'A few nights ago, very late, I got a phone call. A female voice – maybe Kathy's, maybe not – said, "Enjoy the magazine. Come and get me. I survived."'

277

' "Come and get me. I survived"?'

'Something like that, yes.'

'What did she mean?'

'I haven't the slightest idea.'

'What did you think when you first heard about Kathy's disappearance?'

'That she ran away. Decided it was all too much. I thought she'd come back when she was ready. The police thought that too, until they found her undergarments. Then they suspected violence. But I knew the undergarments were probably from the rape, not the disappearance. So in my mind I still considered her a runaway.'

'Didn't the possibility that the rapists wanted to silence her cross your mind?'

'It crossed my mind, yes. But these boys weren't capable of—'

'Rapists,' Myron corrected. ' "Boys" who gangraped a young girl who never did them any harm. You didn't think they had the capability to commit murder?'

'If they wanted her dead, they would never have let her go,' the dean countered steadily. 'That's what I thought.'

'So you kept your mouth shut.'

He nodded. 'That was a mistake. I know that now. I was hoping she had just run away for a few days to straighten herself out. When a week passed, I realized it was too late to say anything.'

'You chose to live with the lie.'

'Yes.'

'She was just a student, after all. She came to you for help during the hardest time of her life. And you turned her away.'

'Don't you think I know that?' he shouted. 'Don't you

278

think this has been tearing me apart for the past year and a half?'

'Yeah, you're a real humanitarian.'

'What the hell do you want from me, Bolitar?'

Myron stood. 'Resign. Immediately.'

'And if I refuse?'

'Then I'll drag you down, and it'll be uglier than you ever imagined. First thing tomorrow morning. Turn in your letter of resignation.'

He looked up, his fingers supporting his chin. Time passed. His face began to soften as though from a masseur's touch. His eyes closed, and his shoulders slumped. Then he nodded slowly. 'All right,' he said. 'Thank you.'

'This isn't penitence. You don't get off that easy.'

'I understand.'

'One last thing: Did Kathy mention any names at all?'

'Names?'

'Of the rapists?'

He hesitated. 'No.'

'But you have a guess?'

'It's not based on anything concrete.'

'Go on.'

'A few days after she disappeared, I noticed a certain student was tossing around a lot of money. A trouble-maker. He bought a new BMW convertible that came to my attention because he drove it across the commons. Ripped up a lot of grass.'

'Who?'

'An ex-football player. He was kicked off the team for selling drugs. His name was Junior Horton. They call him—'

'Horty.'

Myron left without another word, hurrying to get out

of the building. It was a beautiful day. Warm but not humid, the sun weakening in the late afternoon but not quite ready to set. The air smelled of freshly cut grass and blooming cherry blossom trees. Myron wanted to spread out a blanket. He wanted to lie down and think about Kathy Culver.

No time.

The phone in his Ford Taurus was ringing when he unlocked the door. It was Esperanza.

'Dead end with Lucy,' she said. 'Adam Culver wasn't the guy who bought the pictures.'

Another theory blown to hell. He was about to start his car when he heard Jake Courter's voice.

'Thought I might find you here.'

Myron looked out the open window. 'What's up, Jake?'

'We're about to release Nancy Serat's name to the press.'

Myron nodded. 'Thanks for letting me know.'

'That's not why I'm here.'

Myron did not like his tone.

'We also have a suspect,' Jake continued. 'We've brought him in for questioning.'

'Who?'

'Your client,' Jake said. 'Christian Steele.'

Chapter 34

'What about Christian?' Myron asked.

'Nancy Serat had just rented that house a week ago,' Jake replied, 'a day or two before she left for Cancún. She hadn't even unpacked yet.'

'So?'

'So how come Christian Steele's fingerprints – clean, fresh prints – are all over the place? On the front door-knob. On a drinking glass. On the fireplace mantel.'

Myron tried not to looked stunned. 'Come on, Jake. You can't make an arrest on something like that. The press will eat him alive.'

'Like I give a flying shit.'

'You have nothing.'

'We can place him at the scene.'

'So what? You can place Jessica at the scene. Gonna arrest her too?'

Jake unbuttoned his jacket, allowing his belly to expand. He was wearing a brown suit, circa 1972. In a word:

lapels. No slave to fashion, that Jake. 'Okay, smart-boy,' he said, 'you want to tell me what your client was doing at Nancy Serat's house?'

'We'll ask him. He'll talk to you. Christian's a good kid, Jake. Don't ruin him on speculation.'

'Yeah. I'd hate to ruin your commissions.'

'Low blow, Jake.'

'You're not objective, Bolitar. The kid's your most valuable client, your ticket to the bigs. You don't want him to be guilty.'

Myron looked at him but said nothing.

'Leave your car here,' Jake said. 'I'll drive you to the station.'

It was only a mile away. When they pulled into the lot, Jake said, 'The new DA is here. Young hotshot named Roland.'

Uh-oh. 'Cary Roland?' Myron asked. 'Curly hair?'

'You know him?'

'Yeah.'

'He's a publicity hound,' Jake said. 'Gets a hard-on watching himself on TV. He practically creamed when he heard Christian's name.'

Myron could imagine. Old buddies, he and Cary Roland. This was not a good development. 'Has he released Christian's name?'

'Not yet,' Jake said. 'Cary decided to put it off until eleven. Gets a live feed from all the networks that way.'

'And plenty of time to tighten the perm.'

'That too.'

Christian was sitting in a small room, no bigger than eight by eight. He sat in a chair behind a desk. No hot lights. No one else was in the room.

'Where's Roland?' Myron asked.

'Behind the mirror.'

One-way glass, even in a rinky-dink station like this. Myron stepped into the room, looked in the mirror, adjusted his tie, and refrained from giving Roland the finger. Mr Mature strikes again.

'Mr Bolitar?'

Myron turned. Christian waved to him as if he'd spotted a familiar face in the stands.

'You okay?' Myron asked.

'I'm fine,' Christian said. 'I just don't understand what I'm doing here.'

A uniformed officer came in with a tape recorder. Myron turned to Jake. 'Is he under arrest?'

Jake grinned. 'I almost forgot, Bolitar. You're a lawyer too. Nice to be dealing with a professional.'

'Is he under arrest?' Myron repeated.

'Not yet. We'd just like to ask him a few questions.'

The uniformed officer took care of the preliminaries. Then Jake started.

'My name is Sheriff Jake Courter, Mr Steele. Do you remember me?'

'Yes, sir. You're handling my fiancée's disappearance.'

'That's correct. Now, Mr Steele, do you know a woman named Nancy Serat?'

'She was Kathy's roommate at Reston.'

'Are you aware that Nancy Serat was murdered last night?'

Christian's eyes widened. He turned to Myron. Myron nodded. 'My God . . . no.'

'Were you friends with Nancy Serat?'

His voice was hollow. 'Yes, sir.'

'Mr Steele, can you tell us where you were last night?'

Myron interrupted. 'What time last night?'

'From the time he left practice till he went to sleep.'

Myron hesitated. This was a trap. He could try to defuse it, or he could let Christian handle it on his own. Under most circumstances Myron would have stepped in and sounded a subtle warning of what the wrong answer might mean. But this time he sat back and watched.

'If you want to know if I was with Nancy Serat last night,' Christian said slowly, 'the answer is yes.'

Myron breathed again. He looked back at the one-way mirror and stuck out his tongue. The demise of Mr Mature.

'What time was that?' Jake asked.

'Around nine o'clock.'

'Where did you see her?'

'At her house.'

'The one at 118 Acre Street?'

'Yes, sir.'

'What was the purpose of your visit?'

'Nancy returned from a trip that morning. She called and said she needed to talk to me.'

'Did she tell you why?'

'She said it had something to do with Kathy. She wouldn't tell me anything else over the phone.'

'What happened when you arrived at the house at 118 Acre Street?'

'Nancy practically shoved me out the door. She said I had to leave right away.'

'Did she say why?'

'No, sir. I asked Nancy what was going on, but she was insistent. She promised to call me in a day or two and tell me everything, but for now I had to go.'

'What did you do?'

'I argued with her for a minute or two. She started

getting upset and saying stuff that made no sense. I finally just gave up and left.'

'What sort of "stuff" was she saying?'

'Something about sisters reuniting.'

Myron sat up.

Jake asked, 'What about sisters reuniting?'

'I don't remember exactly. Something like "Time for sisters to reunite." She really wasn't making much sense, sir.'

Jake looked at Myron. Myron looked back.

'Do you remember anything else she said?'

'No, sir.'

'Did you go straight home after that?'

'Yes, sir.'

'What time did you arrive home?'

'Ten-fifteen, I guess. Maybe a little later.'

'Is there anybody who can confirm the time?'

'I don't think so. I just moved into a condominium in Englewood. Maybe a neighbor saw me, I don't know.'

'Would you mind waiting here for a minute?'

Jake signaled for Myron to follow him. Myron nodded, leaned over to Christian. 'Don't say another word until I get back.'

Christian nodded.

They stepped into the other room. The other side of the mirror, so to speak. County District Attorney Cary Roland had gone to Harvard Law School with Myron. A bright guy. Law review. Clerk for a Supreme Court justice. Cary Roland had first shown signs of political ambition while exiting his mother's womb.

He looked the same. Gray suit with vest (yes, he'd worn suits to class). Hook nose. Small, dark eyes. Loose curly hair, like a seventies Peter Frampton's, only shorter.

Roland shook his head. Then he made a noise of disgusted belief. 'Creative client, Bolitar.'

'Not as creative,' Myron said, 'as your barber.'

Jake held back a laugh.

'I say we book him,' Roland continued. 'We'll announce it at the press conference.'

'Now I see it,' Myron said.

'See what?'

'The hard-on. When you said "press."'

Snickers.

Roland fumed. 'Still a comedian, eh, Bolitar? Well, your client is about to go down.'

'I don't think so, Gary.'

'I don't care what you think.'

Myron sighed. 'Christian gave you a reasonable explanation for being at Nancy Serat's house. You got nothing else, ergo you got nothing. Besides, imagine the headlines if Christian's innocent. Young DA Makes Major Blunder. Tarnishes Name of Local Hero for Own Gain. Hurts Titans' Chances for Superbowl. Becomes Most Hated Man in State.'

Roland swallowed. He hadn't considered that. Blinded by the lights. The TV lights. 'Sheriff Courter, what do you think?'

Backpedal time.

'We have no choice,' Jake said. 'We have to let him go.'

'Do you believe his story?'

Jake shrugged. 'Who the hell knows? But we don't have enough to keep him.'

'Okay,' Roland said with a weighty nod. Important man. 'He's free to go. But he better not leave town.'

Myron looked at Jake. 'Not leave town?' He laughed. Hard. 'Did he just say not to leave town?'

286

Jake was trying to hold it in. But his lip was quivering pretty good.

Roland's face turned red. 'Infantile,' he spat out. 'Sheriff, I want daily updates on this case.'

'Yes, sir.'

Roland gave everyone his most frightening glare. No one fell to their knees. He stormed out.

'Must be nonstop laughs,' Myron said, 'working with him.'

'Gobs of fun.'

'Can Christian and I go now?'

Jake shook his head. 'Not until I hear all about your visit with Dean Gordon.'

Chapter 35

Myron filled Jake in. Then he drove Christian home. On the way he filled Christian in too. On everything. Christian wanted to know. Myron wanted to spare him, but he knew he didn't have the right to keep things from him.

Christian did not interrupt with questions. In fact, he said nothing. On the field he was famous for his composure under any situation. Right now, Christian had on his best game face.

When Myron finished, neither spoke for several minutes. Then Myron said, 'Are you okay?'

Christian nodded. His face was pale. 'Thank you for being up-front with me,' he said.

'Kathy loved you,' Myron said. 'Very much. Don't forget that.'

He nodded again. 'We have to find her.'

'I'm trying.'

Christian shifted in the car seat so he could face Myron. 'When I was being wooed by all these big agencies, the whole process felt – I don't know – so impersonal. It was all about money. Still is, I know that. I'm not being naïve here, but you were different. I instinctively knew I could trust you. I guess what I'm trying to say is, you've become more than just an agent to me. I'm glad I chose you.'

'Me too,' Myron said. 'This might not the best time to ask, but how did you hear about me in the first place?'

'Someone gave you a glowing recommendation.'

'Who?'

Christian smiled. 'You don't know?'

'A client?'

'No.'

Myron shook his head. 'I have no idea.'

Christian settled back in his seat. 'Jessica,' he said. 'She told me your life history. About your playing days, your injury, what you went through, how you worked for the FBI, how you went back to school. She said you were the best person she knew.'

'Jessica doesn't get out much.'

They fell back into silence. The New Jersey Turnpike had a center-lane closure, slowing them down to a crawl. Should have taken the western spur. Myron was about to change lanes when Christian said something that almost made him slam on the brakes.

'My mother once posed in the nude.'

Myron thought he'd heard wrong. 'What?'

'When I was a little kid. I don't know if they were ever printed in a magazine or anything. I doubt it. She wasn't very attractive by then. She was twenty-five but looked sixty. She worked as a prostitute in New York. On the streets. I don't know who my father was. She figured he was one of the guys at a bachelor party, but she had no idea which one.'

289

Myron sneaked a glance at him. Christian stared straight ahead. The game face was still on.

'I thought your mother and father raised you in Kansas,' Myron said carefully.

Christian shook his head. 'Those were my grand-parents. My mom died when I was seven. They legally adopted me. We had the same last name, so I just pre-tended they were my real parents.'

Myron said, 'I didn't know. I'm sorry.'

'Don't be. They were wonderful parents. I guess they made a lot of mistakes with my mom, the way she ended up and all. But they were kind and loving to me. I miss them a lot.'

The silence was heavier now. They drove past the Meadowlands. Myron paid the toll at the end of the turnpike and followed the signs to the George Washing-ton Bridge. Christian had bought a place two miles before the bridge, six miles from Titans Stadium. A set of three hundred prefab condos loftily labeled Cross Creek Pointe, one of those New Jersey housing developments that looked like something out of *Poltergeist*.

As they cruised to a stop, the car phone rang. Myron picked it up.

'Hello?'

'Where are you?'

It was Jessica.

'In Englewood.'

'Take Route four west to seventeen north,' she said quickly. 'I'll meet you in the Pathmark parking lot in Ramsey.'

'What's going on?'

'Just meet me there. Now.'

Chapter 36

The moment Myron saw Jessica standing in the dusky glow of the Pathmark fluorescent parking lights, looking achingly beautiful in a pair of hip-hugging blue jeans and a red blouse open at the throat, he knew there was trouble. Big trouble.

'Very bad?' he asked her.

She opened the car door and slid in next to him. 'Worse.'

He couldn't help it. He couldn't stop thinking of how beautiful she was. She looked a little pale, her eyes a bit too sunken. She did not have crow's-feet quite yet, but new lines had etched their way into her face. Had they been there yesterday or the day she visited his office? He wasn't sure. But he thought she had never looked so devastating. The imperfections, if you wanted to call them that, just made her more real and hence more desirable. Myron had thought Dean-nessa Madelaine was attractive, but she was nary a penlight next to Jessica's blinding beacon.

'Want to tell me about it?'

She shook her head. 'I'd rather just show you.' She started giving directions. When they reached a road appropriately called Red Dirt Path, she said, 'My father rented a cabin out here.'

'In these woods?'

'Yes.'

'When?'

'Two weeks ago. He had it for the month. According to the realtor, he wanted some peace and quiet. A place to get away from it all.'

'Doesn't sound much like your father,' Myron said.

'Not like him at all,' she agreed.

A few minutes later, they arrived at the cabin. Myron had a hard time believing that Adam Culver, a man he had gotten to know fairly well during his time with Jessica, would want to vacation out here. The man liked to gamble. He liked the ponies, the roulette wheel, the blackjack table. He liked action. His idea of a quiet time was a Tony Bennett concert at the Sands.

Jessica got out of the car. Myron followed. Her posture was arrow-perfect. So was the walk, something Myron had always loved to watch in the past. But there was an unmistakable teeter in her step, as though her legs were not sure they could sustain the lovely torso over the long haul.

Their footsteps creaked on the steps of the wooden porch. Myron spotted plenty of dry rot. Jessica unlocked the front door and pushed it open.

'Take a look,' she said.

He did. He said nothing. He could feel her eyes on him. 'I checked his charge card,' she said. 'He spent over three thousand dollars at a place in the city called Eye-Spy.'

Myron knew the store. This was definitely their handi-work. Three videocameras were sprawled across the couch. Panasonic. All with mounting material, so they could be hung up somewhere. There were also three small television monitors. Also Panasonic. The kind you might see at a high-rise's security station. Two VCRs. Toshiba. Lots of cables and wires and stuff like that.

But that stuff wasn't the most bothersome thing he saw. Alone, those electronic goods could have meant one of several things. But two other items – items that drew Myron's eye and held it like a baby near a shiny coin – changed everything. They were the added catalyst. They completed a mixture that was far too noxious to be ignored.

Propped against the wall was a rifle. And on the floor next to it, a set of handcuffs.

Jessica said, 'What the hell was he doing?'

He knew what she was thinking. The dead girls found near here. The television images of their battered, decayed bodies hovered above them like the most haunting of ghosts.

'When did he buy this stuff?' Myron asked.

'Two weeks ago.' Her eyes were clear, controlled. 'Listen, I've had time to think about this. Even if our worst fears are true, it doesn't explain anything. What about the picture in the magazine? Or Kathy's hand-writing on that envelope? Or the phone calls? Or for that matter his murder?'

Myron looked at her. He knew she was seeking an explanation – any explanation but the one that stared them straight in the face. 'Are you okay?' he asked.

She crossed her arms under her breasts, a hand on each elbow, as if she were hugging herself. 'I feel,' she said, 'unanchored.'

'Can you take more?'

Her hands dropped to her sides. 'Why? What is it?'

He hesitated.

She exploded. 'Goddamn it, don't coddle me!'

'Jess—'

'You know I hate that protect-the-little-lady bullshit of yours! Tell me what the hell is going on!'

'Kathy was gang-raped by some of Christian's teammates on the night she disappeared.'

Jessica looked as if she'd just been slapped with an open hand. Myron reached out. 'I'm sorry,' he said.

'Just tell me what happened. Everything.'

He did. Her clear, controlled eyes went blank, lifeless. She remained uncharacteristically silent.

'Bastards,' she managed. 'The goddamn bastards.'

He nodded.

'One of them killed her,' she said. 'Or all of them. To shut her up.'

'It's possible.'

She paused, thinking. Then the eyes came back to life. 'Suppose,' she began slowly, 'that my father learned about the rape.'

Myron nodded.

'What would he do?' she continued. 'How would you react – if it was your daughter?'

'I'd be enraged,' Myron replied.

'Would you be able to control yourself?'

'Kathy is not my daughter,' he said. 'And I'm still not sure I can control myself.'

Jessica nodded. 'So maybe, just maybe, that explains

this whole setup. The electronics, the cuffs, the rifle. Maybe he was using this hideaway, deep in the woods, so he could grab a rapist and exact a little private justice.'

'Kathy was gang-raped. There were six of them. This place looks built for one.'

'But,' she continued with the hint of an eerie smile, 'suppose my father was in the exact same position we are in now.'

'I don't follow.'

'Suppose he knew the name of only one rapist. Maybe this Horton guy. What might he do then? What might *you* do then?'

'I might,' Myron said, 'kidnap him and make him tell.'

'Exactly.'

'But it's a hell of a reach. Why would I videotape it? Why would I need cameras and monitors?'

'Tape the confession, make sure no one comes down the road, I don't know. You have a better scenario?'

He did not. 'Have you gone through the rest of the house yet?'

'I didn't have a chance. The realtor brought me here. He practically burst a blood vessel when he saw this stuff.'

'What did you tell him?'

'That I knew all this was here. That my father was a private investigator working undercover.'

Myron made a face.

'Hey, it was the best I could come up with.'

'And he bought that?'

'I think so.'

Myron shook his head. 'I thought you were a writer.'

'I'm not good with spur-of-the-moment. I'm a lot better with the written than the oral.'

'Based on past experience,' he said, 'I'd have to disagree.'

'Nice time,' she said, 'for a come-on.'

He shrugged. 'Just trying to keep things loose.'

She almost smiled.

'Let's look around,' he said.

There wasn't much to search. The living room had no drawers or closets. Everything was in plain view – the electronic equipment, the handcuffs, the rifle. The kitchenette held no surprises. Same with the bathroom. That left the bedroom.

It was small. The size of a guest bedroom at a beach house. The double bed took up almost the entire room. There were reading lights on either side of the bed, attached to the wall because there was no room for night tables. No dressers either. The bed was made with flannel sheets. They checked the closet.

Bingo.

Black pants, black T-shirt, black sweatshirt. And worst of all, a black ski mask.

'Ski mask in June?' Myron said.

'He might have needed it to kidnap Horton,' she tried. But her tone would not make the leap.

Myron dropped to the floor and looked underneath the bed. He saw a plastic bag. He stretched out his hand, grabbed it, and dragged it along the dust-blanketed floor toward him. The bag was red. The initials BCME were emblazoned across the front.

'Bergen County Medical Examiner,' Jessica explained.

It looked like one of those old Lord and Taylor's bags, the kind that snapped closed on the top. Myron pulled it back. The bag opened with a pop. He pulled out a pair of gray no-frills sweat pants with a drawstring. Then he reached back in and withdrew a yellow pullover with the letter T in red. Both were covered with caked-on dirt.

'Recognize these?' he asked.

'Just the yellow sweater,' she said. 'It's my dad's old varsity sweater from Tarlow High School.'

'Funny thing to hide under a bed up here.'

Jessica's eyes lit up. 'Nancy's message! Jesus Christ, she said my dad told her all about Kathy's yellow sweater.'

'Whoa, slow down a second. What did Nancy say exactly?'

'She said – and I quote verbatim – "He told me all about that favorite yellow sweater he gave Kathy. Such a sweet story." Those were her exact words. My father never wore it. Kathy did. Like a nightshirt or kick-around-the-house shirt.'

'Did your dad give it to her?'

'Yes.'

'So how did he get it back?'

'I don't know. I imagine it was in her personal belongings at school.'

'Which doesn't explain why he asked Nancy Serat about it. Or why it's hidden under his bed.'

They stood in silence.

'We're missing something here,' she said.

'Maybe your father saw something in these clothes we can't see yet.'

'What do you mean?'

'I don't know,' Myron admitted. 'But these clothes were clearly significant to him. Maybe he found them somewhere unusual. Or maybe the police found them.'

'But Kathy was wearing blue the night she left. That's been established.'

Myron remembered the testimony of the sorority sisters and the photograph. But then again . . .

'One way to check on that.'

'How?'

He ran out to the car. Darkness had finally laid claim on the long summer day. He turned on the phone, hoping they weren't too far out of a calling area. Three of those little bars lit up. Enough for the phone to work. He tried Dean Gordon's office. It rang twenty times. No answer. He tried the dean's house. It was picked up on the third ring.

Dean Gordon said, 'Hello?'

'What was Kathy wearing when she came to your house?' No need for identification or pleasantries.

'Wearing? A blouse and skirt of some kind.'

'What color?'

'Blue. I think the blouse was ripped a bit.'

Myron hung up.

Jessica said, 'Back to square one.'

Maybe, Myron thought. But the flash of an image seared across his mind. He couldn't grasp it, couldn't even make out what it was exactly. But it had been there, and it would come back.

'Let's go,' she said softly, taking his hand. The car light provided enough illumination to see the look in her eyes. They were beautiful eyes, so light colored they were almost yellow. 'I want to get away from here.'

He closed the car door, feeling suddenly choked up. The car light went out, basking them in darkness. He couldn't see her face anymore. 'Where do you want to go?'

From the darkness he heard her voice. 'Someplace,' she said, 'where we can be alone.'

Chapter 37

They found a high-rise Hilton in Mahwah.

Myron checked them in to the best available suite. Jessica stood next to him. The hotel concierge swung his line of vision from Myron to Jessica, eyeing her lustily and Myron jealously. A formal affair was in full swing in the lobby. Men in tuxes, women in long gowns. But every man stared agog at Jessica, who was dressed in jeans and a button-down red blouse.

Myron was used to it. When they were first together, he had taken an almost perverse pleasure in seeing men stare, the familiar you-look-but-I-touch-ha-ha school of macho sneering. But then he started seeing things in the looks that weren't there, and the even more familiar male insecurity burrowed through his rationality.

Jessica was practiced at this. She knew how to ignore the looks without looking cold, bothered, or interested.

Their room was on the sixth floor. They had barely closed the door when they kissed. Jessica's tongue circled and gently darted, making his whole body spasm helplessly. He began to unbutton her blouse. His mouth went dry. He actually gasped when he saw her again. Breathlessness made him heady. He cupped a warm breast, feeling the delicious weight in his hand. She moaned into his mouth.

They moved to the bed.

Their lovemaking had always been intense, all-consuming, but this was somehow more animalistic, needier, and yet more tender.

Later, much later, Jessica sat up, kissed him gently on the cheek. 'That,' she said, 'was awesome.'

Myron shrugged. 'Not bad.'

'Not bad?'

'For me. For you it was awesome.'

She swung her legs out of bed and slipped into a hotel robe. 'I did enjoy myself,' she said.

'Sounded like it.'

'I was a tad noisy, huh?'

'The Who in concert is a tad noisy. You were loud.'

She stood above the bed, smiling. The robe was tied loosely, showing plenty of cleavage and legs that were so long, they were almost intimidating. 'I didn't hear you complain.'

'How could you,' Myron said, 'over all your screaming?'

'What time is it?'

'Midnight.' He reached for the phone. 'Hungry?'

She gave him a look he felt in his toes. Well, not exactly his toes. 'Famished,' she said.

'For food, Jess. Food.'

'Oh.'

'Ever learn about the male's "time for recovery" in health class?'

'Must have been absent that day.'

'The three R's. Replenishment, restoration, recuperation.' He looked at the menu. 'Damn.'

'What?'

'No oysters.'

'Myron?'

'Yes.'

'There's a hot tub in the bathroom.'

'Jess . . .'

She looked at him with who-me innocence. 'We can soak until the food comes. Recuperate. One of the three R's.'

'Just soak?'

'Just soak.'

She had said soak. He was sure of it. Soak. Not soap. But that was how it started. She soaped him back to life. Myron tried to fight it, almost afraid of how good it felt. But he couldn't. Jess toyed with him, pushed him to the edge, let him teeter, then pulled him back. Myron was helpless. Words like *heaven*, *ecstasy*, *paradise*, *ambrosia* floated through his mind.

Total surrender.

With a whispered 'Now,' she let him go. His nerve endings surged and sang. The white-hot explosion was so powerful, his ears popped. The bright light hurt his eyes.

'Awesome,' he managed.

She lay back, smiling. 'Not bad.'

There was a knock on the door. Probably room service. Neither one of them moved.

'Why don't you get it,' she said.

'My legs,' he said. 'They can't move. I may never walk again.'

Another knock.

'I'm not dressed,' she said.

'And what am I, ready for a press conference?'

'Bet you'd get good coverage.'

Myron moaned at the joke.

Another knock.

'Come on, Myron. Just throw a towel around your shapely ass and get moving.'

The second woman to mention his ass in the same day. Yowzer. He grabbed the bath towel and headed for the door. Another knock.

'One second.'

He opened the door. It wasn't their food.

'Maid service,' Win said. 'May I turn down your bed?'

'Didn't you see the Do Not Disturb sign?'

Win glanced at the doorknob. 'Sorry. No speaka da English.'

'How the hell did you find us?'

'I traced down your charge card,' he said, as though it were the most natural thing in the world. 'You checked in here at eight twenty-two P.M.' Win leaned his head in the doorway. 'Hello, Jessica.'

From the bathroom. 'Hi, Win.' Myron heard her stepping out of the Jacuzzi. The image of water cascading down her naked body came to him like a deep punch.

'Come on in,' he grumbled.

'Thank you.' Win handed him a manila folder. 'Thought you might want to take a look at this.'

Jessica came in from the bathroom. The robe was tied tighter. She was drying her hair with a towel. 'What's up?' she asked.

302

'The police rap sheet of one Fred Nickler, aka Nick Fredericks,' Win said.

'Imaginative alias,' Myron said.

'For an imaginative fellow.'

Jessica sat on the bed. 'He's the porno publisher, right?'

Myron nodded. The rap sheet was not very long. He started with the most recent dates. Traffic violations, two DWIs, one arrest for mail fraud.

'Nineteen seventy-eight,' Win said.

Myron skipped down. June 30, 1978. Fred Nickler had been arrested for endangering the welfare of a child. Charges dropped.

'So?'

'Mr Nickler was involved in kiddie porn,' Win explained. 'He was only a small-time photographer back then. But he was nabbed with his hand, so to speak, in the cookie jar. More precisely, taking photographs of an eight-year-old boy.'

Jessica said, 'Jesus.'

Myron remembered their meeting. ' "Just an honest guy trying to make an honest buck." '

'Indeed.'

Jessica asked, 'Why were the charges dropped?'

'Ah,' Win said, pointing a finger in the air, 'that's where things get interesting. In many ways it's not an uncommon story. Fred Nickler was only the photographer. A little fish. The authorities wanted the bigger fish. The little fish ratted out the big fish in exchange for leniency.'

'And they dropped the charges completely?' Myron said. 'Not even a misdemeanor?'

'Not even. It seems that Mr Nickler also agreed to help out the police from time to time.'

'So what's the significance?'

'This entire arrangement was negotiated between Nickler and the officer in charge of the investigation,' Win said. He shot a quick glance at Jessica.

'The officer in charge of the investigation was your friend Paul Duncan.'

Chapter 38

'That's our man,' Win said. 'Mr Junior Horton.'

Horty looked like an ex-football player. Big and wide, all veins and bulges. His arms looked like corded wood. He was dressed for a rap video. His button-down St Louis Cardinals baseball shirt was untucked. His baggy shorts reached down past his knees. No socks. Black Reebok high-tops. A Chicago White Sox baseball cap. Dark sunglasses and lots of jewelry.

It was nine in the morning. One Hundred Thirty-second Street in Manhattan. The street was quiet. Horty was making a drug deal. He had been in and out of jail plenty of times, his one long stint of freedom during his time at Reston U. Drugs, mostly. Armed robbery, once. Two sexual assault charges. Twenty-four years old and a complete punk. Like most inmates he had spent his prison time lifting weights. Pumping iron. Our penal institutions develop violent men's physical strength, so when they get out, they'll be able to intimidate and maim with far greater skill. Nice system.

Jessica was not with them. She was packing her father's office – that is, the morgue – and checking for any additional bombshells. Myron had managed to talk her out of confronting Paul Duncan until they knew a little more. She listened grudgingly, but that was how Jessica usually listened anyway.

Horty finished the transaction with a kid who looked no older than twelve, slapped him five, headed west. He wasn't wearing a Walkman, but he walked as though he were. Very jittery. His eyes were red. Every few steps he would snort the air and wipe his nose with the back of his hand.

'Boys and girls, can you say "Cokehead"?'

'Probably has the flu,' Win said.

'The Colombian strain.'

They ducked out of sight as he approached. When Horty reached the lip of the alley, Myron stepped in front of him.

'Junior Horton?'

Horty gave him a scornful street glare. 'Who the fuck wants to know?'

'Snappy comeback,' Myron said.

'Get the fuck out of my way or I kick your ass.' He spotted Win. 'Both your ass.'

'Asses,' Win corrected. 'One ass. Two asses. Plural.'

'What the fuck—'

'We want to talk to you,' Myron said.

'Hey, fuck you, man.'

Myron turned to Win. 'He's a real badass.'

'Indeed,' Win said. 'I may wet myself.'

Horty stepped toward Win. He had at least six inches

306

and sixty pounds on him. Horty probably thought he was being clever, going after and intimidating the little guy. Myron tried not to smile when Horty spat, 'Gonna fuck you up big-time.'

'If you curse again,' Win said in the tone of a preschool teacher, 'I will be forced to silence you.'

'You?' Horty laughed heartily. He flexed for a moment and then lowered his nose until it almost touched Win's. Win did not move. 'Little piece of upper-crust whitebread gonna shut me up? Fuck—'

Win barely moved. His arm shot up, delivered a palm strike to the solar plexus, and was back at his side in what seemed like a tenth of a second. Horty stumbled back, gasping, unable to get any oxygen into his lungs.

'I asked you not to curse,' Win said.

It took Horty nearly half a minute to recover. When he did, the lips started flapping again. 'Fucking cheap-shot motherfucker,' he said rising. 'I gonna tear you a brand-new asshole.'

He charged Win, his arms outstretched as though tackling a fullback. Win sidestepped him and delivered a quick roundhouse kick, again hitting the solar plexus. Horty folded and went down. His face was a mixture of fury, pain, surprise, and of course, embarrassment. He looked around to make sure nobody was watching. He was, after all, getting his butt whipped by Mr Wonderbread.

'There are two hundred and six bones in the body,' Win said evenly. 'Next time I break one.'

But Horty wasn't listening. His eyes bulged. Rage twisted his face – not to mention his limited ability to reason. Horty stood, stumbling, pretending he was more hurt than he was. The element of surprise. When Horty was close enough, he made his move.

He must have been really coked up, Myron mused. Or really stupid. Probably both.

Win leaned away and snapped a sidekick toward Horty's lower leg. There was a cracking sound, like stepping on a dry twig. Horty screamed and went down. Win raised his leg for an ax kick, but Myron stopped him with a shake of his head.

'Two hundred five,' Win said, lowering his foot gently, 'and counting.'

'You broke my f—' He stopped, holding his leg and rolling back and forth. 'You broke my leg!'

'Your right tibia,' Win corrected.

'Who the – who are you?'

Myron said, 'We're going to ask you a few questions. You're going to answer them.'

'My leg, man. I need a doctor.'

'When we're finished.'

'Look, I just work for Terrell. He gave me this territory. You gotta a problem with that, you speak to him, okay?'

'We don't want to talk to you about that.'

'Please, man, I'm begging you. My leg.'

'You used to attend Reston University.'

A surprised look replaced the pained one. 'Yeah, so? You want my résumé?'

'You knew Kathy Culver.'

Panic now. 'You guys cops?'

'No.'

Silence.

'You knew Kathy Culver.'

'Kathy who?'

308

Win said, 'Number two-oh-five. The left femur. The femur is the largest bone in the body—'

'Okay, I knew her. So what?'

'How did you meet?' Myron asked.

'At a party. Her first week of school.'

'Did you ever date?'

'Date?' Horty laughed at that one. 'No. She wasn't the kind you date.'

'What kind was she?'

'The kind who sucked off my Johnson first night. Willie's too.'

'Who is Willie?'

'My roomie.'

'He play football?'

'Yeah.' Then he added, 'But only special teams,' as if that made him a lower species of being.

'Go on.'

'Man, why you want to hear this?'

'Go on.'

Horty shrugged. The leg was swelling badly, but the coke was numbing the pain enough to keep him going. 'You see, we had this party. At Moore House. Where all the brothers lived. Kathy, she was like the only white chick there. So she comes in dressed like a prime-time ho. I mean, she was all that, you know? We start rapping and shit, you know. Did a little nose-candy like a Hoover vac. She liked the stuff. Then we start slow-dancing.' The grin returned with the memory. 'Grinding, you know. She put her hand on the Black Blade right there on the dance floor. Starts rubbing it and shit. So I take her upstairs, and she sucks me off. But that ain't all. She takes a camera – a fucking camera! – out of her bag and asks me to take

309

pictures. No shit! Close-ups, she wants, of her and the Black Blade.'

Myron's stomach began to churn again. Win looked on with his usual noninterest.

Horty continued. 'Next night, she come back. Takes on me and Willie at the same time. We take more pictures, have a good old time. 'Cept this time I had my camera too.'

'So you took some pictures of your own.'

'Shit, yeah.'

'Did you and Kathy have any more, uh, encounters?'

'Nope. She moved on to other dudes, though. Prime-looking babe for such a ho. All blond and built and shit.'

'You talk to her after that?'

He shrugged. 'Little. Not much. But once she started up with Christian, man, it was a whole other story.'

'What do you mean?'

'She be all nose up in the air, like her shit don't stink no more. Two of them all lovey-dovey and shit, like they was going steady on a TV show. All of a sudden the slut thinks she's some fucking pure-ass cherry. I mean, the ho been riding the Blade like a fucking bronco, and now she don't even say how-do. That ain't right. That just ain't right.'

Mr Etiquette.

'So you decided to blackmail her,' Myron said.

'No way. Unh-unh.'

'We know about it, Horty. We know she paid you for the pictures.'

Horty made a snorting sound. 'Aw, shit, that ain't blackmail. That's a business transaction. I just called her one day and told her I might have to knock her down a few pegs. And then I said a picture was worth a thousand words. She kinda agreed with all that and said she'd be willing to pay for such wonderful pictures. I told her they was real valuable to me. Had a lot of sentimental value and shit. But we finally reached an agreement. A mutually beneficial agreement,' he stressed, 'not blackmail.' He took hold of his leg and winced. 'End of story, man.'

'You left something out.'

'What?'

'The gang-rape in the locker room.'

He did not seem surprised. He half-smiled and said, 'Rape? Man, you ain't listening. This woman had Horty's Three H's: Hot, Horny, Ho. Shit, she'd jump naked into a rock pile if she thought they'd be a snake in it. She loved it. We all had a good time.'

Win looked at Myron. The look said, Keep your cool.

'How many of you?' Myron asked.

'Six.'

'Why,' he said in a low voice, 'didn't you just take the money, Horty? Why did you have to rape her?'

'I just told you, man—'

'She didn't come to that locker room for consensual sex with six people. You raped her.'

'Can't be, man,' he said with a shake of his head. 'She a ho through and through. And once a ho, always a ho. That just the way it is. Fucking cunt acting all high and prissy and shit. Quarterback's girl. Miss fucking all-American cheerleader. Who the fuck did she think she was? So yeah, I showed her. I reminded her where she come from, what she really is. Not some fucking prom queen. A slut. A dick-loving ho.'

Win now stepped in front of Myron. Preventive measure.

' 'Sides,' Horty continued, 'I owed her boyfriend. Big-time.'

311

'Christian Steele?'

'Yeah. He did me wrong. I did him wrong. Passed around his little ho. Just a little payback, my man. To the prick who got me thrown off the team.'

'No,' Myron said. 'It wasn't Christian.'

'What you talking about?'

'I spoke with Coach Clarke. Two guys showed up for a game high. That's why you were thrown off. Christian had nothing to do with it.'

'Oh,' Horty said with a shrug. 'Ain't that something.'

'Your remorse,' Myron said, 'is very touching.'

'I gotta get to a doctor, man. My leg is killing me.'

'Weren't you worried about getting caught?'

'What?'

'Weren't you afraid she'd report the rape?'

Horty made a face as if Myron had suddenly started speaking Japanese. 'You crazy, man? Who she gonna tell? She just gave me major cash to keep it all quiet. She say anything, it all gets out. The whole ugly truth. Everyone would know – Christian, her mammy, her pappy, her teachers. Everyone would know what she just paid all that money to hide. And what if she was dumb enough to tell? There were pictures and witnesses of her doing Willie and me at the party. Who gonna believe she was raped after seeing that?'

Dean Gordon had made the same argument, Myron remembered. Great minds thinking alike.

'Hey, look, man, my leg's killing me.'

'Did you ever see Kathy again?' Myron managed.

'Nope.'

'Were you the one who threw away the panties?'

'Nope. One of the other guys had them. Thought he'd

keep them as a souvenir. When he heard she was missing, he got scared, threw them away.'

'Who?'

'I ain't giving names.'

'Yes,' Win said. 'You are.' He rested his foot against the broken tibia. That was enough.

'Okay, okay. Like I said, they was six of us. Three brothers, two white dudes, one chink.'

Equal opportunity rapists.

'One was the place kicker. Guy named Tommy Wu. Then there was Ed Woods, Bobby Taylor, Willie and me.'

'That's five.'

Horty hesitated. 'Give me a break, man. The other dude was the one who threw away the panties. But he's a friend, man. Still gives me money when I'm down, you know. I can't just give him up. He's big-time.'

'What do you mean, big-time?'

'Plays pro ball and shit. I can't give you his name.'

Win put the slightest pressure on the leg. Horty bucked.

'Ricky Lane.'

Myron froze. 'The running back for the Jets?' Dumb question. How many Ricky Lanes who now play pro football went to Reston University?

'Yeah. Now look, man, that's all I know.'

Win said to Myron, 'Do you have any other questions for him?'

Myron shook his head.

'Then leave,' Win said.

Myron did not move.

'I said,' Win continued, 'leave.'

'No.'

'You heard what he said. You'll never convict him. He

pushes drugs to kids, rapes innocent women, blackmails, steals, whatever, and laughs about it.'

Horty sat up. 'What the fuck is this?'

'Leave,' Win repeated.

Myron hesitated.

'Yo, man, I told you everything I know.' There was a tremble in Horty's voice.

Myron did not move.

Horty shouted, 'Don't leave me alone with this crazy motherfucker!'

'Leave,' Win said.

Myron shook his head. 'No. I'll stay.'

Win studied Myron. Then he nodded and approached Horty, who was trying to claw away but not getting far.

'Don't kill him,' Myron said.

Win nodded. He went to work with the careful precision of a surgeon. His face never changed expression. If he heard Horty's cries, he never showed it.

After a short time Myron told him to stop. Reluctantly Win stepped away.

They left.

Chapter 39

Ricky Lane lived in a New Jersey condo development similar to Christian's. Win waited in the car. As Myron approached the door, he felt rather than heard the bass from Ricky's stereo. It took three rings of the bell and several knocks before Ricky appeared.

'Hey, Myron.'

He was wearing a silk shirt that was either very fashionable or a pajama top. Hard to tell. The shirt was unbuttoned, revealing a well-defined physique. His pants were held up by a drawstring. He was also wearing slippers. Maybe they were pajamas. Or lounging clothes. Or he was trying out for a walk-on role on *I Dream of Jeannie*.

'We need to talk,' Myron said.

'Come on in.'

The music was deafening and awful. Made Pap Smear sound like Brahms. The motif was sleek modern. Lots of Fiberglas. Lots of black and white. Lots of rounded edges.

The stereo took up a whole wall. The lights on the equalizer looked like something on *Star Trek*.

Ricky flipped the stereo off. The silence was abrupt. Myron felt his chest stop vibrating.

'So what's up?' Ricky asked.

Myron tossed him a glass jar. Ricky caught it, looked a question.

'Pee in it,' Myron said.

'What?'

'I want you to urinate into this jar.'

Ricky looked at the jar. Then at Myron. 'I don't get it.'

'Your new size,' Myron said. 'You're taking steroids.'

'No way, man. Not me.'

'Then give me a urine sample. Right now. I'll have it tested at a lab.'

Ricky stared at the jar. He said nothing.

'Go ahead, Ricky. I don't have all day.'

'You're my agent, Myron. You ain't my mother.'

'True enough. Are you taking steroids?'

'It's none of your business.'

'I'll take that as a yes.'

'Take it any way you'd like.'

'Did Horty sell them to you? Or have you gotten a new supplier since college?'

Silence.

Ricky said, 'You're fired, Myron.'

'I'm devastated. Now tell me about raping Kathy Culver.'

More silence. Ricky was struggling to look casual, but his body language was all wrong.

'I know all about it,' Myron continued. 'Your buddy Horty told all. Nice guy, by the way. A real sweetheart.'

Ricky stumbled back. He put the jar down on a shiny

cube that Myron guessed was a table. He turned away. His voice was barely audible. 'I never touched her.'

'Bullshit. You and five other guys jumped her in the locker room. You took turns raping her.'

'No. That's not how it happened.'

Myron waited. Ricky buttoned his shirt, his back still facing Myron. He took a CD out of the stereo and tucked it back into its case.

'I was there,' Ricky began, his voice low. 'In the locker room. I was stoned. We all were. Stoned out of our minds. Horty had just gotten in a new supply, and . . .' He sort of shrugged away the rest of the sentence.

'It started as a dare, you know. We knew we'd never go through with it. We figured we'd walk right to the edge but never jump. We kept waiting for someone to call it off.' He stopped again.

Myron said, 'But no one called it off.'

He nodded slowly. 'It stopped. But too late. It stopped when it was my turn, and I said no.'

'After all the others had gone?'

'Yes. I stood there and watched them. I even cheered.'

Silence.

'You kept her panties?'

'Yes.'

'When you heard the police were investigating, you tossed them in that garbage bin.'

He faced Myron. 'No,' he said with something close to a hint of a smile. 'I wouldn't have been stupid enough to leave them on top of a Dumpster. I'd have burned them.'

Myron considered that for a moment. It was, he thought, an excellent point. 'Then who threw them away?'

Ricky shrugged. 'Kathy, I guess. I gave them to her.'

'When?'

'Later.'

'What time later?'

'Around midnight, I think. After it happened . . . after she left the locker room, it was like someone had given us the antidote. Or like someone turned on the lights, and we finally saw what we'd done. We all went silent and just drifted away. Except Horty. He was laughing like a goddamn hyena, getting more and more stoned. The rest of us went back to our rooms. None of us said one word. I got into bed, for a little while anyway. Then I got dressed and went back out. I didn't have a plan. Not really. I just wanted to find her. Say something to her. I just wanted to . . . shit, I don't know.'

His fingers were playing with his hair, twisting it like a little kid. He looked smaller now. 'I finally found her.'

'Where?'

'Crossing the campus.'

'Where specifically?'

'The middle, I guess. On the commons.'

'What direction was she walking in?'

He thought a moment. 'South.'

'Like maybe she was coming from the faculty housing?'

'Yes.'

After she left Dean Gordon's, he thought.

'Go on.'

'I approached her. Called out her name. I thought she'd just run away, you know. It was dark and all. But she didn't. She just turned and stared at me. She wasn't scared. She wasn't shaking. She just stood there and stared me down. I said I was sorry. She didn't say anything. I gave her the panties. I told her she could use them as evidence. I even told her I'd testify. I didn't plan on saying that. It just came out. Kathy took the panties and walked away. She never said anything.'

'Was that the last time you saw her?'

'Yes.'

'What was she wearing?'

'Wearing?'

'When you last saw her?'

He looked up, trying to recall. 'Something blue, I think.'

'Not yellow?'

'No. Definitely not yellow.'

'She hadn't changed clothes since the rape?'

'I don't think so. No, they were the same clothes.'

Myron headed for the door. 'You're going to need more than a new agent, Ricky. You're also going to need a good lawyer.'

Chapter 40

Jake was sitting next to Esperanza in the waiting area. He stood when Myron and Win entered.

'Got a minute?'

Myron nodded. 'My office.'

Jake said, 'Alone.'

Without a word Win spun and left.

'Nothing personal,' Jake said. 'But the guy gives me the creeps.'

'Come on in.' He stopped at Esperanza's desk.

'Did you reach Chaz?'

'Not yet.'

He handed her an envelope. 'There's a photograph inside. Bring it to Lucy. See if she recognizes him.'

Esperanza nodded.

Myron followed Jake into his office. The air conditioning was on full blast. It felt good.

'So what brings you to the Big Apple, Jake?'

'I was over at John Jay,' he said, 'checking something out.'

'The crime lab?'

'Yup.'

'Find something?' Myron asked.

Jake did not reply. He examined the pictures on the client wall, leaning forward and squinting. 'Heard of some of these guys,' he said. 'But no superstars up here.'

'No, no superstars.'

'Nothing like Christian Steele.'

Myron sat down. He threw his legs up on the desk. 'You still think he killed Nancy Serat?'

Jake did something with his shoulders. Might have been a shrug. 'Let's just say Christian is no longer our main suspect.'

'Who is?'

Jake moved away from the client wall. He sat down and crossed his legs. 'I've been poking into Adam Culver's homicide. Found out something interesting. Seems the cops concentrated solely on the murder scene and surrounding neighborhood. No reason for them to check anything else. They were convinced he was a victim of random street violence. I took a different avenue. I canvassed Culver's neighborhood in Ridgewood. Nice town. Real white. No brothers at all. You been there, I assume?'

Myron nodded.

'Anyway, I talked to a guy who lives two houses down from the Culvers. He says he was walking his dog on the night in question. He wasn't sure of the time, but he guessed it was eight o'clock or so. Seems he heard a big fight going on at the Culvers' house. Major blowup. He said he'd never heard anything like that before. It was so bad he almost called the cops, but he didn't want to pry.

They'd been neighbors for twenty years and all. So he just let it slide.'

'Did he know what the fight was about?'

Jake shook his head. 'Nope. Just loud voices. Adam's and Carol's.'

Myron sat quietly, still leaning back in his chair. Adam and Carol Culver had fought hours before Adam's murder. Myron tried to put it together with what he already knew. For the first time things were beginning to fit.

'What else do you got?' Myron asked.

'On Adam Culver's murder? Nothing.'

Silence.

'There were,' Jake continued, 'a few hairs found at Nancy Serat's murder scene. On the body itself. More specifically, clutched in Nancy's hand.'

Myron sat up. 'Like maybe she tore them off the killer?'

'Maybe,' Jake said. 'But we checked the hairs at our own facilities and got a confirmation this morning at John Jay. There's no question. The hairs belong to Kathy Culver.'

Myron felt his flesh turn to cold stone. He couldn't speak.

'We had some of her hairs on file,' Jake continued. 'From before. In case we ever found a body or wanted to check a location. Got them from her hairbrush at school. Both labs have done every comparison test conceivable. Neither one has any doubt. They're Kathy's hairs.'

Myron shook his head. He felt dizzy. Inside his head the Robot from *Lost in Space* was shouting, 'That does not compute!' over and over again.

'You have any thoughts on this, Myron?'

322

'Just the same ones you're having.'

Jake nodded. 'What Christian said.'

' "Time for sisters to reunite," ' Myron quoted.

'Yup. Kinda takes on a whole new meaning now, don't it.'

'But it still doesn't explain anything,' Myron said. 'Let's assume Kathy Culver is alive. Let's assume that Nancy Serat knows this. Why would Kathy kill her?'

Jake shrugged. 'Sounds to me like Kathy may have gone off the deep end. I mean, first she's got this whole weird past. Then she falls in love with a guy. Then she's blackmailed. Then she's gang-raped. Then the dean turns his back on her. She cracks. Has a breakdown. Runs away. Maybe she tells Nancy Serat, maybe she doesn't. But somehow Nancy finds out. Nancy arranges a reunion – probably a surprise reunion – between sisters. Kathy gets there early. She's not happy about Nancy's surprise.'

'So she kills her?'

'Could be,' Jake said. 'Kathy's loony-tunes. She doesn't want to be found. Shit, she probably killed her old man for the same reason. She's nuts. Maybe she wants revenge for some reason. On her father, on her best friend – even on Christian and Dean Gordon and whoever else she sent that nutty magazine to.'

Didn't feel right to Myron. 'Then what about the big fight between Adam and Carol Culver? How does that fit in?'

'Hell if I know,' Jake said. 'I'm making this shit up as I go along. Maybe the fight was just a coincidence. Maybe ol' Adam was on edge because he was about to meet with his daughter. Maybe the mother knows more than she's saying.'

Myron thought about it. It was confusing, but the last

323

part made sense. Maybe Carol Culver did know more than she was saying. More than maybe. Myron even had some idea now of what she was hiding.

It was time to pay Carol Culver a visit.

Chapter 41

Myron pulled up in front of the familiar Victorian house on Heights Road in Ridgewood. He hesitated. He should have told Jessica about this, but there are things a woman might be more willing to tell a casual acquaintance than a daughter. This might be one of them.

Carol Culver answered the door. She was wearing an apron and those industrial rubber gloves. She smiled when she saw him, but the smile did not reach her eyes. 'Hello, Myron.'

'Hello, Mrs Culver.'

'Jessica isn't home right now.'

'I know. I wanted to talk to you, if you have a minute.'

The smile stayed. But a shadow crossed over the face. 'Come on in,' she said. 'Can I get you something to drink? Maybe a little tea?'

'That would be nice.'

He stepped inside. He and Jessica had not visited here often during their time together. A major holiday or two, that was it. Myron never liked the house. Something about it was stifling, as though the air were too heavy for normal breathing.

He sat down on a couch that was hard as a park bench. The decor was solemn. Lots of religious memorabilia. Lots of madonnas and crosses and gold-leaf paintings. Lots of halos and serene faces looking skyward.

Two minutes later Carol reappeared, minus the gloves and apron, plus some tea and shortbread cookies. She was an attractive woman. She didn't really look like her daughters, but Myron had seen pieces of her in both of them. Jessica's straight posture. Kathy's shy laugh.

'So how have you been?' she asked.

'Fine, thank you.'

'It's been a long time since we've seen you, Myron.'

'Yes.'

'Are you and Jessica . . . ?' She feigned embarrassment. She did that a lot. 'I'm sorry. That's none of my business.'

She poured the tea. Myron sipped it and nibbled on a cookie. Carol Culver did likewise.

'Tomorrow's the memorial service,' she said. 'Adam donated his corpse to a medical school, you know. The spirit was all that mattered to him. The body was worthless tissue, I guess that's part of being a pathologist.'

Myron nodded, took another sip.

'Well, I just can't believe this weather,' she rambled, a distracted smile frozen to her face. 'It's so hot out. If we don't have rain soon, the whole front lawn will be brown. And we just paid to have it reseeded last season—'

'The police will be here soon,' Myron interrupted. 'I thought we should talk first.'

She put her hand to her chest. 'The police?'

'They'll want to talk to you.'

326

'Me? What about?'

'They know about the fight,' he said. 'A neighbor was walking a dog. He heard you and Dr Culver.'

She stiffened. Myron waited, but she said nothing.

'Dr Culver wasn't feeling sick that night, was he?'

The color ebbed from her face. She put down her cup of tea and dabbed the corners of her mouth with a cloth napkin.

'He never intended to go to that medical conference in Denver, isn't that right, Mrs Culver?'

She lowered her head.

'Mrs Culver?'

No movement.

'I know this isn't easy.' Myron said gently. 'But I'm trying to find Kathy.'

Her eyes remained on the floor. 'Do you really think you can, Myron?'

'It's possible. I don't want to give you false hope, but I think it's possible.'

'Then you think she might be alive?'

'There's a chance, yes.'

She finally raised her head. The eyes were wet. 'You do what you have to do to find her, Myron.' Her voice was surprisingly steady and strong. 'She's my daughter. My baby. She has to come first. No matter what.'

Myron waited for Carol Culver to continue, but she fell back into silence. After nearly a full minute, Myron said, 'Dr Culver just pretended he was going to that medical conference.'

She took a deep breath and nodded.

'You thought he'd left that morning.'

Another androidlike nod.

'Then he surprised you here.'

'Yes.'

Myron's soft voice seemed to boom in the room. An antique clock ticked maddeningly. 'Mrs Culver, what did he see when he arrived?'

Tears began to flow. She lowered her head again.

'Did he see you,' Myron continued, 'with another man?'

Nothing.

'Was the man Paul Duncan?'

She lifted her head. Her eyes met his. 'Yes,' she said. 'I was with Paul.'

Myron waited again.

'Adam set a trap,' she continued, 'and we got caught.' The words were once again steady and strong. 'He had become suspicious. I don't know how. So he did just what you said – pretended to go to a conference in Denver. He even had me arrange his flights, so I would be sure he was gone.'

'What happened when your husband saw you?'

Shaking fingers rubbed her cheeks. She stood, turned away. 'Exactly what you'd expect to happen when a man finds his wife and best friend in bed. Adam went crazy. He'd been drinking pretty heavily, which didn't help matters. He shouted at me, called me horrible names. I deserved that. I deserved a lot worse. He threatened Paul. We tried to calm him down, but of course that was impossible.'

She picked up the tea again. Each word was making her a little stronger, making it a little easier to breathe. 'Adam stormed out. I was scared. Paul went after him. But Adam drove off. Paul left after that.'

'How long have you and Paul Duncan . . . ?' His voice just sort of mumbled away.

'Six years.'

'Did anybody else know?'

Her composure gave way. Not slowly. But as if a small bomb had blown it off her face. She crumbled, weeping freely. A realization came to Myron. He felt his blood freeze.

'Kathy,' he whispered. 'Kathy knew.'

The sobbing grew more intense.

'She found out,' he continued, 'during her senior year.'

Carol tried to stop her tears, but that took time. Myron remembered how Kathy had worshiped her mother, the perfect woman, the woman who balanced old-fashioned values with a sense of the modern. Carol Culver had been a homemaker and a shop owner. She had raised three beautiful children. She had instilled in her children more than just a sense of what is now popularly called 'family values.' For her values had been a rigid doctrine that she insisted her children follow. Jessica had rebelled. So had Edward. Only Kathy had been successfully locked in, like a lion kept in too small a cage.

And she had finally broken free.

'Kathy . . .' Carol Culver stopped, shut her eyes tightly. 'She walked in on us.'

'And that was when she changed,' Myron finished.

Carol Culver nodded, her eyes still squeezed closed. 'I did that to her. Everything that happened was because of me. God forgive me.' Then she shook her head. 'No. I don't deserve forgiveness. I don't want it. I just want my baby back.'

'What did Kathy do when she saw you two?'

'Nothing. At first. She just turned and ran away. But the next day she broke up with her boyfriend Matt. And from there – she made sure I paid for what I'd done. For

329

all the years I'd been a hypocrite. For all the years I lied to her. She wanted to hurt me in the worst way possible.'

'She began to sleep around,' Myron said.

'Yes. And she made sure I knew all about it.'

'By telling you?'

Carol Culver shook her head. 'Kathy wouldn't talk to me anymore.'

'So how did you find out?'

She hesitated. Her face was drawn, her skin pulled tight against her cheekbones. 'Photographs,' she said simply.

Something else clicked into place. Horty and the camera. 'She gave you photos of herself with men.'

'Yes.'

'White men, black men, sometimes more than one.'

Her eyes closed again, but she managed to say, 'And not just men. It started slowly. A couple of nude pictures of her. Like the one in that magazine.'

'You saw that same picture before?'

'Yes. It even had the name of a photographer stamped on the back.'

'Global Globes Photos?'

'No. It was something like Forbidden Fruit.'

'Do you still have the picture?'

She shook her head.

'You threw them away?'

She shook her head again. 'I wanted to destroy them. I wanted to burn them and pretend I'd never seen them. But I couldn't. Kathy was punishing me. Keeping them was a form of penitence. I never told anyone about them, but I couldn't just throw them away. You see that, Myron, don't you?'

He nodded.

'So I hid them in the attic. In an old storage box. I thought they'd be safe there.'

Myron saw where this was going. 'Your husband found them.'

'Yes.'

'When?'

'A few months ago. He never told me about it. But of course I knew by the way he was acting. I checked the attic. The pictures were gone. Adam assumed that Kathy had hidden them up there. He had no idea she'd sent them to me. Or maybe he did. Maybe that's how he became suspicious of Paul and me. I don't know.'

'Do you know what your husband did with those pictures, Mrs Culver?'

'No. They were so awful. So painful to look at. I think Adam destroyed them.'

Myron doubted it. They both sat in silence for several minutes. Finally Myron said, 'Jessica is going to want to know.'

Carol Culver nodded. 'You tell her, Myron.'

She showed him to the door. He stopped at his car and turned back around. He studied the gray Victorian house. Twenty-six years ago a young family had moved in. They'd put up swings in the backyard and a basketball hoop in the driveway. They'd owned a station wagon, carpooled to Little League and choir practice, attended PTA meetings, hosted birthday parties. Myron could almost see it all happening, like a life insurance commercial playing in his head.

He slid into his car and drove away.

Chapter 42

Myron was thinking about threads again.

Threads like Gary Grady. Dean Gordon. Nancy Serat. Carol Culver. Christian Steele. Fred Nickler. Paul Duncan. Ricky Lane. Horty and the thugs. But there was one thread he had overlooked.

Otto Burke.

Suppose Jake was right. Suppose the magazines had been sent out to wreak vengeance or maybe to satisfy some misguided or irrational anger. Either way, it meant that everyone who had received a copy of *Nips* was in some way connected to Kathy Culver.

Except Otto Burke.

How did he fit in? Otto hadn't even known Kathy Culver.

Or had he?

Myron got off Route 4 at the Garden State Plaza Mall and took Route 17 south to Route 3. New Jersey, land of routes. He pulled into the Meadowlands and parked near the Titans' executive offices. He found the general manager's office and asked for Larry Hanson.

He was let in almost immediately. He quickly explained the reason for his visit.

Larry Hanson watched him without expression. His huge hands were folded on his desk. His neck strained the top button. Larry was about fifty, but he hadn't gone to flab. He looked, Myron thought not for the first time, like Sergeant Rock in the old comic strips. Should have been chewing on a big cigar.

The office was adorned with trophies. Larry had been named league MVP twice. He'd been All-Pro twelve times. He had been elected into the Football Hall of Fame on the first ballot. There were plenty of his old football photos, from high school through college and into the pros. Black-and-whites and colors. Same crew cut. Same gritty smile. Different poses, including plenty of knee-up, straight-arm favorites from yesteryear.

When Myron finished, Larry studied his big hands for a minute, as if they were something he'd never noticed before.

'Why ask me?' he said. 'Why don't you ask Otto Burke about the magazine?'

'Because he won't tell me.'

'And what makes you think I will?'

'Because you're not a complete asshole.'

Larry's mouth twitched toward a smile, but he caught himself. 'Coming from you,' he said, 'that really means a lot.'

Myron said nothing.

'This is important, huh?'

Myron nodded.

Larry sat back. 'Burke didn't get the magazine in the mail. He heard about it from a private detective.'

Myron shifted in his chair. 'Otto was having Christian investigated?'

Larry's tone was flat. 'A man of Otto Burke's unquestionable integrity would never stoop to such a level.'

'Under the desk,' Myron said, 'you're crossing your fingers.'

Again the twitch/smile. 'This doesn't leave this room, Bolitar. You understand?'

'Cross my heart.' Myron motioned such with his hand.

'Burke has a whole security division,' Larry explained. 'They poke into everyone on the payroll. Including yours truly. They also have a source network all over the place. The credo is pretty simple: If you got dirt on a Titan, Burke will pay top dollar for it. So one of these sources came across the magazine.'

'How?'

'I don't know. Maybe he's a steady reader.'

'Do you know his name?'

'Brian Sanford. A true sleazeball. He works out of Atlantic City. The casino route. Spies on gamblers, that kind of thing. A Titan puts a quarter in a slot machine, he reports it, especially since that whole Michael Jordan thing started. Burke likes to be kept informed. Gives him the edge in negotiating.'

Myron stood. 'Thanks. I appreciate it.'

'Hey, Bolitar. This don't make us buddies or nothing. We talk again, I still hate your guts. You got it?'

Myron said, 'We're having a warm moment now, aren't we, Larry?'

Hanson leaned his elbows on the desk, pointing a finger

at Myron. 'I still think you're a little pissant piece of dog shit. And next time I see you, I'll prove it.'

Myron spread his arms. 'Come on, Larry. How about that hug now?'

'Wiseass.'

'Does that mean no?'

'Do me a favor, Bolitar.'

'Name it, bright eyes.'

'Get the fuck out of my office.'

Chapter 43

Myron called Brian Sanford. Answering machine. Myron said he had a real big case, one that paid ten grand, and he'd stop by his office tonight at seven o'clock. Brian Sanford would be there. For ten grand, a guy like Sanford would let his mother take a bullet in the gut.

Myron dialed his office.

Esperanza said, 'MB SportReps.'

'Did you show Lucy the photo?'

'Yep.'

'And?'

'You found your buyer.'

Myron said, 'Lucy was sure?'

'Positive.'

'Thanks.'

He hung up. An hour to kill. Myron headed over to the county medical examiner's office – Dr Adam Culver's old office. Just a hunch, but worth checking out.

The building was a one-level brick building. Institutional,

almost like a small elementary school. The furniture was metal chairs with thin padding, again like a schoolteacher's. The waiting room magazines were pre-Watergate. The tiled floor was worn and yellowed with age, like the 'before' shot on a Mr Clean commercial. There was nothing even remotely decorative.

'Is Dr Li in?' he asked the receptionist.

'I'll buzz her.'

Sally Li was dressed in hospital scrubs, but there was no blood or anything on them. She was Chinese, approaching forty, but she could have passed for much younger. She wore bifocals. A pack of cigarettes was stashed in her front pocket. Cigarettes with a surgeon's gown. Like bowling shoes with a tuxedo.

They had met a couple of times in the past. Sally Li came to many Culver family functions. She had been Adam's right-hand woman for the past decade. Myron greeted her with a kiss on the cheek.

'Jessica told me you were looking into Adam's death,' she said without preamble.

He nodded. 'Can we talk for a minute?'

'Sure.' She led him to her office. Again, institutional. No personal stuff. Lots of pathology textbooks. A metal desk. Metal chair. A small tape recorder she probably used during autopsies. Her degrees on the wall. She wasn't married, had no children, so there was no picture on the desk. Big ashtray, though. Overflowing.

She struck a match, lit up, and said, 'How's tricks?'

'An MD smoking,' Myron said. 'Tsk, tsk.'

'My patients never complain.'

'Good point.'

She took a deep drag. 'So what do you want to know?'

'Did you and Adam ever have an affair?'

'Yes.' No hesitation. She looked him right in the eye. 'About four years ago. Lasted a week.'

'Did Adam have a lot of affairs?'

'Got me. A few, I guess. Why do you ask?'

'I'm just trying to put a few things together.'

'Vis-à-vis his murder?'

'Right.'

She took off her glasses. 'What does Adam's love life have to do with it?'

'Probably nothing,' Myron admitted. 'How had Adam been acting the last couple months?'

'A bit wacko,' she said. Again no hesitation.

'In what way?'

She gave that one some thought. 'Businesswise, he wasn't letting me help him on a lot of big cases. He was keeping them all to himself.'

'And that was unusual?'

'That was unheard of. We always worked on big cases together.'

'These cases,' Myron said. 'Were they the girls found in the woods upstate?'

She looked at him. 'You want to tell me how you knew that?'

'Just a guess.'

'Hell of a guess, Myron.'

'You said big cases. I read the papers. Those are the big cases they keep talking about.'

Sally didn't believe him, but she didn't push it either.

Myron said, 'So what else was there?'

She took another deep drag. 'He was very distracted. You'd talk to him, he'd nod, but he wouldn't listen.'

'Anything else?'

Sally crushed out the cigarette, though it still had plenty

to go. She lit another. 'A new way to quit smoking,' she said. 'I smoke the same amount of cigarettes, but I take less puffs each day. Gradual slowdown until I quit entirely. At this rate it should take no more than twelve years.'

'Good luck.'

'Thanks.'

'So what else was there?'

Another puff. 'Adam was ordering a lot of weird tests on the last girl they found in the woods.'

'What do you mean, weird tests?'

'Superfluous tests. In my opinion, anyway.'

Myron said, 'You never got a positive ID on her, right?'

'Right.'

'So maybe he was running the tests to see if he could get a handle on her whereabouts.'

'Maybe. But he sent them out one at a time. He'd wait for one test to come back before he'd ask for the next one. Anthropological measurements, shape and size of cranium, pelvic bones, ossification of the bones, fusing of sutures on the skull – all one at a time.'

'So what do you make of that?'

She shrugged again. 'I don't make anything out of that. It's just an example of what I meant by acting strangely. Distracted. The case was a weird one to start off. The girl's skull had been crushed by the perp, but that wasn't what killed her. In other words, she had been buried alive in those woods. She died trying to claw her way out.'

Silence.

'This girl,' Myron said, 'what was she wearing?'

Sally stiffened a little. Then she leaned forward. 'Okay, Myron, what's going on?'

'Nothing. Why?'

'You know why.'

Myron stopped. 'The girl's clothes are missing.'

'Yes.'

He felt his heart crash into the pit of his stomach, like a skydiver with a ripped parachute. 'Oh, shit.'

'What is it?'

'Sally, I need you to run a test for me.'

Chapter 44

The address of Brian Sanford, private investigator, was a go-go bar conveniently located one block from Merv Griffin's Resorts. Atlantic City was like that. The big hotels were like beautiful flowers untouched and unbothered by the unseemly weeds of poverty and sleaze that surrounded them. The big flowers had not beautified the neighborhood as promised by the casino owners. The contrast, if anything, had made the weeds more glaringly hideous.

The go-go bar was called Eager Beaver, and it was exactly what one would expect. Blinking sign with missing letters on the outside. Lots of lowlights around the bar, lots of bright spotlights on the stage. Bored women danced in shifts, most of them unattractive. Lots of flab. Lots of implants. Lots of herpes.

Myron made the key mistake of entering what might loosely be designated a bathroom. The urinals were stuffed with ice cubes – an adequate substitute, Myron supposed, for an actual flushing mechanism. No doors were on the stalls, which did not deter the defecators at all. One man smiled and waved to Myron from a squat.

Myron decided he could wait.

He called over a bartender. 'Could you tell me how to get to Brian Sanford's office?'

'Michelob, Bud, Bud Light, Coors.'

'I just want to know—'

'Michelob, Bud, Bud Light, Coors.'

Myron took out five dollars. The bartender pocketed it.

'Door in the back. Take the stairs up a level.'

He didn't wait for Myron to thank him. Capitalism.

A dancer on break approached him. She smiled. Each tooth was angled in a different direction, as if her mouth were the masterwork of a mad orthodontist.

'Hi,' she said.

'Hi.'

'You're really cute.'

'I don't have any money.'

She spun and walked away. Ah, romance.

The stairs did not creak. They cracked. Myron kept waiting for them to collapse. On the landing there was only one door. It was open. Myron knocked on the wall and peeked in.

Myron called out, 'Hello.'

A man he assumed was Brian Sanford came to the door. All smiles. Dressed in a beige suit that had last been pressed during the Bay of Pigs. 'You the guy who left the message?'

'Yes.'

The office was a minicasino. No desk but a roulette table. A one-armed bandit in the corner. Decks of cards everywhere. Souvenir dice, the kind that have a hole drilled in them, littered the floor. So did racing forms. Keno cards too.

The man put out his hand. 'Brian Sanford. But everyone calls me Blackjack. You know who gave me that nickname?'

Myron shook his head.

'Frankie. That's what I call Frank Sinatra. Frankie. Not Frank. Frankie, I call him.' He paused, waited.

Myron said, 'Good nickname.'

'See, Frankie and me were playing at the Sands one night, right, and I was on one of my streaks, you know. And Frankie turns to me and says, "Yo, check out Blackjack. He can't lose." Just like that. Frankie says, "Hey, Blackjack." Out of nowhere. The name stuck. Now everyone calls me Blackjack. All 'cause of Frankie.'

'Great story,' Myron said.

'Yeah, well, you know how it is. So what can I do for you, Mr . . . ?'

'Olson. Merlin Olson.'

Blackjack smiled knowingly. 'Okay, I can play it that way. Have a seat, Mr Olson.'

Myron sat.

'But before we start, Mr Olson, I have to tell you one thing right up front.'

He was holding dice in his hand, moving them around in his hands the way some people do with those Chinese balls that are supposed to help circulation.

'What's that?'

'I'm a very busy man. Lots of big stuff going on right now. You know how I started in this business?'

Myron shook his head.

'I used to be chief of security for Caesars Palace in Vegas. Head chief. You know how it is. I was in Vegas, right? But Donny – that's what I call Donald Trump, Donny – Donny asked me to head up security for his first hotel on the strip. Then he started nagging me to set up the Taj Mahal's security. I told him, I said, "Donny, I got too much on my plate, you know?"'

Myron looked up. A small crop plane flew overhead, leaving mucho cow manure in its wake.

'So my problem is this, you see. I got a meeting to-morrow morning with Stevie – Steve Wynn. First thing, seven A.M. sharp. Great guy, Stevie. Morning guy. Up at five every day. You know he's practically blind? Got cataracts or something. He keeps it hidden. Only tells his closest friend. So anyway Stevie wants me to do some-thing for him. Normally I'd tell him no, but it's a personal favor and Stevie's a good friend. Not like Donny. I'm not crazy about Donny. Thinks he's some hot stud now that he's got Maria.'

'Mr Blackjack—'

'Please,' he said throwing up his hands, 'just call me Blackjack.'

'I'd like to ask you a few questions, uh, Blackjack. I need your particular expertise on an important matter.'

He nodded. Very understanding. He didn't hitch up his pants importantly, but he should have. 'What's this all about?'

'You performed some work for a friend of mine re-cently,' Myron said. 'Mr Otto Burke.'

A big smile now. 'Sure. Otto. Swell kid. Smart as a whip. He calls me whenever he comes down.'

Probably calls him Ottie, Myron thought.

'You gave him a magazine a few days ago. An issue of *Nips*.'

344

Blackjack looked wary now. He rolled the dice on the table. A three. 'What about it?'

'We need to know how you located it.'

'Who is "we"?'

'I work with Mr Burke.' Even saying it made Myron feel nauseous.

'So why didn't Ken call? He's the usual contact.'

Myron leaned forward. Conspiratorial. 'This is bigger than Ken, Blackjack. We don't feel anyone can be trusted with this but you.'

He nodded. Again very understanding.

'Frankly, Blackjack – and this has to remain hush-hush.'

'Of course.'

'You're our first choice to replace Ken. But we know how busy you are.'

His eyes gleamed a bit. 'I appreciate that, Mr Olson, but for someone like Otto Burke, I could try to open—'

'Let's talk about this case first, okay? How did you come across the magazine?'

The wary look again. 'Don't take this the wrong way,' he said, 'but how do I know you work with Otto? How do I know you're not some schmo off the street?'

Myron smiled. 'I knew it.'

'What?'

'I told Otto you were the right guy for the job. You're not sloppy. You're careful. We like that. We need that.'

Blackjack shrugged. He picked up the dice, gave another roll. Snake eyes. 'I'm a professional,' he said.

'Clearly,' Myron agreed. 'So why don't you call Otto yourself on the private line? He'll confirm everything. I'm sure you know the number.'

That slowed him down a bit. He swallowed, trying to

disguise it, looked around like a cornered rabbit. Myron could see the wheels churning. 'Uh, no reason to bother Otto with this,' Blackjack said. 'You know how he hates that. I can tell you're an honest Joe. Besides, how would you know about the magazine if Otto hadn't told you?'

Myron shook his head. 'You're an amazing man, Blackjack.'

He waved a hand of modesty.

'How did you find the magazine?' Myron asked.

'Shouldn't we talk about my fee? On the phone you said something about ten grand.'

'Otto said you were a trustworthy guy. He said to bill him through Ken. Whatever you think is fair.'

Another nod. He picked up the dice. Rolled again. Another three. Practice, practice. 'I didn't find the magazine,' Blackjack said. 'It found me.'

'What do you mean?'

'I was hired to do a job. Part of it was to send out copies of that mag to some people.'

'Was Christian Steele one of those people?'

'Yup. That's how I got suspicious. I mean, the envelopes were given to me already addressed and sealed. I didn't recognize any of the names except Christian's. Otto had already put out word he wanted anything, *anything*, on Steele. So I opened it up and took a peek. That's when I saw the picture.'

'Who hired you to mail out the magazines?'

Blackjack placed one chip on red, one chip on odd. He spun the roulette wheel. 'You wanna put down a couple of chips?'

'No. Who hired you?'

'Well, that's the weird part. I don't know. I got this big

package in the mail with very specific instructions. Plus cash. But no name.'

'Any return address?'

'Nope. Just a postmark.'

'From where?'

'Right here in Atlantic City. I got it about ten, twelve days ago.'

The roulette wheel stopped. Twenty-two. Black.

Blackjack said, 'Damn.'

'Do you still have the instructions?'

'Yeah, sure.' He opened a drawer and handed him a piece of paper. 'Here.'

The letter had been typed:

Dear Mr Sanford,

For the sum of $5,000 (plus expenses) I would like you to perform the following services:

1. Enclosed find seven envelopes. Two of them should be mailed from the campus mail box at Reston University on Friday. The other three should be mailed from a post office box in their respective towns.

2. Please mail out the following New Jersey Bell literature to each person on the list at the same time.

3. Please arrange a phone number in the 201 area code, one that will work on Return Call. This number should be immediately disconnected should anyone call it back or answer it. I would like you to hook up an answering machine with the enclosed tape to that phone. I would then like you to make calls to each of the numbers listed below from that number. On the first two nights – Saturday and Sunday – you will simply call repeatedly, hold the line when they answer, and say nothing until they hang up. On Monday, you will call and say the following: 'Enjoy the magazine. Come and get me. I survived.' Please make your voice sound female and vague. (As you know, there are phones that can disguise voices and make them sound female.)

4. Enclosed is a money order for $3,000. Upon completion of this exercise I will contact you personally on or around the ninth of the month and pay off the remaining $2,000 plus expenses.

My name must remain anonymous. Thank you for understanding.

Myron looked up. 'I assume the New Jersey Bell literature explained Return Call.'

Nod.

'Who were the seven people?'

Blackjack shrugged. The dice were rolled yet again. Another snake eyes. The guy had the touch. 'I don't remember. Christian was one. Some dean was another. I mailed another from a town called Glen Rock.'

'To a Gary Grady.'

'Yeah, that's the name. I also mailed three from New York.'

'One of those to Junior Horton?'

'Uh, yeah, I think so. Junior. That rings a bell.'

'And the last one?'

'Some other place in New Jersey. Near Glen Rock.'

Myron stopped. 'Ridgewood?'

'Yeah. Something-wood anyway. A woman's name. I remember because all the rest were men.'

Myron said, 'Carol Culver?'

He thought a moment. 'Yeah. That's it. A name with two C's.'

Myron's shoulders slumped.

'Hey, buddy, you all right?'

'Fine,' he said softly. 'What about the phone calls?'

'The numbers were on another page. I threw them away when I finished. I called Steele and hung up a few times. By the time I called him back to give him the message calls, the line was disconnected. Guess he'd moved.'

Myron nodded. Christian had moved from the campus to the condo.

'The guy in New York – Junior – he was never home so I never reached him either. The others all got hangups and then the message calls.'

'How many of them used Return Call?'

'Just two. Christian and the guy from Glen Rock. It wouldn't have worked for the guys in New York anyhoo. Return Call only works for that area code.'

'Have you heard from your client yet?'

'Nope. And yesterday was the ninth. I tell you, he better not stiff Blackjack Sanford.' Another mental pants-hitch. 'If he knows what's good for him.'

'Uh-huh. Anything else you can tell me?'

'About this case? Nope. Hey, you wanna go over to Merv's? They know me over there. I can get us on a good table. Play a little blackjack maybe. Watch the legend in action.'

Tempting, Myron thought. Like having electrolysis performed on his testicles. 'Maybe some other time.'

'Yeah, okay. Say, how much you think I should bill Otto for? Like you said, I want to be fair.'

'Oh, I'd bill him for the full amount.'

'The whole ten G's?'

'Yes. You've been very helpful, Blackjack. Thank you.'

'Yeah, take care. Come by anytime.'

'Oh, one more thing.'

'What's that?'

Myron said, 'Mind if I use your bathroom?'

Chapter 45

It was ten-thirty when Myron arrived at Paul Duncan's house. Lights were still on. Myron had not called to make an appointment. He wanted the element of surprise.

The house was a simple Cape Cod. Nice. Needed a new coat of paint maybe. The front yard had lots of budding flower beds. Myron remembered that Paul liked gardening in his down time. Lot of cops did.

Paul Duncan answered the door holding a newspaper. A pair of reading glasses were low on his nose. His gray hair was neatly combed. He wore navy-blue Hagar slacks and a twist-a-flex Speidel watch. The casual man from Sears. A television played in the background. An audience applauded wildly. Paul was alone, except for a sleeping golden retriever curled in front of the television as if it were a fire on a snowy night.

'We need to talk, Paul.'

'Can't this wait until the morning?' His voice was strained. 'After Adam's memorial service?'

Myron shook his head and stepped into the den. The television audience applauded again. Myron glanced at the screen. Ed McMahon's *Star Search*. The spokesmodels weren't on, so Myron turned away.

Paul closed the door. 'What's this all about, Myron?'

A coffee table had *National Geographic* and *TV Guide*. Also two books – the latest Robert Ludlum and the King James Bible. Everything was very neat. A portrait of the golden retriever in its younger days hung on the wall. Lots of little porcelain figurines adorned the room. A couple of Rockwell plates too. Hardly a swinging bachelor pad or den of lust.

'I know about your affair with Carol Culver,' Myron said.

Paul Duncan played stiff-lip. 'I don't know what you're talking about.'

'Then let me try to clarify myself. The affair's been going on for six years. Kathy caught you and Mommy a couple years back. Adam also caught you two on the night he was murdered. Any of this ring a bell?'

His face went ashen. 'How . . . ?'

'Carol told me.' Myron sat. He picked up the Bible and flipped through it. 'Guess you skipped the part about not coveting your neighbor's wife, huh, Paul?'

'It's not what you think.'

'What's not what I think?'

'I love Carol. She loves me.'

'That sounds swell, Paul.'

'Adam treated her awfully. He gambled. He whored. He was cold to his family.'

'So why didn't Carol divorce him?'

'She couldn't. We're both devout Catholics. The Church wouldn't allow it.'

'The Church prefers marital infidelity?'

'That's not funny.'

'No, it's not.'

'Who are you to judge us? You think any of this was easy?'

Myron shrugged. 'You didn't stop. Not even after Kathy saw you.'

'I love Carol.'

'So you say.'

'Adam Culver was my closest friend. He meant a great deal to me. But when it came to his family, he was a bastard. He provided for them materially, but that's it. Ask Jessica, Myron. She'll tell you. I've always been there. From the time she was a little girl. Who took her to the hospital when she fell off her bike? Me. Who built her swingset? Me. Who drove her down to Duke her freshman year? Me.'

'Did you also dress up as the Easter Bunny?' Myron asked.

He shook his head. 'You don't understand.'

'Correction: I don't give a shit. There's a difference. Now let's go back to the day Kathy caught you two. Tell me what happened.'

His face became irritated. 'You know what happened. She walked in on us.'

'Were you naked?'

'What?'

'Were you and Mrs Culver in the throes of passion?'

'I won't dignify that with an answer.'

Time to rattle his cage a bit. 'What position? Missionary, doggie, what? Were either of you wearing handcuffs or a pig's mask?'

He moved so he was standing directly over Myron.

Everyone thought this was tremendously intimidating, towering over a seated foe. Fact was, Myron could deliver a palm strike to the groin before an ordinary man could even cock his fist.

'Watch it, son,' Paul said.

'How did Kathy react to seeing you two lovebirds?'

'There was no reaction. She ran away.'

'Did either of you follow her?'

'No. Frankly, we were both too shocked.'

'I bet. Did you ever discuss the matter with Kathy?'

Paul stepped away, circled, sat in the chair next to Myron. 'She only mentioned it to me once.'

'When?'

'A few months later.'

'What happened?'

He looked away, his eyes darting about, searching for a safe place to land. 'This isn't easy to say.'

Myron nodded, feigned sympathy. 'Go on.'

'Kathy made a pass at me.'

'Did you catch it?'

'What?'

'As in "catch her pass."'

He flashed the irritated face again. 'Of course not.'

'You turned her down?'

'I pretended I didn't know what she was talking about.'

'Did she persist?'

'Yes. But I kept ignoring her.'

'Bet you were real excited, though. Mother and daughter. Both good-lookers. Your fantasies must have been in overdrive.'

Irritation turned to rage. He finally took off his reading glasses. Very dramatically. 'Last warning, pal.'

'Uh-huh. So now tell me about Fred Nickler.'

Piss him off. Quick subject change. Keep him off balance.

'Who?'

'For a cop,' Myron said, 'you're a lousy liar. Nineteen seventy-eight. You let Nickler plea-bargain a kiddie porn charge. I know all about your connection with him, Paul. What I don't know is how he fits into all this.'

'He helped me out from time to time. With cases.'

'Including the disappearance of Kathy Culver?'

'In a manner of speaking, yes.'

'How?'

'I guess there's no reason not to tell you.' He coughed into a shaking fist. The golden retriever opened an eye but didn't move. 'Adam found photographs of Kathy in his attic. He brought them to me in the strictest confidence. On the back of one was the name of a photography studio called Forbidden Fruit. I couldn't find them anywhere. So Adam and I visited Nickler. Nickler told us that Forbidden Fruit was now called Global Globes. He gave me the address.'

'Then you went and bought all the pictures and negatives of Kathy?' A throwaway question. Lucy had already identified Paul Duncan from a photograph.

'Yes. We wanted to protect Kathy's name. But we also wanted the name of the animal that'd brought Kathy to the studio.'

'Gary Grady.'

'You know about that?'

'I am,' Myron said, 'well informed.'

'Well, I checked Grady out completely. He was shady, no question about it. A high school teacher with all those sex lines. He advertised in at least fifty pornographic magazines. I tailed him for a couple of weeks, did a lot

355

of it on my own time. I also had his phone tapped for a while. But in the end we came up with nothing.'

'How did Adam react to that?'

'Not well. Adam was always coming to me with some new angle on Kathy's case, mostly out of pure desperation. I don't blame him. She was his youngest daughter. The one child he had a decent relationship with. Adam was willing to do anything to find her. He even wanted to kidnap Grady and torture him until he talked. I told him I'd do anything to help, but that we had to keep within the limits of the law. He didn't like hearing that.'

'Tell me about the night Adam died.'

Paul took a deep breath. 'He set us up beautifully.'

'I know all about that. What happened after he caught you and Carol in bed?'

Paul Duncan rubbed his eyes with his palms. 'He went berserk. He started calling Carol names. Awful names. We tried to talk to him, but what could we say? After a while he told her he wanted a divorce and ran out.'

'What did you do then?'

'I went home.'

'Did you stop on the way?'

'No.'

'Anybody who can confirm you were home?'

'I live alone.'

'Anybody who can confirm you were home?' Myron repeated.

'No, dammit. That's why Carol and I didn't tell anyone. We knew how it would look.'

'Not good,' Myron agreed.

'I didn't kill him. I wronged him. I was a terrible friend. But I didn't kill him.'

Myron gave a small shoulder shrug. 'You seem like a

pretty good candidate, Paul. You lied about the night of his murder. You were having a long-term affair with his wife, a wife who could marry you only if her husband died. He confronted you two in his bed on the night of the murder. His missing daughter was the only person who knew about your secret liaison. Her photograph appears in a magazine published by your source. No, Paul, I'd say it looks pretty goddamn shitty.'

'I had nothing to do with any of that.'

'What did you do with Kathy's pictures?'

'I gave them to Adam, of course.'

'Did you keep any for yourself? Maybe as a little souvenir?'

'Of course not!'

'And you never saw any of the pictures again?'

'Never.'

'Yet somehow Kathy's picture ended up in a porno mag.'

Paul nodded slowly.

'A porno mag published by your buddy Fred Nickler.'

Another nod.

'So now comes the big question, Paul: How did Kathy's picture end up in Nickler's magazine?'

Using both arms for leverage Paul Duncan stood. He moved to the television and flicked it off. The junior dancers faded away. The dog did not move. Paul studied the blank screen for a while and then said, 'It's going to sound crazy.'

'I'm listening.'

'Adam arranged it. He put Kathy's picture in that magazine.'

Myron waited. His spine began to tingle.

'I don't understand it either,' Paul continued. 'Nickler

called me yesterday. He was all upset, said you were nosing around and realizing something was up. I had no idea what he was talking about. Then he explained it to me. Adam had told Nickler to put that picture in his magazine. You see, Adam had met Nickler when we were trying to find the photographer's studio. So Adam went back to him, pretended he was still working on a case with me. He told Nickler to put Kathy's picture in Gary Grady's ad. He also told him not to say anything if anybody asked about it – except to give out Gary's alias and address.'

'Enough clues,' Myron said, 'so someone would find Grady.'

'It seems so, yes.'

'Did Nickler tell you why he placed the picture only in *Nips*?'

'No. I can call and ask him, if you'd like.'

Myron shook his head. 'Not necessary.'

'That's all I know. I can't for the life of me figure out what Adam was doing. Maybe he wanted to set up Grady. Or maybe he just snapped. But the truth is, I have no idea why Adam would put his own daughter's picture in that magazine.'

Myron rose. He had a very good idea why.

Chapter 46

Win gazed into the mirror. Despite the fact that the hour was closing in on midnight, his evening was just beginning. He patted his hair, smiled at his reflection, and said, 'God, I am handsome.'

Myron grunted.

'Are you going to call Jessica?' Win asked.

'I want to go over it again.'

'Now?'

'Now.'

'And make my nubile lass wait?'

'She'll survive.'

'You don't understand. This girl is very special to me.'

'What's her last name?'

Win thought a moment, shrugged. 'Okay, what do you wish to review?'

'I've told you everything I know,' Myron said. 'I want to know how you see it.'

Win turned away from the antique mirror. His Central

Park West apartment had been a gift from his grand-father. It was huge, worth millions, and decorated like Versailles. Myron was afraid to touch anything. He was sitting in an antique chair with wooden arms digging into his ribs.

'Do you mind if I break the case down into three separate entities?' Win said.

'Whatever you want.'

'Fine. Then let us begin. Entity one: Kathy Culver's disappearance. During her senior year of high school, Kathy's personality changed for reasons her mother has now revealed to you. Kathy then sought to hurt said mother with promiscuity. Ergo the lewd photographs, which Kathy mailed to Carol. But Kathy Culver did not see the danger in her actions. She took for granted that she could just end it whenever she so desired. But that was not the case. When she wanted to stop – when she met Christian, it seems – she could not just backslide out.'

Myron nodded.

'Enter Mr Junior Horton. He decided to cash in on the new, unsullied Kathy Culver through blackmail. Kathy agreed to pay him in exchange for silence and photog-raphs. On the night in question Mr Horton called Kathy at her sorority house. She agreed to meet him in the locker room. Once there, she was gang-raped by Junior Horton and several cohorts.'

Win stopped and moved toward a decanter. 'Care for a little cognac?'

'No, thanks.'

He poured some into a snifter. 'The rape bent her past the breaking point,' he continued. 'She snapped. She sud-denly craved redemption and justice above all else. So she headed immediately to Dean Gordon's office to report the attack. Dean Gordon had been her employer, and she probably considered him a friend. She told him what had happened to her in the locker room. His reaction was either superfluous or detrimental to her resolve. Take your pick.'

'Probably detrimental,' Myron added.

'Yes, probably detrimental. Either way, Kathy left Dean Gordon's house disheartened. She walked around the campus in a sort of catatonic daze, I imagine. Ricky Lane approached her. He apologized and gave her the panties – that is, evidence of the crime against her. After that – who knows? We slam into a big brick wall. The only thing we know for sure is that the panties were found on top of a waste bin several days later. Are there any questions so far?'

Myron shook his head.

'Then let's move on to Entity two: Adam Culver's involvement. Sometime after Kathy disappears, her father finds the lewd photographs of his little princess in the attic. We know that they were hidden there by Carol Culver. But Adam, I am sure, did not realize that. He would have naturally assumed that Kathy had hidden them there. He would also have naturally assumed that the pictures were connected to his daughter's disappearance.'

'Logical,' Myron agreed.

'Yes, quite.' Win twirled his cognac, studying the color. 'Adam Culver then enlists the aid of Paul Duncan in his investigation. They track down the photographs' place of origin with the help of Fred Nickler. They also find out about Gary Grady. They continue their investigation, but nothing new develops. Paul wants to give up. Adam is desperate – so desperate that he tries to draw out the assailant in a most unorthodox manner.'

Win paused, considering. 'Here,' he said, 'is where it gets very interesting. We know Adam Culver had the photographs. We know he arranged to have them put in a pornographic magazine. I find it significant that the picture was placed only in *Nips* magazine.'

Myron leaned forward. They were on the same wavelength. 'The magazine with the smallest – almost non-existent – circulation.'

'That fact disturbed you from the beginning,' Win said.

Myron nodded. 'Someone didn't want that magazine seen by a lot of people.'

'Like her father.'

'Right.'

'And,' Win continued, 'we know that Adam Culver liked to frequent the casinos of Atlantic City. He might have met your friend Blackjack during one of his visits or at least heard his name. He could have hired someone else to forge his daughter's handwriting. He probably had a tape with her voice from an old answering machine. Ergo, Adam Culver set the whole thing up. He sent out the magazine to everyone who might have been involved in Kathy's disappearance. Her fiancé, for one. People in the picture, like Junior Horton.'

'Why did he send one to his wife?' Myron asked.

'I don't know.'

'And Dean Gordon?'

'Perhaps the dean was in one of those attic photographs. Or perhaps Adam found out about Kathy's visit to the dean's house that night. Most likely Adam was merely considering every possibility. But it's not really that relevant to the case. What is relevant, however, is the question of why Adam did not once again enlist the help of Paul Duncan.'

'Because,' Myron said, 'Adam found out that Paul was sleeping with his wife.'

Win nodded. 'Paul was no longer a friend or trustworthy. Adam was now on his own. He sent the package to Sir Blackjack, making sure it would never be traced back to him. Then Adam set up his second little sting operation, the one on his wife and Paul. He walked in on them, ran out, and was killed.'

'So who murdered him?' Myron said.

Win put down the snifter on a harpsichord from the seventeenth century. He steepled his fingers, bouncing them gently off one another. 'There are two strong possibilities,' he said. 'First, Paul Duncan. We cannot just dismiss him. He had motive and opportunity. Second, Adam wanted to stir up the killer, that much is clear. But perhaps the magazine stirred up more trouble than he'd anticipated.'

'Except for one thing,' Myron interjected. 'The magazines hadn't been sent out yet. Adam was dead two days before Blackjack mailed them.'

'So perhaps someone discovered what Adam was up to before they were mailed.'

'Otto Burke?'

Win shrugged.

'But Otto has no connection to Kathy Culver,' Myron said.

'None that we are aware of. Which leads us to Entity three: the unknowns. A major unknown, as I see it, is Nancy Serat. We can assume that she gave Adam Culver valuable information. But we do not know who killed her. Or what she meant when she told Christian it was time for sisters to reunite. And we especially do not know why Kathy Culver's hair was found on her dead body.'

Win rechecked his hair. Perfect. He smiled, winked, did everything but kiss his own reflection. 'We also have no explanation for Adam Culver's cabin in the woods. He could have become desperate enough to grab suspects and do his own interrogations. Or he could have been seeking retribution for all in the wicked photographs. On someone like Gary Grady. Or Junior Horton. But for some reason my mind cannot fully accept either of these rationales.'

Myron nodded. It didn't feel right to him either.

'And so now we've reached the final unknown. The most significant unknown of all: Miss Kathy Culver herself. Is she alive? Is she behind all this? Is she involved in any way at all?'

Win picked the snifter off the harpsichord. He took a sip of cognac, let it roll around his tongue, swallowed. 'The end.'

They both sat in silence. Myron churned the facts through his head yet again. None of them changed. Win studied his face.

'This was all a mental exercise,' Win said. 'A test drive, as it were.'

Myron said nothing.

'You know what happened. You knew before I said a word.'

Myron handed Win the telephone. 'Cancel your date. We have a lot of work to do.'

Chapter 47

The memorial service.

Myron slipped in late and ducked behind a pillar. He was in desperate need of a shower, a shave, a nap. And he looked it.

He spotted Jessica in the front pew. She sat on one side of her mother, Edward on the other. All three were crying.

The priest delivered the standard death spiel like an actor who knew his lines too well. Nothing new or original was said. There was no coffin, no well-dressed corpse in peaceful repose. The priest seemed bothered by this, by the absence of his customary prop. He kept motioning down on cue, only to draw back when he realized that there was nothing in front of him.

Myron stayed out of sight. The church was crowded. Paul Duncan sat in the second row, directly behind Carol. Every once in a while Paul would put his hand on her shoulder, but he'd never leave it there long. Appearances.

Christian was next to him, head lowered in prayer. Otto Burke and Larry Hanson were a few rows back. Good PR move. The press would undoubtedly be made aware of Otto Burke's heartfelt concern for his players' personal plights. Again, appearances.

Win was near the back. To his right sat Sally Li. Her face looked drawn, as if she could use a cigarette. Myron had spoken to her late last night. She had done the test. It had come out as he'd suspected.

Dean Gordon and his wife Madelaine were off to the left. Dean Gordon looked grim. Madelaine Gordon looked good in black. Myron recognized a few other faces in the crowd, but he couldn't put a name or place to any of them. It didn't matter.

The priest made a few last comments about the hereafter, God's will, and reuniting with the beloved in Heaven. Jessica's sob racked her whole body. No one put an arm around her. No one comforted her. She looked small and frail. Myron felt a lump rise in this throat.

Here we go.

When the ceremony ended, Myron did not hesitate. He walked purposively down the aisle. Jessica ran toward him without hesitation. They hugged, both closing their eyes. The mourners turned away and began to head for the exit. Win kept close to Otto Burke, Larry Hanson, and Dean Gordon.

Jessica finally released her grip. 'Where were you?' she asked.

Myron swallowed. He nodded to Paul Duncan, shook hands with Edward and Christian, lightly kissed Carol on the cheek.

'I don't know how to say this,' Myron said.

'What's the matter?'

He looked her straight in the eye. 'I found Kathy. She's alive.'

The group went silent.

Jessica opened her mouth, closed it.

'I'm meeting her tonight,' Myron said.

Jessica finally found her voice. 'I don't understand.'

'It's a long story. But she's alive. I'll bring her home to you tonight.'

Jessica looked at Carol. Carol looked back. Everyone looked at everyone else.

'I'll go with you,' Jessica said.

'You can't.'

'Like hell I can't.'

'I promised her,' Myron said. 'Just me. Alone. She's scared.'

'Of what?'

'Of the person who tried to kill her.'

'Who?'

Myron shook his head. 'She wouldn't tell me. Not on the phone.' He took hold of Jessica's hand. It was cold and stiff. Like marble. 'I'll bring her right to the house. I promise. We'll all talk then. But we can't risk scaring her off.'

Jessica shook her head. She looked lost. 'Where are you meeting her?'

'It's in the woods.'

'What woods?' Jessica pulled back a little. 'You're not making any sense.'

'I can't tell you, Jess. I promised her. Kathy said it's the spot where she was left for dead. She wants to show me where it happened.'

More silence.

Paul Duncan said, 'Dear God.'

Carol practically fainted into his arms.

'Where has she been?' Jessica asked.

'I only know bits and pieces from my investigation. She spent most of the time recovering from her injuries. She also spent some time in the Caribbean. An island called Curaçao. I picked up her trail from an entry that night in St Mary Hospital's registry. On the night she vanished, a patient was found unconscious in the middle of a road. She gave her name as Katherine Pierce.'

Carol gasped. 'Pierce? That's my maiden name.'

Myron nodded. 'I don't know all the details yet. She was hit over the head. The blow cracked her skull. The assailant thought she was dead. But she wasn't. He buried her in the woods. She woke up and managed to dig herself out. It's a miracle she survived.'

Jessica's eyes filled with tears. 'She's alive?'

'Yes.'

'You're sure?'

'Yes.'

Jessica hugged her mother then. Edward joined in. Christian and Paul watched dumbfounded. Myron turned toward the door. Win was standing there. His nod was almost imperceptible.

Chapter 48

Myron parked his car on the dirt road. He was alone. The car's clock read 8:30 P.M. He grabbed his flashlight and headed toward the meeting spot.

The brush was thick. Several branches whipped across his face. He listened for other sounds. Crickets hummed away. Nothing else. The flashlight sliced through the heavy darkness, carving a path for him to follow. Myron heard his feet crunch on twigs and leaves. His mouth felt bone-dry. It always felt that way at moments like this.

He was getting close now, no more than twenty or thirty yards away.

'Kathy?' he called out.

No answer.

'It's Myron, Kathy. I'm alone.'

No reply. But then Myron heard a shuffling from in front of him. Something came into view. A head. A head of long blond hair.

'It's okay,' Myron said gently. 'I'm here alone.'

She stepped toward him tentatively. Her right hand shaded her eyes from the flashlight's harsh glare. Myron pointed the beam away. 'It's all right,' he said.

She continued to move toward him, a dim silhouette. Her steps were slow, plodding, like a B-movie monster come to life.

'It's okay,' Myron said again. 'No one is going to hurt you.'

'I wish that were true.'

The voice had not come from her. It had come from behind him. Myron closed his eyes. His shoulders slumped. 'Hello, Christian.'

'Don't move, Mr Bolitar. Put your hands up.'

'Why bother?'

'What?'

'You're going to kill us. Just like you tried to kill Kathy. Just like you killed her father and Nancy.'

'I never meant to hurt anybody,' he said.

'But you did.'

Christian cocked the gun. 'Hands up. Now.'

Myron raised his hands slowly. 'Kathy opened up to you that night. She told you everything – every sordid detail of her past. She wanted to clean the slate.'

'She lied to me!' Christian shouted. 'All the time we were together – it was all a lie.'

'So you tried to kill her.'

'Kathy wanted me to still love her, Mr Bolitar. But don't you see? I never loved her. I loved a lie. She wanted me to stand beside that lie while she told her story to the world. She wanted me to sell out my teammates, toss away a chance at a national championship and Heisman trophy – all for the sake of a lying whore.'

'A lying whore,' Myron said. 'Like your mother.'

He nodded. 'Mr Bolitar, tell her. Tell her what that game meant. In terms of money, fame, pride. You understand, Mr Bolitar. It helped get me that contract.'

'So you hit her over the head.'

'I didn't mean to. It just happened. I thought she was dead. I couldn't find a pulse.'

'So you drove her out here and buried the body. You hoped she'd never be found, but if she were, it'd be blamed on a serial killer.'

Christian stepped closer. He raised the gun. 'Enough talk,' he said. 'I'm not going to let you stall around until someone shows up.'

'No need. Someone's been here all the time.'

Win came out from behind a tree, no more than a yard away from Christian. He pressed the .44 against Christian's ear and said, 'Drop it, or your brain becomes squirrel lunch.'

Christian dropped the gun.

'It's over,' Myron shouted.

From a farther distance two uniformed police arrived. They handcuffed Christian.

Jake Courter stumbled behind them, high-stepping through the long grass. 'Too old for this shit,' he mumbled. When he reached the clearing he said, 'Nice setup, Bolitar.'

'Lots of details. The secret to a good scam.'

'Gonna tell me what's going on now?'

'Sure, Jess?'

Jessica took off the blond wig and stepped forward.

Christian's mouth dropped open. 'What the—'

'You killed Kathy,' Myron said, 'but not from the blow to the head. She suffocated trying to claw her way out of the dirt.'

Jake looked confused. 'Where's the body?'

371

'In the morgue. Where it's been since the police found it two months ago. Sally Li confirmed the identity last night.'

'So why hadn't it been identified before?'

'Because the county medical examiner was Kathy's father. He knew who it was right away, but he pretended otherwise.'

'Why?'

'Think about it a second, Jake. From Adam Culver's perspective. Your case had gone nowhere in eighteen months. Adam knew that. He also knew the body provided no new clues. So he figured that the only way to catch Kathy's killer was to draw him out. How? By making the killer think Kathy might still be alive. After all, she'd been alive when he dumped her in the woods. So Adam kept the corpse's identity a secret from everyone – the police, his friends, even his own family. He also figured that the nude photographs were tied into all this. So he used them.'

'You mean he put that ad in the magazine?'

Myron nodded. 'Adam Culver arranged everything. Even the mysterious phone calls saying "Come and get me. I survived." He did everything he could to make it look like Kathy was alive.'

Jake nodded. 'So what you guys were just doing—'

'Was finishing up Adam Culver's plan. Our performance at the church this morning sowed the final seeds of doubt.'

'You were forcing Christian to make a play for you.'

'Exactly.'

'Incredible. So everyone was in on on this?'

'Jessica was,' Myron said. 'So were her mother and brother. It would have been too cruel to lie to them. But

Paul Duncan didn't know. Neither did anybody else, and Win made sure that all the suspects – Otto, the dean, even Gary Grady – knew about Kathy's "survival." '

'Then you weren't sure it was Christian?'

'No, I was sure.'

'You were trying to play it fair.'

Myron nodded. 'That's why I didn't tell you anything. I wanted you to see what happened without any pre-conceived notions.'

'Fair enough,' Jake said. 'Go on.'

'Adam Culver understood that only the killer would know this spot. If he made the killer think Kathy could still be alive, he or she would have to come back here – just to make sure Kathy was dead. That was why Adam rented that cabin nearby. That was why he had all that electronic equipment. To tape him. To have proof.'

'Catching the killer returning to the scene of the crime,' Jake said.

'Right.'

'But I don't get something. Adam was killed before the magazine was mailed out. How did Christian find out about it?'

'He didn't. Remember, Adam was a pathologist. He wasn't an investigator. He overlooked a very important clue. At first anyway.'

'What clue?'

'Kathy's clothes.'

'What about them?'

'When Kathy's body was found, she was wearing a yellow sweater and a pair of gray sweat pants. Yet the sorority sisters said she was wearing blue when she left the house. The rapists said she was wearing blue. Dean Gordon said she was wearing blue. Ricky Lane said she was wearing blue. The sorority sisters were also positive that Kathy never returned to the house. So the question was: Where did the yellow sweater and gray sweat pants come from?'

Jake shrugged.

'It took Adam a while to realize the significance of the clothes. But when he did, he went to the most obvious source. Kathy's roommate.'

'Nancy Serat.'

'Right. But he didn't want to let on that Kathy's body had been found. So he asked Nancy where he could find her favorite yellow sweater, pretending to be a typical dad on some kind of nostalgic tour. But think about it. If Kathy didn't go back to her sorority house, where did she change clothes?'

Jake saw it now. 'At Christian's,' he said with a snap of the fingers. 'Kathy slept there all the time. She must have kept clothes there.'

'Right.'

'And Nancy and Christian were friends,' Jake said, picking up the thread. 'She'd see nothing wrong with telling Christian all about Adam's visit. Probably thought the whole thing was kinda cute.'

Myron turned toward Christian. 'You got scared when you heard Adam had been asking about the yellow sweater. You knew he was getting close. So you followed him that night. You heard him fight with his wife. You saw him storm out of the house, and you figured this was the ideal opportunity to kill him. Another perfect misdirection.'

Christian said nothing.

Jake said, 'What do you mean, "another perfect misdirection"?'

374

'When your investigation of Kathy's disappearance began,' Myron said, 'who did you focus in on?'

'Christian,' Jake said. 'Like I said, we always check out the boyfriend.'

'So what did Christian do? With campus security combing the campus for clues, he planted the panties on the top of a garbage bin.'

'The panties,' Jake added, 'with someone else's semen.'

'Proof he didn't do it.'

'Well, I'll be damned.'

'He also misdirected us with Nancy Serat. He strangled Nancy. Then he planted one of Kathy's hairs at the scene.'

'But where did he get the hair?'

'Kathy slept in his room all the time, right? She would have kept other stuff there besides her clothes. Stuff like a hairbrush.'

'Son of a bitch.'

'It was almost perfect. Blame someone who was dead. And if Kathy wasn't dead – if she had indeed survived – he'd make her look like a lunatic. Who'd believe the ravings of a girl who'd killed her old roommate? But Christian didn't count on Jessica showing up at Nancy's. He panicked. He hit her over the head and ran. Problem was, he'd left his fingerprints behind. But Christian was quick. He even used that to his advantage. When you dragged him in the next morning, he immediately admitted to being at Nancy's house. And then he came up with that wonderful story about sisters reuniting.'

'Another perfect misdirection,' Jake said.

'Except he forgot about the glass.'

'What glass?'

'His fingerprints were found in several spots in the house, including a drinking glass. Yet Christian told us

375

Nancy barely let him in the door, that she practically pushed him away mumbling about the reuniting sisters. Under those circumstances, isn't it odd she'd offer him a drink?'

Myron looked at Christian. He lowered his eyes.

'I – I didn't mean to hurt any of them, Mr Bolitar,' he said.

'You were manipulative and calculating,' Myron said. 'You covered all the bases, even when you hired me. I was small-time. I could be controlled. You knew about my background, that I was an experienced investigator. You knew if any trouble arose, I'd keep things quiet. That I'd keep you informed. That I'd try to protect you. You played me for a sucker.'

Everyone remained silent until Jake said, 'All right. Get him out of here.'

The uniformed officers led Christian away.

Myron looked back at Jessica. She still hadn't said a word. Tears slid down her cheeks. None of this morning's tears had been for her father. Maybe some of these were.

Win shook his head. ' "Squirrel lunch." I can't believe I said "squirrel lunch." '

Jessica stopped crying. She even smiled a little. Myron put his arm around her and pulled her in close. Together they made their way back to the car.

Chapter 49

Three days later Myron drove Jessica to the airport.

'Just drop me off at the terminal,' she said.

'I'll wait with you at the gate.'

'You should head back.'

'I have time.'

'The traffic will be murder.'

'I don't care.'

'Myron?'

'What?'

'Just drop me off. Please. You know I hate scenes.'

'I won't make a scene.'

'You always make a scene.'

Silence.

'What's going to happen to Gary Grady?' she asked.

'I've sent all the information to the school board and the local press. I don't know if he'll spend any time in jail, but he's finished.'

'What about Dean Gordon?'

'He's resigned this morning. He's going to enter the private sector.'

'And the rapists?'

'Cary Roland is the DA. This case means big headlines. He'll do his best. Ricky Lane is going to turn state's evidence.'

'You dumped Ricky as a client?'

Myron nodded.

'And you lost Christian.'

Another nod.

'All in all,' she said, 'this case hasn't had a real positive economic effect on you.'

'I'm more worried about the personal effect.'

'Meaning?'

'Meaning you're back in my life.'

'Isn't that a good thing?'

'It is. Except you're leaving.'

'Just for a month or two. It's a book tour.'

He pulled up to the front of the terminal.

'I'll be back,' she said.

He nodded.

Jessica kissed him. He held on. She finally pushed him back. He released her grudgingly.

'I love you,' he said.

'I love you too.' She stepped out of the car. 'And I'll be back.'

He watched her walk toward the entrance. He watched her pass through the sliding glass doors, watched her walk to the ticket gate, watched her disappear down an escalator. When she was out of sight, he still watched until a security guard knocked on his window.

'Unloading zone, bub. Move it!'

Myron looked back one more time. Then he drove back to the office.

Kat Donovan spun off her father's old stool, readying to leave O'Malley's pub, when Stacy said, "You're not going to like what I did."

The tone made Kat stop mid-stride. "What?"

O'Malley's used to be an old-school cop bar. Kat's grandfather had hung out here. So had her father and their fellow NYPD colleagues. Now it had been turned into a yuppie, preppy, master-of-the-universe, poser ass-hat bar, loaded up with guys who sported crisp white shirts under black suits, two-day stubble, manscaped to the max to look un-manscaped. They smirked a lot, these soft men, their hair moussed to the point of over-coif, and ordered Ketel One instead of Grey Goose because they watched some TV ad telling them that was what real men drink.

Stacy's eyes started darting around the bar. Avoidance. Kat didn't like that.

"What did you do?" Kat asked.

"Whoa," Stacy said.

"What?"

"A Punch-Worthy at five o'clock."

Kat swiveled to the right to take a peek.

"See him?" Stacy asked.

"Oh yeah."

Décor-wise, O'Malley's hadn't really changed much over the years. Sure, the old console TVs had been replaced by a host of flat screens showing too wide a variety of games—who cared about how the Edmonton Oilers did?—but outside of that, O'Malley's had kept the cop feel and that was what appealed to these posers, the faux authenticity, moving in and pushing out what made this place hum, turning it into some Disney Epcot version of what it had once been.

Kat was the only cop left in here. The others now went home after their shifts, or to AA meetings. Kat still came and tried to sit quietly on her father's old stool with the ghosts, especially tonight, with her father's murder haunting her anew. She just wanted to be here, to feel her father's presence, to—corny as it sounded—gather strength from it.

But the douchebags wouldn't let her be, would they?

This particular Punch-Worthy—shorthand for any guy deserving a fist to the face—had committed a classic punch-worthy sin. He was wearing sunglasses. At eleven o'clock at night. In a bar with poor lighting. Other punch-worthy indictments included wearing a chain on your wallet, do-rags, unbuttoned silk shirts, an overabundance of tattoos (special category for those sporting tribal symbols), dog tags when you didn't serve in the military, and really big white wristwatches.

4

Sunglasses smirked and lifted his glass toward Kat and Stacy.

"He likes us," Stacy said.

"Stop stalling. What won't I like?"

When Stacy turned back toward her, Kat could see over her shoulder the disappointment on Punch-Worthy's glistening-with-overpriced-lotion face. Kat had seen that look a zillion times before. Men liked Stacy. That was probably something of an understatement. Stacy was frighteningly, knee-knockingly, teeth-and-bone-and-metal-meltingly hot. Men became both weak-legged and stupid around Stacy. Mostly stupid. Really, really stupid.

This was why it was probably a mistake to hang out with someone who looked like Stacy—guys often concluded that they had no shot when a woman looked like that. She seemed unapproachable.

Kat, in comparison, did not.

Sunglasses honed in on Kat and began to make his move. He didn't so much walk toward her as glide on his own slime.

Stacy suppressed a giggle. "This is going to be good."

Hoping to discourage him, Kat gave the guy flat eyes and a disdainful frown. Sunglasses was not deterred. He bebopped over, moving to some sound track that was only playing in his own head.

"Hey, babe," Sunglasses said. "Is your name Wi-Fi?"

Kat waited.

"Because I'm feeling a connection."

Stacy burst out laughing.

Kat just stared at him. He continued.

"I love you small chicks, you know? You're kinda adorable. A spinner, am I right? You know what would look good on me? You."

5

"Do these lines ever work?" Kat asked him.

"I'm not done yet." Sunglasses coughed into his fist, took out his iPhone, and held it up to Kat. "Hey, babe, congrats—you've just moved to the top of my to-do list."

Stacy loved it.

Kat said, "What's your name?"

He arched an eyebrow. "Whatever you want it to be, babe."

"How about Ass Waffle?" Kat opened her blazer, showing the weapon on her belt. "I'm going to reach for my gun now, Ass Waffle."

"Damn, woman, are you my new boss?" He pointed to his crotch. "Because you just gave me a raise."

"Go away."

"My love for you is like diarrhea," Sunglasses said. "I just can't hold it in."

Kat stared at him, horrified.

"Too far?" he said.

"Oh man, that's just gross."

"Yeah, but I bet you never heard it before."

He'd win that bet. "Leave. Now."

"Really?"

Stacy was nearly on the floor with laughter.

Sunglasses started to turn away. "Wait. Is this a test? Is Ass Waffle, like, a compliment or something?"

"Go."

He shrugged, turned, spotted Stacy, figured why not. He looked her long body up and down and said, "The word of the day is legs. Let's go back to your place and spread the word."

Stacy was still loving it. "Take me, Ass Waffle. Right here. Right now."

"Really?"

"No."

Ass Waffle looked back at Kat. Kat put her hand on the butt of her gun. He held up his hands and slinked away.

Kat said, "Stacy?"

"Hmm?"

"Why do these guys keep thinking they have a chance with me?"

"Because you look cute and perky."

"I'm not perky."

"No, but you look perky."

"Seriously, do I look like that much of a loser?"

"You look damaged," Stacy said. "I hate to say it. But the damage . . . it comes off you like some kind of pheromone that douche bags can't resist."

They both took a sip of their drinks.

"So what won't I like?" Kat asked.

Stacy looked back toward Ass Waffle. "I feel bad for him now. Maybe I should throw him a quickie."

"Don't start."

"What?" Stacy crossed her show-off long legs and smiled at Ass Waffle. He made a face that reminded Kat of a dog left in a car too long. "Do you think this skirt is too short?"

"Skirt?" Kat said. "I thought it was a belt."

Stacy liked that. She loved the attention. She loved picking up men because she thought that a one-night stand with her was somehow life changing for them. It was also part of her job. Stacy owned a private investigation firm with two other gorgeous women. Their specialty? Catching (really, entrapping) cheating spouses.

"Stacy?"

7

"Hmm?"

"What won't I like?"

"This."

Still teasing Ass Waffle, Stacy handed Kat a piece of paper. Kat looked at the paper and frowned:

KD8115

HottestSexEvah

"What is this?"

"KD8115 is your user name."

Her initials and badge number.

"HottestSexEvah is your password. Oh, and it's case sensitive."

"And these are for?"

"A website. YouAreJustMyType.com."

"Huh?"

"It's an online dating service."

Kat made a face. "Please tell me you're joking."

"It's upscale."

"That's what they say about strip clubs."

"I bought you a subscription," Stacy said. "It's good for a year."

"You're kidding, right?"

"I don't kid. I do some work for this company. They're good. And let's not fool ourselves. You need someone. You want someone. And you aren't going to find him in here."

Kat sighed, rose, and nodded to the bartender, a guy named Pete who looked like a character actor who always played the Irish bartender—which is what, in fact, he was. Pete nodded back, indicating that he'd put the drinks on Kat's tab.

"Who knows?" Stacy said. "You could end up meeting Mr. Right."

Kat started for the door. "But more likely, Mr. Ass Waffle."

Kat typed in "YouAreJustMyType.com", hit the RETURN button, and filled in her new user name and the rather embarrassing password. She frowned when she saw the moniker at the top of the profile that Stacy had chosen for her:

"Cute and Perky!"

"She left off *damaged*," Kat muttered under her breath.

It was past midnight, but Kat wasn't much of a sleeper. She lived in an area far too upscale for her— West 67th Street off Central Park West, in the Atelier. A hundred years ago, this and its neighboring buildings, including the famed Hotel des Artistes, had housed writers, painters, intellectuals—artists. The spacious old-world apartments faced the street, the smaller artist studios in the back. Eventually the old art studios were converted into one-bedroom apartments. Kat's father, a cop who watched his friends get rich doing nothing but buying real estate, had tried to find his way in. A guy whose life Dad had saved sold him the place on the cheap.

Kat had first used it as an undergrad at Columbia University. She had paid for her Ivy League education with a NYPD scholarship. According to the life plan, she was then supposed to go to law school and join a big white-shoe firm in New York City, finally breaking away from the cursed family legacy of police work.

Alas, it hadn't worked out that way.

A glass of red wine sat next to her keyboard. Kat drank too much. She knew that was a cliché—a cop

9

who drank too much—but sometimes the clichés are there for a reason. She functioned fine. She didn't drink on the job. It didn't really affect her life in any noticeable way, but if Kat made calls or even decisions late at night, they tended to be, er, sloppy ones. She had learned over the years to turn off her mobile phone and stay away from e-mail after ten P.M.

Yet here she was, late at night, checking out random dudes on a dating website.

Stacy had uploaded four photographs to Kat's page. Kat's profile picture, a head shot, had been cropped from a bridesmaid group photo taken at a wedding last year. Kat tried to view herself objectively, but that was impossible. She hated the picture. The woman in the photograph looked unsure of herself, her smile weak, almost as though she was waiting to be slapped or something. Every photograph—now that she went through the painful ritual of viewing them—had been cropped from group pictures, and in every one, Kat looked as though she were half wincing.

Okay, enough of her own profile.

On the job, the only men she met were cops. She didn't want a cop. Cops were good men and horrible husbands. She knew that only too well. When Grandma got terminally ill, her grandfather, unable to handle it, ran off until, well, it was too late. Pops never forgave himself for that. That was Kat's theory, anyway. He was lonely and while he had been a hero to many, Pops chickened out when it counted most and he couldn't live with that and his service revolver was sitting right there, right on the same top shelf in the kitchen where he'd always kept it, and so one night, Kat's grandfather reached up and took his piece down from the shelf and sat by himself at the kitchen table and . . .

Ka-boom.

Dad, too, would go on benders and disappear for days at a time. Mom would be extra cheery when this happened—which made it all the more scary and creepy—either pretending Dad was on an undercover mission or ignoring his disappearance altogether, literally out of sight, out of mind, and then, maybe a week later, Dad would waltz in with a fresh shave and a smile and a dozen roses for Mom, and everyone would act like this was normal.

YouAreJustMyType.com. She, the cute and perky Kat Donovan, was on an internet dating site. Man oh man, talk about the best-laid plans. She lifted the wine glass, made a toasting gesture toward the computer screen, and took too big a gulp.

The world sadly was no longer conducive to meeting a life partner. Sex, sure. That was easy. That was, in fact, the expectation, the elephant in the date room, and while she loved the pleasures of the flesh as much as the next gal, the truth was, when you went to bed with someone too quickly, rightly or wrongly, the chances of a long-term relationship took a major hit. She didn't put a moral judgment on this. It was just the way it was.

Her computer dinged. A message bubble popped up:

We have matches for you! Click here to see someone who might be perfect for you!

Kat finished the glass of wine. She debated pouring another, but really, enough. She took stock of herself and realized an obvious yet unspoken truth: She wanted someone in her life. Have the courage to admit that to yourself, okay? Much as she strove to be independent,

Kat wanted a man, a partner, someone in her bed at night. She didn't pine or force it or even make much of an effort. But she wasn't really built to be alone.

She began to click through the profiles. You got to be in it to win it, right?

Pathetic.

Some men could be eliminated with a quick glance at their profile photograph. It was key, when you thought about it. The profile portrait each man had painstakingly chosen was, in pretty much every way, the first (very controlled) impression. It thus spoke volumes.

So: If you made the conscious choice to wear a fedora, that was an automatic no. If you chose not to wear a shirt, no matter how well built you were, automatic no. If you had a Bluetooth in your ear—gosh, aren't *you* important?—automatic no. If you had a soul patch or sported a vest or winked or made hand gestures or chose a tangerine-hued shirt (personal bias) or balanced your sunglasses on top of your head, automatic no, no, no. If your profile name was ManStallion, SexySmile, RichPrettyBoy, LadySatisfier—you get the gist.

Kate clicked open a few where the guy looked . . . approachable, she guessed. There was a sad, depressing sameness to all the write-ups. Every person on the website enjoyed walks on a beach and dining out and exercising and exotic travel and wine tasting and theater and museums and being active and taking chances and grand adventures—yet they were equally content with staying home and watching a movie, coffee and conversation, cooking, reading a book, the simple pleasures. Every guy claimed that the most important quality they looked for in a woman was a sense of humor—right, sure—to the point where Kat wondered whether "sense of humor" was a euphemism for "big boobs." Of course, every man also listed preferred body type as athletic, slender *and* curvy.

That seemed more accurate, if not downright wishful.

The profiles never reflected reality. Rather than being what you are, they were a wonderful if not futile exercise in what you *think* you are or what you want a potential partner to think you are—or most likely, the profiles (and man, shrinks would have a field day) simply reflect what you want to be.

The personal statements were all over the place, but if she had to use one word to sum them up, it would probably be *treacle*. The first read, "Every morning, life is a blank canvas waiting to be painted"—click. Some aimed for honesty by telling you repeatedly that they were honest. Some faked sincerity. Some were highfalutin or showboating or insecure or needy. Just like real life, when Kat thought about it. Most were simply trying too hard. The stench of desperation came off the screen in squiggly, bad-cologne waves. The constant soulmate talk was, at best, off-putting. In real life, Kat thought, none of us can find someone we want to go out with more than once, yet somehow we believe that on YouAreJustMyType.com we will instantly find a person we want to wake up next to for the rest of our lives.

Delusional—or does hope spring eternal?

That was the flip side. It was easy to be cynical and poke fun, but when she stepped back, Kat realized something that pierced her straight through the heart: Every profile was a life. Simple, yep, but behind every cliché-ridden, please-like-me profile was a fellow human being with dreams and aspirations and desires. These people hadn't signed up, paid their fee, or filled out this information idly. Think about it: Every one of these lonely people came to this website—signed in and clicked on profiles—hoping it would be different this time, hoping against hope that finally they would meet the one person who, in the end, would be the most important person in their lives.

Wow. Just let that realization roll over you for a moment.

Kat had been lost in this thought, clicking through the profiles at a constantly increasing velocity, the faces of these men—men who had come here in the hopes of finding "the one"—blurring into a fleshy mess from the speed, when she spotted his picture.

For a second, maybe two, her brain didn't quite believe what her eyes had seen. It took another second for the finger to stop clicking the mouse button, another for the profile pictures tumbling by to slow down and come to a halt. Kat sat and took a deep breath.

It couldn't be.

She had been surfing at such a rapid pace, thinking about the men behind the photographs, their lives, their wants, their hopes. Her mind—and this was both Kat's strength and weakness as a cop—had been wandering, not necessarily concentrating on what was directly in front of her yet being able to get a sense of the big picture. In law enforcement, it meant that she was able to see the possibilities, the escape routes, the alternate scenarios, the figure lurking behind the obstacles and obfuscations and hindrances and subterfuge.

But that also meant that sometimes Kat missed the obvious.

She slowly started to click the back arrow.

It couldn't be him.